THE COLD ROOM

The new mystery from the author of
Bodies in Winter

NYPD detective Harry Corbin hasn't been allowed to work on a homicide case for almost a year following his unearthing of corruption amongst his colleagues and superiors. So when a young woman's body is found dumped and mutilated on a sweltering New York morning, Corbin jumps at the chance to redeem his career and solve the case – and finds himself on a journey into the dark and secretive world of illegal immigrants, where humans are exploited and life is cheap...

*Recent titles by Robert Knightly
from Severn House*

BODIES IN WINTER
THE COLD ROOM

THE COLD ROOM

Robert Knightly

Severn House Large Print
London & New York

This first large print edition published 2014
in Great Britain and the USA by
SEVERN HOUSE PUBLISHERS LTD of
19 Cedar Road, Sutton, Surrey, England, SM2 5DA.
First world regular print edition published 2011 by
Severn House Publishers Ltd., London and New York.

British Library Cataloguing in Publication Data

Knightly, Robert. author.
  The cold room. -- Large print edition. -- (A Corbin and
  Bentibi mystery ; 2)
  1. New York (N.Y.). Police Department--Fiction.
  2. Murder--Investigation--Fiction. 3. Illegal aliens--
  New York (State)--New York--Fiction. 4. Detective and
  mystery stories. 5. Large type books.
  I. Title II. Series
  813.6-dc23

  ISBN-13: 9780727896643

Printed digitally in the USA

ONE

I was alone, except for the body, and for a white-hot July sun directly overhead. The sky was milky to the horizon, the atmosphere so charged with ozone, it seemed as if the merest spark would set off an explosion. Before me, strips of yellow tape closed the mouth of a short street paved with cobblestones. The cobblestones ended at the foot of an oblong dirt mound overgrown with dried weeds and yellowing grass. According to Officer Manny Bloom, the body of a deceased white female was positioned between the dirt and a head-high fence that prevented access to the East River.

I stood where I was for a long moment, watching the lights of Officer Bloom's cruiser retreat to the mouth of the Williamsburg Bridge five blocks to the west. The reason for my isolation was up on the Bridge; a derailed, Manhattan-bound J Train that had initially re-kindled the fears unleashed by the attack on the World Trade Center. As all New Yorkers know, these fears do not go away. They hibernate, instead, like frogs in the bed of a dry pond, prepared to regenerate at the first drop of rain.

When the truth finally emerged later in the day, the facts, though bizarre, were far less threatening. A transit cop working in plain clothes had encountered a psycho threatening his fellow passengers with a long-bladed kitchen knife. The officer's adrenals had instantly jumped into high gear, causing him to skip the part in the Patrol Guide about identifying himself as a police officer before taking action. He'd simply drawn his weapon from its holster at the small of his back, then shouted: 'Drop the fuckin' knife, shitface!' But that's the problem with *EDP*s, the *PD*'s politically correct term for psychos, they just can't take a hint, not even when it's reinforced by a 9mm Browning. The *EDP* had lunged at the officer and the officer had fired three times, instantly terminating the *EDP*'s life.

The shooting was justified and the undercover would have been hailed as a hero if the incident had concluded at that point. As it was, a panicked rider at the far end of the car yanked the emergency brake, causing three cars to jump the tracks and slam into the side of a Brooklyn-bound train.

By the time I arrived, at noon, everybody was up on the bridge: bosses by the dozen, every *CSU* and Emergency Service team in the city, the Fire Department, the Mayor and six administrative aides, the Metropolitan Transportation Authority, every morgue wagon, the *FBI*, the Department of Homeland Security and the Secret Service.

That left my home base, the 92nd Precinct

in the Brooklyn neighborhood of Williamsburg, virtually without a police presence, the shortage of personnel so acute that I'd been called out of bed to cover this inconvenient murder. But I didn't mind. This was the first homicide I'd worked in the last nine months and my senses were on full alert.

No more than fifty yards long, the short block was an extension of South Fifth Street running between Kent Avenue and the East River. It was enclosed on either side by the walls of two long buildings, both shut down on a Sunday morning. The building to the south, occupied by Yang Electrical Contractors, was three stories high and almost directly beneath the Williamsburg Bridge, already a hundred feet above the ground at that point. The building to the north, home of Gambrelli & Sons Italian Furniture, was four stories high and constructed of brick. Like its neighbor, all of its lower windows were protected by steel grates.

Behind me, South Fifth Street was solidly industrial, as was Kent Avenue for several blocks in both directions. The only retail business visible from where I stood, a bar on the other side of Kent Avenue, was closed. Williamsburg is a mixed residential and industrial community, with low-rise warehouses and small apartment buildings commonly jumbled together on the same block. That was not the case here. Even Kent Avenue, heavy with commercial traffic during the week, was totally deserted. It was the perfect spot to dump a body on a Sunday morning in July.

I began to walk down the center of the cobblestoned street toward the mound. Twenty yards in, and slightly to the left, I found a pothole created when a number of cobblestones had been removed. I dropped to my knees, then wiped the sweat from my eyes before taking a closer look. At the bottom of the pothole, enough dirt had accumulated to record the impression of a passing tire. I could see the ridges left by the tire clearly enough. Though very faint, they seemed intact.

I rose and walked back to my car, stripping off my jacket and tie along the way. I tossed both onto the back seat, then started the engine, enduring a blast of hot air from the vents in the dashboard. The Crown Vic's air conditioning had long ago ceased to function unless the car was in motion, but the radio worked well enough. I had Central patch me through to the desk officer at the Nine-Two, Sergeant Bill Sabado.

'It's Harry Corbin, sarge,' I said.

'Yeah?'

Sabado's tone was cold, but I was used to that. A year before, I'd exposed a den of vipers nestled in the bosom of the *NYPD*. I had yet to be forgiven.

'Any chance,' I asked, 'that *CSU* is gonna be able to respond?' Ordinarily, the Crime Scene Unit processes murder scenes, bringing their equipment and considerable expertise with them. 'I'm working with some very faint—'

'Negative, detective. *CSU* has no available units.'

And that was that. I shut down the engine, then retreated to the trunk where I removed a cardboard box. The box contained a Polaroid camera, a twenty-five foot tape measure, a few evidence bags, and several pairs of latex gloves. I carried the box to the pothole, set it on the cobblestones, and finally tore off a strip of cardboard. By folding the edge of the cardboard to create a little platform, I was able to stand it upright beside the pothole. Later, when I photographed the scene from Kent Avenue, the strip of cardboard would serve as an evidence marker.

As I straightened up, I felt as if I was pushing against active resistance. There was the sun, a presence I felt in every pore, and the humidity, of course, and a multi-layered wall of noise that hammered me from above. Sirens first, wailing and honking as they rolled up to the wreck, and then the scream of a saw blade cutting into metal. Finally, a steady pounding from the rotors of the news, police and military helicopters stationed above the bridge.

I looked up at that point, my eye drawn to the flashing lights of a hundred vehicles ricocheting across the steel girders of the bridge's massive towers. Red, white, yellow and blue, the lights seemed almost festive.

After a moment, I continued along the middle of the street until I came within a few yards of the mound. Four feet high, the mound was composed of mixed dirt and rubble, most likely deposited when an enterprising truck driver took a short-cut to the dump. But that had been a long time ago, long enough for the city's hardiest weeds and grasses to root. Against the wall of Yang Contractors, slender as a whip, an alianthus sapling rose to the height of my head.

It wasn't my intention to examine the body on my first approach, but my eyes were inevitably drawn to a path, about three feet wide, where the weeds and grass had been flattened. Most of the grass had sprung back up, but the weeds were having a tougher time of it. Their heads faced away from me, toward the river, the stalks broken, and it was obvious that something heavy had been dragged over them. I stepped forward to examine the swath more closely. My reward was a persistent hum that nicely complemented the steady chop of the rotor blades overhead. I recognized the source of that hum, flies drawn to a generous feed and a spot to lay their eggs. If I moved any closer, they would rise in a black cloud, their hum transformed into an outraged buzzing as they circled my head.

I was looking for shoe impressions, but what I found was a furrow that cut through the weeds and rubble. Made by the victim's chin as she was dragged? Or by her foot? I glanced at the victim then, at her back and her buttocks, at the long stretch of her thin legs.

Except for small areas of blanching, her skin was a healthy, glowing pink, the pink of a cherub's rounded cheeks.

I was startled, no doubt about that, but I'd seen this effect years before. A man whose name I've long forgotten had run a length of corrugated tubing from the exhaust pipe of his car through the back window, then stretched out on the seat to catch a final nap. By the time he was discovered in his garage, the force of gravity had pulled his blood down into the lower parts of his body, an effect called livor mortis. Ordinarily, the areas of the body suffused with blood are deep purple in color, but in this case, when I rolled him onto his back, one side of his face was cherry red. He looked as if he'd just been slapped.

I left the body undisturbed and walked the length of the mound, back and forth, but discovered nothing of interest. The grass and weeds were too dense to hold shoe impressions and whoever dumped the victim hadn't been careless enough to leave a wallet behind. Still, I discovered one more piece of evidence before I approached the body. A single link of the fence separating the victim from the river had been cut through. The edges of this cut were sharp, the exposed inner metal of the fence shiny and smooth. Without doubt, the cut had been made recently, and with a tool designed for that purpose.

On impulse, I backed up a few yards, then scaled the fence, dropping down onto a concrete slab, one of several jumbled slabs leading to the water. To my right, behind

Gambrelli & Sons Italian Furniture, a rickety wooden pier extended seventy-five feet into the river. Hauling a body up onto that pier would be no easy task, but if you did get that far, the pier would allow you to drop the body into water deep enough to carry it away. When the tide is running, the current in the East River tops five knots.

The river was quiet now, at low tide, its flat waters dominated by the glare of a sun that reached out for me in a jagged streak that seemed even brighter than its source. In the center of the main channel a dozen boats stood at anchor, their crews and passengers on deck. They'd come to watch the spectacle up on the bridge, no doubt. Perhaps, if their luck was running, somebody would fall off and they'd catch it on video tape.

When I finally approached the body for the first time, the expected cloud of angry flies rose up to circle my head and shoulders. I ignored them as best I could, as I'd been ignoring the waterfall of sweat running from my head to my shoes. By then, my shorts were glued so tight to my crotch, it felt like I was being groped. And none too gently, either.

The victim was lying face down, dressed in a shocking-pink halter and a crimson skirt, both garments of a type commonly associated with prostitutes. The halter was now around her neck, the micro-skirt above her hips. She wore no shoes or underwear, and except for small areas of blanching on her buttocks and shoulders, her torso and legs were a blotchy pink. I knew, now, that she'd been positioned on her back for eight to twelve hours following her death, then moved. Once lividity is fully set, the blood remains in place no matter how the body is turned.

I knew this was a homicide as well, a fact pointed out to me by Officer Murray Bloom when he'd briefed me earlier. 'All you need to do,' he told me before speeding off, 'is take one look. She has a hole in her head, it's gotta be four inches wide.'

The hole, when I finally squatted down to examine it, was almost exactly in the top of the woman's skull, a wound very unlikely to have occurred accidentally. But what struck me was the mass of blond hair surrounding the wound. Though I would have expected the victim's hair to be matted with blood and bits of torn scalp, it was as smooth and glossy as the mane of a runway model.

I left the flies to their dinner and walked back to my makeshift evidence kit, removing the Polaroid camera before tearing off another strip of cardboard off the box. The initial photos I took of the entire scene as viewed from Kent Avenue were adequate. At least the Polaroid was functioning. But I ran into serious trouble when I tried to record the tire impression at the bottom of the pothole. The sun was far too bright, the resulting photograph washed out, the tracks I wanted to record nearly invisible. My first thought was to place my body between the sun and the impression, but I re-considered. My head and hair were dripping sweat and the imprint so faint, no more than a few wavy lines, that a single drop of moisture would mar the pattern. I finally managed to shade the ridges with the piece of cardboard, but the results, although better, were still disappointing.

I briefly considered another appeal to Sgt. Sabado back at the Nine-Two. Maybe if I begged, he'd try to get me a *CSU* van. The Crime Scene Unit employed a number of techniques designed to enhance faint impressions – from laser sidelighting, to spraying with lacquer, to casting with dental stone – and they used high-end cameras to record the results. Meanwhile, my low-end digital camera was lying on a shelf in my closet where I'd put it years before, its batteries too dead even to illuminate the low-battery indicator.

In the end, I muddled along, knowing that even if Sabado was prepared to reward my humility, I wasn't prepared to be humiliated. I'd worked in five different precincts over the past nine months, one in each of New York's five counties. My peers wanted nothing to do with me, my bosses wanted only to be rid of me. As far as I could tell, my transfer out of any given precinct was in the works before I ever reported for duty.

I got several good shots of the cut in the fence, and a pair of shots from the wall of Yang Electrical that revealed the area behind the mound. The initial photos I took of the victim also came out well. Here I was less

14

concerned about dripping sweat and I hovered over the body when I recorded the head wound. Finally, I put the camera and the photos to one side before reaching for a pair of latex gloves in my back pocket. I found them slick with sweat, the powder inside now the consistency of wet plaster, but I struggled into the gloves anyway. Then I squatted down to slide my hands under the victim's right shoulder and hip. Her unyielding flesh was as hard as wood.

Intrigued, I withdrew my hands and manipulated the woman's fingers and wrists, finding both supple. Rigor mortis first becomes apparent in the smaller muscles of the jaw and the extremities, then in the larger muscles of the torso. It recedes in the same order, first the extremities, then the denser parts of the body. In this case, the victim's arms were supple, while her torso was hard, a state consistent with the end of the process and with my initial estimate of how long she'd been dead.

Again, I squatted next to the victim. I was feeling pretty good about myself as I considered my next move, as I again slid my hand beneath the victim's shoulders and hips, as I casually rolled her onto her back. Maybe, I thought, I wouldn't need the Crime Scene Unit after all.

TWO

I can't say exactly how long it took before I realized that the hissing in my ears was coming from the back of my throat, and that I was standing absolutely still, as if any movement would unleash some unspecified demon. Or how long before I accepted the simple – and obvious – fact that somebody had run a knife along the victim's abdomen, pulled the flaps aside, then gutted her.

I once knew a Homicide dick named Mc-Cann who claimed that all victims were the same to him. 'I speak for the dead,' he'd insisted, 'no matter what they were in life.'

I didn't believe him, even then. I didn't believe that all cries for justice were equal. I'd seen more than my share of bodies and knew that the abrupt departure of some victims was an absolute blessing. The world was better off without them. And while I worked their murders diligently, I never felt a moment's sympathy. I spoke, not for the dead, but for the state.

That was not the case here. No, in this particular case, my victim's cry for justice was closer to the howl of a January blizzard.

Eventually, my stomach calmed and my

heart slowed, until I was finally able to remind myself that there was a job to be done and no one else to do it. Like it or not, if I wanted to give this woman a name, if I wanted to make her killer pay, I had to get to work.

I began by examining the victim's abdomen, standing over her for a moment before dropping to one knee. Though it appeared that all of her internal organs had been removed, there was no blood on the upper parts of her body and it was now even more obvious that she'd been carefully prepped for her date with the river.

Satisfied for the moment, I allowed myself to look directly into her eyes. Her corneas were clouded, as expected, but I could see, beneath the film on the surface, two pale blue circles, delicate as the petals of a flower. I raised the camera and took several quick shots, catching the photos as they were ejected. In her early twenties, the woman's appearance was consistent with the first stages of decomposition. Purge fluid, dark as blood, had drained from her nose to form a two-dimensional mustache above her mouth. There was minor bloating evident in her cheeks as well, and some slippage of the flesh along her jaw line. My hope was that, later on, I could use the photos and my computer to create a recognizable likeness of the victim. Unless I got lucky with her fingerprints – assuming they could be taken – I would need something to show around and I didn't intend to wait for a police artist to produce a sketch.

I continued to photograph the body, to record the victim's injuries, including deep abrasions on the point of her chin and the tip of her nose. The abrasions were fresh and flecked with bits of dirt and particles of vegetation. I collected samples of each, placing them in evidence bags, then took more samples from the area surrounding the body. As I continued, the process became mechanical and my thoughts began to focus on an obvious question. Why was the victim...?

I considered this much for a moment before settling on the word eviscerated. I liked the clinical sound of its five syllables. I liked the distance it placed between me and the event.

So, why was the victim eviscerated? The first explanation that sprang to mind, the most obvious, was that she was a dope mule, that she'd swallowed condoms filled with heroin or cocaine, and that her killer had refused to wait for nature to take its course. Perhaps she'd been the target of a drug rip-off, or perhaps she'd been unable to pass the condoms through some abnormality in her bowels. Either way, the product was retrieved.

But that led to another question. If you were only after a few stuffed condoms, why would you remove all her organs, including the lungs and the heart which are tucked up under the rib-cage? To throw me off?

I tried to imagine the dope dealers I'd busted having the imagination or the knowledge to attempt that kind of deception. Most of them, I was sure, would have dumped her in

18

some alley, or tossed her from a roof into a garbage-strewn backyard. Proud as battle-scarred pitbulls, they would have displayed her as evidence of their ferocity.

Of course, there was also a Jack the Ripper scenario out there. But the blunt-force trauma to her head didn't fit. Slow strangulation would have been far more appropriate to a sadistic murderer. Plus, the killer hadn't been fishing for souvenirs like Jack the Ripper. He'd taken everything.

That last word – everything – triggered another thought. Some ten years before, a homeless man had turned up with a missing kidney and a fresh surgical incision. The man remembered nothing of the experience and the case was never cleared, but except for the obvious, there didn't seem to be any other explanation for his injuries. Somebody had needed that kidney.

There's no lack of human beings who need organs. A kidney, a liver, a lung, a heart, a pancreas; recipients far outnumber donors. But gall bladders, colons, spleens? And what about her pink lividity? Where did that fit in? If she'd inhaled enough carbon monoxide to change the chemistry of her blood, why was she struck on the head?

I walked back to the Crown Vic, retrieved a pad and a jug of water from the trunk. A moment later, I was seated in a patch of shade, with my back to the wall, simply enjoying the contrast between shade and sun as I raised the water jug to my lips. The water inside wasn't more than a degree lower than my internal body temperature. Nevertheless, it might have been drawn from an icy stream in the Rocky Mountains. I felt instantly revived.

I had a number of tasks ahead of me, but I was in no hurry. The *ME* would be a long time coming. I sat where I was for a good fifteen minutes, until I finally stopped sweating, and I might have stayed longer if Clyde Kelly hadn't chosen that moment to make his presence felt. I didn't see him at first, but I heard him coming, heard a steady clunk, clunk, clunk, despite the din up on the bridge. The clunking was due to a prosthesis attached to the stump of his right leg, a fact made apparent by his short pants when he finally appeared. Almost the color of tea, the prosthesis was twice as thick as his left leg, which happened to be fish-belly white.

Short and thin, and well past middle-age, Kelly limped to the center of the intersection, then peered over the crime scene tape at the dirt mound and the body behind it. After a moment, he moved on, crossing to the north side of South Fifth Street where he hesitated before making his way back to where he'd originally stopped. Finally, he shaded his eyes before again looking out toward the body and the water beyond.

At no time, despite the sirens and the choppers and the saw blades, did he so much as glance at the activity on the bridge. I got to my feet, imagining the effect my unkempt self would have on the little man standing on the far side of Kent Avenue. My shirt was out, my hair plastered across my forehead, my pants drawn skin-tight across my thighs. Worst of all, from his point of view, at six-three, I towered over him.

The cop from hell. An amusing image, no doubt, but not the one I wanted to project. When he finally became aware of my approach, pivoting on his artificial leg, I displayed my badge, shot him my friendliest smile and gave a little salute. A pure waste of time. His eyes widened in panic and he turned to run.

'Wait a second,' I said, 'I'm not gonna hurt you.'

Clunk, clunk, clunk, clunk.

I caught up with him before he reached the sidewalk, then gently took his arm. 'Slow down, partner. I just want to talk to you.'

He raised a hand as if to shield his head, revealing a prison tattoo on the web between his thumb and forefinger, an uneven black cross. For a moment, I was tempted to excuse his paranoia as the natural reflex of an ex-con, but I finally decided that no matter how many years he'd spent in the joint, his reaction to my appearance was extreme. I took a moment to examine the man before breaking the silence that followed. His shorts and t-shirt were well worn, though clean, his hair recently cut, his face recently shaved. Deep grooves marked the side of his face, running from the inside corners of his eyes down into the soft flesh of his throat. They made his long face seem even longer, an effect enhanced by the sagging skin at his jaw line. His broad nose was also long, while his dark eyes, beneath a pair of brows shaggy enough to cast a veil over his upper lids, betrayed his fear.

'What's your name, partner?' I asked.

'Clyde Kelly,' he responded, his tone hoarse. 'I ain't done nothin'.'

'I'm Detective Corbin. You have to excuse my appearance. I been workin' out in the sun.' I put my shield away. 'You got *ID*, Clyde?'

He looked up at me, his expression tracing a line midway between pleading and resigned. Returning his gaze, I realized that however bad he might have been in years gone by, whatever awful deeds he may have performed, time had taken its toll. He was an old man now, living an old man's fearful life.

'Yeah,' he said, 'I got a card.'

He retrieved that card without my asking, pulling a photo *ID* issued by the Human Resources Administration from a leather wallet as creased and wrinkled as the skin beneath his arms. The *HRA* card revealed an address on Wythe Avenue, one block east of Kent, and his date of birth. Clyde Kelly was seventy-three.

'You live by yourself?' I asked.

He shook his head. 'Senior housing,' he explained. 'Everything's like shared. The bathrooms, the kitchen, like that.'

I think he was proud to have a fixed address, not to be among New York's large population of homeless ex-cons. For my part, I was content to know that I could find him again if I needed him.

'Look, Clyde,' I said after a moment, 'I got a little problem and I think you can help me.' I took out my wallet, withdrew a clammy ten-dollar bill, and pushed it into his hand. 'I don't expect you to work for nothing, of course.'

He stared down at the bill without closing his fingers. 'What do I gotta do?'

'Well, see, this is a crime scene – which I think you already figured out for yourself – and I have to process it all alone.' I gestured up toward the bridge. 'Everybody else is busy'

Clyde nodded once, the gesture slow and steady. 'I hear what you're sayin',' he said, 'and I'm not disrespectin' you or nothin', but what exactly do I have to do?'

I smiled. An innocent bystander would have already inquired into the nature of the crime. 'You have to help me, Clyde. It's as simple as that. Now wait here a minute while I get my flashlight. I'll be right back.' I took a step, then halted. 'You're not gonna run, are ya?'

'No,' he replied, tapping his artificial leg, 'my runnin' days are over.'

I led him down the block, in twenty-five-foot increments, until I was standing with my heels on the edge of the mound. Clyde became more and more upset as we advanced. With his eyes riveted to the ground, he grew increasingly clumsy, stumbling toward me each time I retracted the tape. His fingers

23

were trembling noticeably by the time we completed the last segment.

'What's up, Clyde? You feel okay?'

He stood where he was, his eyes on his feet, until I repeated his name. 'Clyde?'

After another long hesitation, his head finally came up. Though he took a quick swipe at his eyes, it was evident that he'd been crying.

'I can't make it in jail,' he said. 'I just can't do it no more.'

'Who said anything about jail?'

But Clyde was beyond listening at that moment. 'I didn't kill her,' he whispered. 'I swear to God, detective. I didn't have nothin' to do with it.'

'I already know that. I already know you didn't kill her.'

He wiped his eyes, then again looked at me, this time his expression wary. In typical cop fashion, I was messing with his head.

'The victim was killed somewhere else, Clyde, then transported to this location. I know you couldn't have done that. But the thing is, you have to tell me what you saw and when you saw it. You have to, Clyde. You have to.'

Television advertisers claim that the average viewer must see a commercial at least seven times before the message penetrates. By that standard, Clyde was a quick study. He got the point after only three repetitions. He wasn't going anywhere until he came clean.

THREE

I led Clyde over to the Yang Electrical building, figuring he'd be more comfortable away
from the victim. The sun had drifted a bit to
the south, leaving the sidewalk in front of
Yang's wall in shade, another consideration
now that my re-hydrated body was again
pouring sweat.

'I admit it,' Clyde said without prompting,
'I done a lotta time upstate.' He held out his
arms for my inspection, revealing a pattern of
gray lines that rippled over his forearms and
biceps. Faded now, they were the last rem-
nants of a dope habit that must have been
ferocious.

But the point Clyde wanted to make had
nothing to with scoring dope or reformation.
His message was about prison. 'You spend all
those years gettin' up at five o'clock,' he told
me, 'it sticks in ya nerves. I can't sleep no
later than six. Don't even matter if I got
stinkin' drunk the night before. It's like something goes off in my head and I'm awake.'

The upshot was that he'd left his residence
a little after six that morning, intending to
stroll through the neighborhood while it was
still cool enough to be outdoors. His amble

had first taken him to a bodega on Bedford Avenue where he purchased a container of coffee and a buttered roll. From there, he proceeded to South Fifth Street, his intention to gaze across the East River at the finest view of midtown Manhattan that Brooklyn has to offer. Instead, he discovered a man pulling the body of a woman through the open doors of a windowless van. The man wore a gold warm-up suit with black stripes on the pants and sleeves, and he was very large. Fortunately, his back was initially turned to Clyde who quickly retreated, stepping around the corner until just a thin slice of his head was exposed. From this vantage point, he watched the man describe a semicircle, using the woman's chin and chest for a pivot, before dragging her toward the water.

'He yanked her through them weeds,' Clyde told me, 'like she was a bag of garbage, then started cuttin' away the fence. That was when he spotted me.'

'And what did you do next?'

'Whatta ya think I did?' He shot me an incredulous look before answering his own question. 'I got my sorry ass out of there as fast as I could, what with my leg and everything.'

'Where'd you go?'

'Over on the other side of the bridge, there's a hole in the fence. I ducked behind some machinery.'

'Did the man come after you?'

The question produced a shrug. 'If he did,

26

I didn't see him.'

'And what time was this?'

'Around six thirty.'

I think he expected me to respond in some way, perhaps with an accusation, but I held my peace. The crime hadn't been reported until almost eleven.

'Look, detective,' he finally said, 'all my life, the one lesson I learned is that minding your own business is how you stay alive. I mean, I seen guys shanked and I just kept on goin'. In the joint, you don't have no other choice.'

He turned away from me to face the river. The tide was coming in now and the small boats out on the water were in the process of weighing anchor. I watched them for a moment, the chug of their engines, as they fired up, adding still another layer to the din that surrounded us.

'Is that what you did?' I finally asked. 'You walked away?'

'No, I called nine-one-one. I waited till later, but I made the call.'

'Why, Clyde? Why did you wait and why did you make the call?'

'I was gonna forget about it,' he admitted. 'I mean, she was dead, right, and I couldn't bring her back to life. So why should I get involved? For all I know, she done somethin' horrible and deserved what happened to her.'

'That doesn't answer my question.'

He looked up, perhaps for inspiration, at a sky the color of fat-free milk. 'The only family I got is a sister, lives in New Jersey. She ain't spoken to me in thirty years and her kids don't even know my name. I'm not sayin' I deserve nothin' better.' He shook his head. 'No, all the wrong's on my end. I accept that.'

He paused here, while he continued to stare up at the sky. Though I was tempted to prod him, I sensed that he was still working out his motives for reporting the crime, as well as his reasons for returning to the crime scene.

'I'm seventy-three,' he said when it became clear that I wasn't going to speak first. 'I got bad lungs and diabetes, and I got an infection in my liver keeps comin' back. Meanwhile, I don't have two nickels saved up for my funeral. When I go, they're gonna put me in a box and ship me out to the boneyard on Hart's Island. Ya know what they do out on Hart's Island, detective? They dig a trench with a backhoe, then pile the coffins on top of each other. And those coffins, they don't have names on 'em. They got numbers.'

Finally, Clyde turned to look directly into my eyes. I saw that his own eyes were dark and mournful, the eyes of a man who'd been traveling a hard road for a long time, a man who was now close enough to read the *DEAD END* sign at the end of that road. I saw, also, that he was going to tell me the truth.

'I kept thinkin' about her under the water, lyin' in that fuckin' mud, about the crabs and fishes eatin' her. And it just got to me. I mean, the way he was draggin' her. You could see that it was just a job to him, like he mighta been pourin' a bucket of motor oil down a

28

storm drain.' Clyde paused there, his mouth twitching as though he was trying to work up his nerve. Finally, he said, 'Okay, I know you ain't gonna believe this, but when he was pulling her over the weeds, her chin came up so she was lookin' directly at me. And what came into my mind, right there, was that she was askin' me for help.'

I laid my hand on Clyde's shoulder and gave it a gentle squeeze, thinking that cops weren't the only ones to speak for the dead. 'Would you recognize this man if you saw him again?'

'My eyes,' he responded, 'they ain't what they used to be, but I think so.'

'Why don't you begin by describing him?'

'An ugly white dude, around fifty.' Clyde framed his eyes with his fingers. 'His eyes were like slits, like he had a hard time keepin' 'em open. I didn't get the color – he was too far away – but I'm sure about them slits. When he looked at me, it was like I was under a microscope.'

In fact, the man Clyde observed was eighty-one feet from Kent Avenue. I knew because we'd already measured the distance. That's a long way off for a man in his seventies, but my witness did pretty well anyway, replying without hesitation. The shadowy figure to emerge from his description was middle-aged and over six feet tall, with thinning gray hair and tiny eyes made even tinier by a wide face pudgy with fat.

'Like a Chinaman's eyes,' was how Clyde

29

finally put it, 'except they didn't slant.'

But Clyde was less certain about the van. Most of his attention, he told me, at least until he was spotted, had been focused on the victim. Plus, he hadn't driven a car in so many years that he couldn't tell one model from another.

'I want you to come back to the precinct with me,' I finally told him, 'to look at some pictures.'

'Mug shots?'

'Yeah.'

'I don't mind. I already figured you was gonna ask me.'

'Great, but there's a problem. We can't leave here until someone shows up to take the body away.'

'And that's not gonna happen any time soon?'

'Probably not, so what I want you to do is take a hike up to Broadway and get us some sodas and something to eat.'

'You trust me to come back on my own,' he said after a minute.

'Clyde, it's just like you said. Your running days are behind you.'

The first clouds made their appearance some four hours later. They came north from the harbor, long gray tendrils that swung back and forth like questing snakes. The clouds ushered in a gentle breeze, a breeze that became a wind as the clouds gradually took on the yellow-green color of a healing bruise. I led Clyde to the Crown Vic at that point. The air inside was stifling, but the clatter of hail on the roof forced me to keep the windows up.

The hail was followed by a deluge, as if somebody had run a knife across the underside of a water bed. For the next ten minutes, the lightning advanced on our position, until there was virtually no gap between the flashes and the resulting explosions. Clyde was sitting alongside me, his hands over his ears and his eyes squeezed shut. My own eyes were wide open. The hail and rain were pounding on the crime scene, destroying every bit of trace evidence. They pounded on the body of the victim as well, and what I wondered, as I struggled to draw oxygen from an atmosphere as thick as pudding, was whether her open gut would contain the water. Like a bath tub.

The rain stopped as abruptly as it had begun and the clouds receded to the north as if in fear of being left behind. Within minutes, the sun was out and the air again motionless. I exited the car, pausing for a minute to watch a thin mist rise from the hot cobblestones. Then I looked up at the bridge, my attention drawn by the silence. The helicopters were gone, the rescue workers as well, driven away by the weather no doubt. I wondered if there were any civilians still trapped in the subway cars, imagining their terror and the civil damages they would later seek. I was still pondering this question when a morgue wagon, closely followed by a city car bearing a death investigator, pulled up before the crime scene tape. The investigator rolled down the window a few inches. A short black man, he carefully scrutinized my sweat-soaked clothing, his distaste obvious.

'You have a body for me, detective?' he asked.

'I have what's left of a body after nine hours in the sun.'

'Is that supposed to mean something?' he said, staring me down. I turned away without answering.

FOUR

We were in the master bedroom of our Manhattan apartment, Adele Bentibi, my live-in lover, and I, enjoying a meal of hummus, tabbouleh salad, stuffed grape leaves and lamb shawarma. Adele was wearing a blue T-shirt and gym shorts, while I wore only a pair of faded cargo shorts. I freely admit that Adele was quite attractive in this outfit, not to mention erotic, but it wasn't sex that brought us to the bedroom. The air conditioner in the window to our left was the only air conditioner in an apartment that received eight hours of direct sunlight on midsummer days. Although the unit was running full out, and had been for the past week, the room was still noticeably warm at ten o'clock in the evening.

Adele was propped up on one elbow, staring down at me. Nine months before, she'd been assaulted with an aluminium bat as she left her parked car. The blow had been meant to kill her, but had succeeded only in flattening the center of her rather prominent nose. Adele's first instinct was to ignore the defect, no surprise as she was far too vain to admit to her own vanity. But then her breathing became impaired and she was more or less forced into an operating room. The result was a smaller, rounded nose that softened a thin face made thinner by sharp cheekbones and a pointed chin. Myself, I was indifferent to the change, but I remember catching Adele standing before the mirror in the bathroom one day, examining herself closely. Her dark eyes, when she finally acknowledged my existence, were filled with humor, her thin smile impish. Adele liked what she saw in the mirror, a guilt-free result that could only have come about through medical necessity.

'Do you think,' Adele asked as she cut through a stuffed grape leaf with the edge of her fork, 'that Kelly will make a credible witness?'

'Assuming I come up with somebody for him to *ID*, I think he will.' Though Kelly had examined more than a thousand mug shots at the precinct, he'd failed to make even a tentative identification. 'Especially if some defense lawyer is stupid enough to ask him why he didn't report what he saw right away.'

We were analysing the case, our discussion continuing through dinner and while we did the few dishes. I wasn't dealing, we agreed, with a street criminal who acted on impulse, as street criminals so often do. The effort to prepare the victim for disposal had been thorough and systematic. Nevertheless, there were flies in this ointment. The head wound, for example; blunt force trauma is usually inflicted in a moment of passion. And the pink lividity was another problem. If she'd inhaled enough carbon monoxide or cyanide to alter her blood chemistry, why crack her skull?

But the practical benefits of discussing the case with my former partner were beside the point. Nine months before, Adele had been my partner, working the case that put me on the outs with my peers. She'd taken a terrible beating, had come from an emergency ward to confront the man who'd beaten her. Detective Linus Potter had looked directly into Adele's eyes, then surrendered peacefully, knowing that if he resisted, she would kill him.

Now Adele toiled as an investigator for the Queens District Attorney, Kenneth Alessio, and she was bored out of her mind. Mostly, her work consisted of re-interviewing witnesses who'd been carefully prepped by the detectives who'd uncovered them in the first place. Either that or making sure those same witnesses arrived in court on time and sober.

Though she was too proud to say so, Adele missed the streets. I understood this because, to a certain extent, I missed them as well. Literally the odd man out on a squad that was a detective short of full strength, I passed most of my working days without a partner, responding to burglary complaints, or comforting seniors who'd had their purses snatched.

But now I had a mystery on my hands, for the first time in almost a year, and Adele had always been drawn to mysteries. If she wanted to experience this one through my eyes, I wasn't about to deny her. As for me, I was cheered by her interest. For some weeks, I'd felt Adele drifting away from me. Not toward some third party, I didn't fear infidelity. No, Adele had a capacity for solitude, not to mention isolation, and now she seemed to be folding into herself. Only occasionally was I able to draw her out and only for brief periods. Worse still, there didn't seem to be any reason for her withdrawal.

As for myself, I was in love with Adele Bentibi and my fear of losing her was compounded by the simple fact that there was nothing of Adele's in the apartment we shared, not a stick of furniture, not a single picture on the walls, not even a knick-knack. She could be out of my life in the time it took to pack her clothes.

'The taking of the victim's organs, Corbin. You suggested three possibilities: that she was

35

a drug mule; that her organs were harvested for sale; that she was the victim of a sadistic killer. Well, I can think of a fourth possibility.'

'Which is?'

'Which is that she was pregnant and her fetus was removed to prevent a *DNA* test for paternity.'

On that happy note, we retreated to our shared office in the apartment's second bedroom. A few years before, in a moment of foolishness, I'd invested a week's salary in a digital camera, a scanner and an ink jet printer. The camera went into permanent storage on a shelf in my closet after a photography class revealed that I was without artistic ability. But the other part of it, all those little tricks a computer can do with an image, continued to attract me. Not that I'm an expert, though I've spent many hundreds of hours working in Photoshop. But I'm not a hack, either.

I began my work by scanning the best of the photos I'd taken of the victim's face into the computer. I used a filter called Unsharp Mask, which – despite the misnomer – sharpened the Polaroid photograph considerably. Still, the image that popped up on the monitor was marred by decay, by abrasions on the chin and the nose, and by a discharge of purge fluid that stained the mouth and chin.

Starting with the abrasions and the purge fluid, I patiently transferred skin tone from the victim's cheeks to the affected areas until her chin and lips were virtually unmarred.

Then I transferred copies of her eye sockets, nose and the tip of her chin to an underlayer, before squeezing the original photo. The victim's face was bloated and I wanted to narrow it without also narrowing bony prominences less subject to bloating. Returning these features to the original was a fairly simple matter.

'You're bringing her back to life, Corbin,' Adele declared when I'd completed this phase of the job.

I might have mentioned Lazarus at that point, but as Adele was a Sephardic Jew, I didn't waste my breath. And there was no bringing her back to life, either. Like any murder victim, Jane Doe #4805 was beyond even simple revenge. Nevertheless, if I couldn't restore her to life, I could make her lifelike. And that's what I did. I made her cheeks rosy, her lips red, her eyes blue, her teeth white. I sharpened her chin, darkened her brows and restored the shadows bleached out by the Polaroid's flash. The young woman who emerged would not have turned heads on the street. Dominated by a pronounced overbite, her chin was slightly receding, her nose long, her face small and square. A thick head of blond wavy hair had undoubtedly been her best asset, but as I styled her hair with all the attention of a Madison Avenue hairdresser, I could only guess that she'd worn it loose.

Finally, I printed several black-and-white photos, each time sharpening the contrast. I might have printed in color, but there was no way I could be certain that the hues I'd assigned to the victim's cheeks, lips and eyes reflected her normal coloring. Nor could I know if the evident bloating had erased any fine lines around her eyes or at the corners of her mouth. What I did know, however, by the time I finished, was that I had a likeness that would be recognized by anyone who knew her, a likeness at least as good as a police artist's sketch. And I didn't have to beg to get it.

I shut down the computer, satisfied with the result. Long ago, while still in uniform, I'd set my sights on a detective's gold shield. I was at a distinct disadvantage, which I knew at the time. Promotion to the Detective Bureau was strictly at the discretion of the bosses and your pedigree was at least as important as the job you did on the street. That was a given. But if there was nothing to be done about a system that consistently rewarded second- and third-generation cops, at least one variable was still in play. If I couldn't out-influence my competitors, I could definitely outwork them. And that's what I did, collaring so many bad guys in the next ten months that the Precinct union delegate finally told me to lay off.

'You're makin' the rest of us look bad,' he'd explained.

Adele's hand tightened on my shoulder at that point and I swiveled my chair in a half-circle to face her. Although we'd been working for two hours and were both drenched with sweat, I wasn't thinking of a shower at that moment. My mood having instantly turned, I was thinking about the slippery texture of Adele's inner thigh, how her skin would feel beneath my fingers should I slide them from her left knee into the shadow beneath the leg of her gym shorts. I knew that if I lifted her t-shirt just a few inches, I'd discover a tiny drop of salty water trapped in her navel. I wanted to taste that drop on my tongue, to let it roll down into my throat. I wanted to absorb Adele the way the skin of a submerged amphibian absorbs oxygen.

Aroused by death? By violent death, by death undeserved? Looking back, I don't think so. I think I somehow separated the chase from the event that set the chase in motion. But murder was, undeniably, a necessary precondition to the erotic reckless-ness I felt at that moment. And I knew it, even at the time. I reached out to place my hands on Adele's hips, to draw her close, but she was one step ahead of me, as usual. She slid away, then yanked off her T-shirt, smiling that naughty, little-girl smile reserved for me alone. Adele's breasts are small and hard, her nipples like thimbles. That my eyes were drawn to them came as no surprise to either of us.

'Corbin,' she asked, 'what do you think would happen if I stood in front of the air conditioner for a moment or two?'

I don't remember what I answered, or what

I imagined, the end result being at least as grand as any fantasy I could muster. Her nipples became as hard as bullets, her breasts pimpled with little goose bumps that smoothed beneath my tongue. Prior to Adele, my adult relationships had been limited to a series of impulsive affairs that cooled as fast as they began. The pattern was so consistent that I'd pretty much resigned myself to a hit-and-run sex life. Meanwhile, after nine months with Adele, I was as infatuated as ever.

We made love in a frenzy, in a blur of manipulations. Adele is a very fit woman, but I'm also very fit and much larger. Toward the end, when I pinned her wrists to the bed, her legs circled my hips and tightened, commanding me forward, locking me into an arc of no more than a few inches. She was looking directly into my eyes then, her breath coming in short heaves, her mouth curled into a defiant grimace. When I bent forward to cover that mouth with my own, a shudder ran through her body, from the base of her spine up into her skull, and her eyes fluttered momentarily before closing. A moment later, I exploded inside her.

Pillow talk. After the showers and the changing of the sheets, as we lay side by side watching *NY1*, the cable news station, Adele laid her hand on my thigh and cleared her throat. They were doing the subway derailment on the little screen: the eight people dead, the ninety-seven injured, the *EDP*, the plain-clothes cop whose every move was now being judged by a media as anxious as its audience to cast blame. Predictably, the job was acting with caution. No details would be forthcoming until after a preliminary investigation was completed sometime within the next few days.

'Corbin,' Adele said, 'the perp in the case I've been working decided to plead out today. It came as a big surprise.'

Something in her voice, a slight quaver, a hesitation, raised the hair on the back of my neck. 'And?'

'Well, I have nearly a week coming.'

'Compensation for overtime?'

'Exactly. And what I thought I'd do was visit Jovianna. I'm leaving tomorrow afternoon.'

I recoiled, literally, my head jerking back. Jovianna Littman was Adele's sister, an unbearably competitive woman who used her several advanced degrees to lord it over her cop sibling. Ordinarily, Adele avoided Jovianna, who lived with her family in a gated community outside Baltimore, showing up only on the Jewish holy days of Passover and Yom Kippur. And then only for the sake of her parents, who lived nearby and whom she also disliked.

'How will you get there?' I knew the question was inane before the words were out of my mouth.

'I decided to go by Amtrak, so I won't have to put up with the security delays at the

41

airport. The ride's only six hours.' She put a hand on my shoulder. 'Jovianna called me this evening and we just got to talking. My mother hasn't been feeling well, which I think I told you, and I haven't seen them since April. Plus, I know how you get when you catch a case like this. A couple of days from now, you'll barely remember my name.'

'When are you coming back?'

'Maybe in a few days. If I can stand Jovianna even for that long. By the end of the week for sure.'

There was nothing else to say, not unless I challenged Adele's honesty. I wasn't prepared to do that, although much of what she said rang false to my interrogator's ear. So I told her to have a good time and got a hug before she turned out the light.

For the next fifteen minutes, until she fell asleep, I laid quietly beside her. Then I rolled out of bed and went into the living room. Of necessity, Adele and I lived separate lives. She worked normal business hours, while I toiled from four until midnight. I wouldn't have been ready for sleep, even on a normal day, but now my brain was spinning.

I parked myself before the *TV* and tried to watch a movie, *Ocean's Eleven*, but I couldn't follow the convoluted plot. Somehow, I found my thoughts turning, not to Adele, but to the crime scene, to the flies and the body, the heat and the rain, to Clyde Kelly's sad eyes and troubled conscience. Adele was running off to Maryland and there was nothing I could do about it. My Jane Doe was another matter. She was my responsibility. Only I could speak for her.

Eventually, I took those thoughts back to my computer and reworked her likeness. I rotated her head back and forth, tilted her chin up, played with her expression. I imagined her happy and sad, fearful and angry. What would she do with her eyes, her mouth, her nose, her brow, her chin? Finally, after printing what amounted to a model's portfolio, I settled on a three-quarters shot of her right profile, adjusting her eyes until she was looking at me with a sideways glance at once timid and sly. I had no reason to believe that the finished product would be any more effective than the first photo I printed. I really didn't care.

FIVE

I don't like autopsies and I don't ordinarily attend them. I'm not an overly squeamish man, so neither the sounds, the plops, crunches and squishes, or the incredibly foul odor, bother me all that much. It's more a question of loss. You'd think that when an individual is inflicted with an injury sufficient to end her life, there'd be nothing more to take from her. But you'd be dead wrong. At autopsy, murder victims are reduced to meat on a table, to the bare mechanics. The various organs – the ones still left, anyway – are examined, measured and weighed on a scale that might be found in any butcher shop. The stomach is squeezed of its contents, like icing from a pastry bag. The scalp is peeled down and left to hang over the face. The ribs are cut away with shears that might be used to prune the dead branches of trees.

There is no dignity for the victim in any of this. There is only a further reduction, a second stripping away. The Buddhists say that the spirit lingers for a time after death, to watch over the body, to observe the rituals of mourning. As a rule, I'm not one to question another's beliefs, but as I listened to the whine of a Stryker saw cutting away the top of my victim's skull, I found myself hoping the Buddhists were wrong, that her spirit wasn't hovering above that cold metal table, whispering 'help me, help me, help me'.

Like I said, I don't like to watch autopsies, and I didn't watch this one. Though I was physically present on that Monday at three o'clock in the afternoon, a single glance at the victim, now in an advanced state of decomposition, was enough. The rest of the time, I kept my eyes on the floor. Nevertheless, I did learn a number of facts that were to play a key part in the later stages of the investigation. First, the victim was not in her twenties, as I'd concluded after examining her at the crime scene, but in late adolescence, between sixteen and nineteen years old. Dr Kim Hyong established this fact with an X-ray of the long bones of her forearm where they met her wrist.

I listened attentively while Hyong recorded this observation, speaking into a microphone clamped to the autopsy table, but I asked no questions. I was more interested in Hyong's tone of voice, which remained matter-of-fact. There was no doubt in his mind, and nothing to be gained by challenging his conclusion, even if I'd had the expertise to frame a relevant question.

Hyong wound it up with an appropriately grisly flourish. The victim's prints could not be taken because the skin on her fingertips had grown slack, a condition known as slippage. Hyong overcame this difficulty by peeling off the skin of each finger, then inserting his right forefinger into the resulting pouch. By gently stretching this pouch with his free hand, he was able to produce a credible set of prints. 'It's all in the wrists,' he explained. 'All in the wrists.'

The autopsy finally complete, Hyong took the crime scene photos to a metal shelf extending from the wall opposite the door, where he re-examined them under a large magnifying glass. Knowing my place in Hyong's scheme of things, I waited patiently for him to complete this examination. A few minutes later, he called my attention to a full-length photo of the victim as I'd discovered her.

'Tell me what happened here. Tell me why her skin is pink.' Kim Hyong was short and thick, his torso running in a straight line from his armpits to his hips. His hands, by contrast, were very small, his movements precise enough to appear finicky.

'I've seen this before, doctor, with a suicide. The man—'

'Carbon monoxide, fine. What else?'

'Cyanide?'

'Very good. What else?'

My first impulse was to smack him, then count the revolutions before he contacted a solid object, say the far wall. But ever the goal-oriented detective, I merely sighed before shrugging my shoulders.

'I have no idea.'

'Then answer another question. This woman died from blunt force trauma resulting in severe intracranial hemorrhaging. Now, why would anyone strike her with enough force to produce this level of injury if she'd already been poisoned?'

'I've been trying to figure that out from the time I found her.'

Hyong glanced at me before shaking his head. 'Exposure to cold temperatures prior to death will produce lividity anywhere from pink to cherry red. We commonly see this in alcoholics who pass out on the streets in winter, and in cold-water drownings. Of course, we'll test for carbon monoxide and cyanide, but I'd be shocked if either test was positive.'

Now he had my full attention. 'Prior to death?' I asked. 'Is that what you said? Or after?'

'Certainly prior, though perhaps both. Let me explain.' Hyong was smiling now, exposing the yellowed teeth and coated tongue of a heavy smoker. 'Lividity was fully set before the removal of the victim's organs. I know this because the volume of blood in her body would have been greatly reduced if she'd been eviscerated immediately after death, producing a much fainter lividity. I can't be certain, of course, that she was returned to a cold space in the hours between her death and the removal of her organs. But it does make sense.'

Hyong's response directly addressed an anomaly I'd already considered. Blunt force injuries are almost always driven by passion, by the heat of the moment, yet the preparation of the body for disposal had been carefully thought out. A gap of many hours between the two events would go a long way toward resolving the dilemma. Perhaps the killer simply cooled down enough to get his act together, or perhaps a second actor had arrived, somebody more experienced, to lend a guiding hand.

'The organ removal,' I asked, 'do you think it was done by somebody with medical knowledge?'

'No, this is the work of a hunter or somebody who works at a slaughterhouse. The victim's sternum was cut with a heavy-bladed

47

knife, and there are nicks, probably from the same knife, on her ribs.'

I considered this for a moment, before asking an obvious question. 'You said she was exposed to cold prior to her death. How much cold?'

'Thirty-five to forty degrees would be my guess, the internal temperature of a common refrigerator. But I want you to take a look at her dentition.' He pulled down the woman's jaw, then stretched her lips away from her teeth. 'Please, look,' he said.

Though I didn't understand why he could not just describe whatever he'd discovered, I walked over to the table and stared down at my victim's molars, two of which bore gold crowns. But that wasn't what struck me as odd. It appeared that she had no cavities.

'Notice those fillings?' Hyong asked.

'Do you mean the crowns?'

Hyong's face was round and slightly dished in the center. When he compressed his lips, his disapproval apparent, his mouth all but vanished. 'Look closer,' he demanded.

I did as I was told, noticing that my victim's many fillings were white instead of the silver I was used to seeing. 'It's quite likely your victim was born and raised behind the Iron Curtain. In the East, they use composite fillings, the white you see in her mouth; in the West, metal or silver. Notice the gold crowns, common in Europe, while here we cap teeth with porcelain.'

My first thought was of the neighborhood

just to the north of Williamsburg, to Greenpoint and the many thousands of Poles who'd emigrated there following the break-up of the Soviet Union. From even the furthest reaches of Greenpoint, it was only a few miles to where my victim's body was discovered. Now I had a place to begin.

'I hope you're not going to ask me about time of death,' Hyong declared when I turned away from the body and took up a position near the door.

'I don't suppose there's any point.' In fact, every physical indicator of time of death is altered by cold: rigor mortis, livor mortis and insect activity are greatly retarded, while the loss of body heat is accelerated.

'There's a case reported by the DiMaios, father and son,' Hyong announced, 'in which the body of a young boy who'd drowned in a cold lake was still in full rigor when it was recovered seventeen days later.'

I looked back at my victim. Hyong had left her with her mouth agape, her lips folded back in what could have been mistaken for a smile. 'How long will she be here?' I asked. 'If I can't find someone to claim her body?'

'A couple of months.'

'And then what?'

'And then the city will pick up the cost of her burial.'

'On Hart's Island?'

Hyong snorted. 'What were you expecting, detective? A mausoleum?'

I moved toward the door without responding. What questions could be answered had been answered and there was other work to be done. With no tools, I'd been unable to collect the cut link in the fence on South Fifth Street. I'd take care of that now, on my way to work, as I'd prepare myself for the briefing Lieutenant Drew Millard would undoubtedly demand.

'That's it?' Hyong asked.

I turned to face him, suddenly remembering my conversation with Adele. 'One more thing. Will you test her blood to find out if she was pregnant?'

'What makes you ask that question?' Hyong was standing at the sink, washing his hands.

'It's possible that her organs were removed because her killer was after a developing fetus. The idea was to prevent a comparison with the father's *DNA*.'

'Now that is brilliant. Perhaps there's hope for you yet. The blood test in question is for a hormone called human chorionic gonadotrophin. We run it routinely.'

I got a call from Adele on my way to the Nine-Two. She'd used her connections at the *DA*'s office to reach the *NYPD*'s profiler, John Roach, who would grant me an interview on the following morning, should I so desire. I had no more faith in profilers than in Gypsy fortune tellers, but I wasn't about to rain on Adele's parade. There was something in her voice, some hint of regret that I didn't care to acknowledge.

'I think that'd be a very good idea, Adele, because the puzzle has suddenly gotten more complex. According to Hyong, the red lividity was most likely caused by prolonged exposure to cold before she was killed.'

'How much cold?'

'Refrigerator cold.' I hesitated, but Adele remained silent. 'I can't imagine forcing someone into a home refrigerator while they were still able to fight back. The unit has to be commercial. Maybe a restaurant.'

Adele sighed into the phone. 'She's placed in a refrigerator long enough to alter her blood chemistry, then bludgeoned. It doesn't make sense. If you wanted to kill her, why not leave her where she was?'

'That's what I'm supposed to find out, being as I'm the detective assigned to the case. I'll let you know when I succeed.'

Adele laughed, then sighed. 'I've got a train to catch.'

'And I'm on my way to work. Let's both have a good time.'

'Yes, Corbin, let's do that.'

The 92nd Precinct is located on Meserole Street, near Union Avenue, in a two story building erected in 1904, a year after the completion of the Williamsburg Bridge, the second bridge to span the East River. The upper story of the building is of red brick, the lower of limestone blocks. Though not massive by New York standards, the blocks are large enough to impress, especially around the double-doors at the Nine-Two's main entrance where they tilt gradually up to form a true arch. There are other nice touches as well. The fanlight window over the entrance way is dark with age, its rippled panes now more reflective than transparent. Directly above, a weathered terracotta medallion bears the shield of the *NYPD*, while a pair of wrought-iron stanchions flanking the doors are capped with Kelly-green globes.

I'd stood outside the Nine-Two for a good fifteen minutes on the day I first reported for duty. That was on a mid-April afternoon, with a spring breeze riffling my hair. By then, I pretty much knew my fate. One of the cops I'd taken down nine months before, Dante Russo, had been a trustee in the Policemen's Benevolent Association, the union that represents every uniformed officer below the rank of sergeant. For some reason, the fact that Dante was a psychopath who deserved his fate had escaped his *PBA* buddies. The idea, now, was to punish the messenger by repeating the same lie wherever he went: Harry Corbin is an Internal Affairs Bureau snitch.

Within a couple of days, spread by the *PBA* delegates in the precinct, the accusation would be common knowledge in the Nine-Two, and even those cops wise enough to distrust the grapevine would shun me. Knowing, as they did, that guilt by association was another weapon in the *PBA*'s arsenal.

But if I was reluctant to take up residence at the Nine-Two, I was comforted by the building itself. The limestone, grayed by urban soot, and the brick, faded from blood red to rosy pink, had endured for a century, uniting the generations even as Williamsburg's ethnic deck was reshuffled every couple of decades. To me, as I crossed the street and walked through its doors, it appeared ready to endure indefinitely into the future.

Not so the interior. Maybe limestone and brick can withstand long years of neglect, but interiors have to be aggressively maintained. That the Nine-Two's had not was obvious at a glance. A waist-high rail separating the public from the precinct's inner sanctum was without a finish, the raw wood now entirely exposed. Two paths had been worn into the oak floor, one leading from the door to the duty officer's desk, the other to a gate set in the rail. Cracked in a dozen places, the institutional-green paint on the walls and ceiling was overlaid with a greasy, nicotine-yellow film. Worst of all, the interior space on both the Nine-Two's floors had been divided and subdivided many times in order to house other units like Traffic and the School Crossing Guards.

By the time I showed up that spring, the Nine-Two was housing a large contingent of traffic officers, a street narcotics team, Brooklyn North's Vice unit and two shifts of squad detectives. All were expected to share the second floor, which had been divided into a haphazard assortment of cubbyholes and small offices. My own space, into which a pair of battered metal desks had somehow been squeezed, was about the size of a prison cell.

It was almost seven o'clock when I finally walked into the Nine-Two on the day after the murder. The precinct was quiet, as it usually is on a Monday evening. Sergeant Jackson Bell, the duty officer, was speaking with a pair of uniformed officers, both female. He stopped in mid-sentence when I appeared in the doorway, his glance flicking from the two cops to me. The women then turned to check me out and a very staged silence followed, a silence that could only have been more comical if they'd raised strings of garlic to ward off a hungry vampire.

I looked from the two uniforms, whose names I didn't know, to Sergeant Jackson Bell, holding their eyes for just an instant longer than necessary before continuing on my way.

Every precinct has its secrets, and every precinct guards those secrets, however grand or humble they may be. From this point of view, Sergeant Bell's attitude wasn't entirely unreasonable. If I was an IAB snitch, there was always the chance, perhaps even the likelihood, that I'd been assigned to scrutinize some individual, or group of individuals, in the Nine-Two. Perhaps even Sergeant Bell himself.

The corridor I followed to Lieutenant Drew Millard's office took a series of doglegs past the cubbyholes occupied by my co-workers on the four-to-midnight tour. Only one was occupied, by a detective named Robert Bandelone who waved me into the room.

'I heard you caught a homicide yesterday.'

'Yeah,' I replied, 'around noon.' I'd worked with Bandelone for a short time when his partner was out with the flu. Already promoted to Detective Second Grade, I knew him to be obsessed with obtaining First Grade status. If he thought the case was a grounder, he wouldn't hesitate to invite himself in as my partner. On the other hand, if he decided that he was looking at one of those mysteries cops dread, mysteries involving many hours of labor with little chance of a pay-off down the road, he'd keep his distance.

'You come across anybody who might be good for it?'

'No such luck, Bobby. What I got is a seventy-three-year-old witness, I don't think he can see his hand in front of his face, and an unidentified white female with no organs and a hole in her head.' I smiled. 'Would you believe time of death could be anywhere from a few days to a few months ago?'

'That bad, huh?' Bandelone had a habit of patting his bald scalp, very gingerly, with the fingers of his right hand, a gesture I found hopeful. He did it now, while I watched.

'She was dressed like a hooker, so who knows? Maybe I'll get lucky when I ask around.'

'You have a photo?'

'Wait a second.' I opened my briefcase, removed the Polaroid I'd taken of my victim's

55

face at the scene on the prior afternoon and laid it on Bandelone's desk. He stared down at the milky eyes and bloated cheeks for a moment before handing it back. Behind a pair of wire-rimmed glasses that he pushed up onto the bridge of his nose, his dark eyes appeared almost fragile.

'You think anybody's gonna recognize that?'

'What could I say, Bobby? Eventually I'm gonna see what a sketch artist can do with it, but for right now it's all I have.'

SIX

There were times when I felt sorry for my commanding officer. Born into a cop family that traced its roots to an ancestor who'd joined the New York Metropolitans shortly after the Civil War, Drew Millard seemed to pass most of his time playing catch-up. Ranger Millard was the ancestor's name. He'd risen from obscurity, in the course of a career that spanned three decades, to the rank of Inspector, roughly equal to today's Chief. That was just before Teddy Roosevelt forced Ranger to surrender his badge in the wake of a corruption scandal.

Notoriously brutal, Ranger had worn shoes even a hard man would have difficulty filling. Meanwhile, his direct descendant was soft in body, mind and spirit. Drew's gut was flabby, his blue eyes pale, his soft ass shapeless. Wheedling was the tactic he normally used to motivate his detectives, often beginning his sentences with a nearly fawning, 'C'mon, guy'.

Millard was sitting behind his desk when I walked into his office, dealing with his share of the paperwork generated by the train derailment on the prior morning. He seemed unusually cheerful, if a bit harassed, as he motioned me to a chair. 'Let's hear it,' he said. 'Tell me what happened this afternoon.'

Millard wanted to know why I'd attended the autopsy, which I was not obliged to do. I presented him with the mysteries, the pink lividity, the head wound, the evisceration, the possibility that Plain Jane Doe was exposed to cold before and after her death.

'The way the *ME* put it,' I concluded, as I had with Bandelone, 'time of death might be anywhere between a few days and a couple of months ago.'

'So you're saying the case isn't going anywhere until she's identified?'

'The *ME* recovered a decent set of the victim's prints. They'll go over to Missing Persons tomorrow morning. Missing Persons also promised to fax me a list of all females reported missing in the last month. I should have it within the hour.' I shrugged and smiled, my intention to play the role of amiable, semi-competent investigator for all it was worth. No sense, after all, in raising expectations. 'I don't know, boss. I got a bad feeling here.'

'C'mon, guy, don't be so pessimistic.' Millard spread his arms and smiled encouragingly. 'What about the witness?'

'The witness describes a middle-aged white male with squinty eyes and a van that might be any year, make, model and color. Unless I get lucky and identify the vic, I got no way to find either.' I paused for a moment as Millard nodded agreement. I'd returned to the precinct after the body was removed, with Clyde Kelly in tow, then created a case file while Kelly turned the pages of a mug book. The file was now on Millard's desk. Apparently, he'd taken the time to read it.

'What do you make of the way she was disemboweled?' he asked. 'What's that about?'

'I don't know? Jack the Ripper?' I shrugged off the idea, then drove the message home again. 'Until she's identified, it's all a guess.'

Millard began to fiddle with the case file. He opened the cover, sifted through the Complaint Report and my investigator's *DD*5s, then closed the file before rotating it 180 degrees. Finally, he said, 'You got a photo?'

I showed him the same photo I'd shown Bobby Bandelone. He passed it back to me after a quick glance. Again, I shrugged and smiled. '*CSU* couldn't free up a team, what with the derailment. I did the best I could.'

'It ain't the photo, Harry, it's the victim.' He leaned back in his chair. 'Ya know, in a way,

the derailment was a lucky break. The report-
ers would've jumped all over this on a slow
news day. How long until we hear about the
prints?'

I glanced past Millard's shoulder, through
the dirty window behind him. I was looking
west, over a furniture warehouse and across
Union Avenue toward Manhattan. It was
eight o'clock, and the sun had dropped below
the horizon, leaving in its wake a strip of
yellow that brought the upper stories of the
Empire State Building into sharp relief.

'We'll get fingerprint results the day after
tomorrow,' I continued. 'If she was a prostitute or a drug mule, most likely she has a
record.'

Millard nodded judiciously, then laid the
palm of his right hand over his chest. 'So,
whatta ya wanna do here?'

I leaned back in the chair and crossed my
legs. 'Well, boss, showing this photo to the
hookers up on Broadway, it's gonna get us
exactly nowhere. So I think I should concentrate on missing females who fit the victim's
general description, eliminate them one by
one. That way, you won't be second-guessed
somewhere down the line.'

Millard smiled. 'In case she turns out to be
somebody?'

I returned his smile, finally looking up to
meet his eyes. 'Exactly,' I said.

I went home that night to an empty apartment for the first time in many months. There
was a message on the answering machine

from Adele. She'd arrived safely, was very tired and expected to retire soon. I should call her the following evening at my convenience. At the end, she paused for a moment before saying, 'Bye-bye.' Not, 'Love ya, honey.' Not, 'Miss you already. Bye-bye.' And what I wondered, as I heated a can of soup in the microwave, was whether last night's romp had really been a bye-bye fuck. So long, baby, it was fun while it lasted.

I ate standing up by the kitchen window, the cooling soup on the counter before me. Outside, in the landscaped plaza at the center of Rensselaer Village, the leaves on the plane trees lay motionless, as though exhausted. I could smell the dead air on the other side of the screen, redolent of the garbage bags piled in front of the building for collection tomorrow morning. Summer in New York, a condition from which residents have fled for three hundred years. I dumped the dishes in the sink, grabbed a beer and headed for my air-conditioned bedroom, settling on the bed. It was a mistake. My thoughts turned to Adele, to her weary, distant tone, and I couldn't get her out of my head. I told myself that I was reading too much into a brief and simple message. If Adele seemed reserved, so what? Adele was reserved at the best of times; reserve was one of her assets, it leant her an air of mystery and assurance.

But I couldn't convince myself. Like all interrogators, I live by my gut, and my gut was telling me that Adele's sudden trip to

Maryland was more about flight than her mother's gastrointestinal problems. No, Adele had been drifting away from me for some time and now she'd taken that extra step the distance was physical. The saddest part was that I might have asked her what was wrong at any point. And I might have continued to ask until I got an answer.

I hadn't because I had feared the answer. I'd been through the separation process many times, both as dumper and dumped. I knew that what awaited me on the far end of any break-up was a loneliness so intense it bordered on fear. A loneliness that would soon drive me to the bars in search of any female willing to put her arms around my waist.

Long ago, as a boy, I'd gone through a phase where I tried to earn the approval of my druggie parents by transforming myself into the perfect child. (God knows, tantrums and whining were of no use at all.) That meant becoming a little adult, responsible, industrious, eager to please. The effort was doomed from the beginning and I gave up after a couple of years. I would always be an afterthought in my parents' lives and there was no bridging the gap.

'Oh, there's the kid. How's it goin', kid?'

I'm good at self-pity. No surprise, as I lived on it until I was old enough to go out on the streets of the Lower East Side and forge alliances strong enough to substitute for family. Then I abandoned my parents as surely as they'd abandoned me, my rejection of them so complete that I did not – and was not tempted to – attend my father's funeral.

I rolled off the bed, walked to my sweltering office and waited impatiently for my computer to load. Then I pulled up the image of my victim and created a flier I could pass out. I included my name and rank, an untraceable cell-phone number that I routinely gave to informants, and the simple fact that Plain Jane Doe had been murdered.

Though I tried to focus my thoughts on the long search ahead, I couldn't shake off the images presented by Clyde Kelly: the fat man with the narrow eyes; the body dragged over the dirt and weeds; the victim's chin coming up until her dead eyes met Kelly's, until she spoke to him, 'Help me, help me, help me.' If ever anyone had been abandoned, it was my victim, half frozen before her death, eviscerated afterward, finally left to the mercy of the sun and the flies.

In the space of a few seconds, I recalled the late afternoon thunderstorm, the clouds flying up and the hail that pounded her body, and the lightning that burst all around me, listening until the noise overwhelmed every other sense. I told myself to let Adele go, if that was what she wanted. I told myself that my first obligation was to this slain girl and I could not abandon her, come what may. Of course, I knew, even then, that I wasn't about to let Adele go, not without a fight. But that wasn't really the point. No, the point was that

Jane Doe #4805 had a right to justice, my personal problems be damned. Adele was a big girl. She had a good job. She could make her way in the world. For Jane, there was only me.

I went online and dragged up a list of Polish churches in New York. As expected, the largest was in Greenpoint, but there were others in each of the city's five boroughs. Eventually, I would visit them all. I knew this even before Jane's prints cleared every database maintained by New York State or the Federal Government without turning up a match. I knew that if there was even the slightest chance that Jane could be identified through her fingerprints, the men who disposed of her body would have cut off her hands.

SEVEN

I began my work day in the early afternoon at One Police Plaza, *NYPD* headquarters, arriving at two o'clock for a meeting with the *NYPD*'s criminal profiler, John Roach, a meeting arranged by Adele. Roach was in his mid-fifties, a detective first grade who'd been at the business of detecting for thirty years. His thinning hair was too gray even to be called salt-and-pepper, his jowls and forehead deeply creased. His nose was pinched at the end – it dropped almost to his upper lip when he smiled to reveal a half-inch gap between his front teeth. Academic might be a charitable way to describe his overall appearance, though goofy also came to mind as I returned his smile and shook his hand.

Roach gestured to a chair, then took a seat on the opposite side of his cluttered desk. 'Show me what you've got.' His voice was hoarse, barely above a whisper, and I had to actively resist the urge to lean forward, to be drawn into his orbit. '*CSU* was otherwise occupied,' I told him. 'This was the best I could do.' I passed over the crime scene photos I'd taken with the Polaroid on Sunday morning, as well as the autopsy report.

Roach got up at that point and began to pin the photographs to a cork board, one of a series of bulletin boards that ran along the wall behind his desk. He arranged the photos in three groups, the general scene first, then the trace evidence with the tire impressions and the cut fence-link. The victim came last, prone and supine, up close and from a distance.

For the next fifteen minutes, while he examined the photos, then the autopsy report, Roach spoke not a word. Lost as he was in the puzzle, I simply became irrelevant. And the puzzle was what Roach lived for – the puzzle was all he had. Profilers act as consultants, studying the evidence, offering advice, but they neither investigate, nor interrogate.

They're coaches, not players.

When Roach finally turned to face me, he was smiling again. 'Tell me about your witness.'

'His name is Clyde Kelly. On Sunday, he went out for a morning stroll, down to the waterfront in Williamsburg. Purely by accident, he witnessed a fat man with narrow eyes pull a woman's body from the back of a van, then drag her across a dirt mound to a chain-link fence. The fat man severed one link of the fence before spotting Kelly, who took off. That's the end of the story, unless you want Kelly's impressions.'

'I do.'

'According to Kelly, the man could've been "dumping a barrel of motor oil down a storm drain." It was just a job to him.'

At that point, Roach picked up the phone and called the *ME*'s office. Five minutes later, he was speaking to Dr Kim Hyong who'd conducted the autopsy. I'd called Hyong three times before leaving my apartment without getting past his voice mail.

Of course, Roach was a bit of a celebrity. If not with rank and file detectives, at least with Hyong, who also liked puzzles. But if the snub was humiliating, the new elements Hyong added to the mix captured my full attention. Tests for carbon monoxide and cyanide had found no trace of either in the victim's blood, while a third test proved that she had, in fact, been pregnant.

Roach re-examined the photos pinned to

the cork board after hanging up, taking his time about it. 'What do you want to know?' he finally asked.

'How about the name and address of her killer?'

'Sorry.'

'Then tell me how many hands played a part in her death and her disposal.'

'More than one. Perhaps as many as three or four.'

'Does that eliminate a serial killer?'

'That's my opinion.' Roach took a bottle of lemonade-flavored ice tea from the bottom drawer of his desk and drank. 'The exposure to cold, the head trauma, the pregnancy – they're real. The rest is staged.'

'Does that mean you think her killing was unpremeditated, that her killer was enraged?'

'Or panicked, which sometimes amounts to the same thing.'

'Then maybe you should rearrange those elements. First the pregnancy, then the cold, then the death blow.'

Roach smiled as he rose from his chair. My time was up. 'One other thing, detective. There's a sadist in the mix somewhere, an actor who, at the very least, shaped events.'

I took those thoughts with me to Missing Persons where I reviewed eighteen files, all of young white females reported missing in the last three months. Unlike the list faxed to me on the prior night, most of the case files included photographs, which allowed me to quickly determine that my victim was not

66

among them. Still, I took careful notes as I went along. Millard wanted his ass covered and my intention was to generate as much paper as possible, to stuff the case file until it overflowed.

When I finished, I turned to the six files that lacked a photo. Five were either too young or too old to be my victim, while the sixth was of Nina Klaipeda, an eighteen-year-old Lithuanian immigrant. Nina had been reported missing by her mother, Jolanta, five weeks before, and that made her unlikely to be my victim. Nevertheless, I'd have to pay her mother a visit, assuming Nina hadn't returned home. According to the description in the case file, Nina Klaipeda's hair was light, her complexion fair. Weight and height were in the ballpark as well.

I stopped for a coffee break around three o'clock, just before I left for Brooklyn, and took the opportunity to call Adele. I knew she'd be happy to learn that she was right about the pregnancy, a possibility I'd never considered. I also knew that if I waited until I got home, she'd probably be asleep.

'From the beginning, we suspected that the post-mortem activity was purposeful,' she told me upon hearing the news, 'and now we know why. Did you meet with John Roach?'

'Yeah. An interesting guy.'

'What did he say?'

'He said we can pretty much dismiss the psychosexual killer thing.'

'Did he say why?'

'Too many people involved. But he was only giving me a rough impression, not an official profile. By the way, the tests came in for cyanide and carbon monoxide. Both negative.'

Adele paused for a moment. 'So, where are you going with the case?'

'Tonight, I'm heading up to the Bronx, to check out a missing Lithuanian. Tomorrow, it's Greenpoint.'

'Why Greenpoint?'

'Greenpoint has a large population of Polish immigrants and it borders Williamsburg, the neighborhood where the victim's body was dumped. Somehow, I don't think your average, everyday killer would just stumble onto South Fifth Street. You can't even see the pier from the street. At the least, he'd have to be familiar with the neighborhood.'

'True enough, but he might simply work in the area and live somewhere else. Or he might live in the neighborhood, but the victim lived somewhere else. And another thing. Even if the victim grew up behind the Iron Curtain, she doesn't have to be Polish just because she's blond. She might be an East German, a Russian, a Ukrainian, a Czech, or come from the borderlands between Austria and Hungary.'

I found myself smiling. Adele's tone was upbeat and engaged. In this matter, at least, there was no distance between us. 'The dump site is obscure and Poles have been living within a few miles of it for a century. I'm gonna start with the obvious and see how it goes. Unless you have a better idea.'

'Well, there is one thing. If you want, I'm pretty sure I can arrange a meeting with an *INS* Agent named Dominick Capra. You'll have to spring for lunch and put up with his anti-immigrant rants, but Capra's been around for a long time. If you run into a wall, he could point you in the right direction.'

A good detective will take help from anyone. And then there was the matter of Adele's continuing involvement in the case. To which I had absolutely no objection. 'Why don't you give him a call, see if he's willing? If the victim's prints aren't on file and I don't have any luck in Greenpoint, lunch is on me.'

'Done.'

At that point, I turned the conversation to Adele's sister and parents. I was hoping she'd tell me how uncomfortable she felt in their presence, but her tone became wistful, as though she were describing some distant memory.

Adele told me that her mother had lost weight, that she'd be visiting a gastroenterologist on the following afternoon, that the fear – unspoken in Leya Bentibi's presence – was stomach cancer. A lifelong smoker, Leya still consumed two packs a day.

There was nothing I could say to any of this. A sick mother cannot be challenged. Nor could I challenge Adele's obligation to comfort her sister. Jovianna had always been close

69

to her mother. She, too, was frightened.

'What are your mother's symptoms?'

'Pain, acid reflux, gas. And there are traces of blood in her stool.'

'But she hasn't been diagnosed, right?'

'Corbin, what can I say? I'm dealing with the realities at hand.'

At eight thirty, after a long drive in heavy traffic, I knocked on the door of Jolanta Klaipeda's Westchester Avenue apartment. She opened a moment later, then led me to a cracked leather couch draped with a red and green Christmas blanket. The couch was occupied by two elderly men, brothers by the look of them. When Jolanta addressed them in what I assumed to be Lithuanian, they struggled to their feet and shuffled toward one of the bedrooms. Only after the door closed behind their backs did Jolanta turn to face me. Her eyes met mine for a moment, then darted away, then returned. I could see the fear in those eyes, fear dancing in the amber motes flecking her brown irises, and fear in her raised and reddened lids, in the tight line of her mouth, in the flare of her nostrils. On the phone, I'd attempted to reassure the woman. My visit, I'd explained, was routine. I had no reason to believe that the photo I intended to show her was of her daughter. But that strategy backfired when Jolanta, in halting English, told me that she'd provided a photo of Nina to the officers who'd interviewed her five weeks before. Clearly, she didn't believe me when I explained that Nina's photo had somehow been misplaced. Clearly, she thought I was coming to the Bronx only to confirm what I already knew, that her daughter was dead.

I reached into my pocket for the computer-enhanced photo I intended to show her, but Jolanta stopped me. 'Please,' she said, 'for a moment.' Then she followed the two men into the bedroom, leaving me to my own devices.

I can't say for sure how many people lived in the Klaipeda household, but there were two single beds and a cradle in the living room. Half hidden by an upright piano, cradle and beds were lined up against the wall opposite the windows. A young girl, maybe ten years old, sat at the piano. She was play-ing scales, her touch light and delicate, even in the lower registers. An older man sat on a kitchen chair beside her, nodding from time to time, while a metronome ticked away a few inches from her face.

Jolanta returned a moment later with a child in tow, a boy wearing the blue, polyester pants and white shirt of a Catholic school student. Eight or nine years old, his blond hair was cropped to within a few millimeters of his scalp.

'My aunt don't speak English too good,' he explained. 'She wants me to translate.'

Across the room, the girl finally broke free of the relentless scales she'd been playing, her right hand dropping to her side while her left pounded out an equally relentless boogie-woogie.

71

'That's my sister, Alena,' the boy explained. 'She's getting ready for a talent contest. Little Miss New York. At Madison Square Garden.'

I acknowledged his sister's ambitions and talents with a short smile, then handed my victim's photo to Jolanta Klaipeda. Almost without transition, her face brightened. This was not her dead daughter, not the baby she'd raised. It was someone else's dead baby. I saw her look up at a crucifix on the wall to her right, watched her bless herself. Then she laughed, once, a bark of defiance, before addressing her nephew in Lithuanian. He listened attentively until she finished, then nodded.

'She says to tell you that this girl is not her daughter. She says that Nina is beautiful. She says that Nina is a rose and this is a cabbage.'

EIGHT

I got up and out on the next morning in time to catch the tail end of the eight o'clock mass at St Stanislaus in Greenpoint. Afterward, I passed out a dozen fliers to the exiting parishioners before chatting up Father Korda, who stood by the church door. Charm was my weapon of choice in these encounters, humble petitioner my stance. I told the priest, and anyone else who cared to listen, that I had good reason to believe that my victim was a Polish immigrant who'd lived in the neighborhood. Helping her was helping one of their own. I told the same story to Polish storekeepers on both sides of Manhattan Avenue. Murdered innocent, Polish immigrant. Her family was out there somewhere, awaiting closure. Her killer was out there, too, maybe getting ready to kill someone else.

Whenever possible, I tried to buy something. Breakfast at one diner, coffee and a buttered corn muffin at another. I had fifty copies of the flier printed at a card shop. I bought a package of light bulbs at a hardware store and a tube of toothpaste at a small pharmacy. At every moment, I projected an attitude of brotherly cooperation, one common humanity; we're all in this together. My goal was to place my flier in the front window where it would be seen by pedestrians. I'd even brought my own tape.

I was mostly successful, but the going was necessarily slow. Still, by Thursday, I'd covered Greenpoint thoroughly and was out to Maspeth, a Queens neighborhood a few miles to the southeast. I'd gotten two hits by then. Both were false alarms, but ones I'd had to check out. This was a pattern that continued through the week and into the weekend. There were a lot of Nina Klaipeda's out there, women whose daughters bore not the faintest resemblance to Plain Jane Doe.

On Thursday, Millard called me into his

73

office to review the case. 'Tough luck,' he told me. 'Your vic's prints came back negative. And nobody's reported her missing yet.' When I shrugged in response, he leaned back in his chair. 'So, whatta ya doin'? Tell me.'

A case review, at this point, was routine, and ordinarily I'd have progress to report. But there was nothing here and when I described my daytime activities, the effort rang hollow.

'I've got two men out on vacation, Harry,' Millard told me at the end. 'You're gonna have to pick up cases. C'mon guy.'

Later that night, I took the bad news to a *YMCA* swimming pool on Twenty-Third Street. The pool was managed by a man named Conrad Stehle, who'd given me and a few other serious swimmers permission to use it late at night. Conrad had been my high school swimming coach, way back when I was a budding juvenile delinquent. That I didn't suffer the fate of so many of my peers by running afoul of the law was due almost entirely to his intervention. Before we met, my options were limited to my druggie parents or a motley collection of street urchins on the Lower East Side. Conrad offered a third possibility; I could, if I wished, spend my afternoons in his Murray Hill apartment. I don't want to take this too far – I never thought of Conrad as my father, or his wife, Helen, as my mother. Instead, what they provided, and what I needed, was stability, a dependable world equally free of the chaos offered by my parents and the casual violence of the streets.

There was a second benefit to my relationship with Conrad, a benefit still with me twenty-five years later. Simply put, as I learned to swim competitively, water became my preferred element. With my goggles wet and every sound dampened by ear plugs, I was finally able to shut the world out, to turn my attention inward until I eventually became my own object, the insect under the glass. Double-stroke, then breathe. Turn, push off. After a while, you don't have to look ahead to find the far wall, or even count your strokes as you cross the pool. Something inside you, the same something that makes your heart beat and your stomach digest, counts for you.

I swam for an hour on that night, concentrating my attention on the case. I knew, going in, that if Jane wasn't identified, her murder would never be avenged. As I knew that, for the time being, I needed to continue my canvas, gradually expanding the search area, and hope for the best. Still, at some point, assuming I didn't identify her first, the law of diminishing returns would kick in with a vengeance. It's a very big city. Myself, I didn't intend to give up if I crossed that line because there was another possibility out there, a wild card named Bill Sarney.

Now assigned to the Chief of Detectives office, Deputy-Inspector Bill Sarney had been in command of the One-Sixteen when Adele and I worked the case that put us on the outs with the job. Two-faced from the beginning, Sarney pretended to be my rabbi and my friend, all the while selling me out to Borough Command and his buddies at the Puzzle Palace.

It took me awhile, but when I eventually uncovered his game, I'd threatened to expose him to a sitting grand jury. The threat was potent enough to secure a promise that I'd eventually be transferred to Homicide – my long-term goal from the day I stepped through the doors of the Academy – and that we'd meet in public from time to time. About the *PBA* and its whispering campaign he could do nothing.

Working for the Chief of Detectives, Sarney had the kind of juice I'd need if I took the case in a different direction. Unidentified victims are not all that rare in New York, certainly not rare enough to attract attention from the press. True, the media occasionally takes up the cause of a Jane Doe, but cops who reach out to the media without the backing of the job's Public Information Office pay a heavy price. Bill Sarney could get me that backing. All I'd have to do is beg.

Almost from the minute my hands cut the water, I'd been making an attempt to banish Adele from my thoughts. By then I knew she wouldn't return, as promised, by the weekend. On Monday, her mother was scheduled to undergo an endoscopy, a procedure that requires the insertion of a tube through the mouth and into the stomach. Leya Bentibi was beside herself, not least because Jovianna insisted that she make a living will.

Adele could not simply desert her mother. Right? So there was nothing to consider. That's what I told myself, and I almost made it stick. But then, as my stroke became ragged, an image of Adele rose, unbidden, to hang before my eyes. Adele was sitting in the lobby of North Shore Hospital, her face a mask of bandages, her ski jacket matted with dried blood. I'd come to pick her up after an overnight stay because her husband was in Dallas on a business trip that could not be interrupted for so mundane a task.

Adele had been sitting with her back straight and her head up when I entered the hospital, enduring the frank stares of all who passed her by. I fell in love with her at that moment, with her pride, her defiance. You could kill her, but you couldn't break her. A few days later, when she came to me, when I felt her breasts against my chest and tasted her lips, I knew there was no going back. If I lost her, I'd pay a price until the end of my days. Twenty minutes later, after a quick shower, I tried to call Conrad on his cell phone. If I could talk to anyone, it was Conrad, who knew me better than I knew myself. But Conrad was somewhere off the coast of Alaska, on a cruise with his girlfriend, Myra Gardner. He was reachable only when the ship was in port, which it apparently wasn't because I was transferred, after a single ring, to his voice mail. I started to leave a message, then abruptly hung up. There was no point.

NINE

By Monday, I was in the Brooklyn neighborhood of Brighton Beach, popularly called
Little Odessa. Upwards of one hundred
thousand Russians and Ukrainians, most of
them immigrants, are packed into Brighton
Beach, enough to spill over into the communities of Gravesend and Sheepshead Bay.
On the little shops along the streets and
avenues, the signs are most commonly written in Cyrillic, and more business is conducted in Russian than English. There are
grocery stores in Brighton Beach, no larger
than bodegas, which carry ten brands of
pickled herring and a dozen of caviar.

The weather remained hot throughout and
I was grateful for the deep shadow cast by the
el on Brighton Beach Avenue as I made my
rounds. My pitch to these Russian shop-
keepers differed only slightly from my approach to the Poles of Greenpoint. I told the
Russians that I was sure my victim came from
Russia or the Ukraine, a white lie that netted
me zilch, though I managed to post fliers in a
number of businesses. Adele called me that
evening, a few minutes before I entered the
Nine-Two. Her mother's endoscopy had

revealed a small gastric ulcer that would be treated with antacids and a course of anti-biotics. No surgery was foreseen, now or in the future. All concerned were relieved.

Besides a muttered, 'Uh-huh,' I made no comment. I was waiting for Adele to say that she was coming home. Instead, she turned the conversation to the case.

'I set up that meeting with Dominick Capra. He says you should call in the morning and let him know where to meet you.'

It took me a moment to remember that Capra was an agent with the Immigration & Naturalization Service. 'Yeah,' I said. 'I'll call him.'

'Corbin, don't be so negative. He thinks he can help you.'

'I'll definitely call him. So, when are you coming home?'

Adele sighed and I knew the answer: no time soon.

'I need to think,' she told me. 'I have to take a look at my life. I have to take a look at the fact that every day I go out to a job I hate. Do you remember when I told you that I didn't want to live a trivial life? Well, that's exactly what I'm doing. I'm not saying you, Corbin. You'll never be trivial. You don't have it in you. But I'm saying that I need time to think. Time and space.'

This carefully prepared speech presented a line of reasoning familiar to Harry Corbin. You're perfect, darling, the story goes, but my life is fucked up in every other way. So I've decided to leave you. That way I won't be conflicted.

At noon on Tuesday, I met *INS* Agent Dominick Capra at Pete's Tavern near Gramercy Park. About my age, Capra was short and wide-shouldered, with a thickened nose red enough to hang on a Christmas tree. That nose reddened still further when he chugged a double bourbon within minutes of his arrival.

'Be a sport,' he said, the fumes on his breath thick enough to ignite, 'and spring for another.' And another, and another, as it turned out.

Adele had cautioned me about Dominick Capra, and for good reason. Capra was obsessed with the criminality of the new immigrants and the threat they posed to the nation. He spewed bigotry with every breath.

'First of all, there's no Russian mob,' he told me at one point. 'What you got in Brighton Beach is a Jewish mob. And it's bigger than the fuckin' wops ever were.' At another, he declared, ticking the items off on his fingers. 'There's a Rumanian mob, a Bulgarian mob, an Israeli mob, a Nigerian mob. There's mobs from ten different parts of China. Hell, you could just make a list of the world's busted-out countries and there'd be organized criminals emigrating from every fucking province.'

I didn't react to Capra's tirade, probably because my concentration was still focused on my little talk with Adele. But then Capra

80

surprised me with something relevant and my focus shifted abruptly.

Illegal immigrants, he pointed out, aren't hermits and they don't live in caves. They live in ordinary communities, most commonly among individuals they knew in their home countries.

'Bottom line, Harry, even if she was illegal, she should have been reported missing. This is especially true for your ex-commies. Before they're here a month, the kids are in school, the family's on Medicaid and they're collectin' food stamps. They know all the tricks and they're not afraid of authority.'

'What could I say, Dominick? I keep in touch with Missing Persons on a daily basis. If there's anyone out there who cares about her, they're keeping it to themselves.'

'I believe you, Harry.' Capra's head swiveled back and forth, until he caught the attention of a waiter. Then he raised his glass. 'Por favor.' Finally, he turned back to me and said, 'Look, you got two possibilities here, one pretty remote. Let's take the remote one first. You don't see much of this in the US, but every day, thousands of girls from across the third world are drawn into the sex trade against their will. Some are lured into it with false promises and some are purchased from their parents. Either way, these girls become virtual slaves.'

Capra tilted his head back and brought his glass to his mouth, draining the last few drops of Jim Beam. Then he grinned. 'How'd ya like to be sold by your parents in Vietnam, taken to a mining camp in Burma, then forced to screw twenty guys a day? For nothing, right? You're not even gettin' paid.'

This was too much for me and I ignored the question. 'What's the other possibility?'

Capra thought about it for a moment, then said, 'Lemme start by givin' you an example. Four or five years ago, a nineteen-year-old girl, a Philippine national, broke her ankle jumping from the second-floor window of a townhouse. When she got to the emergency room, the docs noticed that she'd been beat to shit and called in the cops. According to the girl, Consuela Madamba, she was recruited in her home village by a woman representing an American employment agency. For a substantial price, to be paid from her wages, Consuela would be smuggled into the United States and guaranteed employment as a domestic. Consuela didn't find out, until she got here, that her employer would be a Saudi family attached to the UN. She didn't know that she'd be watched constantly, that she was expected to work sixteen-hour days, or that she'd be routinely beaten for the slightest failure to maintain the home properly.'

My thoughts flashed to Roach, the profiler, and his prediction: there's a sadist in the mix.

Capra leaned over the table. Though his speech and mannerisms were unaffected by the alcohol he'd consumed, the light reflected from his dark eyes was sharp and fragmented.

'Indentured servants, in colonial times, they only had to work a given number of years until they were free. These days, illegals have to keep going until the debt is completely satisfied. Plus, they're responsible for their upkeep. Funny thing, Harry, but Consuela's living expenses were always just a bit higher than her wages. Call it sharecropping for the new millennium.'

I thought about this for a moment, before asking the obvious question. 'Why didn't she just walk away? It's a big country.'

'First, she was carefully supervised. Second, her family in the Philippines co-signed for the debt. Third, the reason she got her ass kicked was because she tried to escape.'

'But they didn't kill her.'

Capra leaned back as the waiter set a fresh drink on the table before him. He looked at his whiskey for a minute, then caught a single drop running down the side of the glass on the tip of a finger. He brought the finger to his mouth and sucked appreciatively.

'I see what you're gettin at,' he finally said. 'You kill the debtor, you can forget about collecting the debt, which is something no smart businessman wants to do. On the other hand, shit happens now and again, after which you have to clean up the mess.'

Capra's hamburger sat on a dish in front of him. Though he'd nibbled around the edges, it was clear that he was drinking his lunch. 'Anything else?' he asked.

'Yeah, you told me that the international

83

sex trade doesn't operate much in the United States. What about those ads in the Village Voice, the ones for Korean, Thai and Vietnamese escort services?'

'I didn't say never, Harry. What are you gettin' at?'

'I want to know if you think my victim might have been a prostitute? We figure she was around eighteen when she was killed.' I slid my photo of plain Jane Doe across the table to Capra, who stared at her for a few seconds before looking me in the eye.

'Gimme a break, Harry. She was a dog, most likely she was the one who had to pay for it.'

I was still cooling down, when Capra glanced at his watch. 'I gotta get goin' in a minute,' he declared as he chugged his drink. 'I'm supposed to testify at a hearing this afternoon. But there's one other thing I wanted to mention. In my opinion, the best way to reach large numbers of immigrants is through their newspapers. Forget about runnin' from one neighborhood to another. You could be doin' that for the rest of your life. Advertising is what works. I know this because we used local papers to pull off a number of stings. It was very effective.'

I had a sudden vision of shackled deportees being led, in a long line, toward a waiting airplane. Headed for home sweet home.

'How many newspapers are we talking about?'

'Maybe a dozen that cater to Eastern Europeans and Russians.' Capra pushed his chair back and rose to his feet. 'Another thing you might want to consider. Those foreign gangsters I mentioned? Well, they're not civilized, not like your Italian gangsters. You run up against one of them, you shouldn't expect him to act with restraint.'

Capra turned to go, but I held him with a gesture. 'One more thing. The employment agency that placed Consuela Madamba with the Saudi family. Did you run them down?'

'Yeah, we traced them to an apartment in the Bronx. It took about a week, by which time they and their workers were long gone.'

I went from my lunch with Capra to a news store on Second Avenue. I showed the owner my badge and asked a few questions about Polish-language newspapers.

'There's only one with any kind of circulation, *Gazeta Warszawa*. For Polish immigrants, it's the paper of record.'

That was enough for me and I took a ride to the paper's offices in Long Island City. Though I showed my badge and explained the situation in enough detail to draw pity from a psychopath, Lucjan Bilawski refused to discount his advertising rates.

'First thing, I get lots of calls from desperate relatives. If I ran free ads for every one of them, there wouldn't be room for the paying customers. Now, in this case, being as this is a murder, we'd run it as a news story if you could prove that she was Polish.'

I couldn't, of course, and so I paid out three hundred sixty-five dollars for an ad that would run from Thursday through Sunday. At Bilawski's suggestion, I laid out the facts in Polish, him translating: murder victim, unidentified, help the police. On the bottom, I left the number of my cell phone.

Bilawski smiled when he took my check. He shook my hand vigorously. 'If you decide you want the ad to run past Sunday, you don't have to come back. Just give me a ring. I'll take your credit card.'

TEN

I carried Dominick Capra's revelations through the rest of that week, carried them along First Avenue where grown men delivering food on bicycles flew past me. They worked for tips, these men, gathering in small knots outside the many restaurants, their battered bikes chained to meters and no-parking signs. Everybody knew they were in the country illegally. The Mayor knew it. The City Council knew it. The *New York Times* knew it. Dominick Capra knew it. Just as all knew there was a less visible army of illegals out there, sewing dresses, cleaning floors, mowing lawns, busing tables in restaurants all over the city.

But if there's a government agency prepared to deal with the problem, it isn't the *NYPD*. The job, at the direction of a succession of mayors and commissioners, has disavowed the whole business. Illegal immigration, as the job understands it, is a federal, not a local, crime. As for the rest, the debts and the coercion, they don't blip on the radar screens of working cops. It takes something more – a murder victim, for instance, eviscerated and dumped on a street in Brooklyn – to motivate the *NYPD*. Or at least one low-ranking detective.

I can't say that I recall the days following my lunch with Capra in any great detail, but I have a general sense of Adele retreating, of Plain Jane Doe coming forward. I couldn't do anything about Adele. She was in charge of the decision-making process. If I pushed her, she'd only move further away, even assuming I successfully concealed a resentment that had already begun to fester.

The issue was more pressing for Jane. My ad in *Gazeta Warszawa* was not just another turn of the cards. The newspaper, which claimed a proven circulation of forty thousand, was written entirely in Polish. That meant every reader had to be a Pole.

Even as I placed the ad, I'd known that the chain of speculations running from Jane's gold crowns and white fillings to an illegal immigrant from Poland would fall apart if the ad failed to produce a viable lead. A few fillings, a clandestine dump site, a Polish community nearby – it didn't amount to much. Hyong had told me that white fillings were rare in the West. But what about South America? Or South Africa? And while I was sure the man who carried Jane to the Brooklyn waterfront was familiar with the area, I also knew, as Adele suggested, that he might work in the neighborhood and live somewhere else. And then there was the possibility that Jane had only been in the country for a few weeks, or even a few days.

Ordinarily, I don't allow myself to wallow in negativity, not while I'm working a case. After all, any line of investigation can be second-guessed. But I'd laid down a big bet when I placed the ad and most of my chips were on the table. If I busted out, I'd continue to work the case, but the likelihood that I'd ever speak for Jane Doe #4805 would sharply diminish.

The first response came on Thursday evening, when my cell phone kicked out an amazingly tone-deaf rendition of John Coltrane's, 'My Favorite Things'. By then, I had the patter down.

'Detective Corbin,' I answered. 'How may I help you?'

'This girl who is having her picture in the paper. I believe I am knowing her.'

'Can you tell me when you last saw her?'

'One week ago.'

'That would be on July fourteenth?'

'Yes, on Sunday.'

And that was the end of that. The question I'd posed was a screening device. Any date after Jane's body was discovered on July 7th eliminated the possibility of a true sighting. But even if the caller had gotten the date right, I was prepared to add a series of questions about height and weight, country of origin, hair and eye color. Checking false leads was an activity I was determined, for obvious reasons, to minimize.

I continued to field calls through Friday, through torrential rains on Saturday, and into Sunday morning without getting a hit. Although a few of the calls began by asking whether there was a reward – and concluded shortly afterward – most were from desperate parents. Their collective heartbreak poured through the phone lines, as real to me as the air I breathed. They might have been sitting beside me. And I knew what they wanted, these mothers and fathers. They wanted to be made whole, to be restored. I could not restore them, but I doled out the only solace I had to offer. I informed them, after a few questions, that the murdered girl I searched for was not their daughter. They could go on hoping.

At one o'clock on Sunday, after a short lunch, I settled down to watch a Yankees-Mets game, an encounter I'd been looking forward to for some time, having been a Yankee fan all my life. But the game was a dud, and by the third inning, when my cell phone went off, I'd had enough anyway. The Mets were ahead, six-zip, having pulverized

C.C. Sabathia, while the feared Yankee batters had been limited to a single infield hit. I muted the *TV*, then pushed myself to a sitting position and took the phone from the end table. 'Detective Corbin, how may I help you?'

'My name is Sister Kassia Grabski. The girl whose photograph appeared in the newspaper today was here, at Blessed Virgin. I spoke to her briefly.'

'Is that Blessed Virgin in Maspeth, where they have the outreach center?'

'Yes.'

At this point, I was supposed to ask when the conversation had taken place, to screen the call, but several things caught my attention. An authoritative tone, first of all, that conveyed near certainty, and the title, Sister. Then Blessed Virgin Outreach where I'd displayed Jane's photo to a priest named Stan Manicki. Father Stan had examined the photo carefully before looking up. His eyes, as I recalled them, were large and strikingly blue, dominating a hawkish nose and strong cheekbones. They projected sincerity, those eyes, and maybe that's the reason I slipped up.

Honest citizens have a hard time lying to a cop. When they don't want to answer a question truthfully, they tend to evade it. Father Stan hadn't said, 'I've never seen this woman before.' His response had been equivocal: 'I can't help you.' At the time, I'd thought nothing of it.

90

Before I could begin to curse myself for a fool, Sister Kassia asked, 'Are you still there?'

'Sorry, I got distracted for a moment. Maybe you could tell me when you last saw her.'

'On Saturday, June twenty-second.' Again, the confident tone, the precise date.

'Had you ever seen her before?'

'I'd seen her at mass, many times, but I only spoke to her once, and not to her directly. That was on a Saturday when she came here with the other girls, to confess.'

'To confess?'

'Yes, to Father Manicki. They were chaperoned, as usual.'

'Chaperoned by a man?'

'This time, yes. But sometimes they're accompanied by an older woman.'

I told myself to chill out, to wipe that smile off my ugly face. The nun's confident tone might be no more than the natural outgrowth of an assertive personality. 'Now, you said you spoke to her. Would you describe the circumstances?'

'When the girls came into the church on June twenty-second, I was busy arranging the weekly flower delivery. There were five of them, including the girl you're trying to identify. Though I had no real plan, I decided to stay inside the church while they confessed, hoping for an opportunity to speak to them alone. That chance presented itself at the very end when their minder left to use the

91

bathroom. I knew I wouldn't have much time, so I kept it simple. I spoke Polish, telling them my name, and that if they ever needed help, they should come straight to Blessed Virgin and we'd protect them.'

'Protect them from what?'

'I'm sorry, I forgot your name. Would you repeat it?'

'Detective Corbin.'

'Well, Detective Corbin, if you drive out to Blessed Virgin at six o'clock this evening, in time for the Polish mass, you can see for yourself.'

'That, Sister, will be no problem at all. But there's just one more thing I'd like to know for now. Did you by any chance catch the girl's name?'

'No, I'm sorry. This was my first approach and I spoke to the girls as a group. Not that I see how it matters. I'm certain of my identification because the girl had a curious way of looking at you out of the corner of her eye, just as she does in the photograph that appeared in the paper.'

ELEVEN

The community of Maspeth, in Queens, is heavily industrialized, like virtually every other New York community bordering the waters that surround Manhattan. In this case, the water is Newtown Creek, a polluted canal that feeds into the East River. The joke among cops who work near the canal is that a body dumped into the water at sundown will dissolve before morning. I'd never had the good fortune to view a body pulled from Newtown Creek, but I'd been close enough in midsummer to experience the foul odor that seeps from its oily waters any time the temperature rises above eighty degrees. Newtown Creek was an industrial dump site for a hundred years before the first environmental laws were written. Somehow, the near-miraculous rehabilitation of the Hudson and East Rivers has passed it by.

I drove across Newtown Creek that Sunday afternoon, on Metropolitan Avenue, from Brooklyn into Queens, continuing on through the industrial heart of Maspeth and into a primarily residential neighborhood near Fresh Pond Road. The homes were modest here. Semi-detached and two-family for the most part, they bore flat roofs and were sided in a textured vinyl that made only the faintest stab at a wood-like appearance. But their yards were neatly kept, the tiny lawns mowed, the shrubs carefully trimmed. In one, the path to the front door was framed by a trellis overgrown with pink roses. In another, a woman bent over an enormous hydrangea, cutting the purple blossoms and transferring them to a laundry basket at her feet.

Blessed Virgin Roman Catholic Church was as modest and well tended as its neighbors. The stone tower on its northern face rose only a few feet higher than the surrounding homes, and the statue of the Virgin in its churchyard, though crude enough to pass for lawn furniture, was freshly painted.

There were people gathered outside the church when I walked down the block. As they were universally Caucasian, I gussed they were arriving for the Polish mass, as I assumed there'd already been masses conducted in Spanish and English. The Roman Catholic Church in New York is committed to satisfying the demands of believers from nations as diverse as Rumania and Botswana. In the vernacular.

I scanned the crowd as I passed the face of the church, looking for a group of young women escorted by a single man, but found only the expected gathering of families. I was headed for a narrow wood-frame addition jutting from the church's northern face.

Blessed Virgin Outreach was run from this building and that's where I was to meet Sister Kassia.

The large room I finally entered was given over to a motley collection of couches and upholstered chairs. Hand-me-downs, without doubt, their wildly mismatched fabrics, colors and patterns might have filled a manufacturer's sample book. The effect was homey, nevertheless, with the chairs and couches arranged in small groupings that afforded a bit of privacy. Sister Kassia was sitting on one of the couches, speaking to a woman who sat next to her. In her late twenties, the woman's face was swollen and discolored, with one eye closed altogether.

When I shut the door, the nun turned to look at me for the first time, and I knew, instantly, that I'd been right about her take-no-prisoners attitude. Her nose was pointed, her mouth pinched and turned down at both ends, her chin sharp enough to punch holes in sheet metal. Two deep grooves rolled up and out from the bridge of her nose to echo the sharp hook of her pale eyebrows. Beneath those brows, her hazel eyes were as round as an owl's. They appraised me without apology.

Finally, the nun turned to half whisper a few words to the woman on the other side of the couch before crossing the room. Late in middle age and a good thirty pounds above her best weight, she nevertheless moved with grace, coming at me with her shoulders squared, offering her hand for a firm shake.

'Mr Corbin?' she said.

I nodded my head. If she didn't want it known that I was a cop, that was okay by me. 'Why don't you just call me Harry,' I suggested.

'Fine. Now I'm going to need a few minutes here. I have to get Flora settled.'

'Actually, I was hoping to speak to Father Manicki before the mass got started.'

That brought her up short and she paused to reassess the big cop who towered above her. I met her gaze without flinching, the message I wanted to send quite simple. When Sister Kassia picked up the phone to call me, the entrance to the maze had closed behind her. There was no going back.

'Father Stan's in the sacristy, putting on his vestments.' She pointed at a door to my right that fed into the church. 'He won't be happy to see you just now.'

'Father Stan's not gonna be happy to see me any time,' I said. 'Most likely, he was against your calling me at all.'

She smiled then, a thin and grudging smile to be sure, but a smile nonetheless. 'You're very astute, Harry, but don't judge Father Stan too harshly. Our position here is very delicate. It seems the archdiocese approves of Blessed Virgin's outreach to the undocumented, as long as we don't draw attention to ourselves.' I couldn't help but think of the bosses in the Puzzle Palace. They didn't care if you ignored a suspect's civil liberties, as long as you didn't get caught.

'Tell me, Sister, does the parish offer this Polish-language mass on a weekly basis?'

'Every Sunday.'

'And Father Stan, does he usually conduct the mass?'

'Almost always.'

'These women you spoke of, can I assume they show up?'

'Most of the time, they do.'

'I see. Now, I'm not a Catholic, so I don't know the customs all that well. But does the priest who performs the mass go outside to greet his parishioners as they leave the church?'

'He does.'

'Thank you, Sister.'

I discovered Father Manicki in a small room at the end of a narrow hallway. He was standing before a closet that held a variety of robes and brightly colored vestments. There were two children in the room with him. I would have made them for altar boys in an earlier era, but these two were of mixed gender, the girl a foot taller than her companion.

Father Manicki turned to me when I knocked on the open door. He raised a hand to slow me down, then instructed the children to wait outside. When they were safely gone, he closed the door behind them.

'What do you mean, barging in here?' he demanded. 'I'm preparing to celebrate a mass.'

But I wasn't about to be bluffed, not this time, not by the hawk's nose, the square jaw, or the firm set of his mouth. At first glance, Father Stan might have passed for a bare-knuckle prize fighter, but there was something else in his blue eyes, a sense of regret that I knew I could exploit should the need arise.

'I didn't come here to accuse you,' I said. 'But I want you to tell me, right now, whether you recognized the girl in that photo. I want a confirmation or a denial.'

His jaw tightened momentarily – perhaps he wasn't used to being challenged – but then he suddenly deflated, his gaze dropping to the carpet. 'Try to understand,' he said. 'Those young women are virtual prisoners.'

'How do you know that?'

'Because I've looked into the eyes of the men who escort them.'

When I didn't argue the point, he continued. 'And like all prisoners, if they attempt to run away ... well, you know what happened to the girl you want to identify.'

'No, I don't, Father. I don't know what happened to her. If I did, I wouldn't be here asking for your help.'

'But don't you understand? Everything I learned about her life came to me through the confessional, so it's just as I said when you first approached me. I can't help you.' He held up Plain Jane Doe's photo. 'In the Catholic Church, the seal of the confessional is absolute. I'm helpless here.'

The room was very spare, a plain chest of drawers, several ladder-back wooden chairs, a small table. Except for a large crucifix above the door, the walls were undecorated. Father Manicki turned his eyes to the crucifix at that moment, to a stylized Christ whose arms and legs were too long for his emaciated torso, who wore, in lieu of a crown of thorns, an actual crown, as if already risen. 'This girl,' he continued without turning around, 'she's beyond help. But the other girls are still at risk. You may think that you can ride to the rescue, perhaps arrest the men who watch over them. But even if you're successful, it won't help.'

'Why is that?'

'Because in this country, when it comes to undocumented workers, the policy is don't ask, don't tell.'

'You mean they're okay as long as the *INS* doesn't find out about them?'

'Exactly. But if they should come to the attention of the *INS*, say as a consequence of your investigation, they'll be deported.' He hesitated for a moment before delivering the punch line. 'Right into the hands of the gangsters who sent them here in the first place.'

It was Sister Kassia who filled in the blanks, her story essentially the same as that of *INS* Agent Capra. Most likely, the young women in question had contracted a debt which they were now obliged to work off. Most likely, they'd originally been promised wages high enough to settle the debt in a year or two, along with decent housing and an unfettered lifestyle. Most likely, their dreams had been of opulent boutiques and trendy nightclubs that didn't open until one o'clock in the morning, of celebrities, of opportunities.

Bait and switch, a marketing strategy as old as marketing itself. Sister Kassia told me the girls might be working for any employer willing to hire illegals. They might be waiting on tables in Manhattan, or sewing garments in Elmhurst, or dusting furniture in Bayside.

'Church, apparently, is the one solace allowed them,' she said. 'Or, perhaps, the one solace they refuse to live without.'

'Either way, Sister, that provides you with a chance to reach them. Something I want you to do.'

'A chance I intend to take.'

'I don't doubt that for a minute, but if you don't mind my asking, what exactly are you hoping to accomplish?'

We were standing at the window, looking out over the churchyard. The congregation was already inside Blessed Virgin, the mass about to start, but the girls and their escort had yet to appear.

'The first goal is to get them away from their keepers, to separate the slaves from the slave holders. And, yes, I'm willing to use the word slave. I use it because these kinds of debts are commonly bought and sold, because tomorrow morning they could wake up to find a new master in charge of their lives.'

'And the second goal?'

'The second is to put them in control, to settle them in a place where they'll be safe, to find them jobs and to guide them through the bureaucratic maze.'

I recalled my conversation with *INS* Agent Dominick Capra. I'd asked him why these women didn't just run away and he'd explained that the loans had been co-signed by relatives back home. If the workers defaulted, the relatives would have to pay.

'What about the relatives?' I asked. 'The ones in the old country who co-signed for the debt.'

But Sister Kassia had been all over this topic. Once the women were settled into real jobs that paid real wages, they would send money home to those relatives. The point wasn't to avoid the debt. The point was to avoid involuntary servitude.

The nun concluded with a direct appeal to my conscience. 'These women were born with the same hopes and dreams as you and I,' she declared, her tone firm and steady. 'They have a right to their lives, a right we take for granted. Now you have it in your power to affect those lives directly. You've become responsible, whether you like it or not.'

The women came first, five of them in their Sunday best, the oldest in her mid-twenties, the youngest in her late teens. They wore simple cotton dresses, knee-length and brightly colored, and flat-heeled shoes with tiny white socks that barely covered their ankles. Make-up was held to a minimum, a hint of blush in the cheeks, a pale gloss across the lips, a touch of color in the brows.

Snap judgements, especially of strangers, are a hazard for cops. But as I searched their faces, I knew I wasn't making any mistake about these women. There was nothing hard in their expressions, no element of cold calculation. They were not whores.

Pleased with this conclusion, I focused on the man who walked behind the women, the shepherd tending his flock. I watched him turn onto the path leading up to the church, then pass within twenty feet of where I stood. He seemed as ordinary, at first glance, as the women who preceded him. His face was noticeably thin, his cheeks hollow, his mouth squeezed between a strong nose and a cleft chin. Though he appeared no older than thirty-five, the top of his head was bald except for a dark fuzz at the very front which might have been better shaved. As he passed me, I watched his eyes criss-cross the landscape in little jumps. They never stopped moving and only the fact that I was standing well away from the window prevented my being discovered.

'Tell me,' I asked, 'do you know their names?'

'One of the girls is named Katrina. The man is named Aslan.'

'Aslan? Is that a Polish name?'

'No. In Turkish and Farsi, aslan means lion. I know because I became curious the first time I heard the name and ran a search on the Internet.'

'You said they're sometimes escorted by a second man. Can you describe him?'

'Tall, middle-aged, heavy-set, with very narrow eyes. Really, you can't mistake him.'

I stifled a burst of nearly infantile glee, then changed the subject. 'Can I assume they drive to church, the girls and their minders, that they don't take a bus?'

'They come in a van.'

'Can you describe the van?'

Forty-five minutes later, I followed the van back through Maspeth and into Greenpoint, virtually retracing the route I'd taken a few hours earlier. I gave the van plenty of room, passing by the corner of Eagle Street and Franklin Avenue in time to watch it disappear through a roll-up door into the interior of a warehouse. The warehouse was two stories high and no more than twenty feet wide. As decrepit as its attached neighbors to the east and west, the entire face of the building, including the steel door in front, was covered with graffiti. This corner of Greenpoint was mostly Hispanic and poor, a place where folks minded their own business, which was definitely not the plight of a few *blanquitas* who didn't even speak English, much less Spanish.

While Aslan and the women were still in church, I'd briefly inspected the van. I called in the plates, first. They came back registered to an outfit called Domestic Solutions. Jane, it appeared, was somebody's servant. That done, I checked the well-worn tires. I'd photographed a tire impression at the crime scene. Now I had something to compare it with. Finally, I looked inside the vehicle, just in case there was a kilo of cocaine lying in plain view. Instead, I discovered a pair of car seats in the back, one clearly meant for an infant. Children, of course, would add another layer of control, especially pre-schoolers who could be kept out of sight.

As I passed by Eagle Street for a second time, a light went on behind the curtains in the two small windows on the second floor. This was a violation of the building code I could turn to my advantage. Industrial structures cannot be used for residential purposes, not without going through a complicated conversion process that requires a thorough renovation, inside and out. That the home of Domestic Solutions and its workers had not undergone that process was obvious at a glance. A wooden sign running across the building's facade looked as if it was about to drop onto the street below. Eagle Street Roofing was what the sign said, and I didn't grasp its significance until I was on my third circuit of the block. Bottom line, there's very little call for walk-in refrigerators in the roofing business. That meant Jane was killed somewhere else and the only somewhere else she could have been killed was at work. Again, I remembered the Roach's prediction: there's a sadist in the mix.

I kept at it for another twenty minutes, certain of only one thing: come tomorrow morning, bright and early, I'd be staking out Domestic Solutions. The single issue to be resolved was the vantage point from which to do it. Tradition would have me sitting in an unmarked car, pretending to read a newspaper. But this block of Eagle Street, between Franklin Avenue and West Street, was only fifty feet long.

I pictured Aslan as I'd seen him walking into the church, his eyes in constant motion. If I was parked in plain view he'd spot me in a minute. And I didn't want to be spotted, not before I had a better idea of what I was up against.

Eventually, I settled on a place and a plan. Across from Domestic Solutions, a narrow yard was closed off by a chain-link fence topped with barbed wire. The yard ran back at least sixty feet and was littered with everything from bags of garbage to sheet metal boxes and tubes. There was even a cracked toilet. I didn't have to guess where the debris came from. The squat brick warehouse on the eastern side of the yard had been long abandoned and long ago looted. Whether or not it was also unoccupied remained to be seen.

TWELVE

At one time in the not too distant past, I was good-old Harry Corbin, friend to all. My favorite hang-out was a cop bar in Brooklyn where my drink was waiting before I took off my coat, where no one had a bad thing to say about me. That all stopped when I busted Dante Russo and his cronies. Now it was just Adele Bentibi and Conrad Stehle, and Conrad was somewhere off the coast of Alaska with his girlfriend.

Any port in a storm. When I finally arrived home at eight thirty, the first thing I did was pick up the phone and call Adele. I was riding a high which had yet to crest and the urge to blow off steam was too great to resist.

'Corbin, I'm glad you called. I thought you'd forgotten me.'

Adele sounded weary, almost resigned, the effect so pronounced I came close to asking her what was wrong. But I didn't want to go there. I didn't want any distractions.

'I caught a break, Adele. I'm gonna nail the case.'

'You did? Wait, wait a second. I want to take this in my room.' A moment later, she said, 'Okay, I'm alone. Let's hear the story.'

It was as if she'd become another person, engaged now, interested, and I realized, suddenly, that engagement was what I had to offer. Life on the street, where it mattered.

I laid it out for her, taking my time. Sister Kassia, Father Stan, Aslan and the women, Domestic Solutions, the Eagle Street Roofing warehouse. Adele didn't comment until I finished. Then she said, 'You know, Corbin, your victim wasn't killed in that warehouse.'

'No refrigerator, right?'

'Ah, you're already there.'

'Look, starting tomorrow morning, I'm gonna put Domestic Solutions under surveillance. There's an abandoned building across the street. I'll set up shop inside and see what develops. Remember, without the man Clyde Kelly saw at the disposal site, there's no case. So, if he doesn't live in the building or come there to do business, I've still got a long road ahead of me. Sister Kassia told me that she hasn't seen the man in two weeks, which was when he tried to put Jane's body in the water. Did he take off? He had plenty of reason.'

Adele laughed. 'You wouldn't be telling yourself to slow down, would you?'

'It's that obvious?'

'Corbin, you're stoned out of your mind. But don't worry. I'm not putting you down. In some ways, you're at your best when you smell blood in the water.'

'And you? When you were still a detective? How did you feel when you finally got a break?'

'High as a kite.'

'Do you miss it? That high?'

'More than I can say.' She hesitated, her voice dropping off at the end of the sentence. 'But I know I can't get it back. I can't be a cop again. I put that behind me when I left the job.' Another hesitation, then, 'What the nun said about the women. Where are you going with that?'

'Women and children, Adele.'

'What?'

'I looked in the van they were driving. There were a pair of car seats in the back.'

'That only makes the question more urgent.'

Something in her voice warned me to tread softly, but I was too revved up to listen. 'I don't wish those women any harm,' I said, 'but I don't speak for them. I don't represent them. Besides, how do I know one of them didn't kill her? Or play a part in what happened to her after she was killed? And even if you eliminate them as suspects, they might still be witnesses. Down the line, I'll probably ask the *DA* to detain them as flight risks.'

'You understand, they'll be deported once the case is resolved.'

'I didn't tell them to come here in the first place.'

'And the children? What happens to the children? Do they end up in foster care?'

'I'm just a common detective, Adele, who gets paid to arrest common criminals. I don't have the power to right all wrongs, much less solve the world's problems.' I hesitated a moment. According to Dominick Capra, immigrants from Eastern Europe were adept at gaming the system. This was something I could use.

'Look, if the women are detained as material witnesses, two things will happen. First, they and their children will be safe. Second, they'll have plenty of time to find immigration lawyers. Cutting a deal, testimony for refugee status, is a logical next step. Maybe things'll work out for the best.'

'But you can't guarantee it?'

'Adele, you saw the photographs I took at the crime scene. You know what was done to Jane Doe #4805. Where would your priorities be if it was your case?'

'There was a time when I could have answered that question without hesitating. But now, I don't know. Your victim is dead. Nothing you do can change that. But those women and their children are alive. And they're victims, too.'

THIRTEEN

I was up at four o'clock the next morning and out the door by four thirty. By five, I was rolling through the deserted streets of industrial Greenpoint, looking for an elusive parking space, which I eventually found several blocks from Domestic Solutions' Eagle Street warehouse.

I remember taking a minute to collect myself, to reflect, before getting out of the Nissan. I'd slept for less than four hours, but my thoughts were doing a little cancan through my brain, kicking high, flashing a glimpse of lacy bloomers. Eye on the prize, they demanded. Don't fuck it up.

The still air, as I walked along Eagle Street, was damp enough to bead on the peak of the gimme cap I'd pulled down over my forehead. I wore the rattiest shirt in my closet and jeans so frayed they might have been dumped months before. According to Adele, I have a hard time saying goodbye. If so, the quirk had played out to my advantage.

I'd made up a little kit before I left the house, stuffing a six-battery flashlight, a small pair of binoculars, a pair of wire cutters, a jug of water, and a Thermos of coffee into a plastic bag I now carried over my shoulder. I might have left the wire cutters home. A section of the fence that fronted the lot across from Domestic Solutions had been pried away from its supporting post, leaving a gap large enough to squeeze through.

I ducked inside just as a light came on in the upper windows of the Domestic Solutions warehouse. For a long moment, I felt like a cockroach trapped on a wall. Then I began to trudge through the yard as if bearing the weight of the world on my shoulders, taking my sweet time, just another homeless skell in search of a safe place to lay his miserable head. I kept going until I was safely tucked behind a metal box large enough to shield me. Open at the top, the box had been fabricated from four squares of sheet metal joined with hundreds of tiny rivets.

In no hurry now, I took a few minutes to get my bearings. The only street light was at the end of the block, at the corner of West Street, and it was very dark inside the lot. I couldn't be sure I was alone, or that the abandoned warehouse, a few yards from where I sat, wasn't a crack house, or a shooting gallery inhabited by junkies made feral by years on the streets.

My objective was an opening in the warehouse wall, at the very end of the lot, where some enterprising soul had torn away a few dozen bricks. Of one thing, I was certain – the best place to stake out Domestic Solutions was from inside the warehouse.

I looked around the edge of the box, at the

111

light filtering through the curtains across the street. There were no silhouettes behind the curtains, nobody watching as I made my way over to the warehouse, then sat next to the hole with my back to the wall. The sky was beginning to lighten, revealing a network of thin motionless clouds that would burn off by mid-morning. That was another advantage to being inside, a roof to shield me from the elements. According to the early forecast, the temperature would rise into the nineties by early afternoon.

For the next few minutes, I simply listened, my ear a few inches from the hole. Off in the distance, I heard the roar of an accelerating truck, its driver throwing a new gear every few seconds. A car alarm went off closer by, a quick whoop-whoop, followed by a series of beeps. From across the street I heard the raised voices of a child and a female adult, though I couldn't make out the words. But from inside the warehouse there was only silence.

Turning to my left, I dropped onto my knees and crawled through the hole, dragging my gear behind me. I came all the way through, rising into a crouch as I finally drew my weapon. From the other side of the building, a flickering yellow light filled an open doorway, seeming as flat as paint from a hundred feet away. The building was occupied and somebody was at home.

With an effort, I tore my eyes away from the light, forcing myself to systematically probe the darkness around me. I was searching the shadows for any sign of movement, my finger inside the Glock's trigger guard. Eventually my eyes adjusted and I was able to pick out the general shape of a corridor that ran all the way to the faint light at the opposite end. The floor of the corridor was concrete and free of obstacles. That was all to the good because the only view of Domestic Solutions, if there was a view to be had, was from the front of the warehouse. And the only way to get there was to walk.

I swept the room as I stepped inside, keeping my back to the wall, trying to register every detail at once, a mattress on the floor, a lit can of Sterno beneath a grate, an open trash bag holding a pile of neatly folded clothing, a half-dozen air fresheners shaped like pine trees dangling from a clothes hangar, a copper-skinned woman who wore a kimono-like robe that fell to her knees. The robe was the color of heavy cream and there was a heron on the back that fixed me with an impossibly blue eye.

I raised my left hand to display my shield. 'Good morning, ma'am.'

The woman's shoulders flew up and she rose onto her tiptoes, scattering crystals of sugar from the jar she was holding. Then she spun to face me, revealing cheeks filmed with black stubble that contrasted sharply with the green mascara on her upper lids and a well-defined adam's apple that bobbed up and down like a yo-yo.

For a long moment, until I finally broke the silence, her eyes jerked back and forth, from my weapon to my shield, from my shield to my weapon, as if was I offering her a choice, pick one or the other.

'Is there anybody else in this building?' I asked.

She raised her head to look into my eyes. 'Dimitri,' she shouted, 'you best get your sorry Greek ass in here. We got company.'

The door on the other side of room opened a second later to reveal a short muscular man wearing a T-shirt and a pair of blue boxer shorts covered with little red hearts. The man's black hair stuck out in all directions, while his once-prominent nose was flattened at the bridge and bent at the tip. In his right hand, he carried a length of galvanized pipe, maybe two inches in diameter and three feet long.

I let the barrel of the Glock swing in his direction. 'I'm a cop,' I told him, 'and I'm going to be spending some time here. My business has nothing to do with you, but if you don't put down that pipe, I'll kill you anyway.'

Dimitri didn't hesitate. He tossed the pipe into the room behind him where it clanged on the floor.

'If there's anyone else back there,' I said, 'now would be a good time to tell me.'

'There's nobody else in this building,' he replied, his wide mouth twisting into a sneer of defiance. 'I don't allow nobody else. This is

114

my home.'

I turned to his companion. 'Tell me your name.'

'Giselle.'

'Giselle, if I put this gun back in its holster, Dimitri's not gonna do anything stupid, right?'

'Not stupid enough to make you take it out again.'

I holstered the Glock, put my badge away, then removed my wallet. 'Call this rent,' I said, offering Giselle a twenty.

She took the bill, stuffing it into the pocket of her robe. 'You plan to stay long enough for breakfast?'

'What're you making?'

'Making?' Giselle swept the room, her vermilion-tipped fingers somehow at odds with a forearm that would have embarrassed Popeye. 'Do you see a stove? Do I look like somebody's housewife?'

'What she's sayin',' Dimitri said, 'is that if you want breakfast, she could fetch it from the bodega on the corner.'

'Long as you're payin' for it,' Giselle added.

I responded by retrieving my kit, which I'd left outside, then crossing the room to a large window at the front of the building. Several inches thick, the window was made of translucent glass bricks, a few of which had been knocked out, perhaps in a failed attempt to gain entry. I sat down on a milk crate and sighted along one of these holes.

With my field of vision narrow and rounded, the effect was oddly telescopic, but I could see the first floor of Domestic Solutions well enough, both the roll-up door and a smaller doorway on the eastern side of the building. The smaller door was windowless and covered with a sheet of metal that gleamed in the angled sunlight. Both its lock and its outer edges were shielded to resist the insertion of a pry bar.

I fished my Thermos out of the garbage bag and poured myself a cup of coffee. 'Tell me what you know about the people across the street.'

'They'll be goin' out soon,' Dimitri said. 'In the van.'

'They?'

'All I know is every Monday morning, around seven thirty, them girls get driven off. And they don't come back until Saturday afternoon. What happens in between, I can't say.'

'Who drives them?'

'A white man,' Giselle announced. 'A damn foreigner.'

'Does he stay with them, or does he come back?'

'He comes back a few hours later.' Giselle took a pot of water off the grate above the Sterno lamp and poured the water into a bowl before producing a throwaway razor. Finally, she began to soap her face.

'Describe the man.'

'Men, baby, two of them, both ofays, one uglier than the next.'

116

'Describe them.'

Giselle went back to work on her face and Dimitri took over, leaving me to wonder if they also finished each other's sentences.

'The one's got a skinny face and jumpy eyes, bald across the top. The other dude's older. Got a big round face like a pumpkin.' Dimitri squeezed his eyelids together. 'And tiny little eyes that look down at you like you were shit on the sidewalk.'

I took out two more twenties and handed them over. 'Go to the bodega, get anything you want for yourselves, just don't come back until dark.'

That said, I turned my back on them and began to watch the street. It was still quiet outside, but I wasn't fooled. At night, especially on weekends, industrial neighborhoods can seem like ghost towns, like they've been abandoned for decades. But they roar back to life on weekday mornings. The bosses and the managers arrive first, along with a favored employee or two. Lights go on, doors roll up, forklifts begin to move, trucks are pulled out onto the street. Then the workers begin to arrive...

'It's not right, evicting a man from his own house. You're only doin' this because we're homeless.'

Giselle chimed in before I could point out that homeless people, by definition, don't have houses.

'Uh-uh, baby,' she said, 'it's our damn lifestyle the officer don't approve of. Thinks

117

because I'm of a different sexual persuasion I ain't got no rights at all.'

I looked from Dimitri to Giselle, then smiled my broadest smile. 'Okay, you can hang around. Just give me back the sixty dollars.'

Giselle stepped away from me as though I'd just farted. Her eyes opened wide and she pursed her lips in distaste. I continued to stare at her, with my hand out and my affable smile firmly in place. The ball was in her court.

'I ain't about to leave my abode,' she finally announced, 'till I fix my face.'

At seven o'clock, a van pulled into the driveway in front of Domestic Solutions' roll-up door. I could see Aslan in the driver's seat and someone alongside him, a man. I strained to make out the man's features, but the angle was too severe. The view I had was of the back of his head. It might have been the man with the narrow eyes. It might have been anyone.

Aslan leaned on the horn, once, then twice, before the door rolled up. A moment later the van disappeared from view. At seven ten, a woman emerged from the warehouse. She was plump and middle-aged and her thinning hair was dyed a brassy red. Without glancing in either direction, she slapped a magnetized sign on the door, then went back inside. I had to peer through one lens of my binoculars to read the sign. On top, in white letters, it revealed the name of the company: Domestic

Solutions. Beneath that, the address: 532 Eagle Street.

At seven thirty, the larger door rolled up and the Ford Econoline backed out. The van was driven by Aslan and there were five women inside, the same women I'd seen at Blessed Virgin. They were gone a moment later, undoubtedly on their way to work. For the next three hours, until Aslan returned, all was quiet at Domestic Solutions. Aslan parked the van on the street and entered the warehouse through the smaller door without unlocking it. Domestic Solutions was open for business.

I could hear the wheels of industry turning in the other warehouses on Eagle Street, but my limited view was so unchanging, I might have been staring at a picture on a wall. My back hurt, of course, from leaning into the narrow opening in the glass wall, and both my eyes were red and itchy because I kept switching them in a useless effort to prevent fatigue. But my mind kept rolling along, faster and faster as the minutes ticked by, ignoring, even laughing at, my discomfort. It was now possible, I told myself, to collapse the entire house of cards, to bring all the guilty parties to justice. The entire process would take no longer than a few days and it could begin as soon as I determined that the fat man with the narrow eyes was in the Domestic Solutions warehouse.

Needless to say, the sequence of events, as I finally imagined them, didn't pop into my brain fully formed. But once I'd identified the various elements and set them in place, I couldn't find a hole in the logic.

Fabricate a reason to bring the fat man into the precinct, then dig up Clyde Kelly and have him make an identification. Arrest the fat man on the basis of that identification and use the arrest to obtain a search warrant for the van and the warehouse. Domestic Solutions was a business and businesses generate paperwork. An examination of that paperwork would certainly reveal the names and addresses of its customers. If Jane wasn't killed in the warehouse, then she was necessarily killed at her place of work, since she had no other life. And if she was killed where she worked, given the nature of her various injuries, trace evidence would be found.

And then there was the fat man and the charge of second-degree murder I would level against him. Would he cut a deal? If he hadn't killed Jane? If he'd only been involved in the cover-up? Though I couldn't be absolutely sure, I was looking forward to presenting the argument in favor of cooperation.

I didn't forget Sister Kassia's plea or Adele's admonition as I put my strategy together. The women were now at work and wouldn't return until the weekend. Aslan could not round them up in the short time between the fat man's arrest and my obtaining a search warrant for the premises. Once I knew where they were, of course, I'd be after them myself. And I'd give Sister Kassia a heads-up along the way. If Blessed Virgin wanted to hire a lawyer to represent the women, that was fine by me.

I riffled through my notebook until I found Clyde Kelly's information, then dialed the phone number of the Karyn Porter-Mann-berg Senior Residence. The woman who answered told me that Clyde was still a client, though he wasn't in the building.

'Most of the time,' she volunteered, 'he comes back in time for dinner. If not, he always returns for the ten o'clock curfew.'

By three thirty, my lower back nearly in spasm, I was ready to call it a day. I was expected at the Nine-Two and I was in desperate need of a quick shower, not to mention a change of clothes. I hurriedly packed my kit, then stole a last peek through the broken window just as the fat man emerged, carrying a bag of garbage in each hand.

I watched him walk to the curb, his gait quick and graceful despite an extra fifty pounds, watched him look, very deliberately, up and down the block. For just a second, as his head swept from right to left, his narrow eyes crossed mine. No more than slits, they were as disfiguring as a birthmark or a tattoo. Kelly's identification would be quick and sure, and beyond challenge in a courtroom.

The fat man nodded once after completing his sweep, then crossed the street, disappearing from view. A moment later, he returned with his hands empty. The garbage, apparently, had gone over the fence.

FOURTEEN

I was up and moving before the door closed behind the fat man. Down the corridor, through the lot, across the street. I tried to compose myself as I went. A pure waste of time. I entered the small office as though I owned it.

On the far side of the room, Aslan and the fat man sat behind large desks placed at right angles to each other. The woman with the red hair was standing to my right, at the foot of a stairway leading to the second floor. She had a toddler by the hand, a boy wearing a Mickey Mouse t-shirt. Aslan said something to the woman in a language I didn't understand. Without answering, she picked the child up and climbed the stairs. I let her go, not because I wouldn't have relished a conversation with her, but because I was much more interested in the joint Aslan held between the thumb and forefinger of his right hand.

Aslan stared at my badge, then into my eyes. I expected him to make some effort to conceal the joint, even to swallow it whole. Instead, he laid it on the edge of a glass ashtray in a gesture of pure defiance that I would later make him regret.

'Okay,' he said, his tone echoing his earlier gesture, 'you are big-deal cop. Now can put tin badge in pocket and show me search warrant.'

'Hey,' I said, looking directly into the narrow eyes of Aslan's companion, 'what's with your buddy's attitude? He doesn't even know what I'm here for and already he's asking for a warrant. Gimme a break.'

When neither man replied, I inventoried the room, taking my time about it. Perhaps twenty feet square, the office was paneled with sheets of some material halfway between wood and wallpaper. Dark blue tiles, shot with irregular veins of silver, covered the floor.

The tiles were bright and shiny, as they should have been, given the number of servants who lived there.

Above my head, an air conditioner blasted away. A pair of three-drawer filing cabinets to my left were arranged along the front wall. I registered these items quickly, suppressing an urge to open those cabinets and examine their contents, until my attention finally settled on a flag mounted behind Aslan's desk. The flag was bright green, with three stripes – white, red, white – about two-thirds of the way down. At the flag's center, in stark black and white, a large disc contained a semicircle of nine stars. The stars supported a pedestal on which an animal lay with its legs dangling and its head facing outward, so that it stared at me through a pair of ghost-white eyes.

'That a cat or a dog?' I asked Aslan, pointing to the flag.

He stared at me for a moment, then blinked twice before swiveling his chair in a half-circle to face the flag. 'This is wolf of Chechnya,' he told me. 'All Chechen peoples are coming from wolfs. This is in our national song. This is what we believe.'

'Yeah? It must be a pretty wild place then. You do a lot of hunting?'

He broke into song at that point, singing to the flag in a language I assumed to be Chechen. I stepped forward, took the half-smoked joint from the ashtray and put it in my shirt pocket. Then I winked at Aslan's companion, who stared back at me, so unmoving he might have been carved from clay. Dimitri had been right about the man's gaze. He was, indeed, looking at me like I was shit on the sidewalk.

I came forward to sit on the edge of his desk, leaning down to study an open checkbook. I barely had time to register a signature on the top check, Konstantine Barsakov, before Aslan challenged me.

'I have ask you before. In America, man's home is castle. Where is search warrant for castle?'

'Well, it's a funny thing, but your castle is exactly what I'm here about. What'd you say your name was?'

'I don't have to say name. Is unconstitutional.'

'Nope, you're wrong there. Any police

124

officer can ask any citizen for identification at any time. If that identification is not produced, that police officer can detain that citizen until such time as it is.'

This was a complete lie, but not one likely to be unmasked. Aslan's eyes traveled to the ashtray, now minus the joint he'd laid down a few minutes before. Then his eyes jumped to mine, displaying a blind and unreasoning hatred.

'Also,' I added, 'your attitude is really bad here. I just asked for your name. I didn't ask you to submit to a strip search.'

The clear implication, that a strip search would follow a second refusal, didn't escape Aslan. I could see the struggle in his eyes. He was going to have to back down and he didn't like it.

'Aslan Khalid.'

'There, was that so hard?' I glanced down at the second man. 'And what's your name, pal?'

'Konstantine Barsakov.'

'And what do you do for Domestic Solutions? What's your job?'

'I am president,' Barsakov replied, his English much better than Aslan's. 'Now tell us what you want or I will call the lawyer. And remove your ass from my desk.'

'Okay.' I rose to my feet, leaving a sweaty stain behind, then spread my hands defensively. 'See, it's really just a routine complaint. This building is zoned industrial and you have people living here. That's the complaint, anyway. That you have people living here and the conditions are unsafe.'

I might have left all this unsaid. My intention, when I came through the door, was to use the building code violation as a pretext to detain Konstantine. That ploy was no longer necessary; the joint in my pocket was pretext enough. Still, I couldn't resist an urge to needle Aslan, to play to his rage. Turned down at the corners, the man's small mouth had hardened into the sort of petulant frown I associated with a bratty toddler about to launch a temper tantrum.

When Konstantine failed to reply, I turned to his partner. 'Do you deny the charges?' I asked.

Aslan stared at me for a moment, his eyes traveling from my soggy hair, to the t-shirt plastered to my chest, to my frayed jeans. That my mission had nothing to with the building code was obvious and I had to assume he was already thinking of the murdered girl his partner had dumped six weeks before.

'No more I am playing with you this game,' Aslan finally declared, reaching for the telephone on his desk. 'I am calling lawyer.'

'Here, let me help you.'

I hooked my fingers under the lip of the desk and flipped it over. Aslan tried to get out of the way, but he wasn't fast enough. The desk caught him in the hips and his chair went flying. Then the monitor of his Dell computer imploded a few feet from his head and he cried out, despite himself. I drew my

Glock and put on my game face. These were the foreign gangsters Capra had warned me against. I would treat them accordingly.

'You,' I said, leveling the Glock on Konstantine while Aslan struggled out from under the desk, 'get up against the wall.'

When he continued to stare at me, I drew the gun back, fully prepared to slam it into the side of his head. He apparently got the message, pushing his chair away from the desk, rising slowly, turning and walking off to face the wall. I might have demanded that he raise his hands at that point, but there was only one pocket in his warm-up suit, a back pocket which held his wallet.

'You, too. Get up against the wall next to your partner.' I came around the overturned desk to confront Aslan as he rose to his feet, slamming the heel of my left hand into his chest. He staggered backward, but continued to glare at me. Though I was a good five inches taller and fifty pounds heavier, Aslan was powerfully built and obviously unafraid. For a moment, I thought I might have to shoot him, but he finally turned when I stepped forward.

'Put your hands against the wall,' I told him, 'and spread your legs. I'm going to search you.'

'I will tell you story,' he said as he complied, 'of boys becoming mens in Chechnya. Are you wishing to hear this story?'

'I'm interested in anything you have to say, Aslan. That's because you're such an interesting guy.'

Aslan ignored the sarcasm. His expression had hardened by then. 'New Year's Day this story begins, when Russians attack Grozny to drive out rebels. Airplanes they use, mortars, artilleries, missiles, tanks. In one hour, four thousand rounds, boom, boom, boom, boom. This goes on for three months, every day, always bombs falling, house crashing down, glass broken from windows, everywhere flames, everywhere smoke. At end, Grozny is no more a city. Grozny is ruins like of ancient kingdom.'

I searched Aslan carefully, emptying each pocket, tossing items off to the side. He didn't flinch, not even when I confiscated his wallet.

'On first night, mother killed and brother killed. On fifth night, father killed. I run to uncle's house, but house is no more. Boy has only on self to rely. How does boy do this? Fear first, for boy, too scared to think. Then hunger eats at stomach and boy runs through streets, hiding in shadows from snipers, like rat. This is trick Russians play. First bomb, then burn, then shoot when people come out. If civilian, no matter. If child, no matter. All are same to them.'

I moved over to Konstantine and took his wallet as well. He was paying close attention to Aslan's tale and I got the distinct impression that he was hearing it for the first time.

'How survive, huh? For boy? First time boy

128

discovers food, gang of children take it away. Later, boy joins gang, takes food from others. Oldest in gang is fourteen. Youngest is seven. When find wounded Russians, they kill them with knives. No mercy. Kill and take gun. Now grows stronger, this boy. Little more every day. Until no longer is rat. Is wolf.'

At that point, I backed away from the two men, giving myself a little reaction room while I examined Konstantine's and Aslan's green cards. Both appeared to be legitimate and both listed Russia as country of origin.

'Boy can no more be sheep when boy becomes wolf. This is thing about wolfs. Once is wolf always is wolf.'

I can't say how long Aslan would have rattled on if I hadn't chosen that moment to kick his feet out from under him. As it was, his head banged into the paneling as he crashed to the floor and he barely got his hands out in time to break his fall.

'Stay down there, wolfman, while I finish with your partner.'

Finishing with Konstantine meant holstering my weapon while I bent his massive arms behind his back and put handcuffs on his wrists. Konstantine didn't fight me, but I felt his strength nevertheless. We were of even height, with him much the heavier, though most of it – or so I hoped – was fat.

'Why you are arresting me?'

'Marijuana possession.'

Animated for the first time, he looked at me in disbelief. 'I wasn't smoking this joint.'

'Doesn't matter, Konstantine. You're the president of the company and you're responsible.' I drew my weapon. Aslan was behaving himself, but I wasn't taking any chances.

'This is bullshit, this little joint. This is a parking ticket.'

'Not so. Smoking marijuana in a public place is a misdemeanor. Now, check this out, just so we're all on the same page. I'm going to walk you through the door and down the street to my car. You're not going to resist or try to run away. Meanwhile, the wolf of Chechnya will remain inside the building. That's because if the wolf shows his fangs, he not only goes to the top of the endangered species list, he faces the threat of immediate extinction.'

I gave them a moment to think it over, then took hold of Barsakov's right arm just above the elbow, squeezing hard enough to let him know how much it would hurt if I clamped down. We had two blocks to walk and I didn't want him to get ideas. Nevertheless, when we reached the door, I couldn't resist a final diversion. I turned slightly, so that I could see Aslan out of the corner of my eye. He was holding his palm against the top of his bald and reddened scalp.

'Funny thing about detectives,' I told him, 'the best ones have great memories. And what I remember is that the Russian attack on Chechnya took place in the mid-nineties. Now, you, Aslan, you're how old? Thirty-five? And you were how old when the Russians

130

attacked? Twenty? That's a long way from fourteen.'

Aslan continued to stare at me for a moment, hatred still apparent in his black eyes. Then he began to laugh, a phlegmy choking laugh that came within an eye-blink of a convulsion. Still he managed to get his message out. 'Wolfs,' he shouted, to me, to Konstantine, to his thoroughly humiliated spirit, 'do not forget rabbits. Again someday we are meeting.'

I might have added, 'Sooner, rather than later,' but I was already focusing on the tasks ahead.

We made a show of it, Konstantine and I, when we strolled into the Nine-Two. Konstantine with his burgundy warm-up suit and his lime-green socks, his squinty eyes and his great balloon of a head. Me in ratty jeans, a shirt with dark stains under each armpit, humidity-driven hair that rose from my scalp like a fright wig. Konstantine was cool throughout, absorbing the scrutiny of the various cops we passed on our way to the second floor, his expression unchanging, until I finally brought him into an interview room and sat him down.

'I want a lawyer,' he said. 'I have my rights.'

'Speaking of rights, are you right-handed or left-handed?' When he didn't reply, I uncuffed his left hand, then closed the empty handcuff around the leg of a small table bolted to the floor.

I suspect it was this final humiliation that

set him off, that motivated him to throw a clumsy left in the general direction of my head. I avoided the blow easily, then grabbed his wrist on the way back and forced it down onto the table in front of his chair.

Konstantine fought me all the way, his eyes squeezed shut, groaning in frustration. Even when I had his wrist pinned, he didn't give up, struggling on until he finally ran out of energy. Then I leaned down over him, placing my lips a few inches from his ear.

'You were observed on South Fifth Street,' I told him, 'when you disposed of that girl's body, observed by a reliable witness. I'm going to find that witness, bring him into the house, have him make a formal identification, then charge you with the crime of murder. Now, I know you didn't commit this murder, like I know you weren't smoking that joint. But I just don't give a shit. That's because I've been a cop long enough to understand that I work in a give-and-take business. As in, if you don't give me the real murderer, I'm gonna take you instead.'

I wanted to get out the door, right then and there, to begin my search for Clyde Kelly, but I still had a few details to arrange. I went to my locker first, for the spare shirt and trousers I kept for emergencies, then into the washroom where I stripped to the waist and scrubbed myself with paper towels before combing my hair. When I was done, I headed directly for Drew Millard's office.

Millard was at his desk when I came in,

sitting behind a semicircle of 8x10 photographs. The snapshot quality photos were of his wife and his six children. They were all, he'd once told me, that got him through the day.

'I found him, loo,' I announced. 'I found the asshole who killed that Jane Doe last month.'

Feigning a humility that in no way mirrored my inner feelings, I went on to explain that there was nothing miraculous about the break I'd finally caught. It was simply a matter of burning a little shoe leather, of putting the vic's likeness before the community until somebody dropped a dime. Now I had a suspect and an excuse to detain him while I contacted the witness.

Millard disagreed on only one point, the charge against Barsakov. In New York, possession of less than twenty-five grams of marijuana is a mere violation, punishable by no more than a fine. I wanted to charge Barsakov with smoking marijuana in a public place, a misdemeanor, because I needed an excuse to hold him while I looked for Clyde Kelly.

Maybe, Millard pointed out when I finished my pitch, the door to Domestic Solutions was unlocked, and maybe Barsakov was smoking the joint when I walked in. He wasn't doubting my word. But the narrow definition of public space in the penal code did not include place of business.

'Bottom line,' he finally said, 'we can put him in the system, but the judge'll toss the case when it comes up for arraignment tomorrow morning. Assuming you don't find your witness by then.'

'Tomorrow morning will be fine. And you could do me one other favor.'

'What's that?'

'Find someone to fingerprint the suspect. I want to make sure he isn't operating under an alias.'

'No problem.'

I went from Millard's office to Bobby Bandelone's cubicle, there to request a second favor. Procedure required that I show Clyde Kelly a photo array that included Barsakov before I put the suspect in a line-up. I needed someone to snap Barsakov's photo, and the photos of five other white men who looked reasonably like him, with the precinct's Polaroid.

Bandelone put up only a token resistance when I asked him to perform this little service. Maybe it was something in my eyes, something he recognized. Bandelone was a very good detective. Or maybe he was a bit afraid of my reputation as an IAB snitch. Or maybe he just thought it better to stay on Crazy Harry's good side. I didn't much care. I was already focused on Clyde Kelly.

FIFTEEN

The Karyn Porter-Mannberg Senior Residence on Wythe Avenue was typical of others scattered through the five boroughs. Four stories high, the building spread across three lots and was virtually without architectural detail. Red brick, green window frames, white sills beneath the windows, absolutely regular, absolutely functional. But whatever Porter-Mannberg lacked in style, it was clean and solid. The hot water would be hot, the toilets would flush, heat would be forthcoming in the winter. For the elderly poor, like Clyde Kelly, it was the difference between a tolerable decline and the absolute hell of a men's shelter.

The white-tile lobby I entered was just large enough to hold the mailboxes and a small desk. A security guard sat behind the desk. Tall and thin, he wore a blue uniform with a nametag over the left breast identifying him as *OFFICER ROBERTSON*. A thick leather belt around his waist held a canister of mace, a pair of handcuffs and a folding knife.

'I'm looking for Clyde Kelly.' I displayed my shield for the customary three seconds. 'Is he upstairs?'

'Nope. Went out about one o'clock and ain't come back since.'

'Will he return for dinner?'

'Mostly, he does.'

I glanced at my watch. It was almost six o'clock. 'What time is dinner served?'

Robertson smiled. 'Well, it ain't exactly served, but you can get a hot meal between six and seven. After that, it's peanut butter and jelly. But you ain't gotta worry. Clyde always comes back in time for the curfew at ten o'clock. Sleepin' in the street makes him nervous.'

With little choice in the matter, I settled down to wait.

A few minutes before seven, a short black man hustled through the door. I locked eyes with the guard who nodded at the new arrival. He wore a camouflage T-shirt over a pair of cargo pants and he caught an attitude when I stopped him, despite the gold shield I held in my hand.

'Ain't got time for no bullshit,' he declared. 'Ah'm gonna miss my dinner.'

'This'll only take a second.' I stepped between him and the stairs. 'I just need a little help here. I'm looking for Clyde Kelly.'

Officer Robertson spoke up. 'Ain't nothin' bad, Percy. Jus' speak to the detective.'

Percy tossed Robertson a hard look that spoke of grievances past, grievances unresolved. 'Last time I took notice,' he said, 'I wasn't in your army and I don't got to take your orders.'

136

'That's right,' I echoed, 'this is between you and me.' I added a smile to my comment before offering the man a deal. 'By the way, I'm guaranteeing your dinner. You don't get fed upstairs, the Chinese take-out's on me.'

Percy huffed twice, in an effort, no doubt, to show me that he was a hard sell. Then he said, 'I jus' come from Clyde. We was under the bridge, hangin' out.'

'Is he on his way back to the residence?'

'Naw, he went to the festival, watch 'em tote that statue. Clyde's a Catholic.'

'What festival?'

He flared up, his shoulders rising as though I'd deliberately provoked him. 'You know, where the wops carry that statue down the street. I can't pronounce that name they call it.'

Robertson supplied the missing information, his voice dripping contempt for Percy's ignorance. 'The Giglio. It's called the Giglio.'

His pronunciation of the word – *JEEL*-yo – finally kicked my brain into gear. Some weeks before, a long memo from the Community Affairs Officer had circulated through the Nine-Two, a kind of reminder. I'd read the memo from beginning to end, intrigued by the details.

Every year, according to the memo, one of the many Catholic churches in Williamsburg throws a festival to honor an Italian bishop whose name I couldn't recall. The highlight of each day is the 'dance' of the Giglio. This may not seem like such a big deal, but the

137

Giglio includes, among its elements, a seventy-foot tower crowned with a statue of the saint and a wooden platform large enough to hold a brass band, a priest from the parish, the capo in charge, and a few local celebrities. Beneath the platform, more than a hundred of the strongest and most virile men in the neighborhood crouch, their shoulders pressed to aluminium crossbars, awaiting a signal from the capo. They raise the four-ton Giglio when that signal comes, then carry it a short distance before setting it down. This process is repeated a number of times.

I'd put the memo to one side after reading it. From a policing standpoint, the issues were about crowd control and petty crime. They had nothing to do with Detective Harry Corbin.

'You know where this festival takes place?' I asked.

'Up the Northside, on Havemeyer Street. But if you fixin' on locatin' Clyde, you can just put that shit away. Them guineas, they pack 'em in like sardines when they dance the statue. You can't hardly move.'

Percy was right. I approached Havemeyer Street along North Seventh Street, from the Brooklyn-Queens Expressway, only to find the short block choked with pedestrians, road and sidewalks both. I could hear a band playing in the distance. The music was up-tempo, heavy on the brass and so obviously Italian that I was instantly transported to the opening scene of *The Godfather*, a reflex I knew I'd carry into the grave. But I could see neither band, nor Giglio, nor any sign of a procession from where I came to a halt. The hundreds of people pressed shoulder-to-shoulder between me and Havemeyer Street were only the crowd's overflow. The task was hopeless.

I retraced my steps to the end of the block, then called Drew Millard at the Nine-Two. Not only, he told me, was Barsakov still in custody, an *ADA* was expected at any moment to prepare warrants.

'You're not havin' a problem locating the witness, are you, Harry?'

'No, we'll be along.'

'Good, because if Kelly doesn't show up, I'm gonna look like a complete asshole.'

There was nothing more to say, and I headed back to the senior residence, my focus already shifting to Konstantine Barsakov. Interrogation, the duel in the box, is more than my specialty. It's the main reason I continue to carry the badge.

It's never in a suspect's interest to confess to the police. The police cannot, by law, make deals. Deals are the province of the District Attorney. Most suspects know that very well, yet they confess anyway. They confess because good detectives make them confess. And not by any use of physical force more compelling than an occasional slap. No, detectives, the good ones, anyway, know how to unlock the locks, to open the mind, to force all that guilty knowledge through a single outlet. From the lungs, up the trachea, through the larynx, over the lips and gums. Then the leap, through space, into the welcoming ear of the patient detective.

It doesn't always work, of course, but I wasn't expecting Konstantine to be that difficult. The truth, though it wouldn't set him free, would reduce his potential sentence by more than twenty years. That's the difference between second-degree murder and illegal disposal of a body, the worst violation I could charge him with, since accessory after the fact is not a crime in New York. My primary task was to convince him that he'd go down for the murder unless he told me the truth; that was the necessary first step from which all else would flow.

According to Clyde, disposing of Jane's body was just a job to Barsakov, no more distasteful than tossing bags of garbage into a vacant lot. Hardened criminals can't be cajoled. Nor will an appeal to conscience do the trick, not when your suspect doesn't have a conscience. I would have to present the case against him, remaining firm, though dispassionate. Here are the facts of life, Konstantine. Read 'em and weep.

The presentation would begin with my leading Barsakov to a line-up room. There he would be made to pose with five other men, all cops. Step forward. Turn to the right. Turn to the left. Look straight ahead. Konstantine, of course, knew he'd been observed on the night he carried Jane to South Fifth Street. The line-up would only confirm his worst fears.

'It's the eyes,' I'd explain, once I got him back in the little room. 'They're like havin' a tattoo on your forehead. You can't say, "it wasn't me." No jury would believe you. And by the way, we're gonna search the warehouse before the night's over. If the victim was butchered inside, we'll find evidence. I don't care what you cleaned up with. Plus, I have witnesses who put a squinty-eyed, fat man with the woman you dumped on South Fifth Street. You know, back when she was still alive. Whatta you wanna bet they identify you, too?'

By the time Clyde showed up, a little before ten, I was outside on the sidewalk, pacing. He came to within a few yards of me, then stopped abruptly. 'Clyde Kelly,' he declared, his tone cheery, his breath misted with the odor of cheap booze, 'reportin' fa duty.'

SIXTEEN

'Hey, Harry, bad break guy,' Bobby Bandelone called as I led Clyde past his office.

'What're you saying?'

'You don't know? Barsakov's lawyer waltzed your boy outta here ninety minutes ago.' He winked. 'After a long discussion with the lieutenant.'

I closed my eyes for a moment, rocking back on my heels as though I'd been kicked. Millard had promised to hold Barsakov at least until his arraignment on the following morning. Instead, he'd cut the man loose a few hours after I brought him in.

'Bad break, guy,' Bandelone repeated. 'But you'll find him, sooner or later.'

My first instinct was to charge into Millard's office, to vent my frustration in an entirely unacceptable manner, say by slapping his face until he started crying. But something in Bobby's tone, a mocking element he lacked the courage to openly display, brought me back to earth. Bandelone had come through with the Polaroids, snapping the photos before Barsakov's lawyer arrived. Now it was Clyde Kelly's turn.

I set up the photo array in my little cubicle, placing Barsakov's in the upper right-hand corner, then brought Clyde into the room. He identified Konstantine without hesitation.

'You sure?' I asked. 'Take a closer look at the other men.'

'Nope, that's him. I'd know the squinty-eyed prick anywhere.'

Five minutes later, after a quick knock, I stepped through Lieutenant Millard's door to find him in conference with an Assistant District Attorney named Monica Baird. Just a couple of years out of law school, Baird was tall, attractive, and as blond as she was ambitious.

'Spare me the righteous indignation,' she

declared before I could speak, 'there was nothing to be done.'

Millard, apparently, felt I was due a fuller explanation. 'I brought her in,' he told me, gesturing to Baird, 'so we'd be ready with the warrants. Then Barsakov's lawyer showed up.' He sighed. 'If Monica hadn't been here, I would have snuck Barsakov out the back way, shipped him over to the Nine-Four.'

'And faced a lawsuit for false imprisonment,' Monica quickly added. 'The charge was bogus from the beginning.'

I took a breath as I struggled to re-gain control. Monica Baird had no authority to order Millard to do anything. Cops and prosecutors are employed by different agencies of government. Another squad commander would have kicked her (and Barsakov's attorney) out of the precinct.

'My witness, Clyde Kelly,' I finally told them, 'has formally identified Barsakov from a legitimate photo array. That should be enough to get the warrants, right?' I waited for Baird to nod agreement before continuing. 'Barsakov is a foreign national and I'm afraid he'll rabbit. That's why I'm driving into Greenpoint where I can sit on his residence until the warrants are signed.'

'C'mon, guy,' Millard said, 'you don't wanna break anybody's door down. Unless you actually see Barsakov, you gotta promise me you'll stay put.'

In fact, I didn't know what I was going to do, only that I was going. But I promised, nonetheless, as Millard promised to arrive with the Crime Scene Unit and enough cops to make a show of force.

'By the way,' Millard added, 'we did manage to get Barsakov's prints, which we'll run tomorrow morning.'

For a moment, I thought Millard was going to offer his hand, but he simply thrust it into his pocket. His attitude was definitely sympathetic, though, as was Monica Baird's when she called out to me as I turned to leave.

'I've seen the crime scene photos,' she declared, 'and I know how much you want this man. I'll have the warrants ready within the next three hours. I promise you. And I promise you this, too. Once we take Konstantine Barsakov into custody, he won't be going anywhere for a very long time.'

Smiling now, I looked back over my shoulder. 'That's assuming, of course, he isn't already on a plane back to Russia.'

Domestic Solutions was dark, upstairs and downstairs, when I parked on the far side of Eagle Street. I shut off the Crown Vic, then got out of the car and crossed the sidewalk, to the glass-brick window that concealed Dimitri and Giselle's homely residence.

'Anybody inside?' I knocked on the window with the heel of my hand. 'It's Detective Corbin. C'mon out.'

A few minutes later, I watched Dimitri make his way across the vacant lot. He walked up to the fence and gripped the links. 'Giselle ain't feelin' so good,' he explained.

144

'Sorry to hear that.' I registered the dusting of white powder beneath his nostrils, knowing it wasn't sugar and not giving a damn. 'Tell me what's happening.'

'They been takin' shit outta there all night. Musta made three trips in that van they got.'

'They?'

'The skinny bald guy and the woman with the red hair.'

'When did they bring out the last load?'

'A half hour ago.'

'Who was in the van?'

'The skinny dude was drivin', with the redhead sittin' up next to him.'

'That's it?'

'No, the redhead was holdin' something in her arms. I think it was a kid.' Dimitri shook the fence, his mouth twisting back and forth, his jaw locked. He was coked out of his mind.

'Is there something else you wanna tell me?' I asked.

'Yeah, okay, but it's just that Giselle can't be no kinda witness. She's got, like, serious emotional problems. She can't put herself in front of a jury. Believe me, detective, she can't.'

He stopped at that point, and I began to count, slowly. I got to three before he blurted it out.

'Little while ago, we heard a shot.'

'Ah, and when was that?'

'Maybe ten minutes before the van took off for the last time.'

Without saying goodbye, I approached the door leading into Domestic Solutions, wrap-

145

ping my hand in the tail of my shirt before trying the knob. It was open, which came as no great surprise to me. Nor was I surprised, once I got the lights on, to find the computers and filing cabinets gone, or even to discover Konstantine Barsakov in an office chair on the other side of the room.

Barsakov was dead. In his right temple, he had a small entry wound. Behind his right ear, he had a much larger exit wound. A gun lay on the floor beside his chair, a nine-milli-meter Smith & Wesson. It lay in a pool of blood generated by the middle finger of Barsakov's right hand, half of which had been blown away. Undoubtedly when he'd raised it to his temple in self-defense.

As staged crime scenes go, this one was pretty weak. But that didn't surprise me, either, given the haste. No, it was the flag that shouldn't have been there, the green flag of Chechnya, with its lone wolf staring directly into my eyes, positioned directly behind Konstantine Barsakov. Aslan had left it behind to make sure I got the message. As I'd humiliated him, he'd now humiliated me.

I backed out of the building, closing the door, and walked back to my car. Ignoring Dimitri, who continued to grip the fence, I slid onto the passenger's side of the front seat, leaned against the headrest and closed my eyes. I'd been running on adrenalin all day, but now my tank was empty. Domestic Solution's business records were gone, as were all the other victims, the women and the children. I'd moved too fast, committed myself too early, and there was a price to be paid. In the short and the long term.

I waited in the car until midnight, when the warrants and the Crime Scene Unit finally arrived. Though I was anxious to get going, I gave the *CSU* sergeant a heads-up on the Jane Doe homicide in the hope that his unit would turn up trace evidence, especially blood. That done, I conducted a long and fruitless search for any mention of the company's clients or where Aslan had gone, a stray invoice, a business card, an answering machine, a diary, a half-written letter to the home folks. I even went in search of the two bags of garbage I'd seen Barsakov carrying earlier in the day.

I found evidence of haste everywhere. The closets on the second floor were only half-emptied, as if the best garments had been culled and the rest abandoned, and much of the furniture had been left behind. On the first floor, an oily patch of concrete in a large room outside the office revealed a near-perfect set of tire prints. In the same room, along the back wall, a staircase led to the second floor. The stairs were important because they would have allowed Aslan to evacuate the children without leading them past Konstantine's body.

It was all very interesting, but not particularly helpful, until the Crime Scene Unit ripped away the floor tiles in a small bathroom behind the office. There, on the undersides of the tiles and on the floorboards, the techs discovered small quantities of a dark substance with the consistency of dry mud. A few minutes later, a sample of that substance was placed in a test tube before a clear chemical, a reagent of some kind, was added. When the reagent turned blue, a *CSU* sergeant named Palmbach held the tube up for my inspection.

'I'm not callin' it proof positive,' he announced, 'but if this is human blood, which it most likely is, there's more than enough to run a *DNA* test.'

I went from the warehouse over to the precinct where I spent more than two hours, until four-thirty a.m., trying to make up for lost time. There was nothing in the case file about my forays to the outer boroughs, or about Sister Kassia or Father Stan, or even about the ad in *Gazeta Warszawa*. Without doubt, I'd soon have to account for the chain of events that led me to Domestic Solutions and Konstantine Barsakov. I needed paper to back up whatever story I decided to tell.

When I was finally satisfied, I packed it in. But I didn't go straight home. Instead, I drove to the waterfront, to South Fifth Street, parking behind the mound of rubble blocking access to the East River. It was raining, a soft drizzle that reduced the Manhattan skyline to a dim glow on a horizon that might have been a few inches in front of the windshield, or at the outer edge of the universe.

I had no good reason to make the stop. I just felt that I needed some time before I went home. But time to do exactly what? To think? To examine my conscience? To prepare myself for atonement?

But I wasn't ready to go there, apparently, because my attention quickly settled on a pair of photo-hard images. Konstantine Barsakov first, carefully posed before the Chechen flag. Then Aslan with his back to me, singing at the top of his lungs to that same flag.

I kept these images in front of me as I considered my next move, eventually focusing on the worst-case scenario: Aslan decides to round up the women and carry them off, possibly to another country. How fast could he do it? The women were all at work, five women living in the homes of five employers, each employer wealthy enough to afford a live-in servant. Would these employers simply release their maids if Aslan knocked on their door? More to the point, would Aslan risk it? Or would he wait until Saturday and pick up the unsuspecting girls at the usual time?

Aslan had taken his files and computers, along with some of the furniture and clothing, from the warehouse on Eagle Street. According to Sister Kassia, debts like the ones that bound the women to Aslan are commonly bought and sold. Well, that's exactly what I'd do, if I were Aslan. I'd sell them, preferably to an entrepreneur doing business in some far off place. Like, maybe, Cambodia.

I looked out through the windshield at a

gray curtain fragmented by lines of water streaming down the windshield. The rain was picking up, the patter on the Crown Vic's roof more or less continuous. I flicked on the wipers and the headlights, then put the Crown Vic into reverse before making a broken u-turn. This close to the river, my headlights barely penetrated a fog that hung in folds above the deserted streets. I didn't pass a single vehicle on Kent Avenue.

But there was traffic up on the bridge, bakery and newspaper delivery vans and yellow cabs just beginning their twelve-hour shifts. I trailed behind, in the right lane, ignoring the astonishingly bright lights of an eighteen-wheeler that didn't slow down until it came to within a yard of my rear bumper. I ignored the blast of its air horn, too, and the driver's upraised finger as he fell back.

'Thick skin,' I remembered an old partner telling me. 'That's how you do it. That's how you get through the day. Nothing in, nothing out. Keep it from the wife, keep it from the kids.'

SEVENTEEN

I got out of bed at ten o'clock, after five hours' sleep, and set a pot of coffee to brewing. Then I quickly showered and shaved. Though I couldn't be sure that Aslan was contemplating a move – or that he wasn't already in the wind – the need for haste was obvious enough.

At ten thirty, I dialed the number of *INS* Agent Dominick Capra. He picked up on the third ring.

'Dominick, it's Harry Corbin. You remember, we had lunch at Pete's Tavern.'

'Hey, Harry,' Capra said, 'how's it goin'?'

'Can't whine. How about yourself? You put away any foreign gangsters this week?'

'We don't put 'em away, Harry. We just send them back where they came from. So, what's up?'

'Chechens, Dominick. Chechens are up. Or one particular Chechen, named Aslan Khalid, who used to have a Russian business partner named Konstantine Barsakov.'

'Used to?'

'Barsakov's dead, but that's not what I'm calling about. I always thought that Chechens and Russians hated each other.'

Capra took a minute to consider the statement. I could almost hear the little wheels turning.

'First thing,' he finally said, his good-old-boy tone conspicuously absent, 'Khalid is not a Chechen family name. Chechen family names sound like Russian names. Second thing, there's no Chechen immigration quota. Chechnya is a province of Russia. If your man's here legally, he came in under the Russian quota. Third, Chechnya has been penetrated by jihadists from everywhere in the Middle East, so the only way a Chechen could enter the United States under the Russian quota is if the Russian government intervened to get his application approved.'

'I saw Khalid's green card, Dominick. It seemed legit to me.'

'What was his country of origin?'

'Russia.'

'Well?'

I gave it a couple of seconds, than got to the point. 'Aslan's vanished and I need to find him,' I said. 'I was hoping you'd run his name through your database. If he's here legally, he has to have a sponsor. I'd like to know that sponsor's name.'

This time Capra took so long to respond that I thought we were disconnected.

'Dominick?'

'Yeah, I'm here.'

'Well?'

'Harry, listen close to what I'm sayin'. I feel the dead hand of higher-ups in this business.

152

You've grabbed a buzzsaw, but gettin' cut is not on my list of priorities. Not only will I not do this little favor for you, I don't want you to call me again. Comprende?'

Chastened, I refilled my coffee mug before making a series of phone calls, to the Department of Finance, The Motor Vehicle Bureau, and the Department of Consumer Affairs. My hope was to connect Aslan to Domestic Solutions, but the calls were unproductive. Finance told me that Domestic Solutions was not incorporated and had never paid taxes of any kind. Motor Vehicles told me that the Econoline's registration had been signed by Konstantine Barsakov. Consumer Affairs told me that Domestic Solution was unlicensed.

I'm not terribly superstitious, but I'd had enough of the telephone by then. I walked to the living-room window and stood for a moment, looking out on a playground overrun with screaming children. For the past week, the playground had been deserted because of the heat, so whatever the kids had been doing, they'd been doing it indoors. Now all that pent-up energy was pouring out.

The children were in constant motion, running from one apparatus to another, barely pausing to interact.

A few minutes later, I fired up the computer in my office and went back to work. Aslan Khalid had issued a personal challenge to me when he posed Barsakov in front of the Chechen flag. This was a display of ego I could certainly use against him. As for the challenge itself, the case became personal for me when I rolled Jane Doe over and saw what was done to her. I didn't need additional motivation.

I jumped from my server to Google, typed in Chechnya, got 892,000 hits. For the next hour, I bounced from website to website, covering no more than twenty. At one, I discovered a version of Aslan's flag. At another, a history of rebellion that stretched back to 1785 when a Russian army swept south to engulf Chechnya, at the time a virtually autonomous province of the Ottoman Empire. In 1944, a fed up Josef Stalin deported the entire population to the gulags in Kazakhstan. In 1959, a conciliatory Nikita Khrushchev allowed their return. The struggle for independence continued throughout. Not even the 1994 assault on the capitol of Grozny, an attack which left the city looking much like Berlin at the end of World War Two, was sufficient to stop it.

It was all very noble and I found myself in sympathy with the Chechen people. Still, the past ten years had seen a pair of troubling developments. After the rebels were driven out of the capitol and into the hills, Chechnya had been penetrated by Arab jihadists offering money, arms, and a concept of struggle that led to the mass slaughter of Russian school children. At the same time, in the absence of any rule of law, a criminal class had emerged. According to an article in *Le Monde*, Chechnya had become a trans-ship-

ment point for everything from Afghani mor-
phine headed for Europe to stolen BMWs
headed for Thailand. Kidnappings for ran-
som were an everyday occurrence, even now
that the Russians had consolidated what
passed for a victory by installing a sadistic
butcher named Ramzan Khadyrov as president.

I took a break at noon to stand beside the
kitchen window while I ate a slightly overripe
nectarine and collected my thoughts. According to Dominick Capra, Aslan couldn't be in
the country legally unless somebody in the
Russian government requested a favor of
somebody in the United States government.
If so, it must have been a very big favor.
Aslan's description of the Russian assault on
Grozny was too graphic to be entirely rehearsed. Almost certainly, he'd been there, in
his mid-twenties, involved in the fighting. Was
he already working for the Russians? Or was
he originally a freedom fighter?

That was as far as I got before the phone
began to ring. I knew it was from Adele
before I picked it up. Adele was the only one
who called these days.

'Hi,' she said, 'how'd it go?'

I spelled it out for her, summarizing the
facts, my tone neutral. On the prior night,
just before I fell asleep, I'd come to a conclusion: I could not have reasonably anticipated
the events leading to Barsakov's release.
Neither the presence of Monica Baird, nor

the arrival of Barsakov's lawyer, nor Drew Millard's chickenshit decision. Any one, or even two, of these elements would not have been enough to spring Konstantine. It took all three.

But if my plan had been sound, that didn't mean it was the only plan on the table. Far from it.

'What you might have done,' Adele pointed out, 'was take a photo of Barsakov and show it to the witness first. That way, you'd be charging him with murder.'

I was quick to reply. 'For that matter, I could have brought Clyde with me on the surveillance, let him *ID* Barsakov right there, then obtained search warrants before Aslan knew I existed. Or even better, I could have held off on serving the warrants until the women came back to Greenpoint on Saturday evening. Hell, by that time, I might have gotten warrants for them too.'

Adele finally brought me to a halt. 'Alright, Corbin, I'm sorry. I know how you must feel.'

'Do you mean that?'

'Of course.'

'Then why don't you come home, Adele? Or at least tell me what's wrong.' The words were out of my mouth before I could take them back. 'I know I'm supposed to be a new-millennium kind of guy, faithful and understanding, but it's been two weeks and I'm starting to lose hope.'

The inevitable prolonged silence followed, during which I paced from the living room into the rear bedroom and back. Then Adele said, 'Don't give up on me, Corbin. Not yet.'

I noted the quaver in her voice, almost with satisfaction. Adele rarely displays her emotions. Woman of mystery is more her style.

'No,' I said. 'Not yet.'

Another silence, followed by a change of subject. There was to be no revelation.

'So, what are you going to do?' Adele asked.

'About what, exactly?'

'About your Jane Doe, Aslan, the women, the children.'

'Ah, we're back to them. Well, in the short term, there's only one thing I can do.'

'And what's that?'

'I have to break the priest.'

A few minutes later, after a goodbye that might have been warmer, I went back to my computer. There was one more item I wanted to research. Several years before, a Catholic priest had violated the seal of the confessional to free a man unjustly convicted of murder. If it happened once, or so I reasoned, it could happen again. I just wanted to know the exact circumstances before I confronted Father Stan.

EIGHTEEN

By one o'clock, I was on my way to the Blessed Virgin Outreach Center, driving along Metropolitan Avenue, over Newtown Creek, through industrial Maspeth, finally into the small residential community surrounding the center. Again, I was impressed with the resolute orderliness of the neighborhood, with the carefully tended yards and the immaculate gardens surrounding the modest homes. Written off decades before, this little piece of Maspeth was as proud – and ultimately defiant – as it was working class.

The outreach center was up and running when I walked inside. Seven adults and at least as many children were gathered around several of the worn couches against the walls. Curiously, there were no children in the play area.

'Can I help you?' A young woman in jeans and a tie-dyed sweatshirt rose to her feet from a kneeling position.

'I'm here to see Father Manicki,' I said, just as though I'd called ahead to make an appointment.

'He's not here today. He's attending a conference at the Diocese. He'll be back tomorrow.'

'Thanks.' I'd hoped to take the priest by surprise, which was why I hadn't called ahead, but the trip wasn't entirely wasted. There was always Sister Kassia and the pressure I hoped she'd put on Father Stan.

The nun took that moment to make an appearance, entering through a door that led back into the church. She stopped when she saw me, stopped to look into my eyes. I suspect she read the message correctly because her own eyes instantly hardened.

'I need to speak with you for a few minutes.' I was careful to keep my tone firm. There would be no *mea culpas* to confuse the issues. I'd come to make a deal which the good Sister could refuse or accept. There was no third alternative.

'Alright,' she said after a long moment, 'let's go outside.'

We took a slow walk to the end of the block while I related the same sad tale I'd conveyed to Adele only a few hours before. It was a beautiful day. The temperature was in the seventies, the sunlight clear and clean enough to render the cracked roads and worn brick nearly pristine. Above our heads, a steady breeze rattled the leaves and branches of an ancient maple whose roots had broken through the sidewalk.

'I made no promises the other day,' I said, 'with regard to the other women, not to you or anybody else. And I'm not making much of a promise now. Those women are potential witnesses in two homicide investigations. They have a responsibility to come forward and I intend to make sure they honor that responsibility. Nevertheless, I need your help now and I'm willing to put an offer on the table.'

We were interrupted then, by an elderly woman who pushed a walker onto a small porch. The woman called Sister Kassia's name as she skillfully avoided the spring-mounted door by turning in a full circle. Without a word, Sister Kassia went up on the porch to speak to the woman. When she returned a few minutes later, she seemed less tense. I walked alongside her, from the shade of the maple into the sunlight, then simply continued our conversation as though we'd never left off.

'I may have to be hard on the women,' I told her. 'I may have to make them more afraid of me than of Aslan.'

'Why are you telling me this?'

'I'm offering a contract, Sister, and I don't want to conceal the terms. Ordinarily, I'd ask the *DA* to incarcerate the women as material witnesses, with or without their children. *INS* would be notified at that point and deportation proceedings would begin.'

'But that doesn't have to happen?'

'There's no good reason to incarcerate witnesses who are available and cooperative. Undocumented workers testify in court every day.'

160

We continued on, to the end of the street, then began to retrace our steps. Ahead of us, a car backed out of a tiny driveway to block our path.

'I'm going to take those women away from Aslan,' I said. 'All I'm asking is that I have a safe place to bring them when I do. Some place other than Blessed Virgin, which Aslan knows about.'

'I can place them in a temporary shelter easily enough, but if you're trying to make an offer I can't refuse, you're not there yet. You need to spell out my side of the bargain.'

The car finally pulled off and we resumed walking. 'I need a carrot,' I said.

'A carrot?'

'To go along with the stick.'

Sister Kassia mouth turned down and she shook her head in disgust. 'Spare me the drama,' she declared. 'Inscrutable doesn't become you.'

'Then let me state the case plainly. My goal is to isolate one of Domestic Solutions' workers. At that point, I will become the stick. Now there's nothing wrong with sticks. Sticks have produced results many times in the past. But in order for a stick to be most effective, there should be a carrot on the other end, a tangible reward for cooperation.'

'A good cop to complement the bad cop?'

'Exactly.'

She thought about this for a moment, then said, 'You make it seem as if all this is going to happen in the near future. Are you telling me to be ready tomorrow?'

'That, Sister, depends almost entirely on Father Manicki.'

I stopped at a little joint called Driggs Restorante, before heading into the Nine-Two, where I picked up a veal parmigiana hero, a side of spaghetti and a salad laced with pepperoncini hot enough to make your eyes water.

Comfort food was what I called it and my thoughts were on my meal as I threaded the maze passing for a squad room at the Nine-Two. But I wasn't so oblivious that I failed to note Inspector Bill Sarney standing next to Drew Millard in the lieutenant's office. Nor did I fail to note the contrast. Bill Sarney was everything the lieutenant wanted to be, so dominant that Millard seemed lost in his shadow. At various times in the last year, Bill Sarney had been my rabbi, my enemy, and my benefactor. All the while manipulating me with the skill of a practiced con man. I couldn't read him then. I couldn't read him now.

I nodded once as I passed, continuing on to my office where I unwrapped the hero, popped the lids off the spaghetti and the salad, finally opened a can of orange soda. Then I leaned forward and took a deep breath.

'Do you have any idea how much cholesterol there is in that sandwich?'

I looked up at Sarney, then down at my watch. 'I got in a little early,' I said, 'hoping to eat in peace. Now you're in my cubicle, giving me indigestion.'

'Do I hear a guilty conscience speaking?' Sarney looked as if he expected an answer, but when I didn't supply one, he added, 'I read the file, Harry. Unknown to your supervisor, you've been conducting yout own investigation.'

'There are *DD*5s in the case file accounting for every single minute in the investigation.'

'Which you wrote last night.'

'Better late than never.'

Sarney burst out laughing, the thin lips of his small mouth nearly vanishing in the process. Needless to say, I wasn't fooled by his good-old-boy guffaws. Nor did I believe that an inspector from the Puzzle Palace was in a Brooklyn precinct to discuss a case file.

'You think the bosses hate you, but it's not like that,' Sarney explained. 'They think you're a cop's cop, Harry, and they secretly want to be like you. You can trust me on this because I've been among the bosses for some time now. In fact, I'm a boss, myself.'

I demonstrated my indifference with a shrug. Even if true, the compliment was meaningless. The bosses might admire Harry Corbin, but if he threatened them, they'd stomp him like a cockroach.

'What are you doing here?'

Sarney leaned over my desk. 'When Konstantine Barsakov's fingerprints were run this morning, somebody's computer was flagged.'

'Whose?'

'I don't know, Harry, and I don't care. And

you shouldn't care either. What's important is that the somebody whose computer got flagged called a number of other somebodies, and one of those somebodies called me.'

As I awaited the falling of the axe, I kept chomping away. The case, I was certain, would be taken from me. What I would do next was anybody's guess. But Sarney still had some cards to play, including one he'd been hiding up his sleeve.

'I vouched for you,' he announced. 'I told my boss that you'd do the right thing. You hear what I'm saying?'

That caught my attention. 'Yeah, I do.'

'This is the chance you've been waiting for, the opportunity to prove yourself.' Sarney tucked his chin into his chest, displaying a wide swath of naked scalp as he stared at me through his eyebrows. 'If you fuck it up, you'll never get another.'

I thought this over for a moment, then asked, 'You still with the Chief of D?'

'Nope, I'm working out of the First Dep's office these days.' Chief of D is cop shorthand for Chief of Detectives. The First Dep is the First Deputy Commissioner, who sits at the foot of the Commissioner's throne. Power in the *NYPD* flows from the Commissioner, to the First Dep, to the Chief of Department. From there it fans out to the chiefs of the various bureaus, including the Detective Bureau. Thus Sarney's climb, from the Chief of Detective's office to that of the First Dep, was a two-rung advance.

'Do I understand you right? I'm keeping the case?'

'With a little addition. Starting tomorrow, you work with a partner.'

'Who?'

'You don't know him, Harry. His name's Hansen Linde. But don't worry. As long as you play it straight, Hansen won't be a problem, though you'll most likely find him annoying.'

Warning delivered, Sarney turned away. I let him reach the door before I set down my sandwich.

'You wouldn't wanna tell me,' I asked, 'what "playing it straight" actually entails?'

'That's simple,' he said without looking back at me, 'just don't do anything I wouldn't do.'

I finished my dinner and disposed of the garbage before heading for Drew Millard's office. When I appeared in the doorway, I thought he was going to get to his feet and salute. Whatever fears he'd entertained regarding Harry Corbin had been multiplied to infinity by the appearance of an inspector from the Puzzle Palace.

'Sorry to bother you, lieutenant, but I was wondering about Barsakov's prints. Did they get run?'

'Yeah, they were run this morning and they came back clean. Something else, by the way. You're taking the rest of the tour off. Inspector's orders.'

'That anything like doctor's orders?'

165

'More like God's orders, Harry. More like
they were written on the stone tablets. Peons
like us, all we can do is read 'em and weep.'

NINETEEN

The next morning, at ten o'clock, after a restless night, I rang the bell of Blessed Virgin's
rectory, a single-family home to the west of
the church. A buzzer sounded from inside,
followed by a click as the lock on the door
released. I entered to find myself in a small
outer room, facing a slender woman seated
behind a desk. The woman's autumn-gold
dress set off her mahogany skin, as did the
amber stones in her large earrings and a tiny
cross at the end of the chain that encircled
her neck.

'Yes, may I help you?' Her voice held the
merest hint of the Caribbean.

'My name is Detective Corbin. Would you
let Father Manicki know that I'll be needing
a few minutes of his time?'

'Can I tell him what it's about?'

'That won't be necessary.' I flashed my best
smile. 'We're old friends.'

After a short wait, I was ushered into the
priest's spacious office. A large desk set before a window held a computer, an in–out
box and a coffee mug decorated with a photo

of the Vatican. The rest of the space was given over to a long couch and four easy chairs. Two of the chairs were set directly across from the couch, two at right angles. Father Manicki was seated in the chair at the far end of the couch. He didn't rise when I stepped into the room, nor did he offer his hand, and it was obvious that he'd spoken with Sister Kassia. I should have thanked him for the tip, the subject's current state of mind always being of interest to the interviewer. Instead, I took the chair to his right, perching on the edge of the seat, and let my briefcase drop to the floor.

'How have you been, Father?'

'Fine, how about you?' The priest's tone was sharp enough to walk the border of flagrant sarcasm.

'Myself, I'm having a little problem with my conscience, something I need to get straightened out.'

'Are you a Catholic?'

'No, Father, but I'm not anything else, either. Besides, nobody understands that confession is good for the soul better than a detective. I'm talking about the relief that follows a confession. I see that relief, plain as day, in the suspects I interrogate. They always feel better once they get that burden off their chest.'

A portrait of the Madonna holding the infant Jesus hung on the wall facing my chair. The infant's attention was on a book resting on his mother's lap, which he examined closely while his mother gazed down fondly. Above her, a small angel held a gold crown with both hands. I found myself wondering, as the silence built, why the angel, with his black wings and sumptuous charcoal-gray robes, was so dark. Was there a hidden message, something about vanity perhaps? Or was the artist only working a contrast between the angel and the Virgin's blond hair and sumptuous blue robes?

'Are you here to confess?' Father Manicki finally asked. 'Because, if you are, I'll be hearing confessions tomorrow afternoon in the church.'

'I'm not here to confess,' I said. 'Not yet, at least. No, before I can make a confession, I have to know whether or not I'm a sinner. That's the first step, right? To examine your conscience?'

'It is,' he admitted.

'Then that's what I'm here for. I want to know if I'm living in a state of sin.'

Father Manicki looked down at his hands, as if he hoped to find the solution to his dilemma inscribed on his knuckles. He'd made a good-faith effort to be rid of me when he failed to identify Plain Jane the first time I approached him, a charade Sister Kassia had exposed when she called me on that Sunday morning. So where could he go now, this compassionate minister to the downtrodden? Could he throw me out on my ass, perhaps after a dressing down for my impudence? If our positions were reversed, that's exactly what I would have done. I certainly wouldn't have given him the opportunity to plant a wedge and pound away at it.

I took advantage of the silence to pull my briefcase from the floor, to fumble inside for a moment before removing the likeness of Plain Jane Doe I'd planted all over town. Very carefully, I laid the photo on a glass coffee table so that it faced the priest.

'I must care about her,' I said as I straightened up. 'I wouldn't have spent all those hours creating that photo on my computer if I didn't care. Keep in mind, I had very little to start with.'

Father Stan raised his eyes to meet mine. 'What are you saying?'

'I'm saying, Father, that when I found her, she looked like this.' The photo I then removed from the briefcase was a close-up of Plain Jane's face taken a few moments after I'd rolled her onto her back. I laid it on the coffee table alongside the first shot, inviting a comparison. To his credit, Father Stan didn't recoil, though his jaw tightened and his full lips squeezed into a thin line.

'Creating a recognizable likeness wasn't as hard it might appear.' I used my index finger to illustrate as I went along. 'This discharge from her nose and mouth? You can eliminate that in under an hour. Likewise for the crushed portion of her skull. And the main features of her face? Her overbite, her square jaw, her short nose? They're pretty obvious. The only problem I really had was with her eyes. In this shot, all you can see is a white film, but when I got up close at the crime scene, I observed a pair of blue circles underneath. These circles, they were very faint and I couldn't determine the exact shade of blue. That's one reason I printed the final shot in black-and-white. It's like her skin, which was tinged with green. Taking the green out was no problem. But was she originally pale? Was her complexion sallow? Did she have color in her cheeks? Once a victim's in this condition, it's impossible to know.'

I straightened up, drawing the priest's eyes away from the photos and onto myself.

'I thought,' he said, 'there were police artists who did this sort of thing.'

'There are, but I was too impatient to wait for them to get their act together. That's not really the point, anyway.'

Despite my generally bullying attitude, I had Father Stan's full attention. 'Then what is?' he asked.

I again fumbled in my briefcase, making a show of the search, finally removing the original likeness I'd created on the computer. The shot was generic, with Plain Jane staring straight ahead, her face expressionless.

'See, this is what I first came up with. I don't think it took more than a few hours.'

'I recognize her immediately. Anybody would.'

'I knew that Father, but I still wasn't satisfied. I wanted more than recognition. I wanted to find...' I paused long enough to draw a breath and smile ruefully. 'Would you believe it's been more than two weeks and I don't even know her name?'

Father Manicki tugged at his Roman collar, revealing a line of chafing beneath. 'I understand how frustrated you must feel, detective, but I don't see how I can help you.'

I ignored him. 'The point I'm trying to make is that I must have cared for her. If not, I would have been satisfied with my first effort. Recognizable is what it's all about, right? For a cop? But I kept going, hour after hour, turning her head this way and that, widening and narrowing her mouth and her eyes, lightening and darkening the color of her hair. There were times, I swear, when I thought I'd go crazy.'

'If there's something in this story that's sinful, I haven't heard it yet.' Now that he'd gotten over his initial shock, Father Stan's voice was much stronger.

'Tell me something, Father. Have you ever hunted?'

The question brought him up short and his expression became wary. 'When I was a young man, before I entered the seminary, I hunted deer.' He hesitated before adding, 'I was raised near Lake Champlain. Everybody hunted.'

'Were you successful?'

'I dropped an eight point buck in my second season.'

'And how did you feel when you centered the crosshairs on the animal's chest? When

171

you held his life in your hands? Was it a cold day? Could you see his breath in the air? His chest moving as he breathed? The life in his eyes?'

'More than anything, I was afraid that I'd miss.'

I nodded once, then let the silence build. Father Stan shifted uncomfortably in his chair, crossing and recrossing his legs. Finally, he said, 'Do you hunt, detective?'

'I do, Father. I hunt all the time. But not animals. I hunt human beings.'

There was a crucifix on the wall behind Father Stan's chair, so perfectly centered above his head that it seemed to be growing out of his skull. The crucifix was little more than an assemblage of sticks that might have been snapped from the branches of the trees outside the church, but there was no resisting its power. The arms outstretched, the body slumped, the head turned slightly to the side, the chin resting on the chest. By that time, if I remembered right, Jesus had already descended into hell. As if crucifixion wasn't enough.

'Tell me, Father, can sin be a force for good?'

Father Stan weighed his reply carefully. He seemed in no hurry now. 'God is omnipotent,' he said with a smile. 'He can do anything but create a rock so heavy that He can't lift it. But I'd still like to hear about this sin. If it really is a sin.'

'Most of the time,' I replied, 'my job is

172

pretty mechanical. I get cases, everything from burglaries to murders, and I investigate. Sometimes I make an arrest, mostly I don't, but I don't get worked up either way.' I raised my eyes, until I was looking directly into Father Stan's. 'But there are other days and other cases, like this particular case, when I'm as single-minded as a serial killer. I tell you, Father, I've thought about this for a long time, trying to figure out what's going on, and the closest word in the English language for what I feel is lust. That's why I asked you that question. Can sin be a force for good?'

This time Father Stan was ready for me. 'Obsession,' he declared, 'is not a sin. From a purely psychological point of view, Mother Theresa was obsessed.'

'What if you felt as though you'd sacrifice anything to achieve your goal? What if all concern for the victim, along with your duty to society, suddenly vanished? What if you were willing to sacrifice your livelihood? The only woman you've ever loved? What happens when it becomes entirely personal?'

'Are you asking me for absolution?'

'Can you be forgiven for a sin you know you'll commit again?'

'God doesn't ask you to guarantee the future. He only asks you to try.'

'Trying is not an option at the moment. Later, perhaps, after I do what I have to do.'

'Then you can't be absolved.'

'That's what I figured before I came here. But it's okay. I accept the sin and whatever punishment follows. I can do that because I'm certain that the end I seek is good.'

'Certain that the end justifies the means? Is that it?'

I reached down into my briefcase to withdraw the last arrow in that particular quiver, a full-body shot of Plain Jane lying on her back with her abdomen split open.

'In this case, Father,' I said as I laid the photo on the table, 'it surely does.'

I sat back in the chair, leaving Father Stan to contemplate the gruesome reality. I knew all the words likely to be running through his mind at that moment – ghastly, horrid, ungodly, frightful, hideous, evil – as I knew those words would lead to other words, like sadist and serial killer. I also knew the reality, that Jane's evisceration had come after her death, wouldn't occur to the priest. That was because, in an odd way, harvesting a dead woman's organs in order to remove her fetus is even more evil than murdering her for pleasure.

'Can you still remember her voice?' I asked when the priest finally raised his head. 'I mean the sound of it when she whispered her sins to you in the confessional? Was it breathy, husky, musical? Did she have an accent? Did you speak Polish?'

Father Manicki responded by stacking the four photos and handing them to me. 'I cannot be forced to violate the seal of the confessional.'

'Forced?'

'By the law.'

I laughed out loud as I accepted the photos. 'You think I'm going to get a subpoena?'

'No,' he admitted, 'that's not your way.'

'It's not my way and I'm not going to vanish, either.' I held up the photos, fanning them out like a deck of cards before stuffing them into my briefcase. 'Because the man who did this will kill again. He has to be stopped and I think you're the only one who can stop him.'

'Think?'

The subject never controls the interview, even when the interviewer stupidly phrases his remarks. I simply ignored the question.

'Tell me, Father, have you ever heard of a priest named Joseph Towle?'

Father Stan's involuntary recoil was quickly replaced by a grudging smile as he echoed Sister Kassia. 'I underestimated you, detective.'

'Does that mean you're familiar with the details?'

'Every priest in the country is familiar with the details.'

The facts were simple enough. In 1987, two teenagers from the South Bronx, Jose Morales and Rubin Montalvo, were convicted of murdering another teen, Jose Rivera, then sentenced to life in prison. Two years later, in 1989, a fourth teen, Jesus Fornes, approached a street priest named Joseph Towle, asking for guidance. In the course of the private conversation that followed, Fornes told the priest that it was he who'd killed Jose Rivera, and that his conscience was troubling him. Only at the very end of this conversation did Father Towle give Fornes absolution for his sins. For the next twelve years, Father Towle sat on this information while Rivera and Montalvo sat in prison. Then, in 2001, after consulting with his superiors, he finally came forward to inform the appropriate authorities. By that time, Jesus Fornes, the actual murderer, was four years dead.

The law in New York State forbids a minister, priest or other member of the clergy from disclosing a confession or a confidence in a court of law. Father Towle overcame this burden by asserting that Fornes had come to him for counseling. The absolution part was a mere afterthought.

I'd known all this going in, of course. Still, I listened patiently while the priest recounted the various excuses offered by Father Towle. Then I asked a pair of questions.

'If what Jesus Fornes told Father Towle wasn't a confession, why did Father Towle wait twelve years to come forward? Why did he leave Montalvo and Rivera to rot in prison?'

'Those are good questions, detective, ones I've asked myself.'

'And what was your answer?'

'That the questions are irrelevant to this conversation. You see, there's a major difference here. Your victim's confession took place in a confessional. As such, it was formal from

176

the beginning. Every word she spoke falls under the seal.'

'You're right about the difference, Father, but there's another difference, too, and one major similarity. The other difference, of course, is that Jesus Fornes was a killer and Jane Doe was a victim.'

'And the similarity?'

'Fornes was dead when Father Towle came forward. Jane Doe is dead even as we speak. Wherever they were headed, to heaven or hell or oblivion, they're already there. Nothing Father Towle told the court, and nothing you tell me, can harm either of them.'

Father Stan's mouth opened, but I cut off his response. 'And by the way, Father, just in case you're worried about revealing her sin, I already know she was pregnant.'

I crossed my legs and let my eyes wander to the portrait on the wall opposite my chair. The Madonna was looking at the infant Jesus, her head twisted down and to the right, the angle so unnatural I knew she couldn't assume it unless her neck was broken. Still, the line that ran from the hem of her robe, over her son, then around the semi-circle of her hood was compelling. To create her alive would have been to ruin it.

'Tell me what you want.' Father Stan finally said.

'I want to know where she worked and who she worked for.' I spoke without taking my eyes off the painting. 'I want to know who made her pregnant. As I said, I'm not inter-

177

ested in her sins.'

'That distinction is meaningless in the context of the confessional.'

'Why, Father? Why should where she worked be kept a secret?'

'Penitents come to the confessional expecting secrecy. They have to trust us.'

'Ah, I see. Well, if that's your problem, let me put your mind at rest. Nothing you tell me will ever be repeated in public. First, because the Criminal Procedure Law forbids a priest revealing information obtained in the course of a confession. And second, because what you were told in the confessional is classic hearsay. It cannot be used in a trial.'

'Then how did Father Towle testify?'

'Father Towle testified at a hearing where the rules are a lot less strict.' I finally turned to look into his eyes. 'Listen to what I'm telling you, Father, because I mean it from the bottom of my heart. All I want you to do is give me a push in the right direction. I'll take it from there and your name will never come up.'

By then, Father Stan was sitting with his arms folded across his chest, his legs crossed at the knees. He was telling me that his mind was closed, but I still had cards to play.

'What I'm gonna do now,' I continued, deliberately breaking eye contact, 'is run through a scenario I've created in my own mind. The sequence appears logical on the surface, but I could be way off. That's where you can help me.'

'I've already told you that I can't comment.'

'I'm not asking you to comment. In fact, what I'm going to assume, unless you correct me, is that I've got it right. You don't have to say a word.'

Again, putting a stop to the conversation was the priest's best move. I'd made my argument and he'd responded, so long, see ya later. But he merely sat there, his eyes jittery with indecision.

'Okay,' I said, 'let's start with the pregnancy. I'm not thinking rape here, because there'd be nothing to confess if she was raped. I'm thinking that a young girl in a strange country, a girl whose opportunities were few and far between, made a big mistake in the name of love. I'm thinking she became pregnant with an inconvenient child, that she was pressured to have an abortion, by her employers and by Aslan Khalid. I'm thinking that she was confused, that she sought counseling from the only counselor available. That would be you, Father.'

When the priest failed to challenge any of my assertions, I again turned to stare into his eyes. 'Did you tell her that abortion is murder? Did you tell her to resist? To fight for the life of her child? Did you bring about the very conditions that led to her death?'

Father Manicki stared back at me for a moment, then he shook his head as though trying to rid his ears of my words. 'You deceived me,' he declared. 'You led me to believe that she was tortured.'

'According to the medical examiner, she was locked in a refrigerator for an extended period of time right before she was killed. That sounds like torture to me.'

'The cold...' The priest's jaw snapped shut and his eyes lit up with anger. 'Let's ignore the fact that you've been manipulating me ever since you walked into the room. Let's ignore your bullying attitude. The simple truth is that the seal is absolute. If I could have helped you, I already would have.'

I ignored the outburst. 'Father, do you remember the man with the narrow eyes? He accompanied the women from time to time?' I hesitated long enough for the priest to nod. 'Well, his name is Konstantine Barsakov and he was murdered. I know because I'm the one who found his body. The women were gone by then. Aslan, too. That's why I was so certain that Aslan would kill again. He already had.'

Father Manicki rose to his feet, not to throw me out, but only because he could no longer contain the tension. I rose with him, until we were standing only a few feet apart. The advantage, here, was all mine. I was a head taller than the priest and he was forced to look up at me.

'If you violate the seal of the confessional,' I said, 'that would be a mortal sin, right?' When the priest nodded, I continued on, my tone calm and reasonable. 'See, that's what I don't understand. From what I can tell, all mortal sins are equally mortal. So why are you

180

making such a fuss about this one? Why don't you just commit the damn sin, accept the guilt, do your penance and seek absolution? Unless, of course, you're merely protecting the institution.'

Father Stan's mouth dropped open. Without doubt, as a priest who ministered to the poor, he'd fought the hierarchy all his life. 'Get out of here,' he said.

'Sure, but first tell me this. Tell me which mortal sin is the most mortal? To provide a detective with a few facts revealed to you in a murder victim's confession? Or not to provide those facts, knowing that Aslan Khalid will kill again? Bear in mind, Jane Doe is dead, now and forever. Those other women, they're still breathing. And they most likely want to keep it that way.'

I stood there, wearing the most inscrutable expression in my repertoire while I watched Father Manicki, his face red, his hands curled into fists. For a moment, I thought he'd break, but then he abruptly sat and took a series of quick breaths.

'I can't help you,' he said. 'I can't help you.'

I turned away, not to leave, but to cover my disappointment. If the priest chose not to help, the only link to Jane's killer was Aslan Khalid.

'Would it be a sin,' I asked, my tone considerably more gentle, 'for you to tell me her name? Just that, Father, just her name?'

The priest shook his head. 'I can't,' he said. 'It's impossible.'

'Impossible?' I rose to my feet and dropped a business card on the desk. 'The alternative to blind obedience is right in front of your eyes. It won't disappear when I walk out of this room. How could it when what you're looking at is your own conscience?'

Father Manicki waited until my hand was on the doorknob before he spoke. 'Mynka,' he finally said, his voice little more than a whisper, though he pronounced each syllable distinctly. 'Her given name is Mynka. I don't know her family name.'

I turned to look at the priest, hoping this damaging admission would lead to a flood. No such luck. Father Stan's mouth was tight, his jaw locked down, and I had the impression that he'd cut a deal with his good angel. He would give me this much, I would leave, then he'd feel better about himself. And perhaps he would, right up until I returned on the following day, and the day after that, until he realized I might return one day bearing another set of crime scene photos, these of a victim he might have saved.

TWENTY

When I finally got to my cubicle at the Nine-Two, I found Detective Hansen Linde, my new partner, sitting at the front desk. I squeezed by him to get to my own desk at the rear, not even glancing in his direction until I was seated and facing him. Under other circumstances, I would have introduced myself and offered my hand. Instead, I looked him over carefully while he returned the compliment.

Linde was a big man. His face was all forehead, cheekbones and jaw, his narrow smile a tight line, his neck thicker than his skull, his knuckles the size of walnuts. Yet for all his rugged appearance, his skin was almost porcelain white and his stomach curled gently outward to form a little pouch above his belt.

'Hansen Linde,' he finally said, leaning forward to extend one of those hands. 'I'm from Minnesota, ya know.'

As I took Linde's hand, I imagined Sarney chuckling away. Though Linde made no effort to impress me with the power of his grip, his physical strength was obvious enough.

'Harry Corbin,' I said, 'from Manhattan.'

Linde settled back in his chair. 'I tell my partners I'm from Minnesota because they always ask where I'm from anyway. It's the accent, ya know. And the Ole and Lena jokes. I'm an expert on Ole and Lena jokes. I collect 'em.'

I took a moment to consider this, having no idea what he was talking about, and no patience, either. 'What's an OLE-ee?' I finally asked.

'The Prairie Home Companion? On National Public Radio?'

I shrugged.

'See, that's the problem with New Yorkers. That's why people don't like 'em. They think the world begins and ends on their little island.'

The statement was too obviously true to merit a response and I abruptly shifted gears, gesturing to the case file, which was open on his desk. 'That's my case,' I told him. 'You wanna come along for the ride, fine. But you don't get to drive. If that's not okay with you, tell me now.'

He leaned back in his chair, the blood rushing into his cheeks, his mouth curling down at the corners. 'Damn,' he said, 'I just got here. Stealing your case is the last thing I want to do.' He closed the file and pushed it toward me. 'But this Aslan Khalid, he's probably in the wind, if ya get my drift.'

'Wanna bet?'

'Bet what?'

'How about two cows and a corn field?'

184

He stared at me through a pair of corn-flower blue eyes for a moment, then blinked twice before bursting into laughter. 'That's a good one,' he declared between guffaws. 'That's one on me.'

I rose without further explanation and led Hansen through the squad room, down the stairs and out the front door. I made a show of it, nodding hello to every cop we passed, especially those cops who loathed Harry Corbin. Linde was several inches taller than me and a good fifty pounds heavier. Together, we amounted to five hundred pounds of cop, enough bulk to capture the attention of a desk lieutenant named Torres who'd been on the job long enough to remember the Knapp Commission.

'Christ,' he said as we passed. 'I think I climbed the fuckin' beanstalk.'

Behind me, I heard Linde chuckle.

I stopped at Domestic Solutions first, to check for newly-delivered mail. There was none, which didn't surprise me. Then I drove to the Post Office on Meserole Avenue where I cornered the manager, a petite woman named Alfaro. Linde was standing just to my left, his eager, country-boy grin firmly in place.

Alfaro didn't fight me when I asked if a change-of-address card had been filed for 532 Eagle Street. 'Give me a minute,' she said, 'and I'll check it out.'

The minute stretched into five, during which time Linde asked, politely, if he might

185

tell me a joke. I refused the offer, not out of resentment, but because I wanted to see if he could be provoked. He wasn't.

When Alfaro returned, she was shaking hear head. 'Sorry,' she told us, 'no one's been in to have the mail forwarded. Mail to that address is still being delivered.'

Linde waited until we were back on the street, then asked, 'What do you make of that, Harry?'

'You're asking why we didn't find mail at Domestic Solutions?'

'Yeah.'

'Mobility.'

'You wanna explain? Or you just wanna bust my chops?'

I smiled. The priest had blown me off, despite my brilliantly constructed interview, and time was marching on. I was pissed, not least because I'd yet to formulate a Plan B, and I was taking it out on Hansen.

'My best guess, Aslan conducts Domestic Solutions' business on a cell phone and his workers are paid directly by their employers. Maybe there's a bank account somewhere, a place to deposit the checks, but it's more likely that the checks are cashed and the money handed over to Aslan. That would allow him to pick up on a minute's notice without leaving a paper trail, and without jeopardizing his business interests. Which is exactly what he did.'

'But why kill Barsakov? Why not just send him away? That would eliminate any connection between Aslan and your vic.'

'Maybe he asked Barsakov to flee and Barsakov refused. Maybe there's a reason why Barsakov can't return to Russia. Maybe Aslan punished Barsakov for not getting the victim in the water, despite Clyde Kelly's appearance. I don't know how close you read the file, but Kelly didn't call nine-one-one for several hours, so Barsakov had plenty of time to finish the job. Instead, he panicked and left the victim where she was. Two weeks later, as a direct result, I show up and drag Barsakov away on a trumped-up charge. Aslan couldn't have been real happy about that. He had to figure, if Barsakov panicked once, he'd panic again.'

I went on to tell Linde what I knew about Domestic Solutions and its employees and their children, repeating much of what Dominick Capra told me.

'Aslan has to separate himself from those women,' I insisted. 'He has no other choice. First, there are potential charges of involuntary servitude out there. Then there's the issue of what these women know about Jane's murder. I have good reason to believe that Jane was killed at work, but I have no way to find her employer. The other women could fill that gap and many others. They have to go.'

With nothing better to do, Linde and I decided to drive back to Domestic Solutions, to sit on the building in the hope that somebody would show up. We were on route when

Lieutenant Millard hailed us on the radio.

'You might wanna check out a van fire on Kent Avenue and South Fifth Street, if you remember that intersection. According to the uniforms on the scene, the blaze was deliberately set.'

Although the fire was out, the Econoline was still pouring smoke when I pulled up behind a Fire Department pumper. The van itself was a charred shell, its interior, front and back, utterly destroyed. But the license plate was still attached to the rear bumper, and still readable.

'I ran the tags,' one of the uniformed officers on the scene told me a few minutes later. 'The vehicle is registered to a company called Domestic Solutions.'

I thanked him for the information, just as if I didn't already know it, before I led my new partner off to the side and explained that we were standing less than two hundred yards from where the body of Jane Doe was originally discovered. Then I took him on a tour of South Fifth Street, down to the mound of rubble. The pothole was still there and the taller weeds still flattened, but someone had gotten to the chain link fence, prying it away from its supports. It was now possible to squeeze through and approach the East River.

I did just that, but I didn't stop at the river. Instead, I climbed onto the rickety pier behind the Gambrelli warehouse, then walked its length, stepping carefully over broken boards and exposed nails, until I was left gazing out over the waters of the East River. The tide was pulling hard toward the harbor and the surface of the river was deeply furrowed by the five-knot current. Around the footings of the Williamsburg Bridge, patches of white-water threw up a dancing spray that caught the angled rays of the evening sun. Linde was standing next to me, his silky-straight hair fluttering in a steady breeze that smelled of all the lives and deaths concealed beneath the gray waters before us.

'This is where Jane was meant to go,' I explained. 'Good-bye and good riddance.'

'For whatever it's worth,' Linde said, 'I hear you.'

'That's good, Hansen, because there are quite a few things that need doing, and I think you're the kinda guy who can get them done.'

'Oh, yeah,' he answered, 'I'm your fella. What'd you have in mind?'

I turned from the river and began to make my way back to the Caprice. 'I want you to track all the evidence taken from the Eagle Street scene, the blood, the tire impressions, any fingerprints that turn up, any trace evidence found on Barsakov's clothing or his body. And I want you to secure Domestic Solutions' phone records. Personally, I don't think they'll help us, but we gotta look'

'Is that it?' Linde was grinning.

'No. Find out the name of Barsakov's lawyer and give him a call. See if you can track Barsakov's movements after he left the Nine-Two. And one more thing. I want the name of Aslan Khalid's sponsor, Konstantine Barsakov's, too. They couldn't have gotten into the country legally without sponsors. Now, your boss has the juice to get the names, Hansen. Let him make a personal phone call.'

I lapsed into silence as we picked our way between the fire department and police vehicles surrounding the Econoline. There was nothing to be gained by talking to the fire marshals, or to anyone else. The fire had begun in the van's interior, which could not have happened unless it was deliberately set.

'You understand,' I said as I started the Caprice, 'I'm counting on you to expedite these matters.'

He nodded once, then broke into a huge grin, revealing a pair of deep grooves in either cheek. 'Okay,' he said, 'stop me if you've heard this one. Ole is sitting in his back yard one Sunday, in a religious mood after coming back from church. So he looks up at the sky and asks God why He made Lena so soft and round and cuddly. "I did that so you'd love her," a voice rumbles from on high. For a moment, Ole is overcome with awe, but he finally says, "Then why, Lord, did you have to make her so stupid?" A second later, God's voice again rings in Ole's ears. "I made her dumb, Ole," God explains, "so she'd love you."'

Hansen told the joke well, rendering Ole's

dialogue in a thick, Scandinavian accent, but I didn't laugh. I didn't have to. Linde was roaring with delight. He didn't need my help.

New York was enjoying a second day of sunny skies and cool temperatures when I pulled to a stop in front of Blessed Virgin on the following morning. My intention was to take another shot at Father Stan, playing up the institutional aspect of the confessional seal. There's nothing in the gospels, I would argue, about secrecy, or even the ritual of confession. The confessional seal comes not from Jesus, but from men whose greater aim was to preserve the Church. Surely, God's judgment is more sophisticated, less absolute. How could it not be so when the great Commandments, themselves, are open to interpretation? The fifth commandment says, Thou shalt not kill. The seventh says, Thou shalt not steal. There's no wiggle room in either one, yet the Catholic Church finds killing and stealing, under certain conditions, to be without sin.

It was a decent argument, exactly what was needed to move Father Stan, if he could be moved. Or so I thought as I walked into the crowded outreach center. Sister Kassia was seated in a chair to my left, holding a toddler on her lap, a girl. The nun whispered a few words into the girl's ear, then put her down before leading me outside.

'Have you found them?'

The question surprised me, though it was the obvious question to ask. 'No, I haven't.

I'm here to see Father Manicki.'

Sister Kassia smiled, a smile that must, at one time, have struck terror into the hearts of fourth graders. 'Father Stan isn't here, detective. He's at a retreat house on Staten Island. I don't know what you said to him, but he packed up shortly after you left yesterday.'

'Well, that's the problem with having a conscience, Sister. He knew I'd come back and he didn't want to face me.'

Sister Kassia shook her head, then walked me into the deep shadows cast by a towering maple tree. As it was twenty degrees cooler in the shade, I didn't complain.

'Your outlook is typical of the irreligious,' she told me. 'In your view, Catholicism is just another set of arbitrary beliefs.'

'It's not that...'

'Oh, yes it is.' She brought her hands together and folded them at her waist. 'When Father Stan took his vows, after years of prayer, meditation and study, he embraced the doctrines of the Roman Catholic Church, one of which is the seal of the confessional. And you should keep in mind that among the vows he took was a vow of obedience. Tell me, have you ever taken a vow?'

I reached out to run my hand over the trunk of the maple, the bark rough and cool against my fingers. 'When I became a cop, I took an oath to uphold the laws of the State and the Constitution of the United States. Is an oath the same as a vow? I don't know. But I can tell you this. For cops, it's not about absolutes.

We draw our own lines.'

I went on to repeat the argument I'd made to Hansen Linde. Aslan had to put distance between himself and the women, even if he decided to stick around. No, I didn't think he'd commit mass murder, but he would move them along at the earliest opportunity. Maybe he would send them back to Poland. Maybe he would sell them to somebody who ran a brothel in Bolivia.

Ignoring the last part, Sister Kassia asked, 'And how soon would that earliest opportunity be?'

'Saturday afternoon, when Aslan picks them up at their jobs.'

'In that case, Harry, you have a serious problem. Father Stan has already arranged to have his masses covered on Sunday. He won't be back until Sunday night, at the earliest. But if it's any comfort, I've no doubt that he's examining his conscience right now.'

'In the hope of finding a loophole?'

Suddenly, the door to the outreach center opened and a woman exited, holding the hand of a small child, a little boy. The woman glanced at Sister Kassia, then immediately looked away. As she walked up the block, the boy turned to wave goodbye. The gesture was small, no more than a cupping of his fingers, and he seemed, to me, both confused and resigned. Sister Kassia returned the wave, her expression wistful.

'When I became a nun,' she said, 'my intention was to submit to the will of God. I thought it would be easy. Just follow the rules. Now I know enough to look to my conscience for guidance. As for the rules, I obey the ones my conscience tells me to obey.' She paused to smile the brightest smile I'd yet seen her display. 'Father Stan, he thinks I'm incorrigible because I once proposed diverting a small sum of money from the general fund to the outreach center. Really, he was shocked. But I think he's coming around now. I think he's coming to understand that rules have consequences, too.'

I leaned my back against the tree. 'Let's hope it's not too late when he does, because I don't have another way to go.'

'What about finding Aslan?'

'That's not impossible, but it won't do me any good. Aslan won't talk unless I hurt him more than I'm willing to hurt him. And I don't have enough evidence to charge him with the Barsakov homicide either.'

'Well, you need to think of something, Harry, because it's just as I told you on the first day you walked in here. The minute you discovered their existence, you became responsible for the women and their children. You can't blame Father Stan. They're your burden now.'

I called Adele shortly after leaving Blessed Virgin. I had a big decision to make, one that could easily backfire, and I needed to speak to someone I could trust. That wouldn't be my new partner, Hansen Linde. Linde was Sarney's boy and he would do Sarney's bidding.

Though a bit distracted at first – she was sitting with her mother in a doctor's office – Adele seemed glad to hear from me. When I told her about the priest, she honed in on my dilemma. It was Thursday. Thirty-six hours from now, Aslan would pick up the women at their jobs. With Father Manicki out of play, at least until Sunday night, I had two choices. I could do nothing at all and hope for the best. Or I could find Aslan, put pressure on him and ... and hope for the best.

'Sitting around and hoping isn't my strong point,' I told her. 'I'm taking plan B.'

'What happens after you run him down? Assuming you do run him down.'

'Ah, for a minute there I thought you were thinking positively.'

Adele laughed. 'Answer the question.'

'What I'll do, assuming I find Aslan, is make it personal.'

'I think you went down that road when you arrested Barsakov.'

'Then I'll make it even more personal.'

'And what do you hope to accomplish?'

I took a minute before answering. I was sitting in my car outside the Nine-Two, an hour before I was due to report. I had no particular reasons for being early, but I was too restless to sit at home. 'I'm hoping, if I press the right buttons, Aslan will take a swing at me. That'll give me an excuse to hold him in custody over the weekend.'

'And if he doesn't rise to the bait?'

'Then I'll make up an excuse.' I gave it a couple of beats, then said. 'Dominick Capra, do you know anything about his personal life?'

'I know he has a daughter.'

'How old?'

'High school age. Why?'

'When I spoke to Capra the other day, he blew me off. Told me not to call again. I'm gonna call him back anyway, and make a personal appeal. I think he can help me with the name of Aslan's sponsor.'

I didn't have to spell it out. Adele's silence was enough. Even if Capra was willing to cooperate, and even if he furnished the name of Aslan's sponsor, the jump from the sponsor to Aslan was far from assured. Nevertheless, it was a card in my hand and I intended to play it.

And play it I did, after Adele and I hung up. Like the priest, Capra should have blown me off before I got started. Instead, he listened while I turned his own words against him. What had he called it? Sharecropping for the new millennium? Well, these particular sharecroppers were about to be sold on the black market, at which time they would cease to be sharecroppers and become actual slaves.

'How do you know this?' Capra asked.

'Because,' I readily lied, 'when I asked Aslan about the women, he told me that I shouldn't worry about them.' I took a breath and imitated Aslan's thick accent as best I could. '"For these women, American justice will be thing of past." Tell me, Dominick, do you have kids?'

'You're fuckin' with me, Harry.'

'I've seen these women. They're in their late teens and early twenties. Some of them have children.'

'You know that for a fact?'

'I saw a child at Domestic Solutions and there were car seats in the van they used to transport their workers. Look, Dominick, I'm not asking for the moon here.'

'Then exactly what are you askin' for?'

'Anything in Aslan's file that might lead me to him, especially the name of his sponsor.'

It was Capra's turn to pause. 'I don't know, Harry,' he said after minute. 'I'll think about it. See, the thing is, I know that somebody's computer is gonna be flagged if I use my own computer to pull the file up. Now, there's a hard copy, too, and maybe no one's lookin' at it too hard. But maybe someone is. I mean, I got my family to think about.'

TWENTY-ONE

Sergeant Sabado favored me with his customary scowl, which I eagerly returned, forcing
him to look away as I climbed to the squad
room on the second floor, then found my
cubicle. Hansen Linde was in his chair, awaiting my arrival. He greeted me by displaying a
printout that must have been six pages long.

'The phone records for the warehouse,
going back three months. We should have a
lot of fun with these.'

'What about the names of the sponsors?
Aslan's and Barsakov's.'

'Not yet. Plus, I was only able to get a list of
outgoing numbers. Incoming's gonna be
another couple of days.' Linde tossed a *Coles
Directory* onto my desk. 'Whatta ya say we get
crackin'?'

A *Coles Directory* is often called a reverse
directory because it allows you to put a name
and address to a phone number. This was
exactly what we did for the next two hours.
The job was painstaking and tedious, and
ultimately disappointing. There were no out-
going calls to Manhattan addresses where
live-in maids were likely to be employed. In
fact, there were no calls to anywhere in

Manhattan.

'I need new glasses,' Hansen finally declared.

'Don't get comfortable,' I warned. 'We've got a long way to go.' I watched him lay his reading glasses on his desk, then rub his eyes. 'First, I want to record how many times each number was called, then break the list into residential and business numbers, then organize the lists by neighborhood with the most frequently called numbers first.'

Linde groaned. 'Whatta you say we just pick up the phones and start dialing?'

'And ask what? Do you employ a maid from Domestic Solutions in your home? How long do you think it'll take before someone calls Aslan and says, "Yo, wolf-man, the police are looking for your workers"?'

'Alright, I get the point.'

'Good, because that doesn't mean we can't knock on doors looking for Aslan Khalid. Given Barsakov's sudden departure, Aslan'll be expecting me to come calling. But I want the women left out of it.'

Hansen leaned back in his chair and I got the distinct impression that he was sick of my attitude. I wasn't surprised. Linde worked for the First Dep, while I was a lowly squad detective. If life was fair, he'd be giving the orders. Still, I wasn't finished.

'How about a photo, Hansen? Did you, by any chance, make a copy of Aslan's *DMV* photo?

Linde shook his head.

'No photos. No sponsors' names. No out-going phone calls. If I didn't know better, I'd think you were trying to impede this investigation.'

Hansen fixed his baby-blues on me for a moment, then smiled. Not his radiant, prairie-boy smile, but a smile nonetheless.

'Feel free to stop me if you've heard this one, Harry,' he said. 'Ole and Lena decide to get married. They have a big wedding in their home town, followed by a catered reception, then head off to a honeymoon in Minneapolis. As they're nearing the city, Ole puts his hand on Lena's knee. Lena giggles and says, "If ya want to, Ole, you could go furdder." So Ole drives to Duluth.'

It was eight o'clock by the time we left the Nine-Two. With Linde driving, we managed to check out a cluster of twelve residential addresses in the Brooklyn neighborhoods of Brighton Beach, Sheepshead Bay and Gravesend. The addresses were all in apartment buildings inhabited by ordinary workers. That the residents of those apartments were more likely to be maids than to employ them was obvious at a glance. But it was also obvious, given the number of calls from Domestic Solutions, that Aslan was known to these individuals, virtually all Russian, that we interviewed. A few even admitted to recognizing Aslan's photo, the one I'd pulled off the squad's computer. But they hadn't seen him and didn't know where he was. Nor did they care to discuss the nature of their relationship with him.

At one point, as we bounced from address to address, Linde asked an obvious question: 'What the hell are we doing, Harry?'

'We're knockin' on doors, Hansen, in the hope, slim as it may be, that we'll run across somebody with a grudge against Aslan. Someone who'll sell him out for the pure pleasure of doing so.'

'A needle in a haystack?'

Three hours later, we headed back to the house, re-crossing Brooklyn on Bedford Avenue, from Avenue Z only a few blocks north of the Atlantic Ocean, through Sheepshead Bay, through Midwood, though Flatbush and Bedford-Stuyvesant, finally into Williamsburg. There were traffic lights on every corner and most blocks were lined on both sides with closed storefront businesses. On the surrounding streets, the architecture ranged from squat five-story apartment buildings, to single-family homes on spacious lots, to high-rise housing projects. How many thousands of people did we pass? Fifty thousand? A hundred? Five hundred? This was New York stripped of its glamour. This was where all those people who work in the basements of all those New York skyscrapers live out their uncelebrated lives. I knew that Aslan might be anywhere among them. Or in dozens of other equally uncelebrated neighborhoods in Queens or the Bronx.

Thursday was fast drawing to a close. On

Saturday, Aslan Khalid, ever the good shepherd, would gather his flock. I closed my eyes for a minute as Hansen drove across Empire Boulevard, imagining the women I saw at Blessed Virgin, their fresh, hopeful faces, the summer dresses they wore. I imagined them led along a narrow ramp into an airliner. Right this way, ladies. Watch your step.

'Alright,' I finally said, 'let's hear it.'

'Hear what, Harry?'

'Those little tasks I gave you, the ones you mentioned before. Let's hear the results.'

Hansen slowed for the light, then threw the transmission into neutral before producing a small notebook. 'Okey-dokey,' he said. 'First, the lab compared the tire-impression photos you took at the crime scene with tire impressions found in an oil spill at Domestic Solutions. They got a match.'

I shook my head. 'The van can only be tied to Konstantine Barsakov. Let's not waste time on it.'

Linde dropped his eyes to the open notebook without protesting. 'The blood found beneath the bathroom tiles at Domestic Solution is the same type as your Jane Doe's. A *DNA* analysis is ongoing. We'll have results within a week.' He looked up at me, but I waved him on. 'The Barsakov autopsy was done early this morning by a pathologist named Moore. She estimates time of death between nine and ten thirty on Monday night.'

'And the manner of death?'

'Well, Moore's calling it a homicide. That's the good news. The bad news is that Barsakov's prints were found on the gun and a test of his right hand for gunshot residue was positive.'

'How about the finger that was blown off? Did they find gunshot residue on the finger?'

'Don't know, Harry.'

I waved him on.

'I managed to contact Barsakov's lawyer, Martin Cardiff, and, believe me, it wasn't easy. Cardiff says that he and Konstantine split up when they left the precinct on Monday night.'

'Was anybody there to meet Barsakov?'

Hansen shook his head. 'I also called the phone company, hoping that Aslan gave them a forwarding number for Domestic Solutions. As it turns out, the phone's in Barsakov's name and the number's still active.'

Ahead of us, a small cluster of teenagers slouched in front of a deli. The deli was closed and one of the kids was spray-painting a graffiti tag on a steel shutter covering the window. Hansen looked at the kids for a minute, then put the car in gear when the light changed. He drove past without comment.

'The *ME* recovered three human hairs at the autopsy and sent them over to the lab for comparison. The hairs were found on Barsakov's shoulder, where someone leaning over him might have deposited them.'

'Were the follicles intact?' For the most

part, hair evidence is junk science. All you can really say is that a comparison doesn't exclude a given suspect. There are exceptions, however, when hair is deformed in some way, through disease or heredity, or when enough living tissue from the follicle is recovered for *DNA* testing.

'Afraid not, Harry. The lab rat who examined them told me the hairs were unremarkable.'

I left my apartment early on Friday to cruise the streets of Queens and Brooklyn, accompanied by a wispy fog that slowly evolved into a dense summer haze. The temperature was on the rise, the humidity, too, and my Nissan's air conditioning was running full out before the morning was done. I was working with the list of phone numbers secured by Hansen, visiting businesses closed on the prior night, from a pizza parlor in Greenpoint to a plumbing supply house in Flushing. I wasn't expecting much and I wasn't surprised when my canvas ground to a halt at two o'clock in the afternoon, the list now exhausted. But I did learn something. Though I never ran into him, a giant cop, who could only have been Hansen Linde, had already visited a number of these businesses before I got there.

Par for the course. I didn't hold it against Bill Sarney, much less Hansen Linde. They had their interests to protect. As for myself, I'd made no mention, to either, of my encounter with Father Manicki or my deal with

Sister Kassia. And I hadn't told either that I expected the priest, following a thorough examination of his conscience, to find a reason to cooperate, or that my deal with the nun would effectively put five material witnesses beyond Sarney's reach.

Mynka belonged to me. Hansen Linde could not speak for her, even should he wish to do so. Nor could Bill Sarney.

When my cell phone rang, I was down to the last bites of an astonishingly greasy cheeseburger, sitting in a diner on Conduit Boulevard. I was hoping it was Father Stan, calling to say that he'd come back early and his conscience had won the day. Instead, I got Dominick Capra, who turned out to have a conscience of his own.

'If you're tapin' this, ya fuck,' he began, 'I swear to God I'll kill ya.'

'Dominick? That you?'

'Don't say my name.'

'Sorry.'

Though Capra couldn't see it, I was grinning from ear to ear. One day, I decided, I'd express my gratitude with a case of microbrewed bourbon.

'A coupla things about your boy, Harry. First, he has refugee status in the United States. That's supposed to mean that he faces persecution if he returns to Russia. Only the Russian government put him on their immigration quota, which doesn't make a lotta sense if they were persecuting him. Not unless we're talkin' about a very special accommodation for a Chechen who did the Russians some very special favors. Anyway, there's two places you might look for him: the home address he supplied on his application two years ago, and the business address of his sponsor, Nicolai Urnov.'

Capra dictated the addresses, both in Brooklyn. I didn't recognize the first one, but the second, the address of Formatech Money Services, was on the list compiled by Hansen Linde. I'd been to Formatech less than an hour before, only to find it closed, its shutters drawn.

'Promise me something, Harry,' Capra finally said. 'Promise that you won't call me again and that my name will never come up. Swear it.'

Actually, that was two somethings. But I not only promised, I remembered to say thank you.

Five hours later, at seven o'clock, I dialed Bill Sarney's home number from the back of my Nissan. I was scrunched down in the seat with my head pressed against the post separating the side and rear windows. Given Aslan's natural paranoia – fueled, no doubt, by recent events – I might have chosen a better spot for a stakeout. But I hadn't really expected him to show. In fact, I didn't spot him when he came driving down Coney Island Avenue, when he parked his car, or when he got out. I didn't spot him until he opened Formatech's door and walked inside.

'I'm sitting on Aslan Khalid,' I told Sarney,

'and I need something from you before I move on him.'

'Where's Hansen?'

'Probably at the Nine-Two, waiting for me to show up.'

After Capra's call, I'd first checked the residential address supplied by Capra, only to find a hole in the ground and a band of construction workers digging away. I had better luck at Formatech Money Services. The shutter covering the door was rolled up and somebody was inside. My first instinct was to jump out of the proverbial frying pan, to confront Aslan's sponsor, Nicolai Urnov, assuming he was in there. Instead, I decided to sit on the building. If Urnov was inside – or, even better, Aslan Khalid – he'd eventually come out. I knew, of course, that this was my last chance. I didn't want to make the same mistake I'd made with Barsakov.

'I want you to call Hansen immediately.' Sarney's tone reeked of command authority, but I wasn't intimidated. I knew the bastard.

'There's no point and no time, boss. Hansen can't authorize what I need.'

Another silence as Sarney resisted the urge to bite. Finally, he said, 'Okay, prick, let's hear it.'

'I have enough on Aslan to bring him in for questioning, but not enough to charge him.'

'For Barsakov's murder?'

'That's right, and what I want to do is take Aslan out of circulation until noon on Monday. I want him to disappear.'

Technically, any detention is an arrest. Technically, all arrested individuals must be arraigned within twenty-four hours. But these impediments to a long, hard interrogation are easily overcome. All the diligent detective need do is swear that the suspect voluntarily submitted to forty-eight hours of confinement in a small, enclosed place. Since interrogations are not routinely taped, it's the cop's word against the defendant's, and judges almost always rule for the cop. In a law-and-order age, they really have no choice.

'Why?' Sarney asked. 'What's so important about Monday?'

I gave him a quick explanation. Domestic Solutions' workers, their value as witnesses, their current employment. If Aslan was not around to conduct business over the weekend, perhaps they'd be returned to their jobs on Monday, or simply left in place. Or perhaps they'd be shipped to an oilrig anchored off the coast of Nigeria. I was doing the best I could.

Sarney didn't interrupt until I finished. I suspect that the little gears were already turning. There was an intricate cost-benefit analysis to be worked out here. His interests, the job's interests, maybe even Harry Corbin's interests. There were times when Bill Sarney played his brain the way a safe-cracker plays the dial of a locked safe.

'Why not just drag Aslan into the Nine-Two?' he finally asked.

'No good, boss. That's the first place a

208

lawyer would come looking for him. Plus, there's Drew Millard. I need something private and I'm hoping you'll supply it. But, look, this can work out for both of us.' I was talking faster now, but my eyes never left Formatech's door. If Aslan came out, all bets were off. 'Your concern is with Aslan. Mine is with the man who killed my Jane Doe.'

'They're not one and the same?'

'I'm certain that my vic was killed at her job. That lets Aslan off the hook. But what I'm thinking is that if I build a decent case against Aslan for Barsakov's murder, you can talk him into accepting deportation. That way, I get my killer and Aslan's not around to embarrass your bosses. In fact, if I get lucky tonight, he'll take a punch at me sometime over the weekend and you'll have him for assaulting a police officer.'

Sarney chuckled at that. 'Just remember,' he told me, 'if you wanna put that one over, it'd be good if you let him hurt you enough for it to show.'

I sat in my car, alone with my thoughts for the next half an hour until Hansen Linde arrived. I expected him to be pissed off. I'd gone over his head directly to his boss. But Hansen was as jovial as ever, flashing me one of his radiant, corn-belt smiles as he closed the door.

'Hey, Harry, I got to hand it to ya. I never thought we'd find Aslan, even working together, but you went and did it all by yourself.'

I waved him off. 'I'm going inside now, Hansen. You coming along?'

'Yeah, sure, but if it's not too much trouble, would you mind telling me exactly what you hope to accomplish. Just so we're on the same track.'

'Do you remember those pictures that surfaced six or seven years ago, of American soldiers humiliating prisoners in Iraq?'

'Don't tell me you're gonna strip him down and sic a dog on his balls.'

My reply wiped the smile off Linde's face. 'It's a culture thing,' I told him. 'The Chechens have been resisting the Russians for two hundred years. No matter what the Russians do to them, they keep on fighting. Fighting Russians is how boys become men. The widow of a man who died fighting is honored for the rest of her life. All of their national heroes are warriors who fought the Russians. For Chechens, surrender is the ultimate sin.'

I pushed the door open and dropped my right foot onto the running board. 'You still want to come along, Hansen?'

Linde stared at me for a moment, his face solemn, his gaze speculative. Then he grinned and nodded up and down several times.

'You betcha,' he said as he reached for the keys.

TWENTY-TWO

The home of Formatech Money Services was long and narrow, a single open space broken only by a small bathroom at the rear. There was a gray ping-pong table in the center of the room, chest-high workbenches along three walls, and a desk and a velour-covered couch along the fourth. Whorehouse red, the couch was the only spot of color in the room.

Aslan Khalid was sitting at the desk when I made my appearance, followed closely by Hansen Linde. Though Aslan's mouth expanded slightly, he did not rise to greet us. On the other side of the room, two men stood next to the workbench. The older, a Latino, was stripped to the waist. He held a screwdriver in his left hand and his narrow face was streaked with sweat. The younger man was in his early thirties. He wore a white polo shirt over a pair of decently-tailored linen slacks and lattice-work sandals without socks. Silky fine, his carefully-styled hair reached his shoulders, while his beard and moustache were immaculately groomed.

'What's your name?' Linde asked the younger man.

'Nicolai Urnov.' He took a deep breath,

211

then walked to within a few feet of Linde. 'I own this business. Who are you?'

'Oh, yeah,' Linde said, 'I almost forgot.' He reached into his jacket, withdrew the billfold containing his gold shield, then flicked it open for an instant before slapping it closed. 'Now, what about this other guy? The guy standing behind you. What's his name?'

'What do you want with him? He just works here.'

'I want his name.'

The older man turned to face Linde. 'Miguel Sierra,' he said. 'I am not do nothing.'

'Just work here, right?'

'Si.'

'Well, I'm giving you the night off, Miguel. Come back tomorrow.' Sierra didn't have to be asked twice. He was still buttoning his shirt when Hansen closed and locked the door behind him.

Thus far, I hadn't said a word, nor had I turned my full attention to Aslan, though I could feel his gaze boring into the side of my head. Linde had placed himself at center stage and I was content to watch his performance. The fever that had driven me had now vanished. There would be time enough.

'I'm going to call my attorney.' Nicolai's gaze became more intense and I got the distinct impression that he wasn't accustomed to being ordered around. Still, he was a small man, not more than five-nine, and slightly built, a sullen monkey to Linde's menacing gorilla.

'Okay, great, but first I'm gonna have to search you. I mean, a guy could get himself in a whole lotta trouble by not checking a suspect for weapons.'

'Suspected of what crime? I'm a legitimate businessman.'

Linde walked over to the workbench and pointed to a row of *ATM* machines. 'Tell me about these, if it's not too much trouble.'

'I'm a legitimate businessman,' Urnov repeated. 'I place *ATM* machines in stores and split the service charge with the owner. I have a license from the Department of Consumer Affairs.'

Linde held up a slim plastic panel. 'And what's this?' When Urnov didn't answer, Linde said, 'It's a card reader, Nick. You add it to the slot on the *ATM*, it reads and stores the data on every card dipped into it.'

'I want my lawyer,' Urnov half shouted. 'You don't have a warrant. You have no right to be here.'

'And what about these?' Linde scooped up a handful of credit cards and carried them over to Urnov. Though each had a series of raised numbers on its face, the cards were white, the name of the bank conspicuously absent. 'What do you plan to do with these?'

'I'm not saying another word. I know my rights. I was born here.'

'That makes you one up on me. I was born in Minnesota.' Linde allowed the cards to fall through his fingers. 'Now I want you to put

213

your hands on the edge of that bench while I search you, Nick, and I really think it'd be a whole lot better if you did it now.'

Urnov's mouth worked silently for a moment, then his eyes flicked to Aslan Khalid, his gaze accusing. Aslan first frowned, then gave the tiniest of shrugs. Our presence was his fault, no doubt, but there was nothing he could do. Finally, he looked up at me.

'First preliminaries,' he said, 'then comes main event.'

'Alright.' Linde rubbed his hands together, then dropped them to Urnov's shoulders. His fingers clamped down hard, then opened, then closed again as they moved along Urnov's arms, inch by inch. 'Now, stop me if you heard this one,' he said. 'What's the difference between lutefisk and snot?'

'Jesus Christ,' Urnov protested, the words issuing between grunts of pain.

'Nope, wrong answer. What's the difference between lutefisk and snot?'

Linde continued to ask the question and his hands continued to clamp down as they moved from Urnov's arms, to his ribs, to his waist, to the outside of his thighs. It was only when Linde reached Urnov's ankles and started to come up the inside of the man's legs, toward his crotch, that he truly caught Urnov's attention. Was the psycho detective with the vice-grip hands running a bluff? Did he have a stopping point? There was simply no way for Nicky to be sure. Meanwhile, the family jewels were on the line.

'What the fuck is loochapiss?' Urnov finally cried.

'Loo-te-fisk. What's the difference between lutefisk and snot?'

'I don't know, okay. I don't know the difference between lutefisk and snot.'

'The difference between lutefisk and snot,' Linde declared as he finally led Urnov to the couch and sat him down, 'is that kids won't eat lutefisk.'

Urnov's tongue ran across the bottom of his mustache. 'Is that supposed to be funny?' he asked. The question was posed an instant too late. Linde was already beside himself with laughter.

'Oh, yeah,' he declared when he finally caught his breath, 'that was a hot one.'

I gave Hansen a moment to recover by carrying a three-legged stool from the workbench to the front of Aslan's desk. 'What happened to the flag?' I asked.

'Flag?'

'Yeah, the one that hung over your desk at Domestic Solutions.'

'I have never heard of this company.'

'How'd you know it was a company? Why not a rock band?'

'If this stupidness is all you are having to speak, you should be going on your ways. I have living to make.'

'At what?'

'At whatever I am choose to be doing in free country.'

'Fine, let me see your green card again.'

215

The request caught him off guard. Should he refuse? Comply? I watched the wheels turn for a moment, until he reached into his back pocket, withdrew his wallet, then extracted the document. I took it from his hand and passed it over to Linde.

'This is not faking,' Aslan said. 'I am genuine immigrant with right to work in United States of America.'

'I already know that, Aslan. I've spoken to the Immigration and Naturalization Service about your case.' I smiled at him, a smile, or so I hoped, of utmost confidence. 'See, what I remembered, from the last time, is that your country of origin is Russia. Meanwhile, you told me you were a Chechen. That's what I'm trying to make sense of. Why doesn't it say Chechnya?'

I looked into Aslan's eyes, my gaze studiously mild. Though Aslan's features had remained almost immobile, his eyes blazed with hate. I folded my arms across my chest, maintaining eye contact as I waited for him to respond.

'Chechnya is province of Russia,' he finally said. 'Chechnya is not yet country.'

'But it should be, right? Considering how long the Chechen people have been fighting for their independence?'

'One day.'

I turned on the stool to face Nicolai Urnov. 'How about you, Nicky? Are you a Chechen?'

'I'm an American,' Urnov said. 'I was born here.'

'What about your parents? Where did they come from?'

'From Russia.'

I shook my head in disbelief. 'See, this is what's so confusing. There's Konstantine Barsakov and Nicky Urnov, both Russian, and there's Aslan Khalid, the lion of Chechnya.' I snapped my fingers as I turned back to Aslan. 'Oh, I get it. Killing Barsakov was Aslan's way of fighting for the Chechen cause. A little victory for the homeland. One less Russkie to worry about.'

'What is point of this?' Aslan demanded.

'The point of this, Aslan Khalid, is that your buddy has asked for a lawyer twice, but you haven't even asked once. Evidence of a guilty mind, Aslan. That's what they call it in a court of law.'

'If I say to go, you will go? If I say I want lawyer, you will hand me telephone? This I don't think so.'

I got up, walked over to the ping-pong table, picked up a ball and bounced it. 'When was the last time you saw Konstantine Barsakov?' I asked.

'When you place him under arrest for crime of marijuana.'

'Not after he was released?'

'Released? What is this? How am I knowing you have not killed him in your jail?'

'Are you telling me that you didn't see him after he returned to the warehouse on Eagle Street?'

'I am telling you to stick tin badge up ass.'

217

I continued to bounce the ball. 'Relax, I only have a few more questions. I'll be gone before you know it.' When he responded with a grunt and a sneer, I asked, 'Where do you work these days? Now that you no longer work on Eagle Street?'

'I have never work on Eagle Street.'

'Fine, so where do you work?'

'You are big-shot detective. Find out for own self.'

This was one question I would have liked answered, but that wasn't going to happen, not on this pass, and I decided not to push him. Domestic Solutions' workers were at their jobs when I arrested Barsakov. Aslan couldn't be certain that I knew about them. Better to let sleeping dogs lie.

'Okay, so you don't want to tell me where you work. Let's try something else. You told me the last time you saw Konstantine alive was when I arrested him. Now I want to know when you saw him for the first time. Were you still living in your home country?'

Aslan straightened in his chair, his senses on full alert. 'What do you know about this?'

'I know that Aslan Khalid is not your real name. I know that you took your name from Aslan Maskhadov, a hero of the struggle against the Russians. I know that Aslan means lion in Farsi and Turkish. I know that in your dreams, you imagine that you, yourself, have the heart of a lion.' I walked back to the stool, sat down and leaned over the desk. 'Tell me how you came to the United States,

Aslan. Tell me the truth and I'll walk right through that door. I promise, Aslan. I'll walk out of here.'

'How has this to do with Barsakov?'

'I thought maybe he helped put you on top of the quota list.'

'You are fool, Mr Cop. In Chechnya, only you have self to help self. This is lesson of Grozny.'

'Okay,' I said, raising my hands defensively, 'Barsakov didn't help you. But you have to admit, it's a long way from the mountains of Chechnya to the canyons of New York. All I'm asking you to do is describe the journey.'

The tension dropped away from Aslan's expression, his brow softening as his jaw relaxed. He glanced down at his knees, then raised his eyes to meet mine. The body language could not have been more obvious. I was going to hear a tale Aslan had told many times before.

'In Moscow, for right money, can buy whole country. What is exit visa? What is putting name on list? These are nothing.'

'And here?'

'Here?'

'You just said you bribed your way out of Russia. I'm now asking if you bribed your way into the United States?' I looked over at Nicky Urnov to find his dark eyes fixed on Aslan.

'Why do you ask this question?' Aslan said. 'You are miserable New York cop. Immigration is not for you to be concerning yourself.'

'Aslan, please, let's not change the subject. You couldn't have gotten that green card without being scrutinized by the CIA, the *FBI*, and a dozen national security agencies.' I spread my arms wide. 'I mean, you come from Chechnya, for God's sake, a country that's on every terrorist watch list in the entire world.'

Aslan might have taken that moment to claim that he had, indeed, bribed American immigration officials, or that he'd come to the United States before 9/11, when legal immigrants, even from Chechnya, received far less scrutiny. But Aslan was having too much trouble controlling his emotions. He wanted to come off that chair, to vault the desk, to explode in my face.

'Like I already said,' I continued, moving a little closer, 'I spoke to a case officer at immigration about your status. According to her, you got out of Russia and into the United States by...' I glanced at Urnov. 'What do you think, Nicky? What am I gonna say next? I'll give you a hint. The animal I'm thinking of has four legs, a long ugly tail, and a skinny face with sharp little teeth.'

Without waiting for an answer, I swung back to face Aslan. 'Not only did you rat on your own people, you took the name of a true warrior to cover up the truth. Tell your partner, just so he understands, how many died because of you. How many freedom fighters were blown to pieces because the Russians knew where they were hiding? How many villages were burned because you told the Russians that the villagers harbored rebels? How many bodies were dumped in mass graves so you could pursue your American dream?'

By the time I finished, Aslan's eyes were ricocheting from side to side. I'd seen that effect on many a common criminal. The adrenalin pouring into Aslan's bloodstream was demanding that he do something to relieve the tension, but his mind was rejecting every possibility. One of those possibilities became clear to me when he balled up his fists.

'You pissed off, Aslan? You wanna do something about it?' I approached to within a step of where he sat. 'Why don't you do it? C'mon, take a chance. You're the lion of Chechnya, right? You're a true son of the wolf people. Ask yourself, what would Kazi Mullah do? Jokhar Dudayev? Imam Shamil? Shamil Basayev? Would they allow an ordinary cop to label them cowards and rats? Or would they fight to maintain their honor?'

As I reeled off the names of these Chechen heroes, Aslan rewarded me with long slow moan. I'd stripped him of even the pretense of dignity. But he didn't fight me, not when I took him by the shoulder and pulled him to his feet, not when I searched him, then cuffed his wrists.

Finally, I turned to Urnov as Hansen led Aslan out the door; the message I wanted to send was simple, though I felt that it needed driving home.

'You figured this out yet, Nicky? You gettin' this? Well, just in case, let me spell it out for you. If you do business with Aslan Khalid, if you help him in any way, I'm gonna make you a personal project.' I took one of the card readers from the shelf, dropped it to the floor and crushed it with my heel. Then I slapped him in the face, just so there'd be no misunderstanding.

TWENTY-THREE

We took Aslan to the headquarters of a Street Crimes Unit stationed in Far Rockaway. Hansen drove, while I sat next to Aslan in the second of the Ford Expedition's three rows of seats. Aslan's hands were cuffed behind his back and he had to lean forward throughout the forty-five minute drive. He didn't complain, though, nor did he break the silence Hansen and I studiously maintained. Not even when he realized – as he must have at some point – that we weren't headed back to Greenpoint, that we were driving in the opposite direction.

The SCU outpost we finally entered reminded me of Formatech Money Services. A large room with a few desks, lockers and filing cabinets scattered about, a bathroom large enough for a shower, a computer workstation in a corner, a refrigerator and a microwave on a battered table. Except for the wire cage at the far end of the room, it might have been any small business. I checked that cage very carefully, sides, top and bottom, and found it reasonably secure. Nevertheless, I took a further precaution, cuffing Aslan's right wrist to a steel cot, the cell's only furniture. The cot was bolted to the floor.

As I backed out of the cage and locked it, Aslan raised his eyes to me. The hate was still there, but the fire was gone. His gaze was implacable now. He would await a better time.

I broke it off when I heard the door at the far end of the loft open. Our unannounced guest was Sergeant Theobold Anderson, and he came bearing gifts. Our food supply, first, in a pair of plastic bags. Cold cuts, corn chips, a loaf of rye bread, a jar of mustard, a jug of water. Anderson shoved all of it, including the chips, into the refrigerator, then unpacked a billy club, a canister of pepper spray and a stun gun. There was no toilet in Aslan's cage and we were going to have to let him out from time to time. Sergeant Anderson was prepared.

'The sergeant's gonna stay here,' Hansen said when he introduced us, 'to guarantee that somebody's awake at all times.'

And to witness any conversation I might have with Aslan. But that didn't need saying and I gave Theobold's small hand a hearty shake. Tall and heavily built, Anderson might

have plugged a hole in the front line of a professional football team. His face was almost
perfectly round and he had more hair on his
chin than his head.

Theobold didn't smile when he took my
hand. Later on, when I asked him where he'd
worked, he told me that he wasn't a police
officer. He was a Corrections Officer and his
beat was the Isolation Unit on Rikers Island,
home to the most violent prisoners in the
system.

I took Hansen off to the side while Anderson wrestled a folding cot out of a closet. He
accepted the deal I offered without hesitation. I would babysit Aslan until midnight on
Saturday. He would relieve me, then continue
on until Monday at noon when Aslan was to
be cut loose.

That done, I walked Hansen to his car. He
was in an expansive mood and I remember
his cop-to-cop smile as genuine. 'Helluva job
you did on Aslan,' he declared. 'Where'd you
get that good stuff on Chechnya?'

'Forget Chechnya. All I did was memorize a
few names. Plus, it didn't work. Aslan kept his
cool.'

'Maybe so, but he definitely paid a price.'

I accepted the compliment with a nod, then
said, 'Tell me about lootafrish.'

'Lootafrish?'

'The joke about lootafrish and snot.'

'That's lutefisk, Harry. L-U-T-E-F-I-S-K.'

'Fine, tell me about lutefisk.'

Hansen unlocked the door of his Ford, then

turned back to face me. 'Lutefisk,' he explained, 'is dried codfish reconstituted with lye, then boiled or baked until it has the consistency of Jello.'

'Lye? What does lye taste like?'

'I couldn't tell ya, Harry. Lutefisk is a Norwegian dish and my background is Swedish. All I know is that the stuff has a very strong odor and there's as many lutefisk jokes as Ole and Lena jokes. You wanna hear another one?'

Ever the party pooper, I declined.

At eleven o'clock, Theobold produced a tiny portable radio and tuned it to the Yankee game. The Yanks, playing out in Oakland, were at the tail end of a disastrous road trip. Going in, they'd been a game ahead of the hated Red Sox. Now they were two games behind.

I resisted the urge to strike up a conversation, though we were both Yankee fans and at least had something to talk about. Aslan had been confined for several hours and he had to be asking himself three basic questions: what; why; for how long? Thus far, he hadn't even been accused of a crime, much less interrogated. On top of that, the attitude I projected was utter indifference.

At two thirty, the game over, I balled up a dirty blanket to make a pillow, then stretched out on the cot. This was familiar ground. There are cots in every precinct, kept for just this purpose.

I woke up at eight. Not because I wanted to,

but because Aslan, impelled by a pressing need to void his bladder, was rattling his cage.

'You awake?' Theobold asked.

'Afraid so.'

''Cause my orders are the prisoner don't leave his cell unless escorted by two officers.'

'I can see the wisdom in that.'

I got up and headed for the bathroom, leaving Aslan to curse at my back. I didn't mind. I was certain, now, that we'd eventually have a conversation. I used the toilet, washed my face, neck and chest, brushed my teeth with the least ratty of the six toothbrushes I found in a can on the sink. When I came out, I headed for Aslan's cage.

'Uh, detective,' Theobold said, 'I don't mean to tell you your business, but you might wanna put that weapon away somewhere. Prisoners and guns, they don't mix too good.'

Anderson was holding the billy club in his right hand. Leather pouches containing the pepper spray and the Taser hung from his belt. Even in chinos and a polo shirt, he was a supremely menacing figure. I wondered, briefly, as I stashed my Glock in a filing cabinet, how Sarney was connected to Anderson, what favor he'd called in to secure Anderson's services, and how he'd found this very private outpost a few blocks from the Atlantic Ocean.

Only one explanation came to mind. I was witnessing – I was meant to witness – a display of power. Bill Sarney spoke with the authority of the First Dep. The First Dep spoke with the authority of the Commissioner. The Commissioner was obeyed.

I smiled to myself. There was no mystery to Anderson's presence or to this little prison we occupied. Both were readily available because the First Dep had used them before.

When Aslan came out of the bathroom, Theobold was standing with his feet well apart, the left slightly forward. He was holding the nightstick at shoulder height, with the barrel facing backward at a forty-five degree angle.

'Turn around and put your hands on the wall,' he said.

Aslan stopped in his tracks. He looked at Anderson for a moment, wary now. In his Chechen world, the police had almost unlimited power to deal with problems. Commonly, they were problems themselves, there being no clear line between cop and criminal to cross. More like a barely defined no-man's land where bands of predators competed for scarce resources.

'I ain't gonna tell ya but one more time, boy. Turn your ass around and put your hands on the wall.'

Still in control, Aslan slowly complied.

'Now move your legs back and apart.'

Again, slowly, Aslan did as he was told.

Anderson tossed the nightstick to me, then searched Aslan. Good thing, because he found a throwaway razor in Aslan's sock.

The strip search that followed was too gruesome to watch. Open your mouth, raise your arms, lift your penis, lift your testicles, bend over, pull your cheeks apart. At some point, the ritual exceeded Aslan's tolerance for humiliation and he groaned with frustration.

'What, you are getting big hard-on for once in life?'

Though I assume Aslan was speaking to Theobold, he was looking back at Harry Corbin. I ignored him, as did Theobold, who proceeded to search each of Aslan's garments, including a pair of boxer shorts bearing a likeness of Pamela Anderson on each buttock.

'Get dressed.'

Theobold backed away, then reached for the nightstick. I gave it to him and he resumed the stance he'd taken before Aslan emerged. 'Now ah'm gonna tell ya somethin'', and I want you to listen hard,' he said. 'You try to get over on me this one time? I don't take it personal. I figure that's jus' the way it goes. You don't know me. I might be a chump. But that's one time. You hear what I'm sayin'? Cause if you do it again, I'm gonna beat your white ass all over the room.'

A few minutes later, when Theobold settled in for a nap, I made breakfast for Aslan and myself. Sandwiches, ham and cheese, and mugs of instant coffee lightened with some kind of non-dairy creamer and heated in the microwave. The coffee was terrible but I drank every drop.

As for Aslan, he didn't complain. He drank, he ate, he laid back on his cot. Then he suddenly popped up.

'I wish to make phone call.'

I ignored him for a moment, but not because I wanted to prolong the agony. I needed time to suppress a rush of satisfaction. Aslan's pressure cooker had finally sprung a leak. It was nine o'clock on Saturday morning, a few hours before his workers were due to be picked up at their jobs.

'Look, Aslan, the way it's workin' out, you're here until we decide to cut you loose.' Far from confrontational, my tone was sympathetic. 'I think you already know that.'

I settled into a straight-backed chair and picked up a two-day-old copy of the *Daily News*. Aslan held his peace for a good two or three minutes, enough time for me to blow through a story about an accused rapist who'd escaped from a midtown precinct and was still at large.

'You are knowing nothing,' Aslan finally said. 'You are soft American fools. When time comes, Aslan will show you how to die.'

'Show Detective Corbin? Or show the soft American fools?'

Aslan settled back on the seat and closed his eyes. 'In beginning it made sense. Chechens hold Grozny. Chechens hold countryside. But we are now nothing. The Russians attack us village by village, burn crops, kill animals. Childrens, womans, old mens, freezing, starving. Even blind man can see end has come. But there is no stopping for great leaders. Fight must be to death. And all the time

Arabs say to put bomb in schools. Kill Russian children as our children are dead. Great leaders must listen because Arabs have money, because Arabs supply arms and ammunition. Without Arabs, great leaders would be dead.'

Though I'd put down the newspaper, I remained silent for a moment. Then I said, 'Did you kill, Aslan? In Chechnya? Did you kill other men?'

'So soft.' Aslan's head shook back and forth. 'Americans know nothing. In Chechnya, death is every minute coming. Always around corner, in next room. Each day, hear helicopters far away. Will they pass village? Shoot rockets? Will rocket hit house where I am hiding? Will Russian soldiers follow behind rockets? Will I fight free? Or will now be time when I will die?'

'Listen,' I said when he finally slowed down, 'what happened yesterday, at Formatech ... well, you shouldn't take it personally. I was only trying to provoke you.'

'Why?'

'I wanted you to swing on me so I could arrest you for assaulting a police officer. But you didn't bite.' I spread my hands, as I stole a glance at Sergeant Anderson. Though his eyes were closed, Anderson's breathing was shallow, his chest almost unmoving. He was obviously awake. 'That's life for a cop, right? Sometimes you win, sometimes you lose. Nothing ventured, nothing gained.'

TWENTY-FOUR

I let the silence build, hoping Aslan would speak first. Instead, he laid back on the cot with his cuffed wrist behind his head, then closed his eyes.

'My interest,' I finally said, 'is not in Barsakov. Barsakov was a scumbag. My only interest is in Mynka.'

Aslan's eyes popped open when I said her name. He sat up and grinned at me. 'What is Mynka?'

'Mynka worked for Domestic Solutions.'

'Of this company I know nothing.'

'So, you weren't there when she was butchered? You realize, of course, that we found traces of her blood in that bathroom.' I stood suddenly. 'Say, I'm ready for another cup of coffee. How about you?'

I watched Aslan's eyes look up and away. He knew all about the blood, of course. Now he knew that we'd found it. Not a great spot for him. I unlocked the door of his cage to retrieve his mug. As I leaned in, his hands balled into fists. But he didn't come at me, not when I took his mug, or when I replaced it a few minutes later.

'So, where were you when Mynka was

butchered?' I asked. 'If you weren't at Domestic Solutions.'

Aslan thought it over, then his lips slid apart to form an expression vaguely resembling a smile, a smile that didn't come within a light year of his eyes. 'Yes, now I am remembering very well. At this exact moment, I was on rocket ship to moon.'

I didn't respond and he simply continued on. 'Womans. In America is all womans. This is why you are soft. Let womans tell you way to have your life.'

'It's different in Chechnya?'

'In whole world, womans is nothing. Always on men they live. Father sells girl for bride money. Uses bride money to buy wife for his son. Woman with no man for protect her is better off dead.'

I pretended to consider this deep insight for a moment, then said, 'I had a lieutenant once, name of Martha Golson, a real ball buster. All her detectives were men and she was convinced they were out to get her.' I laughed. 'And ya know what, Aslan? She was right.'

This was a complete lie, but my only goal, at that point, was to keep him talking.

'When lieutenant say jump, you are saying, how high?'

'Hey, the boss is the boss.'

Aslan tried to stand, only realizing, when the cuff on his wrist pulled tight, that standing wasn't an option. 'Never in life,' he told me, 'have I had woman for boss.'

'What about your customers? Some of them

must be women? And from time to time, one of them must have called to chew you out. Remember, the customer is always right.'

Aslan started to speak, then stopped abruptly. 'I am knowing nothing of this.'

'Nothing about Domestic Solutions?'

'Nothing.'

'C'mon, Aslan, don't kid a kidder. I have witnesses who saw you empty the warehouse on Eagle Street. You're the one who packed up the furniture, the filing cabinets and the clothes. You packed them into a van that got torched the next day. But like I said, that's not what I'm here about. Barsakov is somebody else's case. My only interest is in who killed Mynka, and that wasn't you.'

Was I offering a deal? Had I brought him to Far Rockaway for that very purpose? Aslan had sold out his comrades to the hated Russians. Why would he hesitate to sell out one of his customers? But Aslan was smart enough to anticipate the only deal I had to offer, and that was not immunity for Barsakov's murder, the only deal he was prepared to accept. Slowly, he raised his head to stare into my eyes. I stared back at him, at a pair of black holes that might have been looking forward or backward, or at nothing at all.

'If go back to Russia,' he said, 'then I am sent to prison. Russian prison? This is very bad place. Better in soft New York prison. Here they are not putting you to death, even if you are killing a policeman.' He hesitated long to produce a second smile, this one amused. 'Next time we are meeting, I will be ready.'

And that was that. Aslan fell back on his cot and I was unable to rouse him. After a few minutes, I picked up the *Daily News* and began to read. My hope was that Aslan would re-think his position during the fifteen hours we'd remain together. If he didn't, it was on to Father Stan.

Six hours later, with Theobold up and about, I approached Aslan's cell. 'I'm gonna take a little walk, stretch my legs. You wanna use the toilet, now would be the time.'

Aslan didn't so much as blink and I took off, walking down a flight of stairs to emerge on Edgemere Avenue. The air, pushed by an onshore breeze, smelled of the Atlantic, only a block away. Behind me, the Ocean Bay Apartments, 1395 low-income units shoehorned into twenty-four buildings, dominated the landscape. I stared at the development, at the prison-block architecture, featureless, forlorn. In fact, it reminded me of Rensselaer Village, except that apartments in Rensselaer Village rented for five times as much.

I stood outside the door for a few minutes, then found a patch of shade. There really wasn't anywhere to go. Gang dominated, this piece of Far Rockaway was the land of the 99-cent store, of decaying bodegas that survived on sales of loose cigarettes, lottery tickets and five dollar bags of reefer, of liquor stores where several inches of bulletproof plastic separated the owner – and his merchandise –

from the customers. Our own little haven, with its wire cage, was above a laundromat that had a good inch of standing water on its concrete floor.

But I hadn't come outside to savor the atmosphere. I wanted to call Adele and outside was the only private place to do it. Adele knew what I was up to with Aslan, knew that I'd take a shot at him before the day was done, and I was more or less obliged to report. Still, I don't recall the conversation we had in any detail. A good piece of my brain was still upstairs with Aslan, reviewing our conversation, formulating tactics. I was rearranging the cards in my deck, but no matter how hard I shuffled, they were the same cards I'd already played. I told that to Adele, and she didn't argue the point. My primary goal, she reminded me, was to keep Aslan out of circulation for the weekend. Breaking him was always the longest of long shots.

As it turned out, Aslan didn't talk, not even to complain. He ate what we fed him and he used the bathroom when it was offered. But he did not talk. Toward the end, I found myself admiring his discipline. We couldn't hold him forever and he knew it. I glanced at my watch. Hansen Linde would arrive soon. Without doubt, he'd take a shot at Aslan, as I'd done. But the only deal on Hansen's table was deportation, a deal Aslan would never accept.

That left it up to the priest.

I was dog tired by the time I got home at

one o'clock, too tired to eat or shower. Too tired, thankfully, to weigh gain and loss, or to contemplate failure. Nine hours later, when John Coltrane's soprano sax announced an incoming call, I was already half awake. I thought it might be Adele getting ahead of the curve, but it was Sister Kassia.

'Father Stan's coming back early, at two o'clock,' she said. 'He wants to see you.'

Nothing ventured, nothing gained. That's what I'd told Aslan. I felt my heart jump in my chest.

'Can I assume he's not dragging me out to Maspeth just to brush me off again?'

'Harry, Father Stan doesn't have a mean bone in his body.'

I took this as an affirmative response, though I didn't know exactly what she meant.

'Our deal,' the nun continued, 'I assume it remains in effect.'

'Sure, Sister, if the women are still around. But six days is a long time. They might be anywhere by now.'

'And that doesn't bother you?'

'Yeah, it does, but I plan to console myself with Mynka's killer and Aslan Khalid.'

When I entered Blessed Virgin, Father Manicki was in the confessional. A wheelchair sat just outside, flanked by a man and woman, both middle-aged. When I approached, the woman asked, 'Are you here to confess?'

'No, I have to see Father Manicki about something else.'

The man laughed. 'That's my mother in there. Every coupla months she decides she's dyin' and she has to confess before it's too late.'

'Swear to God,' the woman said, 'the woman's eighty-eight years old and she ain't been outta this wheelchair in ten years. What could she possibly be confessing?'

I had no idea and I headed off to a pew at the rear of the church. But I was too restless to sit still. Within minutes, I found myself tracing Blessed Virgin's outer walls. This wasn't the first time I'd been in a Catholic church. Like every other New Yorker, I'd toured St Patrick's cathedral on Fifth Avenue. But you could have put Blessed Virgin in one of St Patrick's chapels, and while the stained glass and the statuary at the cathedral were exquisitely crafted, the art-work at Blessed Virgin was as humble as the church itself. Nevertheless, I found myself drawn to a series of small paintings arranged at intervals on both sides of the church.

The paintings depicted events in the final hours of Jesus' life, and each bore a title in script on a small plaque below the frame: The Judgement; Jesus Carries His Cross; Jesus Falls for the First Time; Veronica Wipes the Face of Jesus; Jesus Falls for the Second Time.

That was as far as I got, a view of Jesus lying with his face in the dirt, his left arm extended and limp, his legs trailing in the dust. Help-less was the word that came to mind. Helpless and hopeless. That he could ever get up seemed a clear impossibility. Behind me, I heard a woman praying. Her voice was no more than a murmur, but I could understand the first few words of the prayer she kept repeating: Hail Mary, full of grace...

Father Manicki came up beside me a moment later. His blue eyes were streaked with red, the lids swollen above and below. The lines at the corners of his mouth seemed deeper. I remembered Sister Kassia describing the vows Father Stan had taken. Opening up went against all his instincts. Yet, here he was.

'Father,' I said, 'do you remember a prize fighter named Joe Frazier?'

The priest nodded once. 'Smokin' Joe Frazier. He fought Muhammad Ali three times. What about him?'

'Well, I saw him interviewed on television once, at a Golden Gloves tournament, and I remember he was asked if he had any advice he'd like to offer younger fighters. "Fire back," was what he told the kids. "No matter how bad you're hurt, get up and fire back." '

'Is this another confession?'

I gestured to the painting. 'If I was God, nobody would crown me with thorns, or whip me, or force me to carry my own cross.'

'Not even if you could offer mankind the hope of redemption by submitting?'

'Not even then.'

'Maybe that's because you're only a man.'

'And maybe it's because I've spent most of

238

my adult life protecting society from the unredeemed.'

Father Manicki led me out of the church and down the sidewalk, retracing the route I'd taken with Sister Kassia a few days before. He walked with his hands behind his back, leaning forward as though into a wind. But there was no wind that day, only a layer of haze and humidity that seemed to grow thicker, step by step.

'You're much more subtle than I gave you credit for,' he said, his eyes fixed on the horizon, his voice hinting of a resentment he wasn't supposed to feel.

'How so?'

'When you suggested that Mynka came to me for counseling, I failed to register the comment. Perhaps because you followed it with a very ugly accusation.'

I smiled. In the Fornes case, Father Towle had evaded the seal of the confessional by claiming that counseling, not absolution, had been the purpose of his encounter with Fornes. My lawyerly argument was that counseling and forgiveness were also separate events in Mynka's encounter with Father Manicki.

Because I'd chosen them carefully, I could still remember my exact words: I'm thinking that she was confused, that she sought counseling from the only counselor available. That would be you, Father.

'I showed you a photo of Mynka,' I said, 'with her belly ripped open, but I never told you why she was gutted.'

'Actually,' the priest was good enough to point out, 'you led me to believe that she was mutilated by a psycho.'

'Well, she wasn't. Aslan sliced her because he wanted to be certain we couldn't use her child to establish paternity through a *DNA* test. His objective was entirely rational.'

'Why are you telling me this?'

'Because the man has to be stopped.'

We trudged on, eventually circling the block. Only when we were within yards of the church did Father Manicki speak again.

'The truth,' he announced, 'is that Mynka did come to me for counseling, exactly as you suggested. I've examined my own conscience and discussed the matter with my superiors. We're all on the same page. Nevertheless...' The priest hesitated, his mouth continuing to work. Then he took a deep breath and smiled. 'Nevertheless, my superiors would prefer that my ... my contribution ... not be made public.'

I laughed out loud. 'If I remember right, I already made that offer.'

There was nowhere to go now. We were standing by the church doors. I watched the priest straighten himself, then jam his hands into his pockets and suck on his lower lip. Finally, he said, 'You were right. Mynka was being pressured to have an abortion, by Aslan and by the family she worked for, and she didn't know what to do. But I did not, as you suggested, tell her that abortion is murder and that she was obligated to resist. I told her that if she ran away, we'd protect her and her unborn child.'

'I know that, Father.'

'Then why...'

'It was just a ploy, a wedge, the kind of thing I do every day.' I motioned for him to continue.

'Well, she came into the confessional in early June. She didn't tell me much. I don't even know the name of the baby's father. But she did tell me that she and the baby's father were in love, and she also mentioned the name of the family, Portola. They live somewhere on the upper west side of Manhattan.'

I felt an onrush of powerful emotions at that moment, just as I had when the priest revealed Mynka's name. Though I was careful to show nothing of what I felt – neither joy, nor triumph, nor even cold-blooded calculation – I doubt that I fooled the priest.

'Anything else?' I asked. 'Anything at all?'

'Only this. There's a large refrigerator somewhere in the Portola home, large enough to step into. Mynka kept referring to it as "the cold room." That was the threat, you see. If she didn't work hard enough, if she wasn't properly subservient, if she refused to abort her child, she would be confined in the cold room. Sometimes the baby's father would intervene, but he wasn't always present. Detective, the way she described it, the cold and the absolute darkness, it must have been hell.'

'Who put her there?'

'I don't know. I didn't ask and she didn't say.'

I recalled John Roach, the *NYPD* profiler, telling me that there was a sadist in the mix. Now I knew where to find him. Or her. Or them.

'At this point,' I said, 'I'm supposed to say something like, I know how difficult this was for you. But...'

'But, in fact, you don't give a damn how hard this might or might not have been.'

'I get paid to produce results, Father, and I've lost track of the lies I've told you.'

The priest laughed at that point. 'Most people, every day they go out to a job they don't want to do, motivated solely by a pay check at the end of the week. But that's not your fate. No, no. You're one of a small number of men and women who've found their true calling.'

'One of the lucky ones?'

'Vocation and talent are not free passes. There are always unforeseen consequences, penalties to be paid, a soul to be healed. For instance, didn't you, at some point, think it might be possible to persuade me with reason?'

'I did.'

'Yet you chose to assault me, with the accusations and the photographs.'

'That's right.'

'Why?'

'Because I felt, on balance, you'd be easier to persuade if I softened you up first.'

TWENTY-FIVE

I was up and out at seven a.m., riding the L
Train cross-town, then the A north to 72nd
Street. Both trains were packed on the first
day of the new week, even at that early hour.
I rocked along, alone with my thoughts despite the crush of bodies and the commingled
odors, fair and foul. I'd spoken to Hansen just
before leaving my apartment. Though I didn't
ask, I simply assumed that at some point he'd
explained the facts of life to Aslan, then
suggested deportation in lieu of prison. If so,
Aslan had refused.

'We don't have enough to hold him,' Linde
told me. 'Come noon, he'll walk out the
door.'

I liked the sound of that.

The A Train came to a stop in the tunnel
between Penn Station and Times Square,
remaining motionless for several long moments. Rush-hour delays are common
enough, and I wasn't particularly concerned,
but I found myself looking down at my
watch, shifting my weight from foot to foot, as
if the Portola household would simply vanish
should I arrive at eight o'clock. In fact, the
household was entirely unsuspecting and it

wouldn't matter if I got there tomorrow. All the question marks concerned their maid; assuming they still had a maid, assuming that Aslan was still supplying that maid, assuming all of Aslan's little maids weren't on route to some distant land.

The train began to move, a sharp jerk, first, then the hiss of the air brakes, then a slow steady roll into the station. Automatically, I gauged the number of passengers about to get off, the number coming on, the many directions from which they would go and come, finally adjusting my position to impede as few as possible. I thought of Adele, then, very briefly. Raised in the New Jersey suburbs, Adele hated the subways. Her objections were perfectly reasonable. The subways did stink, and they were always filthy, and the scream of steel on steel when the trains rounded a curve was, indeed, loud enough to cause hearing damage. Myself, I wasn't bothered. I'd been riding the subways all my life and knew that subways were very private places. No one spoke to you, or even looked at you, and the tendency was to withdraw into yourself, as I did on that morning, my focus gradually narrowing. Adele was gone before I climbed to the surface at 72nd Street.

As it turned out, the Portolas lived in a splendid townhouse across the street from Riverside Park, making them far easier to identify and track than if I'd found them living in one of the many high-rise warrens to

244

the east. And then there was Riverside Park itself, the perfect location for a long-term surveillance. In addition to the pedestrians on its winding paths and the traffic flowing north-south along the West Side Highway, there were groves of trees, dense shrubbery and a huge outcropping of bedrock set far enough away from the townhouse to make it unlikely that I would be spotted.

I settled down on a small ledge about halfway to the top of a jagged boulder, sliding out of my backpack, then fishing inside for the container of coffee, fried-egg sandwich and bottle of water I'd purchased at a deli on Broadway. Finally, I removed a small pair of binoculars, settling the strap around my neck.

The atmosphere around me was gray with haze, even at seven thirty in the morning, the air humid enough to virtually guarantee rainfall later in the day. Still, the park was busy, not with strollers who would come later, but with serious joggers, bikers, skateboarders and power walkers. I watched a young woman pass by. She pushed a three-wheeled stroller with extra long handles and sweat dripped from every pore in her body. A border collie trotted alongside the stroller, its tongue hanging out of its mouth, its breath coming in short pants. The dog's head swung in my direction as it passed, looking not at me, or even at my sandwich, but at the bottle of water at my feet.

I pressed the binoculars to my eyes and made a quick sweep of the Portola townhouse. The four-story building, with its lime-stone facade, attic dormer and mansard roof, was typical of the row houses on Riverside Drive. The front was bowed, from the second through the fourth floors, and the main entrance, a narrow archway leading to an elaborate, wrought-iron storm door, was set almost at street level. At minimum, the house, even if the interior had been trashed, was worth a cool five million. And if it had been decently preserved or lovingly restored, the price might be fifty percent higher. I left the binoculars to dangle at the end of their strap and went to work on my sandwich. The Portola family wealth was not something I could ignore. Should one or more be arrested, their dream team would be top-notch and my every move would be carefully examined by attorneys who could recite the Constitution backwards in Sanskrit. Over the past twenty years, the Supreme Court has given cops a lot of room to maneuver, but the line was still invisible. If I crossed it, I was likely to find myself on the losing side at an evidence suppression hearing.

I finished the sandwich, chased it with the last of the coffee, and deposited the trash in a nearby trash basket. Of course, I had no idea when Domestic Solutions' workers were due at their jobs. According to Giselle and Dimitri, a van carrying five or six women left the warehouse around seven thirty on Monday mornings. When any of them might arrive at a given address was far from certain. Still, as time passed, and eight became nine, then ten, I began to get antsy. I told myself that if nobody showed, it would be the priest's fault, not mine. And if Sister Kassia had a beef, she could take it to Father Stan, maybe hear his confession. Arresting Mynka's killer was my first priority. If the fate of these women was taken out of my hands, so much the better. My conscience was clean.

I was still fortifying my argument when a Ford Explorer double-parked in front of the Portola townhouse shortly before eleven. I raised the binoculars to my eyes. They were self-focusing and took several seconds to compensate for the soft edges generated by the fog. By the time I had a clear image, a woman had already exited the vehicle. I caught a glimpse of her red hair, contained beneath a white hairnet, and of a blue skirt and a white blouse. Then she was gone and the door closed behind her.

I shifted quickly to the Ford's driver and found her sitting with her head turned away from me. But I didn't need to see her face to know that we'd met before. The fire-red hair was a dead giveaway. Welcome to the conspiracy. As the SUV pulled away, I wrote down the license plate number. Then I closed my eyes and said a little prayer. Not to the God who lay in the Jerusalem dust, nearly broken by his own cross, but to the God who rained fire and brimstone on those wicked kingdoms, Sodom and Gomorrah. I could put the red-headed woman in the warehouse when Barsakov was killed. She was the key to pinning the murder on Aslan.

At eleven thirty, I moved a hundred yards closer to the Portola home. By chance, the door to the Portola residence swung out twenty minutes later and three people emerged: a middle-aged woman, a man in his twenties and a teenaged boy.

I slid the backpack over my shoulders and headed for the nearest exit, fifty yards to the north. Again, I got lucky. The trio also headed north, until they reached 86th street where they turned east. By that time, I'd exited the park. Tails are easily maintained in Manhattan. There are always pedestrians about and people generally mind their own business. The Portolas, for example, never looked back, not once. They didn't speak to each other, either, content to maintain a steady pace until they reached the doors of a well-known French restaurant, L'Heures, on the east side of Columbus Avenue. I watched them go inside, then headed for a Turkish restaurant called Ishtan on the other side of the street. Ishtan had an outdoor cafe with a perfect view of L'Heures.

I was just finishing my second cup of espresso when the Portolas emerged, followed closely by a man wearing a cummerbund, a starched white shirt and a thin black tie. Obviously a restaurant employee, he engaged the woman in conversation for several minutes, his manner clearly apologetic.

As I brought the binoculars to my eyes,

taking advantage of the family's preoccupation, I felt my heart turn to stone and my world shrink down to these three people. The women of Domestic Solutions, Bill Sarney, Hansen Linde, Drew Millard, even Adele – banished one and all to some anonymous patch of neurons in the recesses of my brain.

The woman was taller than either of her sons. Too blond to be natural, her hair curled in a tight line almost to her shoulders where it hung stiffly, every strand in place. Her cheekbones were very high, her nose short and straight, and while her mouth was naturally full, she'd thickened her lips with a heavy layer of pink lipstick. The make-up on her cheeks was just a bit too thick as well, though it failed to conceal a narrow line of acne-pitted skin beneath her cheekbones.

The older boy's expression was more be-mused than annoyed. He stood to one side with both hands in the pockets of his off-white linen trousers. Although his features were much softer, his resemblance to the woman was evident in his fleshy mouth and his heart-shaped face. Perhaps in an effort to blur that resemblance, he'd grown a skimpy beard and a mustache, neither of which was thick enough to conceal the pale flesh beneath. As I watched, his hand fluttered up to play with an earring, an enamel rainbow, which hung from his left ear.

The teenager had drawn the shortest straw from the gene pool. All three had weak chins, but his was concealed beneath a lower lip that he thrust forward as though in a permanent state of petulance. Meanwhile, his eyes were small and overhung by a heavy brow that only emphasized his receding jaw. The boy seemed uninterested in the ritual humiliation of the restaurant employee. He'd wandered a few yards away and was staring south at the on-coming traffic, his expression sullen, the tension in his cheeks, mouth and neck obvious at a glance. But I couldn't find even a hint of cruelty in his look and it occurred to me that I was probably staring at the father of Mynka's child. Not only was he closer to Mynka's age than the man in his mid-twenties, he wasn't gay.

'Sir, will there be anything else?'

I yanked the binoculars away from my eyes and put them back in the case. The waitress was a twenty-something brunette with her midriff exposed from her waist to below her navel. She was holding an espresso pot in one hand and my check in the other, her professional smile exposing a set of the whitest teeth I'd ever seen.

'Are you, like, a private eye?' she asked.

I watched the Portolas cross Columbus Avenue, then disappear along 86th Street. I might have followed, but I had a better use for my time.

'Private ass is more like it.' I motioned her to leave the check as I retrieved my cell phone and dialed Bill Sarney's office number.

Shaved and showered, I met Inspector Bill

Sarney at five o'clock in a bar on Lispenard Street. Although the bar had a neon shamrock in the window, it appeared not to have a name. Maybe that was because it had no character. The men at the bar huddled protectively over their drinks, mostly drafts and shots. They didn't turn their heads when I came in, as if somewhere on the downhill side, they'd renounced curiosity itself.

Sarney was standing at the end of the bar, leaning back against the wall, grinning. Message sent, message received. This was one joint his boyos from the Puzzle Palace were very unlikely to enter. I walked the length of the bar, my mood so elevated I found myself admiring Sarney's unabashed theatricality. Playful was as much a part of his charisma as inscrutable. After a quick shake, I ordered a bottle of Bud. The bartender fetched it, popped the cap, then laid it on the bar without offering a glass.

'So, what's up, Harry?'

'I didn't report to the Nine-Two this afternoon,' I told him, 'and I don't expect to report for at least a week. I want you to fix it.'

'And what's my motive?'

'There was someone else in the warehouse when Barsakov was killed, another adult. Do you remember?'

He thought about it for a moment, then said, 'The woman with the red hair.'

Credit where credit is due. Inspector Bill had studied the case file. 'I've seen her again, just this morning. Give me a week and I'll turn her. When she implicates Aslan, as I guarantee she will, you'll have enough ammunition to arrest him if he refuses deportation. After a few days in Rikers, he'll likely change his mind.'

Behind me, I heard raised voices. The bartender was evicting one of his patrons.

'Go on, Vinnie' he said, 'go on home. I don't want your psycho sister comin' in here to drag your ass out. She's got a dirty mouth.'

Vinnie slid away from the bar. 'Don't I know it,' he muttered as he stumbled toward the door. 'Don't I fuckin' know it.'

Sarney was smiling when I turned back to him. 'What are we talking about here?' he asked. 'Harry and Hansen? Or just Harry?'

'Forget Hansen.'

'Why?'

'Because neither you, nor the First Dep, wants to be associated with what I'm gonna do. Because if I'm caught in the wrong place at the wrong time, you won't be able to claim ignorance if Hansen's with me.'

Silence is a tool interrogators use to get under a suspect's skin. Sarney and I both knew this. But rank does have its privileges and some tools are definitely bigger than others. I was first to speak.

'This squad you're running, does it have a name?'

Now Sarney was grinning again. 'Not officially.'

'How about unofficially?'

'Unofficially, we call ourselves the Conditions Squad.'

I nodded in appreciation. At one time, there was a conditions squad in every high-crime precinct. The squad was designed to handle acute, short-term problems, from an open-air drug bazaar, to a ring of chop shops, to a crew on a robbery spree, to a serial rapist. Given wide latitude to conduct investigations, each of these squads maintained its own network of informants and was generally made up of the most talented cops in the precinct.

Conditions squads were already disappearing when I graduated from the Academy, replaced with specialized units subject to central control. But the concept had apparently remained alive at the highest levels. Sarney's squad would respond whenever conditions demanded that the commissioner have an ear to the ground.

Sarney sipped at his drink, bourbon or scotch by the look of it, then smacked his lips in mock appreciation. 'So, what did you think of Theobold and my little hideout in Far Rockaway?'

'I was impressed. As I was supposed to be.'

'Well, you're nothing if not dutiful.' Another little chuckle, followed by a searching look. 'Power and the privileges that come with it, Harry. We can reach into any bureau. We can bend Chiefs to our will. I was wondering if that appealed to you.'

I thought it over for a moment, then said, 'Are you trying to recruit me?'

'With a bump to Detective First Grade. That would make your pay equal to a lieutenant's. With overtime, you'll knock down one hundred grand a year.'

The bartender took that moment to wander over. He looked at our glasses, then at Sarney. Finally, he walked away.

'Why me?' I asked. 'Why recruit a man who's been breaking your balls for years?'

'Because I need a talented interrogator to complete the team and Harry Corbin is the best interrogator I know. You've got a gift, Harry. If you'd only use it to benefit yourself...' Sarney's expression hardened as he shoved his hands into the pocket of his nicely-tailored suit. 'I'm gonna fix it for you. I'm gonna put you out there on your own. But one thing you need to consider: the bosses don't trust you because they think you're a boss-hater at heart. Are you? Do you even know? This is your last chance, Harry. You fuck it up and you'll be lookin' for a new career.'

I started to respond, but Sarney was already headed for the door. A moment later, I followed.

My workday far from over, I went from Bill Sarney to the Sixth Precinct where I approached a sergeant named Callahan. I was determined not to make the same mistake twice. I had until the end of the week, when Aslan returned to collect his workers. By then, I would be well prepared.

I flashed my shield. 'Busy night?' Behind me, the squad room was deserted.

'The worst.' Callahan ran his finger along a mustache thick enough to pass for a broom. 'What could I do for ya?'

'I was hoping to borrow your computer, Sarge. I only live a few blocks away, in Rensselaer Village, and I'm on foot.'

Cops like to grant each other favors, especially when those favors entail no costs. Callahan gestured to a far corner of the squad room. 'Knock yourself out.'

I began at the Department of Motor Vehicles, limiting my initial search to the Portolas' street address on Riverside Drive. Within seconds, I had three hits. Margaret Portola, age 45, who owned a 2003 Jaguar, in addition to holding a New York State driver's license. Ronald Portola, age 24, who owned a 2004 Saab convertible and who also had a driver's license. David Portola, age 17, who possessed a learner's permit.

I printed the information, then checked each of the Portolas for a rap sheet. David came up clean. Not so Margaret and Ronnie. Margaret had been arrested twice, both times for assault. Her first brush with the law, a misdemeanor, was dismissed on the following day. Her second arrest, in 1995 for second-degree assault, was more serious. A charge of second-degree assault requires extensive physical injury. Not a black eye or a split lip, but injuries sufficient to require immediate medical treatment. Nevertheless, though it took nine months, this charge, too, was dismissed. But dismissals seemed to run in the Portola family. Ronald Portola had also been arrested twice, both times at a gay bar called Montana, both times for soliciting a male prostitute, and both times the charges had been tossed out. Now closed, Montana was a bar notorious for rough trade.

I printed Margaret's and Ronald's rap sheets, then turned away from the computer to spread out the Portola family photos as they appeared on their drivers' licenses. At some point, I'd be taking a shot at one of them. But which one? I couldn't answer the question, not then, and I didn't try. Still, it was the essential question. Mynka's death had occurred nearly a month before and no cop had come calling. More than likely, they knew nothing of Barsakov's failures, or of the Russian's subsequent demise. More than likely, they were starting to relax, to believe they'd gotten away with it. My sudden appearance would come as a complete shock, and that was all to my advantage, but I wouldn't get a second bite at the apple. If I blew it, the Portola family would lawyer up and that would be that.

Again, I looked from Margaret to Ronald to David. Margaret was staring straight ahead, eyebrows slightly raised, lips and nostrils compressed. Ronald's eyes were fixed on a point slightly below the camera's lens. His soft smile appeared almost regretful and his lips were very red. His brother's mouth, by contrast, was hanging slightly open. David seemed almost bewildered.

I glanced at the issuing date on David's learner's permit: June 17 of this year. According to Father Stan, David and Mynka were in love and I wondered, as I searched David's features, if he'd still been looking ahead on the day the photo was taken, if his hopes and dreams were of happily ever after. Mynka was pregnant by then. Maybe the threats had already started. Abort, or else.

A moment later, I turned back to the computer where I ran the plate number of the Ford Explorer I'd seen on Riverside Drive. The vehicle was registered to Zashka Ochirov, living at 121 North Third Street in the borough of Brooklyn. Brooklyn is a big place, but I didn't need a map to pin down a more exact location. Barely a mile long, North Third Street begins and ends in Williamsburg, home of the Nine-Two.

I pulled up Ochirov's driver's license next. The woman who looked up at me was blond at the time her photo was taken, but I recognized her easily enough. I'd seen her twice before, at the Domestic Solutions' warehouse when I confronted Barsakov, and just that morning when she double-parked in front of the Portola townhouse. Zashka's rap sheet came last, a long record of non-violent offenses, including larceny, forgery and welfare fraud. This was all to the good. Now I wouldn't have to do a lot of talking when I explained that Aslan was tied to the tracks and there

257

was a train coming down the line. Better for her, much better, if she was on it, because that train wasn't—

'Say, you gonna be long?'

Startled, I jerked around to find two detectives, a man and a woman, standing behind me. Intensely focused, I hadn't heard them approach.

'Long day?' the woman asked.

I glanced at my watch. It was eight o'clock and I hadn't eaten since breakfast. I was going to have to slow down. I logged out of the computer and gathered the printouts.

'Long and fruitful,' I said. 'In fact, I haven't had a better day in the last nine months.'

TWENTY-SIX

I was back in Riverside Park at seven thirty on the following morning, striding through a heavy fog in search of a bench close to the street. The sun was a pale orange disc and the morning air, dead still, clung to my body. My pants and the back of my shirt, when I sat on a dew-slick bench were instantly soaked.

Though it was the beginning of the work week, the park was crowded with committed runners tracking their miles before heading off to the job. I thought of Adele then, as I'd thought about her last night after I settled in front of the *TV*. I felt guilty. I should have called her, at least to bring her up to date, but I hadn't. My reasoning was very simple. Suppose she finally opened up, told me what was bothering her. Suppose the issue required my immediate attention at a time when I had no attention to spare. What would I do? Better not to know.

I remained where I was for the next three hours, until I could no longer distinguish between the mist and my own sweat, watching drops of water form on the ends of the pine needles, then drop to the ground. Behind me, the West Side Highway was running full out, but the traffic produced no more than an inconstant hum that seemed part of the swirling fog. On another day, driven by New York's prevailing westerly winds, the reek of automobile exhaust would cover the narrow strip of park between the highway and Riverside Drive, but the only odors to reach my nostrils on that day were of wet earth and decaying vegetation.

At ten fifteen, Ronald Portola, the elder of the two brothers, came out of the house. He wore an off-white linen blazer over a black polo shirt and white pants that bunched around his shoes and ankles. I watched him from a park bench right across the street. He was sporting that same bemused smile and he had that same dismissive look in his intelligent eyes, as though he were observing the game of life the way a scientist observes a colony of ants. I wondered how I'd appeal to

259

him if the time ever came to make an appeal. Ronald would appreciate a creative approach, a bit of high theater, of that I was sure. As I was now sure that bludgeoning was not Ronald's style and I would have to look elsewhere for Mynka's killer. Ronald was glancing at his watch for the second time when a black Lincoln Towncar from one of Manhattan's many car services pulled up in front of the townhouse. The driver popped out an instant later, ran around the vehicle, opened the back door with a little flourish. Ronald shot his cuffs before climbing inside.

David Portola made his appearance a little after eleven, carrying a skateboard. In marked contrast to his brother, he wore a pair of cutaway denim shorts, the hems ragged, and a t-shirt that had once been white but was now a dingy gray.

I was back in the park by then, a good hundred and fifty yards from the townhouse, but I didn't have to shift my position for a better look, or even raise my binoculars. The youngest Portola walked directly across the street, dropped his skateboard onto the sidewalk and came straight down the path in front of my bench. He looked neither right nor left as he passed, his lower lip curled into a nasty pout, eyes hard-fixed on the path ahead. David's hair was moussed into a little forest of quills and he was skimming the few strollers in the park, his head bent forward as if intending to impale them. Finally, he came within inches of a female jogger who yelled at him to slow down. All she got for her efforts was a raised finger.

I knew from experience that sullen can sometimes become outright defiance, that David's hatred for authority figures might extend to all cops all the time. The challenge, if I chose to approach him, was to re-route his anger, to focus it back on his family, on the people who'd provoked his anger in the first place. The rest would be easy. After all, he'd loved Mynka.

A little after noon, I left my post in search of a bathroom and something to drink. I found a reasonably clean restroom several blocks to the north and a vendor near a deserted playground who sold me a can of soda, two bottles of spring water and a couple of boiled hotdogs. I carried the food back to a convenient bench, opened a bottle of water, then leaned forward to pour the cold water onto my head and neck. I told myself that weather is never an excuse, not for a cop; that standing up to the elements is a matter of honor. I wasn't consoled and the water didn't cool me off all that much either.

I was just about to bite into the first hot dog when the door of the townhouse opened and the Portolas' maid emerged. I recognized her without difficulty. At Blessed Virgin, she'd covered her head with a gold kerchief before going inside.

Without pausing, she turned south on Riverside Drive. I dumped the hot dogs and the soda in a wire trash basket and trotted after her, opening and draining the last bottle of water as I went. The water seemed to come out through my skin as I drank, as if my stomach were somehow directly connected to my sweat glands. But I had little choice except to quickstep down Riverside Drive. The little maid was moving right along, arms swinging, legs churning. Without slowing down, she turned left on 74th Street and continued on, pausing briefly on West End Avenue to let the traffic pass, until she finally entered the very upscale Fairway Market on Broadway.

Inside the market, the air was cold enough to bring goose bumps to my forearms. It was refrigerator cold. I let my eyes sweep past stacks of piled grapefruits that looked as if they'd been spit-shined, past strawberries that might have been sculpted by Fabergé, to the back of the store where I found the maid standing with a small group of customers. At that point, I was supposed to call it quits, having verified exactly what I'd come to verify: the Portola's maid was allowed to leave the home unaccompanied. But I found myself moving closer, despite the looks I drew from the other customers.

The maid was standing in front of a twenty-foot counter devoted entirely to salmon – Nova Scotia salmon, Irish salmon, Maine salmon, Scotch salmon, wild Scotch salmon, wild Columbia River salmon, wild Canadian salmon. She'd taken a number and was impatiently awaiting service, shifting her weight from foot to foot. I walked past her, to a display of cooking oils that included walnut, hazelnut and pumpkin seed.

In her twenties, she was as plain as Mynka, with narrow downcast eyes, a long nose, broad at the tip, and a heavy jaw that would become her defining feature as she grew older. She kept glancing back and forth, from a cheap watch held to her wrist by a pink band, to an *LED* screen displaying the number of the patron currently being served. I couldn't tell how far she was from the front of the line, only that there were half a dozen customers standing before the counter. But I could see that she was afraid and I had to wonder whether Aslan charged a premium for a domestic servant who could be abused, as well as used.

I left a few minutes later, heading back downtown to pick up my car. Then it was off to Maspeth, where I found Father Stan in the rectory. He looked me up and down, his smile rueful. The air conditioner in the little Nissan, never all that efficient, had been unable to overcome the heat of the sun pouring through the windows on my side of the car. My hair was plastered to my head, my clothes to my body.

'Still sinning, I see.'

'I'm nothing if not faithful to my obsessions,' I admitted. 'But I didn't come to confess. I'm looking for Sister Kassia.'

The priest gestured to a narrow hallway. 'First door on the left. Her new office.'

Sister Kassia's new office must have been a broom closet in its prior incarnation. Between the desk, the file cabinets and Sister Kassia, there wasn't room for a second chair and I was forced to stand.

'Please don't lean against the wall with your wet clothes,' the nun began. 'It was just painted.'

'Did you ever teach school, Sister?'

'Third grade, at Sacred Heart in Bayside. Why do you ask?'

'I was just trying to imagine what went through a kid's head when he walked into your classroom for the first time.' I hesitated, but she continued to stare at me. 'I didn't change my clothes before coming over,' I explained, 'because I want you to know what you're up against.' I peeled the front of my shirt away from my chest. 'This is what happens when you spend six hours on a stake-out in Riverside Park.'

'Does that mean you've found them?'

'It means I've found one of them. She's working on the Upper West Side and I intend to approach her tomorrow, assuming she leaves the house. If you want to be there, you'll have to put up with the elements.'

I'd underestimated Sister Kassia. Her bird-bright eyes softened at the news and the smile on her face was positively beatific.

'Tonight,' she announced, 'I'm going to collect.'

'Collect what?'

'Collect on that bet I made with Father

Stan. He was certain that we'd never see you again. I told him you'd be back. I told him that underneath your dissembling exterior, there lay a primitive code of honor. Once you gave your word, you'd keep it.'

'That's nice, Sister, but when you made the bet, did you tell him the other part? Did you tell him that I'd also be returning to Blessed Virgin because I still needed you?'

The nun's smile broadened as she arched an already rounded eyebrow, then winked. 'Nope,' she declared, 'I must have forgotten about that one.'

The phone was ringing when I walked into the house. I picked it up a moment too late and the answering machine came on. I listened to the announcement, then heard Adele's voice.

'Corbin, where have you been? I'm dying to know what's going on.'

I picked up the phone and shut off the machine. 'Adele, I just walked into the house.'

'Busy day?'

'Busy two days. But everything's falling into place.'

I went on to describe the various things and the various places into which they'd fallen. Adele responded with an 'uh-huh' from time to time, but saved her questions until I'd finished. Then she asked for the game plan.

'Tomorrow, Sister Kassia and I will make contact with the maid, assuming she leaves the house.'

'Toward what end?'

'What I'm hoping is that she'll be anxious to improve her circumstances. Say, for instance, by getting as far away from Aslan as possible. If that's the way it goes down, I'll pull the women out on Saturday night and hand them over to Sister Kassia.'

'And if it doesn't?'

'Then I'll take her into custody.'

'Sister Kassia?'

Though I didn't laugh at Adele's joke, I finally paused long enough to take a breath. 'It's gettin' a little crazy,' I admitted.

Adele took pity on me. 'I have to give you credit, Corbin. A week into the case, I didn't think you had a chance. Now you're almost there.'

I got off the phone a few minutes later, then took a long shower, finally pulling on shorts and a t-shirt. The apartment was relatively cool, the sun having passed behind my building while the clouds were still thick enough to shade the windows. I settled down in my office, flicked on the computer, finally sat back while it booted up.

I began with an Internet search using the single word Portola. That got me 264,000 hits, for the town of Portola ('Gateway to the Sierras'), for Portola Packaging, for the Portola Railroad Museum, for the Portola School District, for Gaspar de Portola, a Spanish soldier who'd served as Governor of Los Californias from 1768 until 1770.

A more specific search, for Margaret

Portola, produced no hits at all, and I struck out on Ronald and David as well. But I wasn't discouraged. I jumped to the *New York Times* website and ran a general search for the name Portola through their archives. This time I got a mere eighty-five hits, a manageable number that allowed me to plough through several dozen abstracts before I found the obituary of a man named Guillermo Portola.

The abstract revealed only that Guillermo Portola, born in Portugal, was survived by his wife, Margaret, and his two sons, Ronald and David. For the full text of the article, I had to fork over two dollars ninety-five. But the pay-off more than justified the investment. Guillermo Portola had died in 1998, at age seventy-three, five years after suffering a massive stroke. At the moment of his passing, he'd been lying in his own bed, in his own home, surrounded by his loving family.

The obituary included Guillermo's photograph. A man just approaching middle-age, he stood on the deck of a sleek, three-masted yacht, wearing shorts and sandals and a fisherman's cap with a long brim that shaded his face. An Ernest Hemingway beard added a touch of bulk to his weak chin, while a broad smile revealed a set of horsey white teeth. Cradled against his chest, a brass trophy gleamed in the sunlight.

Aside from his support for the usual charities, yachting was Guillermo's one claim to fame. In 1958, he'd won a race from New

York to San Francisco that traced the route of the old clipper ships around Cape Horn. In 1963, he'd finished third in a competition that traced the route of Magellan across the Pacific. In 1974, his yacht had capsized in a squall thirty miles outside of Bermuda. All aboard were rescued after passing several harrowing hours in a life raft, but the vessel was lost.

Oddly, there was no mention of Guillermo's business activities, leaving me to wonder if he'd inherited his money, if he'd lived the life of an aristocratic playboy. Guillermo had been married four times, the last to his personal assistant, Margaret Applewood of Bar Harbor, Maine, in 1984. He'd been fifty-nine on the day of the wedding, his blushing bride a mere twenty-four. Or maybe she wasn't blushing; maybe she was just as bold as could be. Certainly there'd been no hiding the fact that she was pregnant. According to the date of birth on his driver's license, Ronald Portola was born three months to the day after Guillermo put the ring on his mom's finger.

According to his *Times* obituary, Guillermo Portola had died at home. Dying at home, especially if there's no doctor present, raises all kinds of flags for criminal investigators, and so much the worse if the deceased was too feeble to resist an attack. Of course, Guillermo's obituary hadn't mentioned an investigation, but that possibility had reared its tantalizing head when the obituary also failed to mention the name of a funeral home, a memorial service, or the date of the funeral. Maybe the Portola family had instructed a crematorium to drop the old man's ashes into the nearest dumpster, maybe they just wanted to be rid of him. And maybe his burial had been awaiting the outcome of an autopsy.

The *New York Times* prides itself on avoiding sleaze. If the *ME* had termed the death a homicide, the paper would have reported the facts, but the rumor mill was beneath its collective dignity. Not so the *New York Post*, a Murdoch-owned tabloid whose most complex stories begin and end on the same page. The *Post* runs on sleaze the way locomotives run on diesel fuel.

The *New York Post* did not disappoint. The paper's first story, datelined May 17, 1998, six weeks after Guillermo's passage, ran beneath the headline: *'UNDETERMINED!'*

What was undetermined was the cause of Guillermo's death, which the *ME* had failed to pinpoint after an autopsy that included a tox screen. But there was no mention of the *ME*'s findings in a far more pertinent area, manner of death, which includes natural, homicide, suicide and accidental among its classifications. I knew from experience that individuals die for reasons that cannot be divined by even the most thorough autopsy, and that pathologists commonly rule the manner of death undetermined and the cause of death natural.

Nevertheless, my persistence did not go

unrewarded. The story concluded with a description of Guillermo's will, written a full year after his stroke. The estate was to be divided between his wife and two children, with Margaret receiving fifteen percent of the estimated forty million dollars in assets. The kiddies would split the rest, but not until they reached the age of forty. Until that time, the estate's executor, Margaret Portola, would run their lives.

TWENTY-SEVEN

I spent Wednesday in Riverside Park with Sister Kassia, from a bit before nine until a bit after four. Far from the sweat-room I'd described the day before, the weather was delightful, the temperature in the mid-seventies, the breeze steady enough to lure a minifleet of sailboats onto the Hudson River.

Sister Kassia turned out to be a good companion. She didn't complain as the hours dragged by, or when I treated her to a lunch of hot dogs and sodas. Instead, she questioned me closely about life on the job, her curiosity genuine.

I limited my responses to a few amusing anecdotes, including a story about a stoned burglar who'd been apprehended six blocks from the scene of the crime because he'd sat on a peanut butter sandwich, and another about an alcoholic cop fighter named Elvira Menendez. A legend in the Three-Four, Elvira had once been a professional wrestler in the Dominican Republic.

I told Sister Kassia my partner's joke, too, the one about Ole asking God why he made Lena so dumb. She laughed even louder than Hansen.

When I turned the tables after lunch and a trip to the restroom, Sister Kassia was straightforward, even admitting that she had doubts about the whole business of illegal immigration. She didn't believe that the United States could throw open its doors to anyone with a plane ticket, and she realized that illegal workers took jobs that would otherwise go to the poorest Americans. Worse still, from her point of view, she fully understood the extent to which she was acting as a shill for American corporations in search of cheap labor. But illegal immigrants, she insisted, were also human beings, human beings exploited on all sides, human beings in desperate need of aid. Helping them was an obligation imposed on her by the God she loved.

We finally caught a break at three thirty when the townhouse door opened and the Portolas' maid emerged. Again she headed south, this time only to 80th Street where she turned east, toward Central Park. Sister Kassia and I set off in pursuit, but the small woman moved too quickly and we were still a hundred yards behind when she disappeared into a drug store on Broadway.

'What do we do now?' Sister Kassia asked.

'Wait for her to come out.'

A few minutes later, she did exactly that, only to enter Zabar's, an upscale market every bit as pricey as the Fairway Market to the south, and a lot more famous. If you're fond of Namibian goat cheese at twenty bucks a pound, it's the only place to shop.

'This waiting business,' Sister Kassia noted as we stood outside, 'it wears thin pretty fast.'

'Policing is a game of starts and stops. You are always waiting for something, an autopsy, a ballistics report, a witness to surface. There's no end to it.'

This time the wait was only a quarter of an hour; still too long, it seemed, for the little maid. She double-timed along 80th Street as if she'd just snatched a hundred-dollar bottle of grapeseed oil and Zabar's security guards were on her tail. By the time I caught up and took her arm, she was halfway to West End Avenue.

'Police,' I said, displaying my badge, 'I need to talk to you.' She stared at my shield for a moment, through dark blue eyes, while the implications of my sudden appearance made themselves felt. Then her legs buckled as she dropped her parcels and I had to tighten my grip to keep her from falling. A second later, Sister Kassia chugged up, breathing hard. She said something to the girl in Polish and the girl managed to get her legs under her. Nevertheless, she was shivering with fear, her eyes as wild as those of a deer in a forest fire. Her chest had locked up as well, as if she couldn't make up her mind whether to inhale or exhale. When she finally spoke, she spat her words out in short, choppy phrases.

The woman spoke directly to Sister Kassia, gripping the nun's arm. I understood not a word of their conversation, but I didn't interrupt. I knew about fear, of course, having seen it first hand, in the terrified eyes of battered women and battered children, in the eyes of rape victims in hospital examining rooms, in the eyes of the elderly after even a minor assault. Like grief, fear is an emotion cops try to avoid, but this woman was gripped by a terror so powerful that when Sister Kassia finally turned to me, I found it mirrored in her eyes.

'I'll make it simple, detective,' the nun told me. 'Her name is Tynia Cernek. She has a ten-month-old son and she's worried about what Aslan might do to the child if she speaks to the police. She also claims that her chores are timed by her employer. If she's late getting back to the house, she'll be physically punished.'

Again, I wondered if Aslan included an abuse premium in the fee he charged for the maid's services. You want to beat her? Fine. You want to stick her in a refrigerator? Great. In fact, you can even kill one from time to time, as long as you're willing to pay the price. Dominick Capra had told me a story about a servant regularly beaten by her Saudi employers. I remembered it, then, but my attitude didn't change. I was the bad cop here.

'That's not good enough,' I told the nun. 'That doesn't get us anywhere. We can't just let her go.'

When the maid's eyes widened, I knew that she understood English well enough to grasp my intentions. The look in her eyes grew imploring and for a moment I thought she was going to drop to her knees.

'Tell her,' I instructed Sister Kassia, 'that if she cooperates, the police will protect her, her child, and all the other workers. But she has to make a decision right now. She has to convince me that she won't run back to Aslan. Otherwise, I'm going to take her to the Ninety-Second precinct in Brooklyn where I can question her at my leisure.'

Sister Kassia gave me a searching look, but I ignored it. There was no going back.

'What exactly will it take, detective,' she demanded, 'to let her go? Please, be precise.'

'I'm the only chance she has for a normal life, Sister. Me, and me alone. I'm her only hope.'

'That doesn't answer the question.'

By then, I was certain Tynia was following the conversation. 'First, she has to swear that she won't contact Aslan or anyone else. Then she has to name a time and place where we can talk to her without being disturbed.'

Tynia began to speak before Sister Kassia broke eye contact with me. 'Tomorrow in early afternoon,' she said, groping for the words, 'family goes to lunch for museum benefits. I will be in this house alone.'

'Does that about cover it?' Sister Kassia asked.

'Almost.' This time I spoke directly to Tynia. 'I want to know where you stay on Saturday and Sunday when you aren't working.'

Tynia's eyes first grew mistrustful, then resigned. She went into her purse to withdraw a little notebook. The address she rattled off, on 38th Street in Queens, included an apartment number. Though I wasn't familiar enough with the borough to pin the location exactly, I thought it was somewhere in Astoria, near Steinway Street.

'Now, tell me Mynka's last name.'

The fear returned then, followed by an onrushing of tears. 'Mynka, she is dead? Aslan has told us she is running away.'

'Yeah, she's dead. I want to know her last name and how to contact her relatives.'

'Mynka Chechowski. This is her name. Together we are growing up in Poland, in Grodkow. We come here for better life.'

Did the irony escape Tynia Cernek? I was only certain that when I handed her my notebook and she wrote down a phone number, her hands were still shaking. 'Mother's name is Katerina. Of her daughter she is greatly fearing.'

I nodded, then let go of her arm. I was pleased, of course, to finally know Plain Jane's full name. She would have her funeral, in her own country, surrounded by her family. I'd wanted this for her from the very beginning. But there was still that phone call to make, to Katerina who was 'greatly fearing' exactly what I was going to confirm.

'One more question, Tynia. When you were still on Eagle Street, did Aslan live with you?'

'No, there is not room for man.'

'Do you know where he stayed?'

'I am sorry. Aslan, he only speaks to make threatening. If from customer is complaint, he is very angry.'

I nodded to myself as an idea blossomed, then drove home my final point. 'Listen, now, Tynia, to what I'm going to tell you. You must keep this meeting to yourself. Your child's safety depends on it. Speak to nobody, not to your closest friend or your closest relative. Tomorrow, we'll create a plan that accounts for everybody. By the end of the week, this nightmare will be over. I promise you.'

Tynia said nothing for a moment and I turned impatiently to Sister Kassia. 'Please, Sister, repeat what I just said in Polish.'

When Sister Kassia finished, I stepped away. Tynia didn't hesitate. She snatched up her parcels and sprinted toward Riverside Drive.

'You could rescue those children right now,' Sister Kassia said once Tynia disappeared around the corner. 'You don't have to wait.'

'And what would I do next? Hand them over to the social workers? Deliver them into the foster care system?' I turned to face the nun. 'Given the illegal status of their mothers, their missing fathers, and the fact that their mothers knew they were in danger and failed to protect them, the odds are those children would remain wards of the state for the next ten years.'

An hour later, after a quick tour of Astoria, I put Sister Kassia in a gypsy cab, then returned to the Nissan, parked a hundred yards from the address supplied by Tynia Cernek. Nondescript, the building was six stories high, spanned several lots and contained somewhere between forty and fifty apartments. As I'd suspected, it was a block from Steinway Street, the neighborhood's main commercial drag.

The northern and eastern reaches of Astoria have long been the center of New York's Greek population. So much so that natives automatically link Astoria to the many Greek restaurants and groceries along Ditmars Boulevard. But there's another Astoria to the south, near the Grand Central Parkway. This Astoria is a United Nations of ethnicities in which no group predominates. On this particular stretch of Steinway Street, for instance, a block from where I sat, the signs on the storefront businesses were all in Arabic.

Like the warehouse on Eagle Street, the building on 38th Street was an excellent place to hide. For most of the week, apartment 5E would be occupied by Zashka and the children. The workers would arrive on Saturday night. On Monday morning, back they'd go again. This arrangement would not appear terribly unusual to the mostly poor locals, many of whom were illegal themselves.

I sipped at a container of coffee, then got on my cell phone and called Drew Millard. I wanted to locate a detective named Ralph Scott, the arresting officer on Margaret's second bust, the felony assault.

Millard didn't seem all that happy to hear from me. Most likely, he wanted to tell me that I could take my connections and shove them. Instead, he went to his computer and ran the name. Detective Ralph Scott, he told me, now a lieutenant, commanded the squad room at Manhattan North. He was on duty.

I dropped the phone to my lap as the door to the apartment building opened and Zashka Ochirov emerged. She was a hundred yards away, at the opposite end of the block, but I slid down in the seat and stayed there until she disappeared around the corner. Then I called Manhattan North and asked for Lieutenant Scott. He answered his phone on the second ring.

'Lieutenant Scott.'

'Detective Harry Corbin here. I'm calling about a case you handled in 1995.'

'Really? 1995? I can barely remember what I did last week. What's it about?'

'A felony assault. The suspect's name was Margaret Portola.'

'Holy shit. That bitch. I shoulda fuckin'
killed her when I had the chance.'

'That bad?'

'You wouldn't fuckin' believe it. When she
finds out I'm gonna arrest her, she attacks
me. Kickin', punchin', scratchin' at my eyes.
The bitch went all out.' He paused, then said,
'What'd ya say your name was?'

'Harry Corbin.'

'Alright, Harry, lemme just say this. I knew
I was in the home of the rich, if not the
famous. So I didn't go nuts when she came at
me, not even when she spit in my face. All I
did was bring her to the ground and put on
the cuffs. Meantime, she sues me for police
brutality two months later. I still haven't
heard the end of it.'

I gave it a few beats, then changed the flow
of the conversation. 'This happened inside
her house?'

'Yeah.'

'What brought her to your attention in the
first place?'

'She kicked the crap out of a window wash-
er named Pedro Guiterrez for leaving the
windows streaked. Clocked him from behind,
then beat him until her older son pulled her
off. A neighbor heard the guy screaming and
called nine-one-one.'

'How bad was he hurt?'

'Busted arm, busted ribs, cracked skull. He
was lucky she didn't kill him.'

'So, how come the charge was dismissed?'

'C'mon, Harry, I'm sure you figured it out

by now. The Portola family and Pedro Guiterrez reached a settlement on the lawsuit he filed against her, whereupon Pedro went back to Ecuador.'

Under ideal conditions, I would have maintained the surveillance throughout the night, just in case Tynia called Aslan Khalid and he tried to remove the children. But under ideal conditions, I'd have a team behind me and the use of a van designed for surveillance. As it was, I had other work to do and I broke the stake-out a few hours later, at nine o'clock.

I drove directly from Astoria to a section of Williamsburg called the Northside (where I'd almost witnessed the dance of the Giglio). Throughout the 1960s and 1970s, while other white folk, including thousands from surrounding blocks, were retreating to the suburbs, the Northside had maintained its ethnic identity, in this case Italian. The residents' vigilance was the stuff of legend, yet somehow they'd failed to protect their flanks and now were rapidly losing ground to a mixed band of artists, bohemians and yuppies. The end result was much in evidence at 121 North Third Street, a two-story brick building that had once been an automobile repair shop. I only knew about the shop because its name, Elio's Body Repair, was etched into a concrete ledge that separated the upper and lower floors. Otherwise, Dark Passions, the high-end lingerie shop now operating on the first floor, might have been plucked out of SoHo. But I wasn't interested in the lower floor, which was dark in any event. The upper floor, separated from its neighbor by a narrow alley, was obviously residential. This was the address listed on Zashka Ochirov's driver's license and registration.

I drove around the corner, parked, then sat for a few minutes with my hands resting on the steering wheel. As far as I could tell, Zashka lived full-time with the women and their children, first in Greenpoint, now in Astoria. So what need did she have for a second apartment that rented for at least $1500 a month? Was she independently wealthy? I didn't think so. Was she subletting? That was entirely possible. As it was entirely possible that her tenant was Aslan Khalid. After all, he had to live somewhere.

If Aslan was living in that apartment, I needed to know it. One obvious strategy was to establish surveillance, but that was impossible. Not only was Aslan as wary as a three-legged fox, the Portolas' townhouse had a prior claim on my time.

As I weighed my options, I got out of the Nissan and took a walk around the block. It was past ten on a Wednesday night, but the trendy restaurants and bars were still open and there were people on the street. All were young, the oldest appearing no more than thirty, and a number were pierced and tattooed. Their very presence was an affront to the Northside's century-long commitment to hard work and discipline. It was as if the damned hippies had won after all.

My intention was to walk past Dark Passions and the four-story tenement to the east without slowing down, but I hesitated for a few seconds at the mouth of an alley separating the two. In other parts of town, alleys are impromptu garbage dumps peopled by rats and feral cats, by junkies and crack-heads, by whores servicing tricks, by homeless men and women in search of a secluded patch of concrete on which to lay their heads. But that wasn't the case in gentrified Williamsburg. As far as I could tell, there wasn't enough trash in the alley to support an anorexic cockroach.

I continued on to Bedford Avenue, strolling north toward the subway station where I found an open cafe with outdoor seating. The cafe's tables were the size of trivets, the chairs rickety and the staff none too friendly when I ordered a double espresso and a slice of banana cake from the cafe's all-organic menu. The place was deserted, inside and out, and the workers were cleaning up. But I held my ground for an hour, until Bedford Avenue finally grew quiet at eleven thirty.

When I came back to North Third Street, I again took careful note of the human activity on either side of the road, including the upper windows of several apartment buildings. I didn't see anyone in the windows, or in the parked cars, and the only people outside at that moment were a trio of men smoking in front of a bar at the corner. As far as I could tell, they didn't so much as glance in my direction when I ducked into the alley.

I made my way to the end of the alley and turned the corner before squatting down. Across a gap of about fifty feet, the rear walls of the buildings facing North Fourth Street all had multiple windows looking out in my general direction. Two of the buildings were commercial and their windows were dark, but the rest were residential and I knew I couldn't stay where I was for long, much less climb the drainpipe to my left, without risking discovery. I had a strong interest in that drainpipe because it ran past a lighted window on Dark Passions' second floor. There was even a toehold on the lip of the concrete ledge separating the two floors, and handholds on the steel bars protecting the window from invaders. I gave the pipe a little tug. Secured to the side of the building by clamps screwed into the brick, it moved just far enough for me to get my fingers behind it.

In a combat situation, any decision, even the wrong decision, is better than no decision. Climb or retreat. Risk discovery or leave without knowing who resided in the apartment. I think I might have chosen the latter course, if only I could have imagined another way to accomplish my primary goal. I had to know who was living in that apartment and I'd never have a better chance to find out.

After another quick check of the windows across the way, I stood and reached above my head to get both hands around the pipe. Then I began to walk up the side of the wall, digging my toes into the recessed grouting between the rows of bricks, pushing off on my legs, raising my arms, one at a time, to pull myself up. I was enough of a narcissist to be flattered by the ease of my progress; all those hours in the pool were paying off. But the fact that I was able to climb quietly – and that the pipe readily supported my weight – was far more important. Within a few minutes, my head was alongside the closed window.

I shifted my head and shoulders to the right and brought one eye to a corner of the window. When I was certain there was no one in my field of vision, I leaned further in and took a closer look at the small bedroom in front of me. Two things struck me. The place was an absolute mess, with clothing scattered over the floor, and all the clothing belonged to a man.

Was that man Aslan Khalid? When I finally looked through the open door on the other side of the room, the answer was staring back at me. The green flag of Chechnya, with its red and white stripes, hung on the wall over-looking North Third Street. At dead center, the Chechen wolf rested on his pedestal, his head still turned out, ears sharp as knives, white eyes arrogant and dismissive.

My heart literally jumped in my chest, my joy so overwhelming my cheeks reddened as if they'd been slapped. I felt the hairs rise on the back of my neck and my fingers lock onto the pipe. If I'd had a tail, it would have twitched. Then, from somewhere inside the apartment, I heard a toilet flush. Time to go. I hesitated just long enough to give the bars a tug, hoping to discover them loose, but they didn't move by so much as a millimeter. Then I began to work my way back down, finding the descent as easy as the climb.

I was in front of the building, taking note of the lock on the door leading upstairs, when a cruiser turned onto North Third Street. I straightened quickly, easing the billfold containing my shield and *ID* out of my pocket. Hoping the cops inside the cruiser were simply patrolling their sector, I pressed the billfold against my hip. No such luck. As the cruiser approached, the driver trained his six-cell flashlight on my face. I reacted immediately, altering my path until I was walking toward the vehicle, my billfold raised to expose my shield. But the light didn't drop to my chest until I came within a few feet of the door. Now I could see the face of the cop holding the flashlight, Officer Frank Gerhaty, the *PBA* delegate at the very center of the rumors that swirled around me in the Nine-Two. Beside him, in the jump seat, a female officer unknown to me had her arms folded beneath her breasts.

'I hope it wasn't you creepin' that alley, detective,' Gerhaty said.

I responded by snatching the flashlight out of his hand, unscrewing the head, dumping the batteries into the street, finally tossing the pieces back through the window. I would have taken it further if there hadn't been a witness. As it was, I satisfied myself with a cryptic remark before walking away.

'The door you're knockin' on, you better pray it doesn't open, Frank, because what's inside will swallow you whole.'

TWENTY-EIGHT

There was no good reason to get out early on the following morning. The Portolas wouldn't be leaving their home until noon. But I was too restless to sit still. I was up at eight o'clock, scrambling a couple of eggs, washing them down with coffee. Then I dragged the vacuum cleaner out of the closet and went to work. I needed to keep busy.

I was in my office, the vacuum cleaner so loud I failed to hear the house phone until the answering machine kicked on, then off. A second later, the cell phone in my pocket began to ring.

'Corbin, it's me.'

I glanced at my watch. It was a quarter to nine.

'Adele, I was gonna call you later.'

When she hesitated, I felt my stomach churn. I was sure she'd challenge me, that she'd claim I was avoiding her. The accusation would be ironic, of course, since she was the one who had left town. But it would also be true.

Instead, she changed the subject. 'Did you make contact with the maid?' she asked.

I smothered a sigh of relief. 'Tynia Cernek. That's her name. Sister Kassia and I spoke to her on the street for a few minutes. We'll have a longer session today around noon while the family's out of the house.'

'You think she can help?'

'Not with the murder investigation, not directly. She didn't even know that Mynka was dead.'

'What about indirectly?'

'Once I put this business with Sister Kassia behind me, I'm going to take a shot at one of the Portolas. If I pick the wrong one, I'm in big trouble. So, the more I know about them, the better.' I went on to describe the family, each of them, in detail. 'Margaret's out of the question,' I concluded. 'She'll lawyer up right away. It's between the two kids.'

'Do you think Margaret killed Mynka?'

'It's too early for that. Plus, right now, I'm trying to concentrate on the deal I made with Sister Kassia and Father Stan.'

'Actually, that's why I called. I can't stop thinking about what you said yesterday.'

I glanced through the window, at a wall of brick across the way. I told myself not to be distracted, no matter what came next. 'Correct me if I'm wrong, Corbin. You plan to wait until Saturday night, when the women and their children are together, then force an entry in order to pull them out.'

'If there's another option that accounts for them, I don't know it.'

'That's not the point.' Adele gave it a few beats, then said, 'The point is that you're going in alone. And don't deny it.'

'Well, I definitely deny it. I'm not going in alone. I'm going in with Sister Kassia.'

Adele laughed, in spite of herself. 'That's good. That's you. But what about Hansen?'

'First, I promised to keep the priest's name out of it. Second, I have no idea what Bill Sarney will do if he gets his hands on those women before I do.' I stopped for a moment as I collected my thoughts. 'Look, I'm assuming that Aslan's presence in this country, if it ever becomes public knowledge, would embarrass somebody high up on the food chain. But I don't know why or who, and I don't ever expect to know. This does not bother me, Adele. I can live with it. But there's still a question. If I call in Sarney and Hansen, whose interests will they represent? A bunch of illegal immigrants and their snot-nosed brats? Or that top-feeder I just mentioned?'

I paused long enough to catch a breath. 'On the other hand, if I get them away from Aslan and if Sister Kassia supplies them with a lawyer before Sarney knows what's happening, the potential for negative publicity will force the bosses to cooperate.'

There was nothing more to be said on the subject and Adele remained silent for a moment before returning to her original point. 'What you've said, Corbin, doesn't affect the bottom line one bit. You plan to go in alone. How do you know that Aslan won't be waiting for you?'

'Aslan doesn't live with his workers. Most of the time, they're chaperoned by a woman named Zashka Ochirov, who also cares for the children. I'm going to arrange some sort of signal with Tynia – maybe a window up or down – to let me know if there's anyone in the apartment besides Zashka. And I don't plan to kick the door open. Tynia will open it when I knock.'

Adele's tone sharpened. 'Have you bothered to count the number of things that can go wrong?'

'I stopped when I ran out of fingers. But, hey, Tynia gave me the address of the apartment where she stayed last weekend. I went there yesterday and spotted Zashka Ochirov. Now, it just so happens that I have witnesses who can put Zashka at Domestic Solutions when Barsakov was killed. That gives me an excuse to detain her, to put her in the box. Adele, Zashka's a petty con artist. If I was willing to let Tynia and the rest fend for themselves, I could break Zashka in an hour. You hear what I'm saying? If I forget about these women, I can put Aslan behind me in a couple of days without taking any serious risk. Remember, it was you, Sister Kassia and Father Stan who insisted that I protect their interests.'

The outburst surprised both of us. I found myself carrying the phone into the bedroom, too wired to stand still.

'I'm sorry,' I finally said.

'It's my fault, Corbin. I should be there with you.'

The words smacked into me, opening a hole through which Adele poured. I felt a rush of emotion, a longing deep enough to drown in, as though a floodwall had broken. It was the last thing I needed. I glanced at my watch as I pulled myself together. 'I have to go,' I said. 'I have to meet Sister Kassia. This is a big day for us.'

'I understand. It's all right. I only wanted to catch up.'

Sister Kassia and I found seats on a convenient bench in Riverside Park a little after ten. We proceeded to wash down a bag of cheese blintzes with large containers of coffee picked up at a nearby Starbucks. Sister Kassia had prepared the blintzes early that morning and they were incredibly soft and delicate.

'I thought,' she told me as she unwrapped them, 'that we might do better than a bag of stale doughnuts.'

She was right, and I showed my gratitude, once our breakfast was consumed and I'd cleaned my fingers, by reviewing the items I wanted our impending interview with Tynia Cernek to include. Sister Kassia was slated to conduct the interview, which meant she and Tynia would be speaking Polish. The point was to establish trust, to head off any last-minute resistance when I finally came knocking on that door in Astoria.

This time around, I was unable to banish Adele, at least not entirely. She continued to work on me, an itch I couldn't scratch. The worst part was that the dangers she'd described were very real. Aslan would kill me if he could.

The nun and I were still at it when a stretch limo, a white Mercedes, rolled up to the townhouse across the street. Ten minutes later, the Portola family emerged. Margaret was dressed in a dark suit which she'd complemented with pearls at her throat and ears. Leonard also wore a suit, double-breasted, black and immaculately tailored, over a blood-red shirt. By contrast, David's olive-green suit fitted him badly and his striped tie was poorly knotted and askew. Dress-up was not his favorite game and he was unable, or unwilling, to fake it.

I rose from the bench as the limo turned onto 82nd Street, draped my bag across my shoulder, finally offered my hand to Sister Kassia. Together, we walked to the door of the townhouse, which opened before I could knock.

I followed the nun inside, past Tynia, who slid the door closed behind us. Tynia was wearing an apron over her blue dress and she wiped her palms across the front, but did not offer her hand. We were standing in a large entrance hall paneled in dark wood. There were side chairs flanking the door leading into the house, with oval seats and backs, and four oil paintings on the wall above the wainscoting. The paintings, all landscapes, were surrounded by enormous gilt frames and seemed vaguely familiar.

Without a word, Tynia led us to a stairway against the northern wall, then down into a basement kitchen. I came last, hanging back when I reached the bottom of the stairs. For a moment, I failed to register any of the kitchen's details except for one. On the other side of the room, directly across from where I stood, a wooden door rose to the height of my head. The door turned on hinges made of hammered iron and the gap between door and frame was sealed with rubbery gray insulation.

I waited where I was until Tynia and Sister Kassia were seated at a long table, lost in conversation. Then I crossed the room to run the fingers of my right hand over the front of the door. The faint mahogany stain was flaking and the surface felt dry and rough. Around the handle, a black semicircle attested to decades of wear. Setting down my bag, I gave the handle a yank. It released with a satisfying *ka-chunk* and the door turned effortlessly on its hinges. I was left staring into a room about ten feet deep, with shelves and bins, some open, some covered, to my left and right. The room was narrow, not more than four feet wide, including the bins, and I had to turn my shoulders when I stepped inside.

Instinctively, I reached out to keep the door from shutting, but I needn't have bothered. Unlike most refrigerator doors, which close by themselves if left ajar, this door was weighted to swing outward. Just as well, because there was no inner latch. If the door shut behind me, I'd have to rely on a red button, labeled *EMERGENCY*, mounted on the wall.

The button was a great idea, no question, but as a means of escape, it depended entirely on the good will of the individual, or individuals, on the other side of the door.

The cold air cut its way into my skin as I edged toward the back of the refrigerator. I found myself wanting to jam my hands into my pockets. Instead, I began to pull out the bins, to examine them closely, along with the shelves beneath them. I was looking for blood evidence, which I didn't find, but I was struck by the number of empty bins. There was a lot of food in the refrigerator, including a dozen varieties of cheese and enough fruit to stock a pushcart, but the unit was only a third full. Clearly, it was too large for a single family.

My fingertips and toes were growing numb by the time I gave up the search. My forearms were rapidly following suit. I was wearing a short-sleeved polo shirt, loosely woven, and lightweight tropical slacks, both seemingly as porous as fishnets. The temperature inside the refrigerator could not have been more than a few degrees above freezing.

For a moment, I stood in the doorway,

letting warm air from the kitchen wash across my body. Sister Kassia and Tynia were still seated at the table, still engaged in intense conversation. But now the empty space in front of Tynia was taken up by a set of silverware, a service for twelve by the look of it. Tynia was working on the knives, one at a time, coating them with polish, then buffing them until they gleamed. She worked quickly, leaving me to suppose that she'd been assigned a number of duties, and that she faced consequences if they were not completed before the return of her employer.

'Sister?' I waited until the nun turned to me. 'I'm going to close the door. I want you to open it in five minutes. Not before, understand?' I shifted my gaze to Tynia. Initially, I found her eyes questioning, but then her doubts were replaced by simple recognition. We understood each other now.

When the door closed and the refrigerator went dark, I took several steps back. I couldn't shake a feeling that the room was contracting around me and I instinctively hunched over, as if avoiding a blow. In that moment, the cold became organic, an alive and hungry parasite burrowing down through my skin.

I was tempted to fight back, to jog in place, to flap my arms, as I knew Mynka had been tempted, as Tynia had been tempted. But there was just so much oxygen in that little room and the harder I worked the sooner it would be exhausted. The only question was which would kill me first, would I freeze to death or would I suffocate?

But these were questions that didn't need answering. After a time – which I was unable to measure – I began to shiver, a reflex which became more and more intense as the seconds ticked by. Eventually, conserving oxygen ceased to be a viable option. I started to run in place, slowly at first, than faster, until my body produced enough heat to drive the cold away. The effect, as I well knew, would only be temporary. As long as that door remained closed, the cold was an enemy that couldn't be defeated, or even kept at bay for any length of time.

Literally blind, I groped my way toward what I hoped was the room's door, only to discover myself up against the back wall. I turned on my heel, aiming to re-trace my steps, but was unable to walk a straight line. I kept lurching into the bins on either side as I shuffled along. By the time I reached the door, I was breathing hard. Because the adrenalin was pumping? Or because my lungs weren't getting enough oxygen?

I let my index finger rest on the emergency button, wondering how many times Mynka had stood here, how many times she'd push-ed the panic button? I wondered if she'd become angry when no one responded. Whether she'd held the button down, smash-ed her fist on the door, demanded release. Or if she was in fear of some greater punishment, something worse than the cold room.

When I pressed the button, a buzzer sounded on the other side of the door. The buzzer was loud even in the sealed refrigerator; in the kitchen, it must have been ear splitting. I tried to imagine Mynka's tormentor on the other side of the door, knowing it might have been Margaret or Ronald, or both.

The sound of the buzzer, of course, would only inspire a true sadist to persist, to confine Mynka long enough, before she was killed, to produce an unforeseen consequence. I'd noted this consequence at the crime scene, as had Dr Hyong at the autopsy: lividity that should have been purple-black was rosy pink. That single anomaly, more than any other factor, was responsible for my presence in the Portola townhouse.

I didn't panic, didn't pound on the door or repeatedly press the emergency button, as I imagined that Mynka and Tynia had, but I felt an overwhelming sense of relief when Sister Kassia opened the door and I stepped out. The nun was holding a mug of hot coffee and smiling faintly, while Tynia stood by the table, polishing cloth in hand.

I took the mug, cradling it between my fingers until I stopped shivering. 'Who did it?' I asked Tynia. When she shook her head, I added, 'Who put you in the cold room?'

'Madame,' she answered.

'Not Ronald?'

Her sudden smile was contemptuous. 'Never.' She turned to Sister Kassia and spoke in rapid-fire Polish.

'Tynia says that Ronald is a coward, that he only does what his mother tells him to do. She says that when Margaret's angry, she calls her son, "La Bamba." '

'What about David? Did she have a pet name for David?'

'Jerk,' Tynia responded. 'Always she is saying, "Jerk, do this, do that." David is hating this, but is also fearing the mother. She is beating her sons from time they are babies.'

'How do you know that?'

'Mynka is telling me this and I am seeing Madame for myself. When becomes angry, she is crazy woman. Punch, kick, slap. Her sons are pushing her away, but they are never fighting back.'

I nodded, then turned to Sister Kassia. 'Are you and Tynia finished?'

'We have a bit more ground to cover. I've spent most of the time describing what comes after the women and their children arrive at the shelter.'

'What'd you tell her?'

'I told her that we'll get them jobs as soon as they're settled in, that their children will be cared for by professionals while they work, that we'll help them find housing, that legal assistance will be available.'

I left it there and began to search the kitchen for any trace of blood evidence. I didn't know whether or not a servant has the right to allow a cop into her employer's home, or if a cop, once admitted, has the right to seize evidence. But if I discovered

297

traces of Mynka's killing in that kitchen, I intended to document them. Unfortunately, the only evidence I found was evidence of a thorough cleanup, a cleanup that included the floor beneath the refrigerator and beneath a huge dishwasher. In the broom closet, every item, from the dustpan to the mop, was new. That didn't mean there was no evidence to recover, only that recovery demanded a level of expertise that excluded Harry Corbin.

When I took a chair at the kitchen table next to Sister Kassia and settled down, Tynia was finishing up the last of the teaspoons. By then, we'd been inside the townhouse for about an hour.

'You're not going to like this, Harry, so let's get it on the table.' Sister Kassia's brows formed twin arches above her eyes, arches that mirrored the curve of her downturned mouth. 'Tynia has been in touch with some of the other women.'

I looked over at Tynia. She shrank back in her chair and dropped the spoon she was polishing. I listened to it clatter on the tabletop, thinking that she was right to be afraid.

'Harry?' The nun tapped my arm. 'There are five women staying in the Astoria apartment. Tynia only contacted two of them...'

'On whose phone?'

'The Portolas'. But she made the calls when the family was out of the house.'

'And how do we know somebody wasn't eavesdropping on the other end? You understand, if Aslan gets wind of our plans, not only will the women and the kids vanish, the Portolas will be notified, at which point they'll lawyer up and my case against Mynka's killer will also vanish. Even if I eventually prove that she was murdered in this very room, I'll never be able to prove who did it. My entire strategy is based on catching the family unaware.'

Sister Kassia's eyes dropped to her hands. I can't be sure, but I suspect that she'd finally grasped the magnitude of the risk I was taking. In any event, it was Tynia who broke the silence. 'Mynka, this is where she was dying?'

'Yes, Tynia, your friend died in this very room. Does that frighten you? Do you want to leave right now? Because if you do, I can arrange to have you taken directly to a detention center.'

Tynia took Sister Kassia's arm and began to speak in Polish. She spoke very quickly, but her tone was even. I settled back in my chair and waited until she paused.

'Tynia says that last weekend she and the other girls were taken to a place they'd never been. Aslan wasn't there, nor was a man named Konstantine. But there were other men there. They offered the girls new jobs at a motel in Los Angeles.'

'They say to us it will be better,' Tynia interrupted. 'Time off every day to be with children. These men, they have nothing in their eyes. They are looking at you like you are dead.' Suddenly, she reached over the table to take my hand. 'We are ready, all of us. For a long time we have been ready. We cannot live more like this, every second afraid. Help us.'

The refrigerator's motor kicked on at that moment and I listened to what might have passed for a death rattle before it finally settled into a low-pitched hum.

'Listen, Harry,' the nun said. 'The women Tynia contacted are old friends of hers. They knew each other in Poland and came over together. They're eager to cooperate.'

'Fine, now tell me the rest of it. What, exactly, have these ladies cooked up?'

'On their day off, when they're in Astoria, they're watched by a woman named...'

'Zashka Ochirov.'

Tynia jerked back in surprise, but Sister Kassia merely smiled. 'Tell me about Zashka,' I continued. 'Is she armed? Will she fight?'

'Zashka takes care of the children when the women are at work. According to Tynia, she treats the children kindly and they respond to her without fear. The only threat she's ever made against the women is to call one of her bosses.'

I nodded. 'Did you make arrangements for a signal?' This was another topic I'd asked her to explore.

'There's a window in Tynia's bedroom that faces the street. If Ochirov is alone when you arrive at ten o'clock, the window will be raised. If there's someone else in the apartment, but Tynia will be able to let you in, the window will be closed. If she can't let you in,

300

the window will be halfway down.'

'Good. Did you tell her that you won't be there when I come through the door?'

'I told her that I'd be waiting downstairs, ready to take her and the others away. She was suspicious at first, but she finally accepted it.'

I turned back to Tynia then. My sense was that I'd done about as well as I could have, given the constraints, and it was fast closing in on the time for Sister Kassia and me to leave. I just had a few more questions.

'Tell me how old Mynka was?'

Tynia's expression clouded for a moment when I said Mynka's name, but then she grew sober and her eyes lit up. I liked what I saw in her eyes. When the time came, she would not back down.

'Are you knowing Mynka is pregnant?' she asked.

'Yes, I am.'

'Then this is two peoples who are dying. Two lives are being killed.'

I nodded agreement, then repeated my question. 'How old was Mynka?'

'She was eighteen years, still a girl only.' Tynia rattled off several sentences in Polish, which Sister Kassia promptly translated.

'She says that Mynka loved romance novels, that she dreamed of true love. Mynka thought that love would save her.'

Yeah, right.

'One last item, Tynia, and we'll be gone. David Portola. Tell me what he's like?'

As she considered her reply, Tynia put the last of the spoons into a mahogany chest and closed the top. Then she rose to put the chest away.

'David is father of Mynka's child.'

'I already know that. I want to know what he's like, as a person.'

Tynia thought it over for a moment. 'This boy is with anger every minute. Sometimes, I think he is ready to blow up, like bomb. But on nights when I am coming past his room, I can hear him inside and he is weeping. It is for Mynka that he weeps.'

TWENTY-NINE

I went for a swim that night, hoping to work off some energy. No such luck. I fell asleep late and woke up early, feeling like a prize-fighter on the day before a big match. All those weeks of training, of devising strategies to negate my opponent's skills, to maximize my own. Would there be a payoff? Or would I end up on the canvas, eyes glazed, tasting my own blood? There was no way to know. After breakfast, I took a small toolbox from a closet shelf, fiddled through the screwdrivers and pliers, and finally withdrew two items: an L-shaped bar about the thickness of a tooth-pick, and a specialized tool the size and shape of a glue gun. The bar was called a tension bar, the tool a snap gun. They were designed for folks, like myself, who sometimes need to get past a locked door but never mastered the art of picking locks.

I went to the door of my apartment, to a multi-pin, deadbolt lock similar to the one on Aslan's door. I inserted the tension bar first, rotating the lock slightly, then the blade of the snap gun. When I pressed the gun's trigger it lived up to it's name, making a distinct snap, like the snap of a finger, as the blade flew up. The point here was to kick the upper pins into the cylinder. If they became trapped above the shear line, the lock would open. If they didn't, you could always try again.

The nicest thing about a snap gun is that you can't screw it up. The lock opens or it doesn't. In this case, I got lucky on the third try.

I kept at it for two hours, moving from the upper to the lower locks on the door. The point was not just to open the lock. Eventually, I'd be doing this in public. I needed to be quick and casual. Over time, I improved on both counts, but there was no way to get past a snap gun's ultimate flaw. The process was entirely random. On one pass, it took me twelve attempts before the lock opened.

When my fingers began to cramp, I finally brought the gun to my office and left it on the desk. It was now eleven o'clock. For the first time in weeks, there was nothing I absolutely had to do. Over coffee, I checked the movie listings, considered driving up to Yankee Stadium for an afternoon game, checked the hours of the Metropolitan Museum, considered a long walk in Central Park or a trip to Jones Beach on Long Island. The last was especially attractive. It had been a long time since I'd taken a swim in heavy surf.

But I didn't drive to Jones Beach, or choose any of the alternatives in Column A. Instead, I took the subway to Riverside Park and once again settled down across the street from the Portola townhouse.

Ronald and Margaret Portola made an appearance at noon, cabbing off to place or places unknown, while David emerged at three o'clock, his skateboard tucked beneath his arm. As before, he headed north. I watched him until he disappeared behind a hill, then sat back.

Tynia's story had confirmed Father Manicki's. David had loved Mynka. He loved her still. Men have a powerful need to protect the women they love. The urge is visceral, an impulse as physical as hunger or thirst. David, of course, had failed to protect his beloved. Most likely, he was currently protecting her killer. It had to hurt.

Love and guilt. These would be my weapons, if I chose to interrogate David Portola. But I wouldn't use them right away. Initially, I'd hold myself in check, endure the vitriol sure to flow from David's mouth. Only after he wore down would I drive in the stakes. You loved her, David. I know that. But you have to face the facts. You failed to protect her in life. Are you willing to fail again?

I would pound the message home, without raising my voice, over and over, until I felt him give. Then I would show him what happened to his beloved after she left the townhouse. I'd lay the photos out, one at a time, saving the close-ups for last. Are you willing to fail her again?

The sun was going down by the time I broke off the surveillance. I felt more relaxed by then. The lights were on inside the Portola townhouse and I'd caught occasional glimpses of the family through the curtains on the windows. Nothing was out of order, as far as I could tell. Tynia's resolve hadn't weakened.

I went from the Upper West Side to dinner at a First Avenue restaurant in the East Village and it was almost nine when I settled the check and walked back to Rensselaer Village. I picked up the mail in the lobby of my building, glanced through it, separating the bills from the usual run of unwanted junk as I rode up in the elevator. I think I was feeling sleepy, from fatigue or from a third glass of wine, but I can't be absolutely sure. That's because, when I entered the apartment to find Adele Bentibi asleep on the couch, my heart took off like a rocket and I was overwhelmed by successive waves of emotion. Hope, first, then gratitude, then relief, then fear. For all I knew, Adele intended to stay just long enough to pack her things and quit

New York for good.

I draped my bag over the back of a dining room chair, then walked to the couch and dropped to my knees. I didn't touch Adele, didn't want to disturb her sleep. There were dark circles under her eyes and her face was pale, as though she'd spent the last few weeks indoors. She was lying with her arms folded across her chest, her fingers curled as though about to make a fist. I'd been thinking of Adele all day, trying to evade little bullets of guilt. I knew I'd relegated her needs to a category that might be called, 'I'll worry about it tomorrow.' Now, tomorrow was lying on the couch.

'Corbin?' Adele rubbed her eyes, then sat up to give me a chaste peck on the cheek. 'If my breath smells anything like my mouth tastes,' she announced, 'watch out for your fillings. I need to brush my teeth.'

I observed her march down the hall the way soothsayers watch birds in flight. I was looking for a sign, but I could make nothing of her confident stride. Then the door closed and I went into the kitchen to set up the coffee maker. The shower came on a moment later.

The next fifteen minutes were long and difficult, but when Adele finally emerged, wrapped in a sea-green towel, I began to relax. Adele had made a similar appearance in the hallway ten months before, on the night we first made love. That she hadn't forgotten was clear from the amused sparkle in her eyes.

'Did you really think I'd let you confront Aslan without backup?' she asked.

The question was entirely unexpected and it took me a moment to recall our last conversation. Adele had forced me to admit that I'd be on my own when I liberated Domestic Solutions' workers and their children.

Though I wasn't sure I'd need help, I was definitely touched. I reached out to lay my fingertips on the side of her throat, to take the pulse of her life. 'I don't care why you came,' I told her. 'I'm just glad to have you back.'

Adele smiled. 'Do I smell coffee brewing?' she asked.

'Decaf. You look tired as hell.' A few minutes later, I walked out of the kitchen to find that Adele had replaced the towel with a flowered Japanese robe. I sat down next to her on the couch and was immensely gratified when she reached out to take my hand. 'I wasn't kidding about the main reason for my being here,' she announced. 'I won't let you play lone wolf. I don't care if the part is dear to your soul.'

'I can accept that, but I was wondering, besides the main reason, what were your other reasons for coming home? If there were any.'

Adele was nothing if not direct, but this time she chose to evade the question. 'We have to let it go, Corbin, until this whole business is behind us. I'm not here to distract you. The stakes are too high for that.' She leaned back and closed her eyes. 'You know what I want, Corbin? Right now, more than anything else in the world? I want to lie next to you in bed. I want to feel your body next to mine, to hold you in my arms, to feel your heart beating in your chest.'

I hastened to grant Adele's wish, and without complaint. True, I was anticipating a bit more action after we got through with the heart-to-heart thing, but it didn't happen, not then. Adele settled down next to me with her leg across my belly and her head tucked beneath my shoulder. She was in a mood to talk.

'You're so big, Corbin,' she said as she ran a finger across my chest. 'You're an immense man. Why don't you act your size?'

I thought about it for a moment, then said, 'I'm whatever size I need to be.'

'I know. In the box, I've seen you shrink down until you're smaller than the suspect, until you're no threat at all. How much do you weigh?'

'Somewhere between two-twenty and two-thirty.'

'I feel small lying next to you. I never felt that way with my husband.'

'Small and helpless?'

Adele pinched my nipple and I jumped. 'No, not helpless,' she said. 'Not while I still have a gun.'

A few minutes later, she fell asleep. I stayed as I was, on my back with my arm encircling her head and shoulders, finally drifting off. It was still dark when I awakened. Adele was already astride me, mouth open as she rose and fell. I reached out to take her breasts in my hands and she looked down at me for a moment. Then she said, 'I missed you, Corbin. I missed you every fucking minute.'

THIRTY

Adele and I spent a good part of Saturday on a little tour. I took her first to Aslan's place on North Third Street in Williamsburg, then out to the apartment building in Astoria, finally to Riverside Drive and the Portolas' townhouse. Margaret and David made an appearance shortly after we settled down in the park. She and her son stood in front of the house for a several minutes, their conversation entirely one-sided. Margaret's lips moved in rapid bursts. David endured the barrage. He stared off into the distance, a small act of defiance, perhaps, but he didn't move until she was done. Then, like a dog let off the leash, he dashed across Riverside Drive and headed south. Margaret watched him for a moment before stepping into the street to hail a cab.

Adele watched it all, her attention locked on the encounter. When she finally turned back to me, her eyes were sparkling. The case had grabbed her. She was fully engaged.

Ronald came out a short time later. He posed in front of the building for a few seconds, looking up and down the block as though in search of an audience. His eyes were lidded, his movements slow, almost dreamy, and it was obvious, to both of us, that he was stoned.

'He's the one,' Adele said.

'You think so?'

'Yes, I do. But he's soft, Corbin. We have to remember that. Soft people don't break, they bend. If we put too much pressure on Ronald, he's likely to withdraw.'

We returned to the apartment a short time later. Adele went off to give her weapon a quick cleaning, while I phoned Sister Kassia to make sure things were proceeding smoothly on her end. She assured me that she'd meet her obligations, though the tension in her voice was obvious. Taking a civilian into an inherently dangerous situation is a big-time no-no, but it couldn't be avoided. I'd used Sister Kassia to gain Tynia's confidence, used her well. Now I was stuck with her.

But the job could only hang me once. Taking a *DA*'s investigator (currently on a leave of absence) into a potentially life-threatening encounter isn't encouraged either. If things went wrong ... Well, if things went wrong, I'd just have to blackmail Inspector Sarney into protecting me. All that bullshit about denying any knowledge of Harry Corbin's activities? Harry knew where the bodies were buried and he didn't intend to become one of them.

After a light supper at seven o'clock, Adele and I headed into the bedroom to dress. I saw Adele glance into the office as she passed the open door, then stop suddenly.

'What's that for?'

I followed her eyes to the snap gun lying next to my computer. 'That's a snap gun.'

'I know what it is. I want to know what you plan to do with it.'

'Simple. If I confront Aslan in a public place, there's a good chance that civilians will be endangered, if not injured or killed. I'm hoping the snap gun will get me into his apartment.'

Adele folded her arms across her chest, her expression bordering on grim. 'Simple? Corbin, we've been together too long. I know simple isn't part of your game plan. There's more to this than a threat to public safety.'

'I want a few minutes alone with Aslan. A polite conversation that might include the odd damaging admission, or even a full disclosure of the facts.' I winked. 'And I also want to control the situation, which is why I plan to be waiting inside the apartment when he enters.'

I was hoping the last part would get me off the hook, but Adele continued to study me for a long moment before leading me into the bedroom. I watched her rummage in the closet, sliding hangers back and forth. Finally, she emerged bearing a pair of Grade *III*-A Kevlar vests. Thick and heavy, *III*-A body armor is designed to stop any handgun round

and most rifle rounds, and to minimize the
blunt force trauma associated with bullet
impacts, even when there's no penetration.
Myself, I would have been content with
something lighter, something less confining,
but this decision was clearly out of my hands.
I pulled the vest over my head, fastened the
straps, stared at myself in the mirror. I'd
acquired the vests long ago, while assigned to
the Manhattan North *SWAT* Team. Now I
felt like a posturing fool.

Adele and I arrived at Blessed Virgin to find
Sister Kassia standing next to an elderly
Latino. I introduced Adele before turning to
the old man whose job was to drive the small
yellow bus parked at the curb. I told him that
under no circumstances was he to leave that
bus.

'I don't care what happens, don't be a hero.
Stay in the bus.'

'Hey, man, I'm just...'

'Listen to me, the only thing I want you to
say is yes.'

'Si.'

The issue settled, I led the bus through
south-eastern Queens. We took the scenic
route, along surface streets lined with storefront businesses, Maurice Avenue, 69th
Street, Broadway. It was raining just hard
enough to loosen the oil and grit on the
asphalt, to transform the roads into shiny
black sheets that reflected the rainbow of
neon to either side.

The districts we passed through were com-

312

mercial and there were traffic lights on every block, with no apparent effort made to synchronize them. As often as not, the light ahead turned red just as the one in front of us turned green. Meanwhile, I wanted nothing more than to jam the gas pedal to the floor even though I knew the four-cylinder Nissan was more likely to stall than accelerate.

At Roosevelt Avenue, I was brought to a stop by a screaming fire engine double-timing beneath the elevated tracks that carry the 7 Train. Roosevelt Avenue was never designed for traffic. The el's girders come down almost in the middle of the street, narrowing the road into a pair of lanes, and it's always slow going. But the ladder truck's driver seemed not to notice. He continued to run the siren full blast as he shifted into the left lane, effectively blocking oncoming traffic. When that traffic came to a screeching halt, everything stopped, including Harry Corbin. Hurry up and wait. The city demands activity. You can sense its frantic pace in the foul air you breathe as you hustle down the street. But at the same time it puts an endless series of obstacles in your way. The ladder truck, with its driving-challenged pilot, was just another example.

Or so Adele explained. 'Get used to it, Corbin,' she said. 'You're looking at your heritage.'

I nodded agreeably, but didn't fail to note the gleam in her eye or the flush in her cheeks.

'Feel good to be a cop again?' I asked.

'Yeah,' she admitted, 'it feels great.'

As Adele and I walked toward the brick apartment building on 38th Street, I pulled out the chain concealed beneath my shirt and let it fall against my chest. What with the shield dangling at the bottom of that chain, and the Kevlar body armor, my status must have been obvious to the superintendent, who opened the lobby door after I rang his bell. The super was a wizened man from the Middle East who might have hailed from any of a dozen countries. For just a moment, when I told him to return to his apartment, I thought he was going to become difficult. But then Adele flashed her billfold, revealing her Investigator's shield, and said the magic word, 'Immigration.' Seconds later, we were alone.

Ignoring the elevator, we climbed the stairs to a featureless second floor hallway – cracked tile floor, brown walls, yellow ceiling, green doors. I paused for a moment to get my bearings, then followed the corridor to apartment 2B where Adele and I drew our weapons.

'You ready?' she asked.

'Yeah.'

As I'd driven past the building in search of a parking space, I'd noted the closed window on the second floor. That meant there was somebody else in the apartment besides Zashka and the women, but that Tynia would open the door when I knocked. Though we'd

314

have to go in hard, we'd have the advantage of surprise. Still, my heart was pounding away. And drawing my Glock didn't slow it down, either.

I took a deep breath, glanced at Adele, then tapped on the door. It opened immediately and I stepped into a large room, shouting, 'Police, police, police.'

Zashka Ochirov was sitting on a chair at the far end of the room, her mouth hanging open. Tynia was standing to my right, still holding the door as Adele made her entrance. To my left, two male Caucasians were perched on opposite ends of a couch. They seemed to levitate, eyebrows shooting up, hands rising as though yanked by a string.

'Anybody else in the apartment I should know about?' I asked Tynia.

'No.'

'Then get moving.'

Tynia disappeared into a rear bedroom and I focused my attention on the two men. Wary now, their eyes reflected a measure of calculation that required my immediate attention. I didn't know them or what they might do. Better to take precautions early on.

'Get on the floor.'

I grabbed the first man by the shoulder and yanked him off the couch. Tall, wiry, and much the younger of the pair, he was most likely to resist. When he did, reaching out to grab my arm, I slammed the Glock into the back of his head and he went down hard.

'Now you,' I told the older man. 'Get on the

floor.'

'We have not done nothing,' he said as he complied. 'We are abiding the laws.'

I searched both men for weapons. They were clean. Then I pulled the cushions off the couch, discovering a manila envelope where the older man had been sitting. The envelope was stuffed with cash.

I wanted to kill them, right there, and I might have done it if Adele hadn't laid a hand on my shoulder. Tynia had come into the room, along with the rest of the women and two children, an infant and a toddler. The toddler's eyes were wide with fear. His hands were balled into fists and his jaw was quivering. Suddenly, he turned away from his mother and flew into Zashka's arms. She stroked his head and kissed him.

'Little Teddy,' she said, speaking without an accent, 'you have to be a brave boy now. You have to help your mother. She needs you.'

'Why can't you come, too?'

Zashka looked up at me, her dark eyes beseeching. I stared at her for a moment, then glanced at Tynia. Tynia nodded once. I couldn't have asked for more.

'Go.'

As Zashka came abreast of me, she stopped momentarily. 'Aslan's on his way over,' she said. 'He's going to kill you if he gets the chance.' Then she followed the other women out the door.

I watched from the window until the bus pulled away, feeling instantly lighter. If an

316

unsuspecting Aslan walked through the door, now that I'd done what I'd come to do, it was odds-on that he wouldn't walk out.

'What were you going to buy with this money? A few slaves?'

I turned to find Adele standing over the older man. Though still prone, he'd turned his head far enough to fix her with a pale blue eye. 'I have not done nothing wrong. You cannot do nothing to me.'

'No?' Adele crossed the room, opened the window, tossed the money out into the rain. The old man groaned, but kept his mouth shut. He was being treated to a dose of curbside justice and there was nothing more to be said.

It was raining hard when Adele and I came out of the building and the streets were deserted. There were bills plastered to the roofs and windshields of the cars parked on the block, more bills on the sidewalk. I had a crazy urge to pick them up, but then Adele tapped me on the shoulder and I saw the SUV as it turned onto the block and began to accelerate. The vehicle was running with its brights on. Magnified by the wet streets and the falling rain, the glare stretched from curb to curb.

My universe contracted into a single frame encompassing only this street at this moment in time. I reached for the Glock tucked behind my hip, knowing I didn't have a chance. A bare fifty feet away, the truck was closing fast. We were going to come out second best here. The window was already sliding down. Behind the glare of the headlights, Aslan's face and the gun he held leaped into focus. The pounding rain effectively drowned out the blasts when Aslan opened up, reducing the gunshots to barely audible thuds. But I saw the gunfire, a trio of muzzle flashes so distinct they might have been separated by light-years. And I saw Adele drop to the pavement and the truck's brake lights come on as the SUV flew past me, then skidded to a halt thirty yards away.

As I raised my weapon, I fought a surge of adrenaline. I wanted to help Adele. I wanted to kill Aslan. I wanted to fly to the fucking moon.

The truck's door opened, a foot dropped to the asphalt, a shoulder emerged. I was aiming for the head that followed when I pulled the trigger, but the round missed by a few inches, slamming through the truck's side mirror. That was enough for Aslan. He jumped back inside and shot off toward the far corner.

I waited until the truck was out of sight before turning to Adele. She was lying on the pavement, clutching her abdomen, her breath coming in short quick gasps. I dropped to one knee beside her, remembering her Kevlar vest only when I actually touched it. The hollow-point bullet was right there, caught in the fabric and severely deformed. I pulled it out as though withdrawing a tumor.

Cradling the bullet in the palm of my hand, I offered it to Adele. I wanted to say something, but couldn't seem to get the words past the constriction in my throat. Adele stared at the flattened chunk of lead, her face reddening as she fought for breath. Then her lungs suddenly emptied, the whoosh of air loud enough to be heard above the steady slap of rain on the sidewalk. Slowly, her breathing became more regular and she stopped gasping.

'I'm okay,' she said. 'I had the wind knocked out of me. That's all.'

'Can you walk?' I asked. 'If you can't, I'll carry you. But we really need to get out of here.'

She started to rise, then slid back onto her butt, finally made it on the second try with a little help. I took her arm and we started down the street. We were soaked to the bone long before we reached the car, but Adele was moving freely by then. I slid behind the wheel, started the Nissan and turned on the heat.

'I'm not shivering because I'm cold,' Adele explained. 'I'm shaking because I was frightened.'

I glanced at my left leg. It was going up and down like a piston. Alongside me, Adele removed her vest. She patted her stomach gingerly.

'How do you feel?' I asked.

'A little bruised. That's about it. Let's just do what we have to do.'

What we had to do was drive into upper Manhattan, to a school on Amsterdam

Avenue that'd been converted to a shelter for battered women. On an upper floor, in what had once been a gym, we found the women of Domestic Solutions. The setting was grim – floors, walls, cots, a pair of cribs – but the women seemed in fine spirits as they unpacked their few possessions and discussed the sleeping arrangements. Zashka was with them and she appeared comfortable.

'Zashka?' I said.

She turned to look at me, wary now. 'Yes?'

I crooked a finger. 'We need to talk.'

I led a resigned Zashka to a small office on the first floor. Adele remained behind. She was going to speak to the women, just in case they knew anything about Barsakov or Mynka. It was a long shot, but we were covering all the bases.

'Sit down, Zashka.'

I pointed to a chair on the far side of a desk, waited for her to sit, then sat down myself. Though my fingers were still trembling, I made an effort to appear casual. I crossed my legs at the knee, dropped my hands to my lap, let my shoulders fall back.

Zashka held up a pack of cigarettes. 'You mind?'

'Knock yourself out.'

She closed her eyes when she inhaled, opened them when she blew the smoke out through her nose. 'I got in trouble,' she said, 'with a Russian shylock out in Brighton Beach. I was working it off.'

'With Aslan?'

'Aslan needed somebody to stay twenty-four-seven with the kids and mind the ladies when they were at home. It wasn't like he could advertise in the papers. The shy was a friend of his and they made a deal. Aslan got me for a year, me and my debt.'

She paused then, her chin coming up, mouth tightening. I waited patiently, certain she had something else to say. Finally, she cleared her throat and smiled.

'I was good to them. To the kids. I didn't think I would be, not havin' kids myself, but they got to me right away. Their mothers were gone all the time. If I didn't love them, nobody would. I know what's that's about, detective. I know what it is to be little and have no one to love you.'

'Okay,' I said, 'but what about their mothers? What about Tynia? How could she leave her child in the care of stranger, even a nice stranger, for six days a week?'

Zashka thought it over, then looked at me, looked straight into my eyes. 'Two reasons. First, poor women all over the world leave their children, sometimes for years, in order to provide for them. Second, Aslan Khalid is a frightening man. You fuck with him, he will definitely kill you. One time, when the girls staged a little revolt, he threatened to blow up the warehouse with everyone in it. Myself, after listening to all his bullshit about Chechnya, I believed him.'

The window behind Zashka was covered by a white shade. Someone had painted a pic-

321

ture in crayons on its smooth surface, a bunny rabbit hopping through a field of crudely drawn flowers. I stared at it for a minute, then got to the point.

'I think you were in the house when Mynka was butchered. I think maybe you even know what happened to her organs, though I can't prove it. But what I can prove, through independent witnesses, is that you were present when Konstantine Barsakov was murdered. So there's no room for bullshit here. You know what happened that night. The only issue is whether or not you want to tell me.'

Zashka took another pull on her cigarette. In her forties, she was fairly attractive once you got past the red hair. Her cheekbones were high, her features small and regular.

'God, I hate that prick,' she said.

'Aslan?'

'Yeah, Aslan.' She nibbled at her lower lip for a minute. 'What's the threat? There has to be a threat.'

'If you don't cooperate?'

'If I don't cooperate now. If I cooperate somewhere down the line, say after I get a lawyer.'

'I need a statement tonight. If you don't give it to me, I'll charge you with extortion.'

'Extortion?'

'Any time you compel an individual to refrain from any lawful behavior, you commit the crime of extortion, a D felony. You'll be charged with five counts and there'll be a strong recommendation that you be held without bail.' I ticked the items off on my fingers. 'You're a material witness in a homicide, you're an extreme flight risk, you'll almost certainly face charges in a federal court that could land you in prison for decades.'

Zashka looked at me for a minute, then laughed. 'Know something? You're a prick, too.'

I shrugged. I'd kept my tone matter-of-fact and Zashka seemed relaxed. 'Zashka, you're entirely too negative. Remember, you can cooperate now and lawyer-up later. There's no law against it.'

'Fine. And if I do cooperate? What then?'

'If the written statement you give me is complete and truthful, you retain your liberty. That's assuming you convince me that I'll be able to find you again when I need you.'

Zashka thought it over, her mouth working as she weighed her options. 'I have an aunt in the Bronx, in Kingsbridge. She'll take me in.'

'And after she does,' I encouraged, 'you'll contact a lawyer and cut a deal.' I spread my hands apart, palms up. What could be simpler? 'Keep in mind, anything you tell me is useless without your testimony at trial. So, you can always back out if you don't like the offer.'

In fact, once she committed herself in writing, the pressure from the *DA*, should Aslan be arrested, would only grow more intense. Zashka most likely knew that. But the fib I'd told was a social fib, the kind you might tell at a cocktail party. Oh, I just love that tie.

'First thing,' she said, 'me and Aslan, we weren't partners. I only worked for the guy.'

'And now you work for me.'

About Mynka's fate, Zashka knew little. On the night before Mynka's body was discovered, she'd been roused from sleep by Aslan and Konstantine when they entered the warehouse around midnight. This was unusual since they didn't live there, but it was none of her business. On the following morning, she was again awakened, this time by a loud argument. Aslan was clearly in a rage, Barsakov more defensive, but as they spoke Russian, she had no idea what they were fighting about. She had her suspicions, of course, because Mynka hadn't returned from the Portolas on Saturday morning, but she wasn't about to face off with Aslan. When he told her that Mynka had run away, she'd accepted the explanation and gone about her business.

I broke it off at that point, instructing Zashka to write everything down, then went upstairs to check on Adele. I found her sitting on a straight-backed chair next to Sister Kassia. They were leaning toward each other, engaged in a conversation that ended abruptly when I stepped into the room.

'How are you feeling?' I asked.

Adele probed her abdomen with the tips of her fingers. 'A little sore. No big deal. You almost finished?'

'Not even halfway. You wanna take the car,

go back to the apartment, feel free. I can find a gypsy cab later on.'

'No, I'll wait. Sister Kassia and I are having a very interesting talk.'

'Can I ask what about?'

'About husbands and lovers.'

I smiled. 'Well, let me know what you decide. Right now, I'm kinda focused on Konstantine Barsakov.'

As expected, Zashka was eager to distance herself from Barsakov's fate. She'd been upstairs, she explained, when Barsakov entered the warehouse after his release. Aslan was upstairs as well, packing linen into a cardboard carton.

'Wait here,' he'd told her. 'Don't come down.'

A half hour later, a single shot was fired. Then Aslan came pounding up the stairs. He loaded her and the children into the van and they drove away. She never saw Barsakov again.

I was far from satisfied with a speech Zashka had obviously been composing for some time. I took her over the details. What was she doing when Barsakov arrived? Packing? What was she packing? Where were the children? What were they doing? How did they react to the move? To the shot? To Aslan's appearance? Was Aslan composed? Agitated? Was there blood on his skin or his clothing? Do you know where Aslan is currently staying?

The last question, which came from left field, was a test of truth. I knew where Aslan was living. If Zashka lied, if she was still protecting him, I'd arrest her on the spot.

'In Williamsburg,' she said after a moment. 'On North Third Street above a lingerie shop.'

I left with a hand-written statement ten pages long, each page signed and witnessed. That was enough to buy redemption. All I had to do was hand the statement and Aslan's address to Bill Sarney. What happened next – whether or not Aslan agreed to deportation – was none of my business. Just pass on the information and become the bosses' fair-haired boy.

But I didn't call Sarney. I put Zashka's statement in a manila envelope, then shoved it in a file when I got home. Aslan was for the future. For now, there was only Ronald Portola, a man who wore thousand-dollar blazers and paid to have men abuse him sexually. Earlier, I'd guessed that Ronald was the sort of guy who'd appreciate a bit of theater. When I explained this to Adele, then asked her if she was up to putting on a show, she replied with a grin. We were inside by then. Adele was holding an ice pack to a small bruise just above her navel.

'What's my role?' she asked.

'Bad cop.'

'Do I get to slap him around?'

'Sparingly. Remember, this guy likes a beating now and then. You hurt him bad, he's liable to get a hard-on.'

'And that would be counter-productive?'

'Let's just say, Ronald being attracted to men, not women, it would put me in a ticklish position. Being as my goal is to make him happy.'

THIRTY-ONE

On the way home that night, at her request, I took Adele to Beth-Israel Hospital's emergency room, only a few blocks from my apartment. Just in case, was how she put it. I was relieved, although Adele claimed not to be in any real pain. I knew that a bullet stopped by a vest transmits energy forward into the body. Internal injuries are fairly common and deaths are not unheard of, especially when a round impacts the left side of the chest.

That hadn't happened to Adele. Plus, she'd been well prepared. Not only was her Grade *III*-A body armor much heavier than that generally worn by cops, it was specifically designed to minimize post-impact trauma. In addition, when I examined Adele's vest, I found a gouge running across the fabric. The bullet had struck at an angle and some of the force had dissipated as it slowed down.

We used our badges to get immediate treatment, but kept the cause of Adele's injury to ourselves. A fall on stairs, a collision with the point of a cast-iron handrail, we just wanna be sure she's okay.

A few minutes later, Adele was sitting on a narrow bed separated from a line of other narrow beds by a set of flimsy curtains. I was standing beside her when the doctor came in, a tall blond who seemed on the point of collapse. She listened to Adele's story, then asked me to step outside while she conducted an examination. The wait was short, as was the message. Adele would go to Radiology for a few tests. It would be better if I returned to the waiting area.

'Don't worry,' she assured. 'I haven't found any injury beyond the contusion. But let's err on the side of caution.'

Then she was gone, leaving me with no choice except to comply. I'd been out-copped.

It was three o'clock on Sunday morning and the waiting room was fairly crowded. There was the usual collection of the wounded and the overdosed, along with a half-dozen women of varying ages, all accompanied by children. A wheelchair backed against the rear wall was occupied by a man so ancient he might have been a mummy. The old man sighed from time to time, though he never moved. Nor did his aide, who was asleep in the wheelchair next to him.

Adele came out an hour later. 'All clear,' she told me. 'I'm just gonna have to suck it up and stop whining.'

This was news I was glad to hear. It was four o'clock in the morning. We were both dead tired and we weren't going to get more than a few hours sleep. Still, I'd come up with an idea while I sat in the waiting room, a way to establish rapport when I interviewed Ronald on the following day. I wanted to know whether I could bring it off before I turned out the lights. I took Adele's vest from where it hung on the back of a chair and slid it over my head. The vest was too small for me, which was why Adele had worn it, but I managed to fasten the Velcro straps. Though the fit was tight, I could breathe well enough.

As it turned out, we slept for five hours, until nine, then bolted down a hasty breakfast and got out the door. We were eager, the both of us. Personally, I had no thoughts of failure. Adele and I were going to play with Ronald Portola's psyche. We were going to twist his mind until the truth popped out. We could not be defeated. It was all familiar stuff, remembered from my high school days when I'd competed on the swimming team. My coach, Conrad Stehle, was big on positive thinking. And I have to say, I won a lot more races than I lost. But I wasn't good enough to win the big ones, the statewide competitions. Positive attitude or not.

David Portola emerged from the townhouse a little before noon, his trusty skateboard tucked beneath his arm. Adele and I were parked at a fire hydrant a mere fifty feet to the south, but David looked neither right nor left as he crossed the street, dropped the skateboard to the ground and vanished into the park.

Margaret Portola came out to hail a cab an hour later. As before, despite the designer frock, the gold jewelry and the strawberry-sized diamond on her left hand, the pitted cheeks and narrowed eyes gave her away. She was not the princess, or even the dowager queen. No, at best she was an ill-tempered wannabe.

Screened from outsiders by the misted windows, Adele was sitting beside me in the Nissan, on the passenger side. The humidity, if anything, was even worse than on the prior night, and it was again threatening to rain. Across the street, in the park, the leaves on a little stand of young maples all pointed downward, as if only awaiting the first touch of autumn to give up the ghost.

At three thirty, David Portola made his way back home. His mother followed a half hour later. Then all was quiet as the sun, an indefinite presence behind a ceiling of gray cloud, moved to the Jersey side of the Hudson River. Adele kept shifting in her seat. She'd made a quick foray in search of a restroom several hours before and now it was time to repeat the experience. The plan called for us to maintain the stakeout well into the night. From our point of view, the later Ronald came out, the better. As long as he did, eventually, come out.

The suspense ended abruptly when Ronald emerged, along with his mother, at five thirty. This was the worst possible news and I muttered a curse which Adele echoed. But then Margaret stepped into a cab and Ronald closed the door behind her, hesitating for just a second as the cab pulled away before walking in our direction. Adele waited until he was almost alongside the Nissan before she got out and flashed her tin.

'Hi, Ronny,' she said. 'My name is Bentibi. I'm an investigator with the District Attorney's office and I want to talk to you.'

I came up on his blind side, but didn't display my shield. I was wearing Adele's vest and the letters stenciled across my chest, *NYPD*, made my identity clear enough.

'Detective Corbin,' I said before repeating the essential message. 'We need to talk to you.'

As I drew Ronald's attention, Adele wrapped her hand around his right arm, her fingertips coming to rest in the hollow space between the bicep and the elbow. From this position she could execute, with a simple squeeze, what the bosses at the Puzzle Palace call a pain-compliance technique.

'What about?'

'What do you think?' Adele asked.

Up close, Ronald Portola seemed incredibly soft. But he was not only unafraid, he seemed oddly comfortable. He stared directly into my eyes, and I stared back. Patience was, after all, my game.

Finally, Ronald turned to Adele. 'I suppose I'm expected to ask for a lawyer,' he finally said.

'Why, did you commit some crime? Have you been messin' with that rough trade again?'

Ronald made a small move, as if to leave, and Adele clamped down, squeezing hard enough to draw a little grunt of pain.

'You're disappointing me, Ronald,' I said, stepping in. 'Where's your spirit of adventure? Your basic curiosity? I figured you for a player, a man eager to walk that fine line between pleasure and pain. Was I mistaken?'

Ronald's only prominent feature was the long, straight nose he'd clearly inherited from his father. He gave the tip of that nose a series of quick strokes, as if searching for a pimple. 'I just know there's more to this story,' he said.

'How about you and me all alone in an interrogation room? There probably won't be anybody else around, not on a Sunday night. That means nobody to overhear our conversation, nobody to misinterpret the direction it might take.' I put my arm around his shoulders and led him toward the car. He went more or less willingly, ducking his head as he slid onto the back seat. 'I promise, Ronald, I'll show you a good time. I promise.'

I walked around the car to get in on the other side. When I closed the door, I found Adele and Ronald locked eyeball to eyeball. Adele wore a half smile poised mid way between amused and sneering, her eyes so laid back she might have been looking at a freshly killed insect pinned to a specimen board.

'Tell me,' Adele asked, 'because I'm dyin' to know. How old were you when your mother started callin' you "La Bamba"?'

Ronald's eyes jerked open. He'd been blindsided, not only by Adele knowing his pet name, but also because she was a woman. In his world, a woman had always held the whip.

'Ya know,' Adele continued, 'I just don't get it. If you'd knock her on her ass, just once, she'd respect you. Just once, La Bamba. Just one fucking time. Then you'd be a man.'

'I want a lawyer.' Ronald's head began to rotate in my direction, only to stop abruptly when Adele corrected him.

'Don't you dare turn away from me when I'm talking to you.' She reached over the back seat to grab him by the chin, forcing his head back until their eyes were again locked. 'First, you're not a suspect, so you don't get a lawyer. Second, you're not goin' anywhere until we're finished with you. Do we understand each other?'

Ronald jerked his chin out of Adele's grip, but didn't look away. I could almost see the little gears turning in his mind as Adele regained both her contemptuous smile and her equally contemptuous tone.

'See, here's what I don't get. My father liked to slap me and my brothers around when he was in a bad mood, which was mostly all the time. And I'm tellin' ya, Ronnie, when you got beat up by my dad, you really got beat up. Now, when I was kid, what could I do? I hadda take it. But the day I graduated high school, I left his house. You hearin' this? I didn't have ten dollars in my purse, but I packed my things and left. Now here you are – twenty-four years old with a freakin' trust fund – and you're still livin' with a crazy bitch who calls you La Bamba. How is that possible?'

'Are you suggesting that I'm a faggot?'

'Please, don't hide behind that one. Gay has nothing to do with your spineless attitude, not a fucking thing.'

Suddenly, Ronald's face lit up. 'Of course,' he said, 'you've gotten your hands on Toad.'

'Toad?'

'Toad. That's the name we have for the little creatures who hippity-hop through the house doing all those nasty chores the rich don't have to do.'

'So, you're referring to Tynia Cernek?'

'I'm referring to them all. They were all Toad.'

'Does that include Mynka Chechowski?'

'Toad, I'm afraid. Toad, Toad, Toad.'

Adele leaned over the seat and backhanded Ronald across the face, a really nice shot that spun his head around. I waited a few seconds, then kicked the back of Adele's seat.

'That's enough. Start driving.'

Adele complied meekly, which brought a smile to Ronald's fleshy mouth, a smile that revealed several blood-stained teeth. I gave him a little poke.

'Hey,' I said, 'didn't I promise to show you a good time?'

The squad room at the Nine-Two was deserted when I led Ronald though the maze of corridors that fronted the little cubbyholes we called home. As I'd worked on Sundays in the past, I knew that only one pair of detectives was on duty. Who they were and what they were doing, I couldn't say. I was just glad they weren't at their desks, counting the minutes until they clocked out. Their presence wouldn't have changed the outcome, but it would have ruined the atmosphere.

'In here, Ronnie.' I opened the door to a small interrogation room, waited for him to enter, then followed, closing the door behind me.

About the size of a prison cell, the eight-by-ten room was everything Ronald could have wished for. Cracked floor tiles, tan walls, a recessed fluorescent fixture, a small table, three plastic chairs. There was even a sprinkling of dark stains on the wall. The stains resembled blood spatter, but were actually marinara sauce from a carelessly handled meatball hero.

Ronnie took the chair behind the table without prompting. He slumped down in the seat of his chair and crossed his legs. One arm dangled in his lap, the other played with his skimpy beard. I followed him around the table and dropped to one knee slightly behind him. Across the room, a one-way mirror reflected our images. Adele was on the other side of the mirror, watching carefully. Her role in the performance was not yet over.

335

I stared at Ronald for a long moment, allowing a half smile to play across my face. Despite the air of indifference, Ronald's eyes, when I found them, were jittery. And why not? Adele had spoken Mynka Chechowski's name aloud, so there was no doubting our ultimate purpose. A murder had been committed, Ronald knew the identity of the killer, we were here to make an arrest. For Ronald Portola, those were the only certainties. He couldn't know, for instance, despite our assurances, that he was not the prime suspect, that ten minutes from now I wouldn't put him on a bus headed for Rikers Island.

THIRTY-TWO

'Didn't work, right?' I began.

'What?'

'The bit with my associate. She was supposed to soften you up.'

'No, it didn't work. But she was very good.'

'Wasn't she?'

'She was.' In lieu of applause, he raised a languid finger to his swollen lower lip.

'That's why I like usin' her. She's such a piece of work. Still, she was in over her head, which was what I told her in the first place. I said, "This kid's been smacked around by a woman who makes you look like Mother

Theresa. You won't lay a glove on him." '

'Then why did you go through with it?'

'Hey, nothing ventured, nothing gained. Besides, I knew you'd appreciate the gesture.'

I stood at that point, then picked up the nearly weightless plastic table and carried it to the wall. As I set it down, I suddenly grabbed my left side and dropped to one knee, my eyes squeezing shut as I gasped in pain.

Adele opened the door and looked inside, but I shook my head and waved her away.

'I'm alright.'

'You sure?'

'Yeah.' I waited for her to leave, then struggled to my feet and offered Ronald an apologetic smile. 'Ya gotta cut me some slack, Ronnie. I got shot yesterday.'

'Shot?'

'By Aslan Khalid. You wanna check it out?'

Ronald's quizzical smile expanded at the mention of Aslan's name. 'Yes,' he said, 'I would.'

I took off the vest and laid it in his lap. 'See here? This gouge? That's where the bullet hit me' I pointed to a tear in the vest where the fabric was blackened. 'The doctors tell me that if I hadn't been wearing my vest, I wouldn't be talking to you now. You or anybody else.'

Very slowly, very softly, Ronald slid the fingertips of his right hand over the hole in the vest, tracing its edges first, then easing his pinky into the opening. Prurient is the first word that came to my mind as I watched.

Perverted was the next. Ronald Portola was a sick puppy and he didn't care who knew it.

Clutching my side, I re-positioned myself behind him, then waited patiently until he dropped the vest to the floor.

'Can we talk about Mynka?' I whispered in his ear.

'Toad?'

'Think twice, Ronnie. That mirror over there, it's a window for anybody standing on the other side. Getting your face slapped once might be a thrill, but I guarantee it's an activity that wears thin pretty fast.'

Ronnie put his hand on his heart. He was staring at the mirror now, clearly fascinated. 'My sincere apologies,' he said, 'but I'm afraid I didn't keep track of their given names. Which one was Mynka?'

'Mynka was the one who got murdered in your kitchen.'

I put my right hand on his shoulder, my fingers reaching around just far enough to sense, very faintly, the pulse at his throat. Ronald's heart was racing.

'I was just wondering if you'd like to hear a story, Ronald, a kind of travelogue that begins with Mynka Chechowski's body, then follows a trail to Margaret Portola and her children. It's a very entertaining story.'

'Certainly.' He sounded relieved, almost grateful. I'd turned up the pressure, then eased back. Maybe everything would be all right. I began with the forensic details, the pink lividity, the foreign dentistry, and especially the evisceration. Then I told him about the witness who'd happened on the scene a moment before Mynka's body was to be consigned to the sea, and about the advertisement in *Gazeta Warszawa* that broke the case open, and about my consultation with Aslan Khalid in the Eagle Street warehouse. Finally, I described Barsakov in the chair behind Aslan's desk with half his head blown away and the flag of Chechnya pinned to the wall behind him.

'Swear to God, Ronnie, when I looked into the wolf's eyes, it was like he did it. I'm talkin' about the wolf. It was like the wolf came down off the flag and drilled his fangs into Konstantine's skull.'

Ronald and I were both staring at the mirror on the other side of the room when I finished the tale. I was watching him, watching him closely, but Ronald was gazing directly into his own eyes.

'It's your turn, now,' I finally said, my voice a whisper, 'to tell me a story.'

'About what?'

'Start with the cold room. Tell me what it was like.'

Ronald tilted his chin up, his eyes shifting slightly to meet mine. Did he want to play this game?

'Did you ever tell anyone, Ronnie, anyone at all? A friend, a teacher, a therapist?'

'I had no friends as a child. I hated my tutors. Margaret would never allow me to see a therapist.'

'Then it was a family secret.'

'Yes, a secret.'

'Well, I've been there, Ronnie, in the cold room. I already know.'

'The trick is to make yourself little. I used to imagine that I was a ball of cheese, all folded on itself, with a thick, waxy skin for a blanket.' Ronald's tongue appeared between his lips and he sucked in a deep breath as his shoulders relaxed. 'But the cold room was only for special occasions. Usually, Margaret was more hands-on. Besides, you can get used to anything if you have to.'

'Don't bullshit a bullshitter, Ronnie. I was in the cold room with the door closed for five minutes and I nearly panicked.'

'Panic? Yes, of course, at first. But panic only excited Margaret. Begging, too. No, you had to make yourself infinitely small, so tiny there was no self for the cold to penetrate. Jerk never understood that.'

'Jerk?'

'My brother.'

'Can you say his name?'

'Jerk.'

'And what didn't he understand?'

Ronald's hands began to wash over each other. He was breathing through his mouth now. 'Do you know why the cold room is there in the first place? Were you clever enough to find out?'

'Actually, that was one of the things I was going to ask you.' I was encouraged by Ronald's attitude. He was now volunteering information. 'Why have a refrigerator that big in a private home?'

'The cold room is there because in the nineteen twenties, the house was a speakeasy, with an upstairs brothel, owned by Dutch Schultz. In nineteen twenty-eight, two gangsters were killed in the cellar, Blintzy Reznick and Little Moe Cohen. Margaret has newspaper clippings documenting the whole episode. According to the *Herald Tribune*, Little Moe and Blintzy were refrigerated for three days after the actual murders. I think that's where Margaret got the idea. Otherwise, who would even think about putting a child in a...'

'In a refrigerator?'

Ronald's laugh was soft and dry. 'Jerk was a fighter,' he added, 'and what did it get him? I was a ball of cheese, and look at me now.'

'What about your father. Why didn't he protect you?'

Once he got started, Ronald couldn't stop, and bit by bit, I assembled a portrait of the Portola household. The only child of a prominent, Brazilian family, Guillermo Portola had used up three wives, along with innumerable mistresses, in an effort to produce an heir. His marriage to the secretary he'd occasionally boffed was motivated solely by the need to legitimize that heir. According to Ronald, aside from impregnating Margaret a second time, Guillermo had very little to do with his wife and children. His life was lived in a suite at the Pierre Hotel, where he passed his nights with the high-end call girls he preferred to his psycho spouse. Nevertheless, Guillermo supported his family in style, which left Margaret to do as she pleased, the absolute master of the house.

And what a master she was, given both to sudden rages and calculated cruelty. Her children were initially cared for by nannies, then privately tutored through high school. Subject to Margaret's temper, the nannies and tutors came and went, leaving in their wake a montage of faces and names that Ronald chose not to remember. As they, the nannies and the tutors, chose not to remember, or even recognize, the obvious bruises on the frail bodies of the children.

'What about friends?' I asked.

'I went to birthday parties sometimes, and sometime a luckless child would be sentenced to pass an afternoon in my company. Needless to say, they rarely came back. I belonged to clubs, too. A chess club on the East Side and a gem club at the Metropolitan Museum. I have friends now, a collection of oddities who share my interests, but my early years were passed in solitude.'

Ronald paused, gave his head a tiny shake, then abruptly changed the subject. 'For Margaret,' he said, partitioning the syllables of his mother's name as if sounding out a word in a foreign language, 'Father's stroke was a stroke of luck.'

I wasn't expecting much to come from the revelations that followed, though I listened attentively for any mention of the circumstances surrounding Guillermo's death. But Ronald wasn't going there. This was all about a will Guillermo had somehow created, despite being completely disabled, a man whose speech was limited to a series of unintelligible gurgles. That the will would eventually be challenged was inevitable; that Margaret would be up to the challenge was also inevitable. At the first hint of a lawsuit, she'd produced an impeccably credentialed attorney named Mason Livingston. A direct descendant of the Livingstons so prominent during the revolution, Mason swore, under oath, that he'd read the document aloud to Guillermo, clause by clause, and that Guillermo had indicated consent with a series of nods confirmed by eye-blinks. Three other witnesses, attorneys all, then leaped forward to confirm Mason's account. The will was unbreakable.

'And now she runs your life,' I said. It was time to make the turn.

'And now she runs my life.'

I leaned even closer, until my chest brushed Ronald's back. 'Remember what my partner said, about you being afraid to stand up to Margaret? I know it isn't true. I know you stopped being afraid of your mother years ago. Like I know you would have left home years ago ... except for the money. I'm talking about the forty million dollars, and the will, and the trust fund. Margaret knew exactly what she was doing when she made herself

343

executor of a fund that ties you up until you reach the age of forty.'

'How can a person,' Ronald asked, 'be so crazy and so crafty at the same time? Margaret's fucking Mason Livingston, who administers the trust. If I displease her, Mason will invoke the will's morality clause. I've got a record, which I'm sure you already know, a record that brands me a cocksucker and a pervert. My claim to any part of my father's estate hangs by a thread.'

'And Margaret's standing right there with a pair of scissors?'

'Exactly.'

'Well, it seems pretty obvious to me that you have to take those scissors out of her hand.'

I stared for a moment at the sheen of perspiration on the back of Ronald's neck, at tiny drops of moisture no bigger than grains of sand that clung to the black hairs fanning out from a natural parting. 'What would you do, Ronald, if you got control of the estate? How would you live your life?'

Ronald answered without hesitation. 'My favorite word is debauchery, followed closely by depravity. I want to drown myself in sensation. I want to use every drug there is to use. I want to have sex on three-masted yachts, and in filthy alleyways. I want to keep going until I'm dead.'

I rose to my feet at that point and gripped my side. No more whispering. Time for business. 'I can't kneel anymore,' I told him. 'My

344

wound is killing me.' I set a chair in front of him and sat down. 'Now, the sex part you can keep to yourself, but tell me, is heroin your drug of choice?'

'It's that obvious?' he asked.

'I'm afraid it is, Ronnie, but we can forget about that. For now, anyway.' I leaned back in the chair. 'Ya know, there's a way out for you. A way to make all those fantasies come true.'

'Tell me.'

'Mynka Chechowski died in your mother's kitchen. The cause of death was a blow to the top of her skull with a blunt object, a blow universally associated with an enraged perpetrator. That perpetrator can't be you, Ronald, because blind rages are beyond you. And it can't be your brother, either, because he was the father of Mynka's child and he loved her. That leaves Margaret holding the bag, and her elder son to put her in it.'

Ronald rocked back and forth, his eyes still closed. He was breathing through his nose again. 'Dreams are the best things about dope,' he told me. 'Evil dreams that fly around your mind like cobwebs in a breeze. I believe I've dispatched Margaret in every way there is to dispatch a human being. In my dreams, I've skinned her alive.'

He bent forward to look into my eyes. 'You've taken the time to know me. That's an act of respect and I'm thankful. But I can't give you what you want, as much as I'd like to. That's because you've misread the tea leaves. Margaret didn't kill Toad. Jerk killed

Toad. Margaret wasn't even there.'

I jumped to my feet, grabbed Ronald's shirt and ripped him out of the chair. I wasn't faking anything this time. Ronald had given the wrong answer and I didn't care whether it was a true answer or not. For those few seconds, until Adele opened the door and I saw the look of utter distress twisting her features, I was out of control. Still shaking, I dropped Ronald into his chair and waved Adele off.

Unlike my partner, Ronald seemed more bemused than afraid. He waited until Adele closed the door behind her, then began to speak.

'Ridding myself of Margaret? Well, the gods are having too much fun to let me off that particular hook. But when you're talking about tens of millions of dollars, losing a brother is no small thing. For a time, right after Jerk killed Toad, I thought Jerk would commit suicide. But he rallied.'

I re-positioned my chair in front of Ronald's and sat down. Ronald nodded, then simply continued. He was off and running now. He wouldn't stop until the tank was empty. This was a phenomenon I'd witnessed many times in the past, but I still couldn't shake the feeling that he'd been playing me all along.

'Margaret approved of Jerk's relationship with Toad—'

'Use their real names, Ronald. That would be David and Mynka, in case you've forgotten.'

346

'David and Mynka? It could be the title of a romance novel. The second son of a fabulously wealthy South American aristocrat falls for the Polish maid his mother loves to abuse. Miraculously, the Polish maid responds to the second son's overtures with a previously unrevealed passion. Desire wells, of course, and juices flow, until they can stand it no longer. Until the second son creeps up to the little maid's attic room and is not rebuffed.

'Mother eventually finds out, but, amazingly, she doesn't object. In fact, she tells her older son, whom she knows to be a practicing homosexual, "Why can't you be more like your brother?" '

Ronald stopped there, his eyes moving down and to the left as he retrieved a memory. I watched his tongue wash across his lips and his eyes harden, but his voice was almost without inflection when he resumed speaking.

'The maid is impregnated by the second son a few months later, even though his mother supplies him with boxes of condoms, condoms in a wide variety of colors, textures and flavors. Predictably, the mother becomes enraged when the second son reveals his love's delicate condition. Predictably, she berates her hapless son. Fade to black. Ho-hum.

'Enter a new actor, a catalyst, a man to stir the pot, to ratchet up the tension. He is Aslan Khalid, the entrepreneur who supplied the little maid to the Portola family. Initially, Aslan is as outraged as Margaret, insisting that his property has been damaged and compensation is in order. But then, in the course of a single hour, he abruptly switches tactics. Maybe, he tells Margaret, the little maid should be allowed to give birth. The resulting child would carry David Portola's *DNA* and be entitled, not only to his support, but to his lifestyle.

'Much discussion naturally follows, a period of bargaining, of hard, hard bargaining, until both parties agree that abortion, followed by a liberal outflow of capital from the mother to the entrepreneur, is the only rational solution to their mutual problem.

'From that day forward, the pressures on Mynka, when she flatly refuses to consider an abortion, are unrelenting. Her religious objections – so sorry, God wouldn't approve – are instantly dismissed. She's beaten and threats are made against her life. Not only by the procurer, but by the mother as well.

'It's as hard for David. He's still a child, barely seventeen and home-schooled. Except for Riverside Park and the few clubs Margaret let him join, he knows nothing of the outside world.

'Margaret assaults him by the hour, a two-pronged attack designed to sap his will. The first attack is entirely personal. She tells him the little maid is less than nothing, a toy to be discarded once the novelty wears off. He loves her only because he, too, is less than nothing, an utter failure whose manhood is a lost cause.

' "Why can't you put it together, Jerk?" she demands to know. "That buck-toothed whore doesn't love you. How could she when you are what you are? No, that bitch smelled money all the way from Poland. Just find a rich asshole, a punk kid who's never seen a woman naked, and get him hot enough to screw you without a rubber. Face it, Jerk, you don't even know if the kid's yours."

'At the same time, she offers him a way out, a solution. If she wishes, she explains, she can have Mynka shipped to a country where doctors perform abortions without asking too many questions. With Aslan, it's only a matter of money. And, of course, once shipped out, Mynka will never return.

' "Do you understand what I'm telling you, David? You'll never see her again. It'll be the same as if she died.

' "But that doesn't have to happen. Things can go back to the way they were. You can screw the little Polack from morning to night. In fact, you can even pretend that you'll live happily ever after. All Mynka has to do is refrain from giving birth to a child bearing Portola genes, a child the family will be supporting for the next twenty fucking years."

'The saddest part is that David and Mynka can never return to "the way it was," to those first hot days when their bodies and emotions were perfectly synchronized. David probably knows this, but knowing and accepting are two different things. And David is so young, so isolated. He wants to believe the past can

349

be restored and who can blame him? Besides, the child in Mynka's womb isn't the issue. The fetus will be dealt with, one way or the other, of that he's certain. The issue is whether David and Mynka will be forever parted.

'Eventually, though he claims to love her still, David joins the merry chorus: abort, abort, abort. Do it, let it be over, let equilibrium be restored. He begins to wonder if Margaret isn't right, if he isn't being played for a fool. Surely, if Mynka loved him, she'd do this little thing rather than be parted from him forever.

'Love, hope, resentment, suspicion, rage. David has always been volatile and now these emotions rocket through his brain almost from moment to moment, seizing him by turn. When he's alone with his beloved, his heart melts. When Margaret is present, his blood boils. At all times, he's afraid. He's afraid that he'll be left all alone, that he'll again become a trapped and helpless child.

'That particular Friday is one of the worst. Aslan will come to fetch the little maid on Saturday afternoon and Margaret wants the whole mess over and done with. Twice during the day, she slaps Mynka. Then the dinner is late, the soup tepid, the roast charred, the soufflé too rich, the coffee burnt.

'Finally, toward the very end of the meal, Margaret again becomes violent. David makes a half-hearted attempt to intervene, but finally backs away. Mynka is dragged to the cold room and forced inside. I'm watching, of course – watching is the only thing I'm really good at – and I find myself wondering if David will find the courage to at least open the door. He's too strong for Margaret, even at seventeen. He can stop this if he wants to.

'But then, I'm also strong enough to make my will felt, yet I sit and watch, all the while molding the events into a single, seamless anecdote I intend to share with my friends.

' "I'll let her out when I'm ready," Margaret tells David. "And you, Ronald, you make sure Jerk doesn't open that door. If he does, I'll beat the child out of that bitch myself."

'Jerk is beyond himself. As the seconds tick by, he begins to sob. He has to do something, but he doesn't know what. He paces back and forth, toward the cold room, away from the cold room. He has to let her out. He can't let her out. She has to abort her child. She won't abort her child.

'Ten minutes pass, then twenty. The emergency buzzer rings again and again. Help me, help me, help me.

'When Jerk can stand it no longer, he yanks the door open and Toad comes forth on her hands and knees, shivering uncontrollably. Jerk begs her: "Please, please, please. You have to. You have to."

'I'm sitting at the kitchen table, watching, waiting. I know that Jerk has gone over the edge. I know because I've been to the edge so many times myself. The pressure is tearing

Jerk apart and he has to relieve it. If not, he will explode, literally, into a million pieces. He hops around Toad as if the floor is hot. He groans and pounds his hand into the wall until his knuckles bleed. "You've got to," he keeps repeating. "You've got to."

'Then it's done. A cast-iron pot, an antique, sits against the wall only a few steps from where Toad kneels. Also cast iron, a ladle rests inside the pot. Jerk doesn't hesitate once he's made up his mind. There is no moment of indecision. He grabs the ladle, raises it up, brings it down.

'Toad collapses without a word of reproach. Maybe she knows it's coming, maybe she's known all along. Jerk looks down at her for a moment, at the little river of blood that makes its way toward his feet. Then he drops the ladle, raises his head and howls at the ceiling. He doesn't stop until Margaret comes downstairs, until she steps into the room and says, "Do you have any idea how much this is going to cost us?"'

THIRTY-THREE

Adele walked into the room and directly up to Ronald, ignoring me altogether. 'You have the right to remain silent,' she told him. 'Should you waive that right, anything you say can be used against you in a court of law. You have the right to be represented by an attorney. If you cannot afford an attorney, one will be appointed for you.'

This was the big surprise. Only Ronald didn't look all that shocked. When he turned to me, his lips were pursed, his eyes flat and impenetrable. 'I don't get it,' he said. 'I thought we understood each other.'

'You did a good job, Ronnie,' Adele said. 'You've convinced me that you were in the room when Mynka Chechowski was killed. But the other part, the part about who swung that ladle? How do I know you're not covering up for your mother? How do I know you didn't swing it yourself?'

With no choice, Ronald turned to Adele. 'Margaret wasn't there and I'm just not capable.'

'That's good, La Bamba. That'll work fine. You'll get up on that old witness stand and tell the jury, "I'm so, so sensitive. I couldn't possibly have committed such a horrible crime. Please acquit me." '

Ronald took a moment to consider his situation, then said, 'What if I deny this conversation ever took place?'

'Too late. We've recorded every word.'

'But you didn't read me my rights.'

'You weren't informed of your rights because you weren't a suspect.'

'But I'm a suspect now?'

'Listen to me, La Bamba. We couldn't know you'd incriminate yourself until you actually incriminated yourself. Once you did, you were immediately informed of your right to remain silent. There's no Constitutional issue here.'

Thus far, everything Adele had said, with a single exception, was a lie. There was, indeed, a constitutional issue – more than one, in fact – and we hadn't recorded a single word of the conversation. The exception was the threat of arrest.

After a moment, Ronald nodded twice, then turned to look directly into my eyes. I expected to find him afraid; for a man of Ronald's passive temperament, Rikers Island would make his mother's house seem like paradise. But he wasn't afraid, not at all.

'Am I under arrest?' he asked.

'Technically,' Adele replied.

'Technically?'

'Well, you can't leave, so the situation is obviously custodial. On the other hand, nobody's in a hurry to start the paperwork.'

'So there's still a way out?'

Adele carefully avoided the question. 'Why don't we begin with you telling us what happened after the murder. In great detail.'

I sat back and let Adele finish up. I was already convinced that Ronald's tale was essentially true, that the wrong perpetrator had, indeed, murdered the wrong victim. My little fantasy had been murdered as well. The one that had me plucking Margaret Portola and Aslan Khalid like rotted tomatoes from a vine, that had me tossing them into the compost heap of a maximum-security prison. Given all that had gone before, I made the odds against David Portola surviving in jail at least five to one.

Though it was no consolation whatever, I'd gotten the aftermath right. According to Ronald, Margaret had wasted no time. Within minutes of discovering Mynka's body, she'd shrouded the girl's head and torso with a black garbage bag, then dragged her into the refrigerator for safekeeping. Aslan Khalid showed up late the following morning, appearing cheerful. He huddled briefly with Margaret, viewed the body, then took his leave, returning at ten o'clock that night with Konstantine Barsakov. Without fanfare, they carried Mynka to a waiting van and drove away. Supposedly forever.

The physical clean up began within minutes of the door closing behind Aslan. With David in his bed, virtually unmoving, Ronald was assigned the task of scrubbing the kitchen from top to bottom. Margaret wasn't about to pick up a scrub brush, though she subjected his work to several critical evaluations.

'I hope that doesn't make me a criminal,' Ronald finally said.

'Why would it?' Adele asked.

'Because I'd be obstructing justice.'

'Just like mom?'

This time, Ronald's smile was genuine. 'Well, it did occur to me that covering up a murder can get one into trouble. That's why I want to put this on the record. I cleaned the kitchen because I knew my brother's mental health was in jeopardy. I was afraid that the sight of his lover's blood would finally break him.'

'That was noble of you, La Bamba, but we only have your word for what happened. How do we know you didn't contact Aslan yourself?'

'Margaret's checkbook.' Ronald scratched his chest and yawned. 'Margaret wrote a series of checks after Aslan took the body away. Each was in the amount of $3,000, and each was cashed by Margaret at her bank. I know because I sneaked into her office and looked.'

'How many checks so far?'

'Eight.'

'And you're certain you can put your hands on this checkbook?'

'Of course.'

'How about the murder weapon?'

'The pot and the ladle? In the front parlor

356

next to the fireplace.'

'She kept them?'

'Pre-revolutionary, both pieces. Margaret would never part with anything so valuable, especially after Aslan told her that Toad's body had been successfully disposed of.'

I chose that moment to interrupt. Ronald Portola had made a choice, a choice he could not take back. The state would profit by that choice, no doubt, and Ronald would profit as well. I'd been a cop long enough to shake off most of the grime associated with the moral sewer in which I work, but this outcome was truly revolting. Nevertheless, I stirred the sludge running through that sewer without hesitation.

'Suppose we do this. Suppose we all go back to Riverside Drive and ask Margaret and David for their versions? If their stories agree with yours, David will be arrested.'

'And me?'

'You'll go back to being a witness.' I leaned forward. 'But, look, just to be completely fair, I'm even willing to let you ask the questions. As long as you're willing to have a small recording device taped to your bare skin.'

Ronald hesitated only for an instant before nodding agreement. I nodded back, then said, 'If you need to use the facilities, now would be a good time.'

Ronald Portola's eyes lit up, as I'd hoped they would. I hadn't searched Ronald because he was witness, not a suspect. Now I knew he was carrying dope and that he would

357

use it in the bathroom. There would be no elegance to the act – he would not inject it into a tiny vein below his ankle with a needle small enough to pierce a hair. No, this was about need, about the effort necessary to maintain a facade of indifference when your real future is really on the line. Ronald would stick that heroin up his nose and be glad for it.

When the bathroom door closed behind Ronald, Adele came into my arms for a hug. I held her close, neither of us having to say a word. We both knew that some evils can't be addressed in a court of law. That sometimes what cops do is rough enough to leave scars.

'You think he's using in there?' Adele asked.

'That's why I suggested a trip to the bathroom in the first place. Ronald's ultra-cool stance? He'll need some help if he's going to maintain that stance when he has to face his mother.'

'That's good. You're going to let Ronald confront David.'

'Not David. Margaret. Ronald's finally going to confront his mother.'

'How do you know that?'

'Call it prophecy.'

Ronald took that moment to emerge. The pupils of his eyes were reduced to a pair of black dots, but he was still in control. That, too, was predictable. For all his talk of wretched excess, Ronald Portola was a young man who kept a close watch on his best interests.

Margaret Portola's eyes flew up like yanked window shades when Adele and I followed Ronald into her front parlor. She was sitting on a pale yellow sofa, a sectional that effectively partitioned a corner of the room. David was sitting off to the side, slouched in a leather chair with one leg thrown over the arm. Quicker than his mother, he knew exactly why we were there. His eyes flickered for a moment, then grew resigned as his sullen expression vanished. He'd been waiting a long time for his punishment, trying and convicting himself over and over again. When finally pressed, he'd offer no resistance.

'I've told them everything about Mynka,' Ronald announced as he took a step toward his mother. 'The before, the after, the event itself.'

Margaret's lower jaw bobbed up and down as she struggled to frame a response. In an instant, her world had come crashing down, all her fears realized. Still, she made a stab at gaining control of the situation.

'Get out of my house,' she said to me and Adele, 'before I call my lawyer.'

I ignored the remark as I dropped to one knee beside David's chair, leaving Adele to follow Ronald as he drifted in his mother's general direction. Given Margaret's volatility and Ronald's determination to provoke her, Adele was prepared to intervene if Margaret became violent.

'You're not listening to me,' Ronald continued. 'I told them how Toad became pregnant and how Jerk was the father. I told them about Aslan and the abortion you wanted Toad to get. I told them how you beat Toad and locked her in the cold room.'

By then, Ronald was close enough to capture Margaret's full attention. I watched her closely as she met her son's eyes. Despite her rage, the sadist at her core was still weighing costs and benefits.

'I don't know what lies you told these officers,' she said, 'but you might want to consider that whatever you said amounts to no more than the word of a convicted pervert.'

Still on his game, Ronald didn't hunch his shoulders or curl his hands into fists. I leaned toward David, gave him a little nudge, then whispered in his ear. 'Your brother's playing her like a violin.' When David looked at me, I winked.

'I told them about the checks you wrote,' Ronald continued as if his mother hadn't spoken, 'and how you cashed them to pay Aslan off. I told them about Aslan and Konstantine wrapping Toad's body in plastic and carrying Toad out to the van.'

'Stop calling her Toad.'

Ronald raised a finger to his lips. 'And I told them how you murdered Toad in the kitchen.'

Margaret's jaw dropped and her eyes literally bulged from her skull. She looked at Adele, who had her arms folded across her chest, then at me, then at Ronald's finger as it described a leisurely semi-circle, only coming to rest when it pointed directly at the kettle and ladle resting by the fireplace.

'I told them how you picked up that ladle, raised it high above her head, then brought it down. I told them how upset you were by the blood that spattered on your dress and how you made me scrub the kitchen afterwards. I told them everything.'

Her timing impeccable, Adele stepped forward and took a pair of handcuffs from the pocket of her jacket. 'I'm placing you under arrest,' she said to Margaret, somehow failing to mention exactly what for. 'You have the right to remain silent. If you waive that right, anything you say can be used against you in a court of law. You have the right to an attorney. If you cannot afford an attorney, one will be appointed for you. Now, turn around and place your hands behind your back.'

'I didn't kill anyone,' Margaret said. 'You can't do this to me.'

'Listen carefully, Mrs Portola. I'm an investigator with the office of the Queens District Attorney and I have peace officer status throughout the state of New York. If you don't allow yourself to be handcuffed, I'm authorized to employ all necessary force to make you comply.'

Margaret's eyes jumped from Adele to Ronald and back again. She had no idea what to do. I again whispered in David's ear.

'You understand, David, that you also have the right to remain silent. If you say the wrong thing, it'll definitely come back to haunt you later on.'

I watched Margaret's body describe a series of small, involuntary jerks. Maybe submission wasn't her game, but no good would come of fighting cops. Adele waited patiently until Margaret's wrists were crossed behind her back, then slipped on the cuffs.

'I swear I didn't do it,' Margaret said. 'I didn't kill anyone. You've got to believe me. He's lying. I swear it.'

'Then what about those checks you cashed?' Adele asked. 'Are you telling me you didn't write them?'

The questions caught Margaret off-guard and she hesitated as she framed a reply. Finally, she said, 'I had business dealings with...'

'Stop right there. How do you expect me to believe that you didn't kill Mynka Chechowski when you start out with a lie? See, I know those checks are in addition to the checks you cut for Domestic Solutions. And the amount? Twenty-four thousand dollars in a little more than a month? You're not paying that much for any housekeeper.'

'I swear to you,' Margaret said. 'I didn't kill her.'

'Then why did you write those checks?'

Margaret was over-matched. Silence was her best move, as it usually is for anyone accused of a crime. But Margaret was a rich and pampered civilian, accustomed to having her way, a woman who now believed herself about to be charged with murder. That transi-

362

tion, from supreme mistress of her safe little world to involuntary ward of the state, had blown apart the little dots that connected her universe. Their place had been filled by an irresistible urge to shake off the nightmare, to crawl out from under.

'I did what any mother would do,' she finally claimed. 'I protected my child.'

'Which child?'

Margaret didn't hesitate. 'David,' she said, 'you have to tell them the truth.'

David Portola rose to his feet. Short and slightly built, he looked younger than his years. Nevertheless, he clearly wasn't afraid.

'Call me by my name,' he demanded.

'For God's sake, this is no time to play around.'

'Call me by my name.'

'David, please, you know I didn't do it.'

'Call me by my name.'

Margaret's body shook, literally, a shiver that seemed to run up from her toes. Then, despite the cuffs, she lowered her head and charged Ronald, only to be brought up short when Adele kicked her legs out from under her. For a moment, she lay sprawled on the carpet, seeming almost helpless, and I thought she was done early. But she finally rose to her knees, blood dripping from her nose, her features distorted by rage.

'Alright,' she screamed. 'Jerk, Jerk, Jerk, Jerk, Jerk. Tell them what happened, Jerk. Tell them what you did.'

David was smiling when he turned to look

into my eyes. 'I loved her and I killed her,' he explained. Then he repeated himself, as if bewildered by a truth he'd just discovered. 'I loved her and I killed her.'

THIRTY-FOUR

I remember the rest of that evening as a succession of isolated scenes. First, the shock on Margaret Portola's face – and the look of utter rapture on Ronald's – when Adele enumerated the charges she intended to file against the woman: two counts of involuntary servitude; two counts of extortion; four counts of assault; one count of obstruction of justice; one count of tampering with evidence; one count of conspiracy.

Bill Sarney came next. As his annoyed tone made clear, Harry Corbin was the last person he wanted to hear from at eight o'clock on a Sunday night. But he didn't shirk his duty. Damage control was in order.

It was Sarney who arranged to transport the prisoners, including Ronald, to the Fifth Precinct, Chinatown, in lower Manhattan, and it was Sarney who brought in an *ADA* named Wilson Bird. Bird was beyond accommodating and I had to assume that someone of considerably higher rank than Bill Sarney had cashed a marker with the Manhattan *DA*.

364

By the time I got David Portola in the box, I was resigned to the task at hand. I wanted to tell him that he'd already said too much, that hiring a lawyer to cut a deal was his one and only move. Instead, I listened to a confession that might better have been made to Father Manicki. Only David wasn't after absolution. He wanted to dig a hole in which he could lay down and die.

I did my best to prevent this outcome by telling Wilson Bird that David had threatened to commit suicide, a fact I intended to document in my written report. Hopefully, the boy would be placed on a suicide watch and kept far away from the Rikers Island wolves. But you can never be sure with the Department of Corrections. *DOC* is a world onto itself, cultivating a level of secrecy that makes cops appear frank and open by comparison. Disregarding a simple request from the Brooklyn District Attorney's office was not beyond its capacities.

I carried David's confession to Bill Sarney and Wilson Bird, who were huddled inside a small office. I nodded to Bird. 'Give us a minute. The Inspector and I need to talk.'

'Sure.'

I waited until the door closed behind him, then told Sarney about Zashka Ochirov and the other women. I needed Tynia Cernek, of course, to make a case against Margaret. Sarney was predictably suspicious, but I assured him that any and all would testify voluntarily, should their testimony become necessary. In the meantime, being as they'd lawyered up, it was better to keep them in the background. The last thing anybody wanted was publicity.

'Look, between Zashka and the Portolas, you can put Aslan away for the rest of his life. If that doesn't convince him to leave the country, nothing will. All you have to do is find him.'

Sarney stared at me for a long moment, but I only smiled. I wanted Aslan for myself and I think he knew it. As I knew that Hansen was running his own investigation on the side. Call it a friendly competition. Whoever finds Aslan first gets to take him into custody. And what fun that would be.

'Okay, Harry, you've done what you said you were gonna do. You've handed me Aslan Khalid's head on a platter. I have no complaints.' Sarney dropped his butt to the edge of a desk. 'Are you still considering my offer?'

'It's tempting, for a lot of reasons.'

'Like?'

'Like the rumors are gonna follow me for the rest of my life. I'll never get back what I had. So why not become the First Dep's rat? Why not accept the promotion and the pay raise that comes with it?'

Sarney grinned. 'Well put, Harry. Why not?'

'Because sooner or later, most likely sooner, you'll ask me to do something that I won't be able to do. Then what?'

'Then we'll deal with it.'

I had more to say, much more, but I froze when Adele cried out, froze with my mouth hanging open. Adele's cry was closer to a moan than a scream, a cry of immense loss, a ghost's cry. I had to gather up all my courage before I opened the door, and to step around Wilson Bird before I was able to see Adele. She was sitting on the floor tiles, her back slumped against the side of a desk, her tan slacks red with blood.

I knew, then, even as I gathered her up in my arms, as I followed Bill Sarney out the door and down to his car. I knew on the ride to Beekman Medical Center and when I was ordered to wait outside and when Bill Sarney came to sit next to me. I knew when Sarney left, at my insistence, an hour later. I knew when Doctor Morris called out my name. Morris wore bloodstained green scrubs and a white mask that hung around his neck.

'I'm sorry,' he said, 'but we couldn't save the pregnancy.'

'And Adele?'

'She's had a miscarriage. She'll be out of here within a couple of days.'

Morris started to turn away, but I put my hand on his arm. 'A boy or a girl? Which was it?'

'A boy.'

Time and space. That's what Adele claimed to need. But time to do what? Space to do what? I couldn't get these questions out of my mind as I made my way down a long corridor. Adele was in room 2A and I ticked off the rooms as I went: 2G, 2F, 2E, 2D, 2C, 2B. Then I heard her, heard Adele. I heard her

367

sobbing as I imagined David and Ronald must have sobbed, years ago, when they were utterly helpless, as I imagined Mynka sobbing when the cold began to penetrate her bones.

I rushed into the room, dropped to one knee by the side of the bed and took Adele's hand. I didn't know where any of this was going, but I felt an overwhelming need to protect her. That was impossible, of course. Nobody can be protected from an event that's already happened. But if I couldn't protect her, I could definitely avenge her.

Adele gripped my hand, but didn't stop crying or look at me. Instead, she fixed her eyes on a bag of whole blood hanging from the arm of an IV pole. I wanted to tell her that we'd make it. I wanted to tell her that love would conquer all. But I was too old for that. Eventually, we'd file our grievances. And it would be all the worse if our conversation was polite.

'Corbin?'

'Yes.'

'My *IUD* slipped. I didn't become pregnant on purpose.'

This was one grievance that never crossed my mind. 'I know that, Adele.'

'I wanted to say it before you left.'

I rose to my feet when a nurse entered the room. She held up a syringe and said, 'You'll excuse us?'

I don't know what the nurse gave her, but Adele was almost asleep when I returned. Her eyes fluttered when I entered her field of vision, but she didn't really focus. I stood above the bed for a moment, staring down at her pale face, her hollow cheeks. I wanted to take her in my arms, carry her home, tuck her into her own bed. I wanted to care for her.

But I did nothing of the kind. I waited until she was asleep, then walked away.

It was raining hard when I turned onto North Third Street to find the front windows of Aslan's apartment dark. I circled the block, to get a look at the rear windows, finding them dark as well. Finally, I parked the Nissan about fifty yards from the apartment and leaned back. A dog walker, a woman, was coming toward me from the other end of the block.

I don't believe the woman spotted me, not even when she paused to let her drenched husky pee against my front tire. The wind had picked up and she was far too preoccupied with her striped umbrella. The umbrella was gigantic, wide enough to protect her legs, but nearly impossible to control in the wind. Meanwhile, the dog was pulling her down the street and her arms were extended in opposite directions. She looked like a Hong Kong traffic cop.

I waited for her to stumble off before retrieving the tension bar, then the snap gun, from my coat pocket. For the next few minutes, I rehearsed the sequence of actions that would unlock Aslan's door. My aim was to be just another pedestrian hurrying home on a miserable September night. To that end, I would stand erect, with my head raised, close enough to conceal my hands while I worked on the lock. I would have to grope for the keyhole, to rely almost entirely on my sense of touch. If I'd been a little smarter, I'd have practiced in the dark. I closed my eyes for a few seconds, holding the tension bar between my fingers. The snap gun rested in my palm, the blade jutting out. This was the end of the game, the point of the exercise, what my life had been about since that July morning when I first came upon Mynka's decaying body.

I opened my eyes, checked the mirrors, checked Aslan's still-darkened windows, scanned the street ahead of me. The block was entirely deserted.

I didn't hesitate. I walked directly up to Aslan's door, glanced quickly down at the lock's keyway, finally raised my head and let my fingers go to work. Fumbling just a bit, I slipped the tension bar into the bottom of the keyhole before applying torque. The snap gun's blade followed, sliding in above the bar.

When I pulled the trigger, the blade shot up into the lower pins. Whatever noise it made was obliterated by rain and wind. But the lock stayed locked.

I pulled the trigger again, then again, then again, waiting for a slight release in the tension to indicate that the upper pins were trapped above the shear line. But there was no release and I had to fight the instinct to grab for my gun when a car turned onto the block. The car's lights swept over my body as it approached, casting an elongated shadow across the face of the building, a shadow that steadily retreated, then disappeared as the vehicle passed me.

Despite my best intentions, I found myself holding my breath. Maybe Aslan coming home while I was standing in front of his door with my back turned was a long shot, but it was far from impossible. Meanwhile, the car didn't slow down until it reached the stop sign at the end of the block. A moment later it was gone.

The pins lined up and the bolt retracted on my twelfth attempt. By that time, my legs were soaked, from mid-shin to ankle, and rainwater was streaming from my coat. I pushed the door open, stepped inside, glimpsing a narrow flight of stairs before closing the door and plunging the space into utter darkness.

I felt instantly reassured. Stairway, hall and door were windowless – Aslan would step into the same darkness (assuming he wasn't asleep in his bed) when he returned to his apartment. If I positioned myself halfway up the stairs, I'd have him in my sights before he knew I was there. That was important because my raincoat was dripping water onto the linoleum floor and every step I took on those stairs would leave a puddle behind.

I retrieved my flashlight and flicked it on. About the size of a cigar, the flashlight was set to cast a very narrow beam. I ran that beam over the wall to my left, discovering a light switch. Good news. Aslan would reach for the switch with his left hand, while closing the door behind him with his right. The sequence would be automatic, leaving both hands far from any weapon he might have on his person.

It was a nice fantasy. Aslan opening the door, the light coming on to reveal Harry Corbin sitting on the stairs. I could even picture myself, coat open, weapon in hand, smiling my brightest gunslinger smile when I pressed that first button: 'Yo, Aslan, what's happenin'? I thought you'd never come home.'

I flicked the light switch, but nothing happened, hall and stairs remained as dark as ever. I was about to throw the switch a second time, then checked myself as I remembered Zashka's warning; Aslan would kill me if he got the chance. Then I recalled something else she'd said. Faced with a mini-revolt, Aslan had once threatened to blow up the Eagle Street Warehouse with everyone in it. At the time, he'd also claimed the expertise to bring it off.

Surely, replacing the bulb at the head of those stairs, if it blew out on its own, would be one of those household chores that gets taken care of right away. Otherwise, you'd have to climb the stairs and find the lock with your key in total darkness. I widened the beam on the flashlight, examined the area at my feet, finally began to move forward. When I got to the stairs, I dropped to my knees before I began to climb. I was looking for a trip wire, or an electronic sensor that would mark my passing, perhaps set off an alarm, or something far worse. I didn't find anything like that, just a series of painted wooden steps that rose to a landing barely wider than the door it fronted. Nevertheless, I checked the door carefully before turning my attention to the light fixture on the ceiling above my head. I could see the outline of a bulb through the frosted glass, but that didn't tell me what I needed to know.

Rising onto my toes, I was just able to reach the light, to unscrew the pins holding the globe in place, to finally expose a single bulb. Gingerly, I took the bulb between my fingers and gave it a slight twist. It was loose in the socket, but I didn't test it by screwing it down. Instead, I removed the bulb, then examined the filament, positioning the flashlight behind the bulb to maximize the contrast. The filament was perfectly intact and there was no carbon build-up on either pole.

I dropped the bulb into my pocket, next to the snap gun and the tension bar, then closed up the overhead fixture before turning to the door. By then, my brain was rocking along. Aslan's home country was the place where booby-traps were perfected, especially as they applied to urban guerrilla warfare. According to the Russians, explosive devices of one kind or another were found in every third building when they re-took Grozny, along with a host of lesser goodies, like ceilings and floors rigged to collapse, and light bulbs filled with gasoline.

I sat down on the landing, my legs on the stairs, facing the door at the bottom of the steps. A little voice in my head was insisting that I stay the hell out of Aslan's apartment. Do it just the way you said, this voice insisted. Wait for him on the stairs. Take him down the minute he steps through the door.

But there was another voice, too, a nasty little voice that whispered, Aslan killed your son. Over and over and over again.

Of one thing I was certain. The loose bulb was not some sort of trigger mechanism. Not unless Aslan had imagined me clever enough to check the bulb out, then stupid enough to screw it back down. There had to be another reason.

I sat there, in total darkness, until I thought I knew that reason. Then I got to work.

I wasn't surprised to find the door un-locked, though I admit to a flash of bladder-clenching fear when the hinges squealed as it swung away from me. I was at the back of a long room, facing a narrow table set against a wall fifteen feet away. Light streamed into the apartment through a pair of windows and the room seemed well lit compared to the hallway. There was enough light, for instance, for me to pick out a shadow beneath the table, a shadow mounted flush to the wall. I could even see little pinpricks of light, so faint I might have imagined them, within the shadow.

But I wasn't imagining the wires running from a light switch to my left, down to the floor, then out along the wall in both directions. To Aslan, the sequence must have seemed obvious. You climb those stairs in the dark, the first thing you'll do, when you finally get into his apartment, is grope for that switch. The light at this end of the room, furthest from the windows in front, was extremely dim. It had to be, otherwise the shadow between the legs of the table would be revealed for the pound or so of plastic explosive it actually was. And that would ruin all the fun.

I leaned through the doorway and looked around. The space was large, easily fifteen-by-thirty, and sparsely furnished. The Chechen flag caught my eye first, just to the right of the rain-spattered windows. I couldn't see the wolf's eyes – the walls to either side of the window were in deep shadow – but I knew his gaze was as mean spirited as ever.

A worn leather sofa, an end table supporting a painted ceramic lamp, a small *TV* set on a rolling stand, and a coffee table littered with newspapers and *DVD*s were clustered before the windows. Along the near wall midway between where I stood and the windows, an open notebook computer, along with a stack of floppy disks and a small printer, rested on a metal desk.

Facing the desk, an L-shaped serving bar partitioned off a small kitchen, its metal sink piled with unwashed dishes. A pair of doors to my right led to interior rooms. The room closest to me was the bedroom, the one I'd looked through when I climbed the drainpipe. The second room was undoubtedly the bathroom.

I registered each of these items carefully, in search of anything out of order. When I was satisfied, I squatted down to examine the open spaces between the furnishings. I was looking for trip wires and the light was very dim, especially along the walls. But I kept at it, until I was sure I could enter the apartment without blowing myself all the way back to Manhattan. Then I stepped inside and took another survey, this one limited to the explosives, mounted six feet apart and six inches off the ground, on all four walls.

From close up, those pinpricks of light I'd observed when I first opened the door were obviously the heads of common nails. The nails had been pressed into bars of what looked like molded clay, the intention to shred the flesh of anyone caught in their path. But the nails were pure overkill. There was enough explosive material in that room to take out the building. If it went off, I wouldn't live long enough for the nails to reach my body.

Still, I appreciated the theatrical touch; as I also appreciated the way Aslan had rigged the trap after I found a second set of wires, in addition to the wires leading from the light switch. These wires began at a *DVD* player positioned on the floor where the eastern wall of the building met the kitchen's service counter. They ran the full length of the room and were connected (as were the wires from the light switch) to detonators on each of the little bricks fastened to the wall.

I stood over the *DVD* player for a moment, staring down, until I finally hit upon its purpose. Then I began a search of the room that ended when I found the Sony's remote control next to the computer. Needless to say, I was careful not to press any of its buttons. Instead, I carried it to the door through which I'd come, back to the rigged light switch.

I'd had some formal training in the handling of explosives while I was in the military. Enough to know that Aslan had created a dual system. The explosives could be triggered by turning on the light switch or the *DVD* player, either one. Thus, an intruder, like myself, entering while Aslan was out, would be the immediate cause of his own death when he switched on the light. On the other hand, if I'd made an appearance while Aslan was at home, he'd literally have his finger on the button.

Still, there was a definite bottom line here: no current, no explosion.

I went into my pants pocket, removed a small folding knife, and opened the blade. I told myself that the remedy here was apparent. If there was a break in the wire, no circuit could be completed, no matter what you did with the switch. But despite all that macho bullshit about inviting Aslan to the dance, I couldn't bring myself to cut those wires. My knowledge of explosives was limited. For all I knew, Aslan had rigged his bombs to explode when an already established circuit was broken. How he'd do it, given the simplicity of a light switch, was beyond me, but sometimes the consequences of a mistake are so great, it doesn't matter how great the odds against it. I'd surveyed the apartment, done my job, and fulfilled my obligation to protect the public. Who would fault me if I waited on the stairs? I'd give the bomb squad a heads-up, of course. Right after I finished with Aslan.

Good thinking, no doubt, but my timing was awful because I was still standing there, looking down at the open blade of the knife, when the outside door opened and I heard raised voices in the downstairs hall. I was seconds away from a confrontation. I had to act.

THIRTY-FIVE

Aslan came into the apartment first, edging sideways through the door. Hansen Linde followed. Though he wasn't bearing down, he had a grip on Aslan's trailing arm, an obviously custodial grip. A third man trailed behind. I didn't get a good look at his face, but his vested suit, his crew-cut hair and the attaché case he carried virtually screamed Fed.

I was in Aslan's bathroom, peering through the crack between the partly open door and the frame, and the first thing I noted was that neither Hansen, nor his companion, had drawn a weapon. This was a mistake for which Aslan would surely make them pay.

He didn't wait long. They were barely five feet into the room when Aslan yanked his arm free and made a dive for the remote control on his desk. Hansen and the Fed both grabbed for their weapons, only to stop when they realized that the plastic object in Aslan's hand wasn't a gun.

Aslan's lips were moving, but nothing was coming out. Maybe he was considering the effect on his own body, on flesh and bone, should he press that button. Finally, he swept the room with his arm. A wasted gesture. Hansen and the Fed had already figured it out. I knew that because I saw the Fed's knees buckle momentarily, while Hansen withdrew his hand from beneath his jacket, then raised it, palm out.

'We don't wanna do anything stupid here,' he said.

'Why? You are fearing death?'

'You betcha.'

'This is good. Now please to put guns on floor.'

The Fed hastened to comply, removing a pair of weapons, the first from a holster, the second, presumably Aslan's, from the waist-band of his trousers. He put them on the floor and took a step back. Hansen didn't move a muscle.

'Are you not hearing me?'

'I hear you,' Hansen said, 'but I'm not gonna surrender my weapon. That's the first rule of policing, ya know. Never surrender your weapon. Plus, I just can't take the chance that I'll die in this room while you continue living. I don't wanna go before the pearly gates with that crime on my con-science. Oh, yeah. I'd be too ashamed even to beg forgiveness.'

I fell in love with Hansen Linde at that moment. Not so the Fed.

'What's the matter with you, Linde?' he demanded. 'Are you crazy?' When Hansen ignored both questions, he turned to Aslan. 'Look, we didn't come to arrest you, Aslan. I'm not even a cop. I work for Immigration. Here.' Very slowly, he unbuttoned his suit jacket and removed a business card from his vest pocket. When he held it up, his hands were shaking so hard the print couldn't have been read, even in sunlight, even if Aslan wasn't standing fifteen feet away. 'My name is Horn, Jack Horn. I work in the Deportations Division of the *INS*.'

Aslan smiled for the first time. 'You are tired with Aslan in your country? You want no more to be seeing him?' He paused, his eyes flicking to Hansen, then back again. 'Where is it you want Aslan to be going?'

'To Russia.' Horn shifted his weight from one foot to another. Though I couldn't see his face, I was certain that he was smiling, and that his smile was fawning. 'Use your common sense, Aslan. It's the only way. You can't stay here, not with a murder hanging over your head. It's time to move on.'

Aslan sat down in front of his desk, the light from the lamp bathing the side of his face and his shoulder. He seemed at peace as he crossed his legs and let his weight fall against the back of the chair.

'Is not only way,' he told the Fed. 'Is another way I am holding this minute in my hand.'

'Yeah, but...'

Aslan shook his head, bringing Agent Horn to an abrupt halt. 'Where is partner?' he asked Hansen Linde.

'You mean Detective Corbin?'

'Do not be fucking with Aslan. From his life you are ignorant. Dead is nothing to Aslan. Honor is all. Tell me where is partner.'

'I don't know.'

Aslan nodded. 'Now, please to put down gun. No more bullshit.'

'Do what he says,' Horn demanded. His hands were curled into fists, his shoulders squared. For a moment I thought he was going to attack Linde, though Hansen was much larger.

'What you said about honor?' Hansen spoke directly to Aslan. 'I agree with you one hundred percent. Honor is everything. That's

381

why I'm gonna tell you, for the last time, that either we all walk out of here, or nobody walks out.'

'You think I will not do this?'

Hansen's adam's apple gave a quick bob as he shook his head. 'I'm not giving up my weapon, Aslan. It's your move.'

The Fed grabbed Hansen's arm, only to be shoved away. 'I have a wife and children,' he pleaded. 'I haven't done anything to anybody.' Then he hesitated for a moment, his breath coming in near-convulsive heaves, before he made his final argument. 'I'm an innocent bystander. I don't deserve this.'

'Aslan doesn't care about innocent bystanders,' Hansen explained. 'There's enough explosive material in this room to collapse the building on anybody in the store downstairs. Maybe it's Sunday night and the store's closed, but we might easily have come along on a Saturday afternoon. To Aslan, it doesn't matter.'

I watched Aslan's mouth compress and his eyes narrow as he sought the courage to make good on his threat. He didn't like having his bluff called – that much I knew from experience – but dying, apparently, didn't have all that much appeal either. In any event, it was Hansen who broke the silence.

'See,' he said to Horn, 'Aslan has the same problem I do. I don't want to go to my death knowing that Aslan's still breathing. Aslan doesn't want to go to his death knowing that Harry Corbin's still breathing.'

Aslan considered this for a moment, then rose to his feet. 'Choice for Aslan is simple. Surrender and become prisoner of state, or go to Allah. Prisoner of state is not possible. In Russia, prisoner of state means Gulag. I have been to Gulag. Never again is what I have said to myself at this time. If once I am out of here, never again.'

'Suppose we find someplace else?' Horn asked. 'Or you just walk away right now. I mean, if you left, there's not much we could do about it.'

Aslan and Hansen both rejected the Fed's suggestion with simple shakes of the head. 'Here is better deal,' Aslan declared. 'I will make trade. Bring to me Detective Corbin and I will give to you back your lives.'

The offer was a transparent lie, but Hansen didn't dispute it. Instead, he stroked his knobby chin for a moment, then said, 'I could try him on his cell phone.'

'No, do not try. For to go on with living, you must succeed.'

'My cell phone's in my coat pocket. My phone book too.'

Aslan grinned. 'I am not afraid you will pull gun on me. That would be suicide.'

Hansen made a show of thumbing through his phone book, although he had to know that he didn't have the number of the cell phone I was using. I'd purchased minutes in bulk, instead of buying into a phone company plan, and the number wasn't listed in any registry. But that didn't discourage Hansen. He punched away at the number pad, raised the phone to his ear, waited a few seconds, then said, 'Show time, Harry. Get your ass inside.'

I straightened, stepped through the door and walked up to stand between Hansen and the Fed. Horn's jaw was bobbing helplessly, his teeth clacking together, his eyes rolling in his head. Aslan Khalid wasn't in much better shape. His eyes were saucer-wide, his irises a pair of black dots lost in a milky sea. As I approached, he riveted those eyes to mine. Linde immediately took advantage of Aslan's fixation, his left hand snaking up to unbutton his jacket. Now he could get to the .357 he carried in a shoulder rig.

'How'd ya know?' I spoke directly to Hansen.

He rolled his eyes, his mouth curling into a little circle of distaste. 'You left a goddamned swamp in the hallway downstairs.'

'I was gonna clean up, only I didn't get a chance. But what I'm asking is how you knew it was me who left the puddle?'

'Well, I knew Aslan didn't leave it, because we've been tailin' him all afternoon.'

'Fine,' I insisted, 'only that doesn't explain how you knew it was me. Or how you knew I hadn't come and gone.'

Hansen laughed. 'Some things in this life you gotta take on faith, kiddo.'

Aslan rose from the chair, displaying the remote control as through it was a cannon. 'Enough from this crap...'

'Will you shut up,' I said. 'I'm speaking to

my partner.' I didn't wait for a reply. 'Who'd you break?' I asked. 'Nicolai Urnov?'

'Yeah, Urnov. I put him in the hot seat and melted him like a stick of butter. He told me that Aslan owns a piece of a bar in Canarsie, so I gathered up Agent Horn, drove to Canarsie and there he was. It was only a matter of waiting for him to leave.'

Aslan was virtually incoherent by then, the hate in his eyes all-encompassing. I addressed Horn for the first time. 'Take your weapon,' I ordered, 'and get the fuck out of here. And don't call the cops.'

Horn looked from me to Aslan. I don't know what message he took from Aslan's contorted features, but he finally snatched up his gun and took off like a shot. I listened to his feet on the stairs, to the door slam behind him, then I raised my left hand to expose the AAA batteries in my palm. Aslan stared at my hand for a moment, then jabbed the ON button anyway. When nothing happened, he pressed it again, then again. Finally, his eyes darted to his left, to the *DVD* player still lying against the far wall.

'Why,' Aslan asked, his tone genuinely perplexed, 'you have done this thing to me?'

I marveled at the question as I watched Hansen's fingers move toward his weapon, thinking that the list of reasons, should I give them voice, would go on for hours. But the question was never meant to be answered. Instead, it was an attempt to divert our attention, and it might have been effective if Aslan hadn't paused long enough to throw the remote in our direction before diving for the *DVD* player. Linde's hand was on his .357 even as the remote sailed over his head. He got off his third shot before Aslan took his third step.

The muzzle flashes were predictably blinding in the darkened room, inducing a series of images that persisted in my retinas – Aslan turning, Aslan rising suddenly on his toes, Aslan halfway to the floor, eyes open, lips parted, the back of his head a spray of red particles fanning out across the room.

I dwelt on these flashes, on the entire sequence and my part in it, until my wildly expanded pupils again contracted, until the roar of Hansen's .357 gave way to the patter of rain on the windows. Hansen was kneeling beside Aslan. His fingers were pressed to Aslan's throat, the gesture somehow ritualistic, as though he were blessing the body.

'You realize,' I said, 'what would have happened if one of those bullets you fired off had ploughed into one of those bricks on the wall, right?'

'What was I supposed to do, let him get to that *DVD* player, maybe turn it on?'

'It wouldn't have mattered, Hansen, because I cut the wires before you made your grand entrance.'

Linde rose to his feet and slid his revolver into the holster tucked beneath his arm. For a long moment, he regarded me with his hands on his hips. Then he grinned a grin that bore all the marks of his boyhood, towering blue skies, golden sunlight, fields of tasseled corn that ran all the way to heaven.

'Okay,' he said, 'so one day Ole and his cousin, Sven, rent a boat and go fishing on Lake Chimmawabbee. They don't have much luck at first, so they keep moving from one spot to another until finally, in the middle of the afternoon, they start catching fish. For the next half hour they're pulling them in as fast as they can re-bait and cast off. Then they finally take a rest. "Sven," Ole says as he lights his pipe, "we just better mark this spot so we can find it again." After due consideration, Sven takes out a magic marker and draws a circle in the bottom of the boat. Ole stares at the circle for a moment, then shakes his head in disgust. "Ya big dummy," he says, "how do ya know we'll get the same boat tomorrow?"'

This time, not even Hansen laughed.

THIRTY-SIX

There was nothing to do but wait there in the dark, wait to see if the shots were reported, if uniformed officers would come knocking. Sheets of rain continued to rattle against the windows and on the roof above our heads, rain that seemed to grow louder as time passed. In the kitchen, a wall clock in the shape of a black cat ticked away, its long tail and dark eyes twitching from side to side with every tick.

'What next?' Hansen finally asked. He was standing before the front windows, looking up and down the street as though expecting a *SWAT* team to appear at any minute.

I held him off with a raised forefinger, then took out my cell phone and punched in the number for Beekman Hospital as I walked into Aslan's bedroom. The operator I got was as nasty as she was uncooperative, even when I identified myself as a police officer. I had to demand a supervisor before I was put through to the nursing station in Adele's unit and found a sympathetic nurse. Adele was asleep, she told me. She was doing just fine.

'Look, detective, I know it's none of my business, but I want to offer my condolences. It's a hard thing to deal with, a miscarriage, but it's not the end of the world. There's no reason why Mrs Bentibi can't become pregnant again.' I looked through the doorway, at Aslan Khalid's shattered skull. No, no reason at all, I thought. No reason at all.

Hansen was standing over Aslan's body when I came back into the room. 'I didn't have any choice under the circumstances, but Sarney's gonna go nuts,' he announced.

'I'm a man of conscience, Hansen. I got you into this and I'm gonna get you out.'

I walked into the kitchen and searched beneath the sink, unearthing a bucket, a scrub brush, two rolls of paper towels and a roll of duct tape. In a cabinet next to the refrigerator, I found a box of garbage bags and a bottle of floor cleaner. I gave bucket, brush, paper towels and cleaner to Linde, then proceeded to wrap Aslan in the garbage bags, to create a fitting shroud for a man of his character. It wasn't as easy as I'd imagined – Aslan's limp body had the consistency of an under-stuffed sausage. But I finally got it done, without contaminating myself (so far as I could tell) with Aslan's blood.

Hansen's job lasted a bit longer, though his goals were modest. Given the low light, a clean up that would bear the scrutiny of the Crime Scene Unit was impossible. Hansen hoped only to deceive those who didn't know a shooting had taken place, or who didn't care. Our story, in the event that Agent Horn couldn't be controlled, was that Aslan had used the threat of annihilation to make good his escape. Undoubtedly, he'd meant to kill us, but clever Harry Corbin had cut the wires before the dastardly villain got clear of the building.

'Where do you think he got them?' I gestured to the bricks on the wall. 'I thought we kept track of plastic explosives in this country.'

Hansen shrugged, then went back to his scrubbing. 'Plastics are used for demolition sometimes, so they could have been stolen off a construction site. Or he might've made the bricks himself. That's something a Chechen guerrilla would learn how to do. Plus, from what I know, it's not that hard.'

By the time Hansen finished wiping the plastic taped to Aslan's body, he'd filled a trash bag with paper towels. I didn't know what he intended to do with it, only that it was his and Sarney's problem, as were the explosives. By then it was one o'clock and the bar on the corner was closing. I could understand why. I'd been watching for a half hour and I hadn't seen a customer go in or out. Across the street, almost every window was dark.

'You got a police radio?' I asked Linde. He seemed more rattled now than he had when Aslan was alive. Myself, I was caught in the downside of an adrenaline rush. I felt heavy and lethargic, and oddly indifferent, though I knew my night was far from over.

'I have a radio in the car.'

'A portable?'

'Yeah.'

'You think you can get it, bring it upstairs?'

Hansen looked at me for a moment, then nodded. 'I never killed anyone before,' he said. 'I never even shot anyone.'

'Well, if you feel like holding me responsible, it's okay.'

'Does that mean you wanted me to kill him?'

'Yeah, I wanted him dead and I wanted you to do it.'

'Why?'

'I wanted him dead because he killed

Adele's baby. I wanted you to do it because now Sarney can't blame me for the fuck up. In fact, the way it's playing out, Bill Sarney's gonna be in my debt for the rest of his career.'

Hansen turned up the collar of his jacket, then stuck his hands into his pockets. 'Sarney told me what happened with your wife. I'm sorry, Harry.'

'Adele's not my wife.'

'I'm still sorry.' He smiled. 'Something else Sarney told me. He said you were crazy and he was right.'

'Not crazy, Hansen. Gifted. What you see, in Harry Corbin, is the perfect marriage of talent and vocation.'

'What's that supposed to mean?'

'It means I beat you to Aslan. And a good thing for you and Agent Horn that I did.'

Hansen broke into laughter at that point. 'What do ya call it,' he asked, 'when a bull-shitter gets so good he can bullshit himself?'

'Enlightenment.'

I set the radio on channel 4 when Hansen returned, to a dispatcher covering three precincts in Brooklyn North, including the Nine-Two. I was waiting for the unit working Sector A to be assigned a job, or to announce a meal break. Instead, at one thirty, Nine-Two Adam contacted Central to announce that a pair of suspects were under arrest and they were headed for the house. That would leave this little section of Williamsburg un-patrolled for the next several hours.

The rain was flowing in long, nearly

horizontal lines when I came through the front door with Aslan's body slung across my shoulder. My face and hair were instantly wet, despite the hood I'd yanked down over my eyes, and cold water was trickling down the back of my neck. Still, I was doing better than Hansen Linde. Hatless, he stood behind the car, holding the trunk open, his navy-blue suit plastered to his thick body.

I had to pull Aslan's feet tight against his buttocks and force his head into the wheel well before Hansen was able to close the trunk. I think Hansen wanted to say something, maybe even give me a hug, but he settled for a simple nod as I got into the car. Only when I was about to pull away did his lips begin to move. I dutifully lowered the window, but whatever Hansen was going to say had already been said. He turned and walked off toward Aslan's apartment.

I drove straight down North Third Street, to Kent Avenue, where I made a left. I saw no one, neither car nor pedestrian, and the warehouses to either side, distorted by the rain and the sweep of the wipers across the windshield, might have been the remains of some dead civilization. Every opening to every building was closed off by steel gates, every gate had been tagged with graffiti, again and again, and every brick was coated with soot.

I turned right a block before I reached the Williamsburg Bridge, onto South Fifth Street, and drove fifty yards to a mound of dirt that blocked the road. I was already switching into a higher gear as I slid to a stop. In quick succession, I shut off the headlights, pulled the trunk release and got out of the car. I could be seen here, by anybody driving along Kent Avenue. The last thing I needed was another Clyde Kelly to call the police.

The wind tore the hood of my raincoat away from my head as I forced my way to the trunk of the car, as I unfolded Aslan Khalid, as I dumped his body onto the cobblestones, as I seized him by the ankles and dragged him over the weeds covering the mound. The weeds grabbed at my legs and I lost my footing once, but Aslan came easily, sliding along on his plastic shroud like an otter on a mudslide. Mynka, I knew, would have offered a good deal more resistance. Aslan hadn't bothered to wrap her body and her chin would have dug into the earth, as her arms would have pulled away from her sides to hook the weeds. But Aslan's job was to butcher Mynka Chechowski. Disposal was Barsakov's problem.

I yanked Aslan's body through the breech in the chain-link fence and down a short incline. We were out of sight now. Just a few steps away, the East River was driving small persistent waves against the rocky shoreline. I stared out at the river for a moment, tempted to be rid of Aslan then and there, but the water was too shallow, the current too weak. A body dumped into water this shallow wouldn't drift more than a few hundred yards before it came to the surface.

I finally turned to the long pier tucked behind the Gambrelli warehouse to the north. I'd have to lift Aslan above my head to get him on the pier and I wasn't sure I could do it. Aslan had to weigh a hundred and seventy pounds. Even balancing him on my shoulder long enough to get him into the trunk had been difficult.

For a time, I simply stood where I was, looking down at the body next to my feet, no longer moved by any sense of urgency, any need to get it done and get away. I felt at that moment as though Aslan and I were the only two human beings on the planet; that we'd built ourselves a space inaccessible to ordinary human beings, a space they could not enter, a space they could not even detect. Above me, the lights of the bridge rose in the fog, gradually becoming more and more faint, and the skyline of Manhattan across the river was reduced to a faint glow more imaginary than real. I listened to the great moan of a foghorn that seemed to come from everywhere at once, though I couldn't find the lights of any vessel on the black waters of the river.

I tried it the easy way first. I lifted Aslan to my shoulders and attempted to move with my arms alone. But I couldn't raise him more than a few inches. His weight kept rolling away from me and the wet plastic wasn't helping either. I would have to squat down, to use my legs to gain momentum, to toss Aslan onto the pier with one quick push.

My first attempt landed me on my ass with Aslan sprawled across my lap. At another time, I would have found the situation grisly, or even humorous, but I wasn't feeling much of anything. There was the river and the pier and Aslan's body. There was a ritual to be performed that involved all three, performed as written before, and I had no energy, physical or emotional, to spare.

I took more care on my next attempt. Once I got Aslan over my shoulder, I tested his weight, eventually sliding my right hand, palm up, from his waist to his sternum. Then I wrapped my left hand in the plastic surrounding his thighs and squatted down, making a conscious effort to center my spine between my ankles. When I was sure I had it right, I pushed up as hard as I could, barely aware of my closed eyes and the scream that issued from my lips, a scream that was lost on the wind before it reached my ears.

Aslan's head and back went up and over the pier, but I had to get under his legs to keep him from sliding back down. We hung there for a moment, my arms wrapped around his thighs, my head pressed into his groin, until I finally inched his hips past the tipping point and the pier took his weight. A moment later, I was standing beside him, his ankles in my hands.

Splinters of wood tore at the trash bags enclosing Aslan's body as I dragged him the length of the pier. I assumed they were also tearing into his flesh, and that he was leaving traces of himself behind, but I no longer had the energy to lift him. On the river, the darkness was near absolute and the running waters of the outgoing tide might have been the heaving back of some prehistoric beast.

For reasons I couldn't know, and for a time I couldn't begin to measure, I stood where I was, staring out at the rain and the river. I was soaked, now, every article of clothing, every inch of my flesh. Water streamed from my hair into my eyes and down the back of my neck. As far as I could tell, I offered no resistance, my body a mere conduit for an element seeking nothing more than its own level.

I kept thinking that I should feel something, anger, maybe, or satisfaction. But when I finally squatted next to Aslan's body and rolled him over the edge of the pier, I felt nothing at all. I handled him like he was so much trash.

Aslan hit the water head first and his body went completely under. I expected him to pop back up, figuring there was enough air trapped in his shroud to keep him afloat, at least initially. But the East River claimed Aslan as utterly as the whale claimed Jonah. Perhaps, somewhere down the line, Aslan would be disgorged. Or maybe the ocean would fully digest him. It didn't really matter that much to me, one way or the other. The prison doors had opened and my thoughts were already turning back to the living. I was done now. I could go home. I could try to pick up the pieces.